THE ENGINEER'S MECHANIC

BOOK 1 OF THE METICITY SERIES

L. K. WINTUR

YELLOW PANDA PUBLISHING

CONTENTS_

CHAPTER ONE_

"Can't we wait outside?" I ask, looking over at the glass door that leads to the balcony.

"Why? There's only one person in front of us," Migo gestures to a woman sitting a few chairs down. Her eyes are fluttering slightly but never completely open. Leaning back in the chair, she rests her head against the wall behind her. She's completely gone. Tapped-in.

I stare blankly at Migo as if I didn't hear him. After an awkward moment of silence, he gives in, shrugging defeatedly.

"...I guess we'll wait outside then. Zeesh, Ren. You're really a walking stereotype, you know that?" He groans, getting up from his seat.

"Stereotype? What stereotype?" I ask, following his lead.

"The one that says sandscavengers can't ever stop moving."

"The settlement hasn't moved since you left, and we haven't been nomadic since the '90s. You're runnin' on outdated software, Migo," I explain.

"Yeah, yeah." He begrudgingly leads the way outside to the balcony of the repair facility he's brought us to. Because only his credentials can open the door, it feels sort of like I'm being chaperoned. We probably look like an odd pair, too. I'm still in my dirty mechanic overalls from work; Migo, on the other hand, is wearing MetiCity-6's latest fashion, equipped with advanced coolant tech and vital monitoring. They're '2120 exclusives'; he loves to remind me every new year. The number seems to keep rising in tandem with his ego.

"You've got this glacious view of the city, and you want to sit inside watching that zombie surf?" I say, leaning up against a guardrail that borders the balcony we're on.

He rolls his eyes.

I peer out over the cityscape and fix my gaze upon the large semi-transparent dome that covers it all. I follow the light shining through as it cloaks everything in a yellowish hue. Buzzing transports fill the sky with movement and life. The ground itself exists in constant motion as the various Mag-Lev lines slice their way through the compact arcology. It's stunning.

"Every time we get a few floors up, you wanna dangle off some balcony like it's your first time above ground," Migo groans.

"But from up here..."

From up here, it's easy to believe this city is endless. From home, it looks like a waning moon, mirroring its reflection over the open ocean. I shift my gaze to the white shimmering buildings blanketed by earthy green foliage and vegetation. Vines twist their way throughout the entire cityscape, connecting everyone and everything.

"I just think you guys get too busy looking forward to look around," I say.

"You guys?" Migo has a feigned look of offense.

"You've been here half a decade, domehead. You're a full MetiCitian now," I stand up on my toes to mess up his dark, slicked-back hair, rubbing my fist into it and twisting at the wrist. He pushes me off and vigorously attempts to make the disheveled look work. He's obsessed with his hair, which makes messing it up even more satisfying.

"I mean, look at this place. They never dreamed anything like this up in those old movies," I think back to crashing at his place when my foster home got too heavy. We'd watch twenty-first century movies at max volume to mask the sound of the superstorms rumbling through the Outskirtz landscape.

"Yeah. We're short about one alien invasion, two AI takeovers, a few zombie apocalypses, and my personal favorite, a robot rebellion," Migo says through a smile, counting each on his fingers.

"Yeah, and there'd be nothing here but a vast wasteland of decaying, rusted ruins torn apart by war, famine, and Earth itself. You know, just like home," I joke back. "They dreamt of the apocalypse, blind to the little green oasis that was just beyond it."

"That's because they were stressed, depressed, and oppressed. They wanted to tear it all down. They dreamt of places like the Outskirtz so they could fantasize about running wild and being free. Don't you feel free, Ren? Don't you!?" he says, grabbing me by the shoulders and shaking me up teasingly. I'm the one pushing him off this time. Migo's personality isn't for everyone, and at the moment, I'm everyone.

"I've signed nothing. I am free," I say, not sure if I'm trying to convince him or myself.

"You know Ren, you're right. And truly, I'm just jealous. All that sand. All that junk. The outlaws with no morals, and you sandscavs with too many. If my parents didn't force me to live in this wretched place of rules and order, I'd come back. I miss it," Migo says, dripping with sarcasm.

"You miss the women with no morals," I correct him.

"Speaking of women, you're going to love this new girl I

met, Tovah. She's the cream of the MetiCity crop. You know, you really gotta move out here, 'scav. I wouldn't call this a paradise, but it's definitely the greener of the two sides. Thank the Allspirits," he says, placing his hands together to imitate prayer. More devoid than devout.

"Thank him," I gesture to the massive skyscraper positioned behind Migo.

"Who?" he asks, turning his head to face the towering building.

"Go heads up," I urge him, pointing to my own credentials, which I've just activated. He pulls his off his wrist and places it over his ear. Pulling on the edge of the device, a thin piece of translucent flexible glass stretches out across his eyes.

"Oh, shit," he says, stepping back slightly to get a better view of the large, holographic, statue-like figure in front of him, now visible due to his augmented view. "Thank you, Zelius, sir! Looking very sinister today, sir! Happy Birthday, sir!" He laughs, standing at attention and saluting the floating monument.

The looming figure is an older man with a white beard in a General's uniform, casting his gaze out over the city skyline towards the setting sun. He is The Engineer. Founder of Meti-Corp. Zelius Metihand.

"I saw a bunch of these murals on my way into the city scattered all over the place. I guess when you up the ante every Engineer's week for thirty years, something like this is inevitable. I wonder if it's the same in all the Meticities?" I ponder aloud.

"Probably. I can't imagine what they do in the first cities," Migo says, turning back to me.

"He looks sad to me. Honestly, I feel bad for the guy. Imagine starting a Company that saves humanity from the brink of total destruction, only for that very same Company to betray and kill you. What a tragedy," I say.

"Is that the conspiracy of the week? I thought he went nuts and tried to blow up MetiCity-1?" Migo questions.

"Who knows."

The man's life is tantamount to mythology at this point. As I study his face, I notice someone on a FlyBike go screeching past. He's covered in UnderGround tattoos. I thought he might be an augmented visual until I push my credentials slightly above my eyes to confirm he's actually there. The pale-skinned biker makes a sharp u-turn before speeding past again. He brakes quickly, stopping in front of the section of the hologram showing years of Zelius's birth and death. I let the credentials slip back over my eyes and can see his avatar begin striking out the year of Zelius's death. He's replacing it with the letters U and G, similar to the style of his tattoos. These guys are obsessed zealots. They think Zelius was some kind of God and worship him like one.

"Yo, look! UG's taggin' the mural," I point out to Migo.

"I can't believe he's tapped-in fifty stories up on a FlyBike. Is he nuts? These guys will do anything for some publicity."

"Here come the controllers!" I shout.

"Good. What did he think was going to happen?" Migo laughs. The Company Control Officers descend upon the tagger, throwing a small disruptor that latches onto and disables his bike. They're able to easily gain control of him while he's still tapped-in and tagging online. "Why didn't they just tap-in at home and travel here virtually?" he asks.

"They do it to make a statement, but he's going to end up a deadcred and get tossed out of here."

"Yeah, maybe he'll be your new neighbor," Migo returns a favor by rubbing my head and messing up my already unkempt hair. His credentials suddenly flash a notification signal. "That's us. We're up."

As we make our way back towards the waiting room, Migo reminds me why we're here.

"Ok, Ren, just remember, you were a witness to a hit and run."

"Yeah, I'm sure after you hit the ground, you ran. To me. How do you even crash a FlyBike? It's all automated."

Aerial crashes are super rare for everyone here but him. My guess is he was high or drunk and ran into something, then tried to paint over the impact. He'd be nothing but a noso in a nice fit if it wasn't for me.

"Shhhh," he hushes me.

"I told you I can fix it, and they'll never know," I whisper.

"It's not like I don't trust you, Ren. I just don't have the record to make that bet."

He's not worried about the social credit as much as he is about his pilot's license. These MetiCorp-owned facilities are credit-neutral, so it's not like he'd have to lose anything on the repair. MetiCorp runs credit-neutral versions of just about every business in the cities. They allow private businesses to fill the cracks, providing various niche products and services. But if you have a MetiCorp vehicle, and you bring it to some third-party repair shop like mine in the Outskirtz, MetiCorp won't fix it after that. They'll argue some 'amateur' tampering with it voids their service agreement.

The majority of repairs completed in MetiCity are done by machines. Only mechanics like me who work in the Outskirtz really get a sense of what's going on under the hood. Technology gets replaced more than repaired, so I've gotten really good at finding various scraps to reverse-engineer and rebuild. When you grow up with nothing to your name, everything you touch was either once someone else's or a gift.

One man's trash is another man's dinner.

"There's nothing wrong with used parts," I say as I follow him back into the repair facility. "Let's make it quick, it's freezing in here."

"You sound like you're from the Outskirtz," Migos says, walking up to the front desk to check-in.

"I am?" I say, confused. He ignores me.

Migo is real selective about when he wants to claim being from the Outskirtz. If he wants to fit in, he's MetiCity-6 born and raised. He wants to intimidate someone? Then he's fresh out the 'skirtz. We both know there's not enough credit in this city to get him to go back to sand and unfiltered sun. He was happy to sign the MetiCorp contract and leave as soon as he could.

He'd never admit it, but at this point, I'd say his ratio is probably ninety percent dome baby to ten percent sandscavenger. He's probably even forgotten how to dig. And us sandscavs have a saying; 'you only stop digging when you've dug your own grave'.

After ranking, he decided to become a disposal worker. A once-ridiculed career has become an important essential infrastructure role that comes with a ton of responsibility. Along with some personal discretion when it comes to deciding when things are dumped and when things are recycled.

The best kind of a friend for a scavenger.

I look over to see the same woman sitting in the waiting room is still tapped-in, surfing the internet on her credentials. I never like tapping in while in public. I don't mind going heads up; the augmented overlay gives the green and pristine MetiCity the look of a neon dynasty. But when you tap-in, there's something slightly off about the way you look. Like your brain was beamed out into space and there's no one home. A state I'd never be caught in outside the city, especially considering how rare credentials are out there. Only settlers who have em' are the ones who don't mind getting paid in social credit, like my boss, Frank.

We're instructed to follow the tech through the door to a garage port where Migo's FlyBike is waiting. It's a mess. The bike and the garage. At any given time, my shop could have ten to fifteen violations by MetiCorp standards, but this place has more, and we're not even regulated. Regardless, there's no way the tech is going to think this was some hit-and-run accident. The only thing strong enough to do that to a FlyBike is the Earth itself.

Before the tech can speak, Migo tries to convince him he doesn't know how it happened.

"Are you kidding? Look at this thing," the tech says, lifting one of the flimsy panels and letting it drop, "to be honest, you should thank the Allspirits you're alive."

"I wasn't even driving it. It was parked! I have a witness," Migo says, pointing to me.

"Like I'm going to trust the word of some Outskirtz kid with sand for brains?" the tech scoffs.

"It's true. I think he may have parked a little crooked and... well, it was an accident," that's for sure, I think to myself.

"Wait right here. I'm going to get a second opinion," the tech smiles, walking over to a coworker who is elbow-deep inside the engine of some old cruiser. "Hey boss, check this out, will ya?"

"One second! This damn thing..." he grunts, trying to twist his way through detaching a locked bolt. This is what I'm talking about. These guys replace everything. They rarely have to get their hands dirty.

"Excuse me, sir?" I say, walking up behind his boss and tapping him on the shoulder. He jumps and the wrench he was using flies out of his hand into the air, just barely misses Migo's head.

"Whoa! Kid, are you crazy? I'm working here!" His boss yells.

"Hard, but not smart. There's a release just behind the air filter," I say, pointing to the switch he needs to hit. They both exchange confused glances before the boss hits the release. The storage area he was trying to get to clicks and he's able to pull it out easily.

"Holy shit! Kid, I've been working on this for hours."

"Don't sweat it," I say.

"What are you doing here anyway?" his boss asks.

"They said it was a hit-and-run accident," the tech laughs, pointing to Migo's wrecked bike.

His boss grimaces at the damage. He looks back over at me and smiles before shrugging.

"If they say it was an accident, I guess it was an accident."

"But he-" the tech starts.

"Might trip and fall walking around this place? Punch it up, and when you're done, I want this place cleaned up. Oh, and hand me that wrench. Please?" he says with a smile.

"Yes sir," the tech grumbles, walking over to grab the wrench. He hands it back before opening his credentials to scan the FlyBike and create the repair order. "Give me a day. Enjoy the loaner, asshole," the tech says, punching up the order.

"Bruh, you saved my ass. Drinks on me tonight. Well, 'drink' on me tonight," Migo corrects himself and laughs.

After waiting a few minutes, the garage door opens and the tech comes rumbling in on a FlyBike that looks like it's being held together with shoestring and bubble gum.

"Nice." Migo isn't fazed in the least. "Hop on. I'll take you to the loading docks so you can go home, shower, and change before I come get you. And don't tell me you don't have anything else to wear."

"You think I'm going to a bar? With you? On that?" I ask, pointing to the loaner.

It's a certified piece of scrap. Older generation and showing its wear. When he starts it back up, it's loud and vibrates so much I think it's going to give him a concussion.

"Fine. See you tonight 'scav," he says, zooming off before I can talk my way out of it.

CHAPTER TWO_

The public Mag-Lev takes me as far as the MetiCity docks, where I go through the standard security scan. Wouldn't want us taking anything too fancy back home. The 24-hour travel pass Migo gave me has restricted access anyway, so it's pretty limited as to where I can go and what I can get. It comes with enough social credit for things like hotels and food, but because of the time penalties, I don't ever risk using the full day. Break that rule once, and I may never see the city again.

Once I'm through the gates at the docks I have to foot it to the massive parking lot built for visitors. The old Jeep I drove in stands out so much that I spot it immediately. When I first dug the thing out, I had to gut it, update the engine to run off our biodiesel blend, and firm up the suspension for the rugged terrain. I modified the AC too, but I rarely use that anymore. It's a waste, considering there are no doors or windows. It's not the prettiest, but it handles great in the sand and has no trouble scaling dunes. I've had dreams about driving it through MetiC-ity, just to enjoy the shocked faces gasping at the sight of tech-nology from the old world still running. Even if I was approved to drive, I doubt they would let me use something so archaic on their autoways.

I start the Jeep up and the radio blares out over the old engine. The radio signals from the city are blocked, so it must be someone transmitting from the Outskirtz. Lethal Weather's old stuff; I like their taste. I drive to the edge of the parking lot and dock it in one of the free transport carts. After locking in, I turn the Jeep off and sit back reclined in the seat. The warning buzzer sounds and the cart is propelled through the airtight Mag-Lev tube leading away from the city at five hundred miles an hour. The transport cart runs atop an extensive bridge that rises high above the open sea. After about an hour and a half, I begin to see an end to the ocean and our encampment comes into view in the distance.

I restart the Jeep, leaving the transport cart at the end of the bridge, hit sand, and speed off. Most of the camp is dug in below ground, but because we haven't had to move recently, it's grown a bit since I was young. What was once just a small roaming settlement has become a city home to thousands of settlers, deadcreds, criminals, ex-rebels like Frank, and sand-scavengers like me. Cities like mine aren't unique, so much so that we don't even have our own name. Because wherever there is a MetiCity, there is always an Outskirtz.

The shop just feels like home to me. I can't explain why. Ever since I can remember, I just wanted to fix all the broken little things left from the old cities. Give them a home. A better home than the orphanage my parents dumped me in. A better home than the one my fosters gave me. We all just want to feel useful at the end of the day. It's been years since something came into the shop that I couldn't fix. In that, I find solace.

I'm almost there when I notice some punks beating the shit out of a poor guy right in the open road. As I pull up, I realize it's actually a Droid. I could *really* use a fucking Droid. Even if it is an older generation, it could help Frank run the shop. By the look of it, it's taken some heavy damage, but it's nothing I can't repair.

"Where you think you're going?" one of the punks says, grabbing the Droid by its legs and pulling it back. It tries its best to crawl away.

"Hey!" I call out. I'm outnumbered and I don't want to start a fight here, but I can't watch this senseless violence and not say anything.

They turn to me like blood-thirsty wolves protecting their prey.

"You got a problem, kid?" one asks angrily. He sets his foot on the Droid's head and crosses his arms.

"No problem. I just so happen to need a Droid, and it doesn't look like you guys are going to use that one."

"You need an eye mod kid? We're using it now!" he says, stomping on the Droid. The Droid is mostly unbothered, but I can't help but see a look of hope in his faceless expression.

"Maybe you'd be willing to part with it for some fresh MetiCity social credit? There's still plenty of time on em'." I'm not sure that'll work. They aren't sandscavengers, UG, or anyone who might travel to MetiCity. They're the bottom of the barrel. Misery pulling company down with it. And if they never leave the Outskirtz or trade with MetiCity, the social credit goes from plat to rat crap. Unfortunately, it's all I have on me, save for my wrench and credentials. And those aren't for sale.

"Why would I go all the way up ta' MetiCity when I'm havin' so much fun down 'ere? You best be 'bout your business, 'fore you become *our* business," he warns.

"Come on! How about a trade?" This pisses him off even more.

"What I say, kid? Noro, shut this guy up," he says, signaling to one of his friends.

Shit.

A fat bag of sand, who I assume is Noro, cracks his knuckles and slowly makes his way over to me. He walks up and stands in front of me with his hands at his side, smiling.

"Sure you guys don't want to negotiate?" I plead. There are four of them in total, including this smelly slomper. Maybe I can take them one on one. But not all at once.

Noro pulls his ham-hock arm back slightly, looking to deck me with a hook to the side of the head. I lean back and bend at the knee as his punch goes shooting past. I pull my wrench off the magnetic strip on my overalls and activate it, extending its size from a foot to nearly three. I spin it around, then swing at his elbow. It hits, throwing him off balance due to the force of his swing. Too much wind-up. Too much time. I adjust my weight onto the bent back knee and lift my front foot slightly, just enough to trip him at the ankle, sending him to the ground face-first. His head hits the concrete hard and he lays there out cold with his ass up to the sky. I watch as the others' faces shift from shock to anger.

"Noro!" they yell as they run over to and make sure he isn't dead before turning their focus back to me.

One comes at me while the other tries to wake up Noro. Another one-on-one. This one doesn't throw any punches. Instead, he has a size advantage, so he walks straight up and goes two-hands-on-one, trying to get control of the wrench. Incorrect assessment. While he is pulling at my arm, attempting to get to the wrench, I crouch and pull back to feign resistance. Once he gives it a good pull, I push off my feet, driving the top of my head into his chin. This throws him back and he releases his grip on my arm. I'm still in the air when he does, so I'm able to spin around before hitting the ground, driving my heel right into his chin where I had just headbutted him. He drops onto the other guy, who is still on the ground trying to revive Noro. He looks up at me, trying to get free from the weight of the limp body.

Out of the corner of my eye, I can see that the leader has snuck up and is about to swing on me. I'm not sure I can react in time, but I try to angle off and fade back slightly. Just before his punch lands, it stops. The Droid grabs his fist in mid-air. They aren't supposed to do that unless they're protecting an owner. I'm as shocked as he is.

"What the fuck? Is he decoded? Let go! Get off me!" he yells at the Droid. The Droid loosens its grip enough so that he can free his hand. As soon as he does, he winds up for another punch, this time aiming at the Droid. Before he can throw the punch, I kick the back of his knee, causing him to kneel. I raise my wrench and stop.

"Enough?" I ask, smiling.

"Fuck this. Let's get outta here. This Droid 'bout fully fucked up," he says, backing away and grabbing at the other guy's arm. The two on the ground are just regaining consciousness as they are dragged away. Humiliating.

"Can you go into carry mode?" I ask the Droid, but I'm met with silence. "Yeah, I didn't think so." He's in no condition, but I know these things have a setting that makes them easier to travel with. I'm able to find a rusty wheelbarrow that I have him sit in so I can get him to the shop. He seems to enjoy the ride and opens his hands out to let the breeze pass through his fingers. The skinny bipedal Droid is old in age and appearance, its wires exposed, peeking out from what little exo-layer is left on him. I've heard people say some of the oldest prototypes had faces, but this isn't one of them. MetiCitians didn't like their Droids to look too human, weirded them out. So this one had to have been made after the rebellion, even if it looks like it's been through one.

Like all Outskirt settlements, the shop is set in the ground, and there's a stairway leading down into the entrance. I help the Droid up and let him lean on me to keep him standing, although he's at least two feet taller than I am. As we walk down the stairway, he can't seem to stop staring at me. Maybe he's trying to utilize facial recognition but is having trouble?

Once we're inside, I'm able to tap-in and I realize this isn't a generation one. It's... older. Maybe an original prototype? The code is weird, too; it's nothing I've seen before. It's simple and cleaner than the new code but also more primitive. It's also missing some major updates that allowed these guys to become the commercial successes they are today.

Why would this thing be in the Outskirtz and not a museum? Maybe someone brought it here to get repaired since the Company would likely replace it? I figured they would have recalled all the prototypes a long time ago. Odd.

I'm still working on getting the Droid back to full function-ality when Migo calls.

"INCOMING!" Migo yells. I lost track of time.

"A'ight, meet you at the docks at 8:00," I say to dead air.

From the Outskirtz, you can see the city lights for miles. As more MetiCities pop up across the oceans, the various Outskirtz around them fade, and populations dwindle. What were once massive cities with vastly different populations and cultures are now uninhabitable crumbling relics. What was once an ocean teeming with life under the surface is now just an empty foundation for the cities above it. The wreckage is most dense near the coastlines, and as we pass over, I can still make out certain landmarks like the infamous Statue of Liberty. Now resembling someone in neck-deep water, holding a torch up in the hopes that they can be saved by a passing ship.

When I arrive, I can hear Migo coming in for a landing next to me, the loud FlyBike rumbling as he lands and idles. I assumed he had another at home, but I guess that was his second or third wreck. Honestly, I've lost count.

"I can't believe you're still riding that thing." I don't know why I'm surprised. He gets a kick out of people watching him, even if they are laughing.

"This *thing* may be damn near a prototype, but it's still got the gas." Migo smiles and slaps the side of the loaner.

Once I get on, and we get going, we *really* get going. Now I know what he means. It looks like shit, but the performance is amazing. Much smoother than I'd imagined. It only rumbles and vibrates heavily when sitting still. Like it's dying to take off. I can tell, even with Migo's terrible driving, that it has great handling. It automatically adjusts its own pitch and yaw, so we stay upright as we head back into MetiCity-6.

CHAPTER THREE_

Once we park, Migo sends me some social credit so I can get into this fancy place without too much issue. He makes his way to the bar immediately. It's loud and stuffy. I'm not a big drinker, but I indulge anyway. Not every day does Migo swing down and rescue me from the Outskirtz, and offer to buy.

Migo hands me a colorful bottle with a rainbow on the label. I take a tentative sip. It burns on the way down, but once it goes away, I'm impressed enough by the taste to take another swig. Migo points to my face, laughing. I'm smiling ear to ear. I don't even know why, but I can't stop and I start to worry my face is going to get stuck like this.

"What was that?" I ask, looking down at the bottle he had handed me.

"A LiteRay. How you feelin'?" Migo says through laughter.

"Like someone shoved a rainbow up my ass."

"You look so happy about it, though." He grins, chugging back another before making his way through the crowd.

I follow. I'm always following.

"HEY! There they are!" He addresses two young women sitting at a table. Both are attractive if you're into the MetiCity look, loud and artificial. One is platinum blonde, the other's hair is a dizzying mix of neon colors, similar to the empty bottle I'm for some reason still holding. "This is Lucy, and this is-" Migo starts.

"His girlfriend," she cuts him off, giggling. "My name is Tovah." She reaches to shake my hand.

"And this is-" Migo starts.

"His boyfriend," I interrupt with a smirk. He rolls his eyes.

"Guys, there's enough of me to go around. Calm down." Migo gestures for everyone to mellow out. "Speaking of rounds, didn't you say you were paying tonight, Ren? Why don't you and Lucy go grab us some beers? Get the girls one of those fancy gin cocktails they love so much," he says, nudging me.

"Actually, we like the new Company spritzers. They're so refreshing," Tovah says with an odd exaggerated smile.

"Yes. We like the new Company spritzers," Lucy parrots back in an obsequious tone.

I sneak a glance at Migo to see if he thought that was as weird as I did, but the obnoxious look on his face reminds me of his setup. It's not the first time he's brought me to meet one of his 'girlfriends' and their cute friend.

I'm stuck waiting with her at the bar and I try some small talk to kill the awkwardness.

"Is tonight your first time meeting Migo?" I ask.

"He and Tovah have been talking for a while, so I've met him a few times. To be honest, he seems like a player to me. Is he going to break my friend's heart?" she asks half-jokingly.

I hesitate, "Nah. Of course not. I've known him for years, and I can tell already he likes her. Otherwise, he wouldn't have dragged me out of the house on a work night."

"Hmm, I don't know if I'm convinced, but you do look like a hard worker," she purrs. "You're not from MetiCity, are you?"

"Nope," I say as the bartender hands over four drinks on a metal disk. "I'm from the Outskirtz. So is Migo, or he was. That's how we met, in ranking," I explain.

"I knew it. I can always tell! So what do you do?" she asks as we make our way back to the table.

"Well, I'm a mechanic."

"So you're good with your hands?" she says coyly. It's an obvious pass, but I'm skeptical.

We take our seats and I hand out the drinks, fielding a smile from Lucy as I do. Migo is sitting facing Tovah and Lucy is sitting facing me.

"Lucy, didn't you say you were into boys from the Outskirtz? Said they were more...real, remember?" Migo jeers. She turns red immediately.

"Fuck off, Migo!" she says to him, avoiding eye contact with me. "I mean, they are. A lot of guys I meet in MetiCity haven't worked a day in their life," she argues.

"Lucy, *you* haven't worked a day in your life!" Migo laughs. This isn't a surprise. The creation of new jobs has been a huge problem for the last few decades. Because of advances in robotics and automation, food scarcity has been almost completely eliminated. Unfortunately, because of that, many jobs have been eliminated as well. A lot of women have given up dreams of a career to instead focus on finding a partner who can provide a cushy life for them.

"Yes, okay, but I've always been a fan of...traditional gender roles," she explains. This notion of traditional gender roles is a farce. Most of what was once 'traditionally' a woman's role has faded out in the last century as the social credit system was established and Droids took over the work. She wants freedom but seeks it in the hands of another instead of her own.

"You have nothing to be ashamed of, Lucy. Don't let him pick on you," Tovah says, smacking Migo in the arm.

"I'm just messing with you, Lucy. Nothing wrong with focusing on...keeping your man happy," he smirks. She turns red again, this time out of anger rather than shyness. Tovah again assaults Migo for his coarse tongue.

"What?" he says, lifting his arms to defend himself.

"Allspirits, Migo, you have no filter. Ugh," Tovah says, putting her credentials over her ear. "Let's dance! You can't talk when you're dancing."

Tovah grabs Migo by the arm and drags him to the dance floor platform. There's another couple dancing under a lit circle on the floor. While it looks empty, that's all going to change once they open their credentials and peer through their glass displays. By now, they're likely seeing a dance floor full of tapped-in people from all over the world. I can see them fidgeting with the music settings, most likely scrolling through an assortment of genres to find the right mood. As they scroll, they'll be able to see a different group of people for each station who are either tapped-in or are being broadcasted from another club in another city. Tovah finds the right station and a light from overhead marks an open spot for them to dance in.

"Do you ever...?" Lucy says, pointing to the dance floor.

"Not since ranking. It's been a long time. I wouldn't even know what to do," I reply, looking over at the couple dancing.

"That's okay. I never know what station to pick anyway," she says, looking down. We sit for a moment, awkwardly watching Migo and Tovah dance before I muster up the guts to make a move.

"We can always hop on their station?" I stand up and hold out my hand for her to join me.

We make our way over and Migo and his girlfriend cheer us on. Putting on our credentials, we join the now crowded dance floor as a vaporwave retro remix of some old song I've never heard fills our ears. I try moving slightly but can't keep up with her. The hook hits and the three of them start singing the lyrics. We become four people dancing instead of two pairs. Not sure if it's the LiteRay or what, but I'm starting to enjoy myself. It's honestly nice to block everything out and just live in the moment.

The next song is slower. Migo and Tovah immediately close the distance, forehead to forehead, wrapped in each other's arms. I look over at Lucy, who has opened her arms, inviting me to join her, so I do.

"You're not a bad dancer. A bit stiff, but I've seen worse," she says.

"Thanks?" I ask, looking down while closing my arms around her.

"Oh. Can you get us another drink?" she says suddenly before I can join my hands together. I glance over at the table where our drinks still are, shrug, and head to the bar. I order two, and when I walk back toward the floor, I can only see Migo and his girlfriend still slow dancing.

"Where did Lucy go?" I ask him.

"Oh. Umm..." he says, surveying the room. "Oh shit... Hilson." He and Tovah have stopped dancing and are looking at a couple making out near the entrance.

"Sorry, my guy. They're an off and on kinda thing," Migo says, scratching the back of his head.

"I told her not to call him. She always does this," Tovah says, sighing. They stop making out long enough to walk their way towards us.

"Hey guys! Look who randomly showed up," Lucy says, showing off Hilson.

"Randomly. Right," Tovah says under her breath while rolling her eyes.

"Hey Migo. Long time no see," Hilson says, waving at Migo and Tovah.

"Yeah, like, a week ago, right?" Migo says sarcastically, but well enough that it doesn't sound so.

There is a moment of us all standing there awkwardly before Lucy breaks the silence.

"Oh, thanks Ren," she says, grabbing the drinks out of my hands and handing one to Hilson.

"Oh yeah, thanks bud," Hilson says, chugging my drink.

"No problem," I say softly as they make their way to the dance floor and start to dance inappropriately.

"Gross," Migo says. "Here. Drink up." He hands me the beer from the table, slapping my shoulder.

"I'm good. I'm going to head home. Long trip and I don't want to be late for work."

"Aww. You sure man? Frank won't be upset."

"Nah, I actually scrapped a Droid from some punk in the 'skirtz, so I'm going to get to work on that."

"A true 'scav!" he says, smiling. He looks over at Tovah and shrugs. "Shall we join them?"

"As you wish, my good sir," Tovah says with a little curtsy.

"Sorry Ren," they both say in almost unison, heading back to the dance floor.

I wave them off and head out. If I got social credit every time he headed home to get laid while I left thinking about work in the morning, I'd be able to buy him the entire bar. For a moment there, I got excited at the possibility. I'm usually so good at not getting my hopes up. I try to keep my head out of the clouds as much as I can, but the more I visit MetiCity, the more I feel like I'm missing out on something. I'm not mad at Migo for trying. The fact that he's always included me as much as he can since he moved to MetiCity lets me know he isn't ashamed of his friend from the Outskirtz. I've always admired him for that. And for his ability to adapt so quickly to MetiCity life. I take one last glance back at the dance floor from the exit.

He's a natural at it. Sometimes, I'd rather have that talent than mine.

I step out of the bar and can see that the nearby stadium is lighting up the night sky. I still have my credentials on, so I'm able to see the City filled with projections of people visiting as well as the actual populace. It's a dizzying mess but somehow comes together as a spectacle to behold. I'm standing in the middle of the walkway, taking it all in, when I'm bumped into by a tall man in a Biosuit. The bump knocks me on my ass. Who the hell would wear a full military-grade Biosuit in public?

"Oh, sorry kid, you ok?" he asks, looking down at me. "Didn't even see you there."

He's Asian, with a buzzcut, and he's got scarring on his neck where it meets the Biosuit collar.

"Help him up, Koujin!" I didn't realize it, but he's accompanied by a woman with light green hair pulled back into a ponytail, contrasting against her smooth, caramel skin. I can't help but stare, and not just because she's stunning. I've never seen a Jardinera in real life. They were discovered on a remote island in the 2040s and have a separate evolutionary tree from modern humans, completely unique.

"Right, come on kid," Koujin says, offering out his hand to help me up. It takes me a moment because I'm mesmerized by the girl's eyes, which are the same soft green as her hair. I place my hand in his and when he tightens his grip, it feels like it's going to break my hand.

"Arrgh," I cry out.

"Oh shit. Sorry kid!" he says, releasing his grip.

"It's fine," I say, making my way to my feet. I look up at them and for a moment, I'm not sure if the suit or the girl is more beautiful. The man has a menacing presence, a few inches taller and wider than me in the Biosuit. The girl is around my height, but her frame is slender and feminine. Not that I'm looking too hard. She's wrapped up in a MetiCity white academic coat with a light blue trim. They look like MetiCity elites.

"Um. To be honest, it's probably the actuator for the hand grip. Have you tried taking it off and repairing it?"

"Not an option, kid." He says sternly. He's one of 'them.' I've heard that some of the hardcore military guys never get out of the Biosuit. Not to shower, not to shit, not even to fuck. That explains the scarring on his neck, a sign that he's fully committed. Which means he is actually military, and it's not just a Biosuit; it's Paladin armor.

"Of course. Sorry. Well, if you disable the actuator manually, I may be able to adjust it externally." I offer.

"Yeah? You sure you know what you're doing, kid?"

"I know this is a Paladin armor Biosuit and the locking mechanism is adjustable from the outside once the actuator is disabled," I say, putting his hand in mine. He looks over at the Jardinera girl and they both shrug. We step off to the side of the walkway and he explains that he's been having issues with it since his last fight.

"To be honest, I'm surprised you didn't recognize me," he says, putting his credentials on to disable the mechanism in his hand.

"Don't watch the fights much."

"What's wrong kid? They don't get the fights in the Outskirtz?" he says, chuckling.

"Koujin, he's trying to help. Don't be rude," the girl says to him, and she smiles at me. "I'm sorry."

"Ok, it's disabled. But I'm watching closely." He glares at me.

"An audience doesn't bother me," I say, taking out a small tool I keep on me, apparently for situations just like this. I'm just happy to be able to work on Paladin armor. It's not something you see every day. Neither is she.

"That should do it," I say, finishing up my work. He makes a fist a few times, then smiles.

"Not bad, kid. I'm impressed."

"Well. Um. See ya, I guess," I say, starting to turn around. She's staring at me, looking impressed, and it's starting to make me nervous.

"Hey kid, wait. You should come check me out tomorrow. I have a fight a few blocks from here, in the HFL."

"Couldn't afford it, even if I wanted to. But thanks." I solemnly turn to walk away again.

"No worries. Here, open up a com-link," he says, fidgeting with the credentials on his wrist. I open the message and get a notification saying I've received two tickets to his fight. VIP tickets, whoa.

"Are you serious!? Thanks!" I say, staring at the image of the tickets.

"No sweat. Bring a friend. Ask them about me," he says, turning to walk away with the girl. I hear him say something about needing to bump into random people on the street more often.

I break away from staring at the tickets for a moment to do a search on 'Koujin' and find out he's the champion. Tickets to a championship fight? I could eat off these for months if I sold them.

You know what, I'm starting to see what Migo sees in this city.

CHAPTER FOUR_

Was it all a dream? It's the first thing I can think of as I awake. I open the credentials on my wrist and see the tickets still there in my inventory. I let out a sigh of relief. My head turns to one side and I can see the Droid sitting there, staring. It startles the shit out of me.

"Sheesh, you almost made me short-circuit there for a second," I say, placing my hand over my heart to make sure it's still beating. I had worked on him last night until the sun rose, so I couldn't have been out that long. "Are you fully operational?" I ask him. I can't exactly remember how far I got.

He lifts his hand and tilts it side to side as if to say 'so-so.' That's right, his voice box is crushed. I need to get it replaced. Looks like he can see me, but from the distance he's staring, I think he may need to have that repaired as well.

"What kind of piece of shit did you drag up in here, boy?" I couldn't see him until I turned, but Frank had been sitting at a workbench in the back of the shop for who knows how long. Again, startling the shit out of me.

"What's up with you two?" I huffed, getting to my feet.

"I'm not the one passed out at work doing Allspirits know what, with some junker Droid," Frank huffs back.

"I always sleep here," I say, throwing my hands up and shrugging.

"My shop ain't no motel, boy."

"You wouldn't turn me towards a dusty road, would ya' Frank?

"The hell I wouldn't," he grumbles before lurching towards the Droid to get a better look.

"Some punks were beating the shit out of it for fun. I took it off their hands." I smile slightly.

"Wasn't worth the hassle. The hell you need a MetiCity Droid for? This thing might as well be older than me. As a matter of fact..." he says, leaning close to the Droid. The Droid responds by leaning back slightly in an uncomfortable effort. "This thing's a damn prototype boy. An original. Might be able to get some money for it. Get you a ticket to MetiCity, where you should be. 'Bout time you started taking care of yourself," he says, turning back to face me.

"I do take care of myself."

"Yeah? Well, why don't you take care of the customer that's been waiting for the last ten minutes."

"What? Why didn't you help them?" I say, heading towards the front of the shop.

"If I have to deal with another scavrat looking to sell his friend's fridge for some greesha, I'm going to sell this place and retire off land," Frank hollers as I get out of earshot.

Frank is the only person I've known almost as long as Migo. I used to come through his shop when I was young, selling things I had dug out and repaired. When I was good enough, I started buying his crap gear, upgrading it, and selling it back to him for a profit. By then, I was old enough to work for him. He's a centenarian now, and since it's become increasingly challenging to access safe life-extension treatments out here, he seems resigned to let nature take its course. He wasn't always so willing to let go, though. About forty years ago, when Frank was in his sixties, he joined a rebel force that tried to topple Zelius's regime. He often brags about the time he almost killed Zelius with a rocket launcher. He says that MetiCorp turned a blind eye to those still outside who were suffering on the deteriorating planet. The rebellion lasted through much of the 2080s until they were forced to start worrying more about where to get food and clean water. They decided they would rather roast in the high sun than sign the contract. Since then, he's been slompin' out here in the Outskirtz with the rest of us. That's what happens when you're on the losing side of the war.

As I get to the front, I can tell immediately it's a MetiCitian, well-kept and meticulously groomed. He even looks familiar. I just can't place it.

"Sorry about the wait. What's going on?" I ask him. He continues looking around the shop. "You know what you're looking for?"

"Actually, I believe I'm looking for, well, you," he says, looking me over.

"Me?" I say. I've built a bit of a reputation around here for being able to fix broken tech. Only a few know I can mod Meti-Corp tech; it's not exactly something I've been advertising. Modding Company tech may be something I can do, but not for some rando off the street. Especially one who looks like he's never seen sand in his life...

"Do all Outskirt folk have a scar like you and work in repair shops?" he asks, pointing at my face. I brush my hand against the side of my head where my scar is. Sometimes I forget about them. They streak from just past my eye to the side of my head. No idea where I got them from. The only gift my real parents left me. I'll be sure to ask them how I got the scar when they come back and tell me I've been a prince this entire time.

"Gotta love MetiCity folk, coming through the Outskirtz to stop and stare at us like zoo animals," I say.

"No, no, no. I meant no offense. I was told to look for a boy with a scar here who may be able to help repair my vehicle."

"From who?"

"She was stranded and you helped her get back airborne in a flash. She was told by someone when looking for help you could fix anything. That's why she came to you."

"The old lady with the clueless security guard?" I say. It's got to be her. I was stunned to see an elder from MetiCity out this far, but it turns out she was just passing through and got stranded outside the city. It was an easy fix, but something her security was completely useless to help her with.

"That old lady is my mother, but yes. Her security has a high turnover rate. I'm not sure who is more insufferable. Now, if that wasn't enough, a friend of mine said he bumped into a kid from the Outskirtz last night. The kid, who also had a scar like yours, repaired his Paladin armor in seconds."

"Koujin? The guy in the Paladin armor?" I ask, thinking back to last night.

"So it is you. One and the same. And is it true? What they said."

"Only one way to find out. What 'chu got? Although I don't usually work on Company tech." I backtrack.

"Well, it's not *really* Company tech. More of a new proto-type." I am expecting something similar to the one Migo got as a loaner. Not even close. We step out into the loading dock and he shows off this gorgeous one-seater. Brand new tech. Something a professional O-Racer would use.

"I remember where I know you from now. Zander. O-Race Cup runner-up two years in a row." I recall.

"Three years in a row, but who's counting? Can you fix it?"

I lean down, admiring the craftsmanship. You don't see tech like this in the Outskirtz. Hell, you don't see tech like this, period. I am basically drooling. "What's wrong with it? It looks like you could win your fourth Cup with it."

"Start it up," he says, passing his credentials over the monitor.

"Really?" I'm perplexed. To bring this kind of tech to the Outskirtz, his security must be sweating outside. To let someone he doesn't know operate it? Is he insane or just dumb? I don't give him time to answer. I start it up and hop in.

Man, this thing is eerily quiet. Runs smooth and feels fast. Part of me wants to know how fast. After a moment, though, my senses kick in. I hop out. I press my hand against the side and slowly move it towards the back of the jet.

It's like a magnet, sometimes. I can feel the pain calling out to me. Something's wrong, and this O-Racer jet is begging me to find it. I slowly glide my hand over the frame, and about halfway down, there it is. The heating coil is burnt. My understanding is they use them to heat specific surfaces so the jet can modify airflow patterns, reduce drag, or enhance lift. These things can withstand extremely high temperatures. Even when maneuvering at all those g-forces, he shouldn't get this kind of damage. Damage like this could be life-threatening, depending on the situation. How the fuck did his overpaid bubble baby crew miss this?

"How the hell does someone overheat a heating coil?" I ask.

"That was quick," Zander says with a huge smile. "It's something that most techs wouldn't even check for, and you went right to it." He chuckled.

"I don't even know if we have any heating coils. It's not

something we often have to replace, but I can check," I say, turning to go back into the shop.

"It's fine. I brought one with me."

"You already know the issue? Then why-"

"A test. I've been looking for a different set of eyes for my pit crew this year. I've been having random issues like this and need someone capable. Someone...unconventional. Interested?"

"Nah. I've already got a job. Besides-"

"HE'LL DO IT!" Frank screams out of nowhere.

"What? But what about the shop?" I yell back.

"I'm going to sell this dump, remember? I was planning on cutting your shifts anyway." He says, walking up and slapping my back harder than necessary.

"Well, if your Grandfather says it's okay and you're interested, you'll have to fill out these forms." He airdrops them over to me on my credentials. That cut Frank's smile short. "You'll need to be at the MetiCity-6 stadium tomorrow morning at 8:00 a.m. We can give you a test run and see if you fit." He heads to the door to tell his team to load the jet into the cargo carrier they had strapped to one of their transports. He turns back to me in the doorway. "Oh. What's your name, kid?"

"Ren. Ren Unkno."

"Unkno Eh? Poor kid." Zander sighs.

"Yeah, he is! That's why you're gonna give him a travel pass for this fancy MetiCity job of yours."

"Frank, don't be rude," I say, trying not to ask for too much.

"What? Migo ain't gonna just gift you a travel pass every day," Frank argues.

"It's no problem. Open a com-link," Zander says, fidgeting with his credentials. I received the message.

"A week-long travel pass?" I exclaim. I didn't even know

that was possible. It's not cheap to get travel passes, and he just sent me seven.

"Do you think you'll only need one? You must have more confidence in yourself, Ren."

"He's right," Frank says, pushing at my shoulder.

"You have my information if you have any questions. Otherwise, I will see you in the morning," Zander says, waving before passing through the doorway and out of sight.

I look over at Frank in shock.

"What? It's about time!" Frank huffs before fading into the backroom. "And clean that damn Droid up!" he yells loud enough for me to hear.

I have to tell Migo. He's not going to believe it. I open a com-link and invite him. I get no response, so I go to check if he's streaming. He likes to stream himself playing games from time to time, but it's usually just a bunch of cursing and throwing his game stick. He's not very good. I tune in just in time to see him waiting to respawn. I type in his chat, 'CHECK YOUR PHONE DOME HEAD.' He pauses the stream and finally accepts my com-link invite.

"Mushi mushi Ren, are you enjoying the stream? I almost had em'!" Migo groans.

"Hey. Didn't mean to interrupt. I was just wondering, have you heard of Zander Thorne?" I know he has. He's been into O-Racing since we were in ranking. Everyone in MetiCity-6 was proud to have the number 2 O-Racer in the world, and Migo is no different.

"Good one. Of course I have, have you? I hope you didn't waste your social credit on tickets to the Opening Cup next week, because I've already got them, of course," he cockily claims. I want to one-up him for once.

"Oh yeah? We'll then maybe you'll see me at the Cup. I

might just be working. Pit Crew. For Zander," I say, chopping the sentence up to build suspense.

"You'll be doing WHAT? FOR WHO?"

"I thought you said you knew who he was?" I laugh.

"ARE YOU SERIOUS? Wait...is this some kind of prank? I could have got it on stream. For the clout, man! For the clout!" he groans.

"No prank."

"WELL?"

"He heard from his friend Koujin that I could repair anything. So he came out and tested my knowledge on some glacious new jet, and I passed. I've got to be there early tomorrow."

"Wait...Koujin...THE Koujin?" he stutters.

"Oh, you've heard of him?"

"Of course I've heard of him! Tonight's his first title defense! How does he know YOU?" His bewildered excitement was palpable.

"After I left the bar last night, I bumped into him and did a quick repair on his Paladin armor." I tried to sound nonchalant.

"Allspirits man, I'm stunned! Actually, no, I'm not. Everyone knows you're the best mechanic in the Outskirtz. You deserve this. We need to celebrate! I'll come get you and we can hit a scrapyard or something. Or maybe a brothel?" he says, giggling to himself. "Then back to my place and we can watch the fight?"

"I've got a better idea. Why don't we go to the fight?"

"You never want to go to the fights. I mean, maybe I can swing some last-minute tickets, but it's a title fight. It's probably sold out."

"Well, I didn't want to go because it's a luxury I usually can't afford."

"Usually?"

"Remember when I said I repaired Koujin's Biosuit?"

"Yeah?"

"Well, he gave me two free tickets. And I don't think Frank is up for it."

"I never said that!" I could hear Frank call from the back. He's always listening.

"Think fast, Migo."

"Be there in two hours," Migo says, closing the com-link. I can't help but smile. It's not every day I get to be the one to treat Migo.

From just outside the shop, I can see the outline of the MetiCity-6 dome peeking out over the horizon. I finish cleaning the Droid just before Migo arrives. His FlyBike isn't really meant for two people, like a cruiser, but I fit snugly in the back where one would keep cargo. I stun him again when I tell him I don't need a travel pass.

"Wish you would have told me that before I bought one!" he groans.

"Why not invite Calli? I'm sure she'd love to see you," I say smirking.

"I'm exclusive now, remember?"

"Oh right, to Tovah?" I ask.

"No. Exclusively MetiCity girls only." He grins whilst revving the engine.

CHAPTER FIVE_

When we arrive at the ArenaSphere, we're greeted by security, whom we flash our VIP tickets to. They scan the tickets off our credentials and usher us into a separate entrance. We're a little late, so there's no one outside. Inside, I can hear there's a fight going on, the crowd roaring with excitement.

"Follow me Ren!" Migo says cheerily. "I'm not sure I can record here, but I wanted to show you guys that I am backstage at the Koujin fight!" Migo says, broadcasting the empty hallway to his stream through his credentials. "What do you mean I'm lying? Look!" he says, pointing the camera around at random doorways and people.

"You can't film back here," one of the security guards says, covering Migo's credentials with his hand.

"See. I told you guys. Look for me in the crowd!" Migo says before shutting down the stream. I shake my head.

"Koujin was supposed to meet you guys, but he's still busy warming up. Go ahead and take your seats." The security guard says, directing us through the door to the arena. We find our seats in the front row, right in front of the ArenaSphere. The

Sphere is used to contain the violence of the fight, with both combatants locked inside until one submits, passes out, or dies. As we sit, we can see the medical crew drag the loser of the previous match out.

Sanitation Droids swarm in, getting it ready for the main event, but they aren't fast enough. I can still see trails of blood dripping their way down the inner walls.

The maximum offensive output these guys can produce is more than a person can take, even with armor. Frank said that during the 2080 rebellion, these guys would rip tanks apart and tear off limbs like they were pulling pages from a book. I can't imagine what it was like for him to see one of them on the other side of the battlefield.

Loud music blares overhead, and the crowd talks amongst themselves. Most people are probably using some kind of noise cancellation, but I am not modded, so I don't have anything to lessen the volume. Even with the background noise, I'm close enough to make out the middle of an argument going on near the loading area. It's Koujin, his girl, and his manager talking to who, I can only imagine, is the challenger and his own manager.

"Then why don't we make a wager if you're *so* confident? Whoever loses, loses their gear," the challenger's manager yells, cutting the bickering to a silent halt. Koujin and his girl trade glances while his manager shakes his head behind them.

"Hell no. Winning is enough, Koujin." Koujin's manager says, trying to get him to decline the offer. Wise. Something feels off about those two. Koujin comes off as confident, but he's committed to the life, so he's not going to wager something so important.

"I'm in. I could use some upgrades, and there's not a single human alive in MetiCity who can beat me, especially not some noso in a bird suit," Koujin says, pushing away his manager. I am shocked, as is his girl. I can't really make out what she whispers to him after, but I can see her face. She isn't as confident as him. Just as they shake hands on the deal, the announcers introduce them.

"Whoa. Is that the girl you were talking about? She's hot!" Migo says, finally noticing them in the corner.

I get a better look at the challenger before he dons his helmet. Pale and pasty like a walking corpse. Something you rarely see in the Outskirtz, but it's more common in MetiCity. Some guys spend entire months tapped-in, completely outside of direct sunlight. That isn't him, though. I'm thinking it is a designer drug addiction. To be fair, you would probably have to drug me to get me into the ArenaSphere. These professional leagues have a ton of doctors and med Droids around in case someone gets seriously injured, but even then, there will still be casualties.

They announce the challenger's name as Raven. It's a fitting stage name. His Biosuit is mostly black with dark purple highlights. It's similar to the Paladin armor Koujin is wearing, but it's been modified to give Raven a more bird-like appearance. He's got black wings jutting out of his back, talons for feet, and sharp claws at his hands. I know that the Robot Fighting League tends to get theatrical, but I thought the Human Fighting League was more serious.

"Dammit. That reminds me, I forgot to put some money on Koujin. Wonder if I can still make it in time," Migo says, looking around the room for a timer. It is up. Both fighters make their way into the ring. No flashy entrances. The ArenaSphere closes, and they waste no time.

Raven immediately takes flight to the top of the sphere, digging his talons in and damaging it slightly when he lands upside down. He quickly dives down to Koujin's flank like a bird of prey. Koujin smiles, falls to his back, and suddenly thrusts both feet up, crashing into Raven's helmet. The force of the blow sends him back into the air. This might be over quickly.

The durability of his Biosuit kept him alive, but the output of power would have been enough to punch a hole through most classic metals. It's not odd to see someone with armor made of full MetiMetal. Almost everything is made of it these days. What separates the champion from most other competitors is how he utilizes the reflex boosts. Bursts of enhanced power and agility that only the most skilled can perform. Before Raven can reorient himself, Koujin grabs him by the ankles and pulls him back down to the floor. The thud of Raven's body slamming into the ground shakes the entire ArenaSphere.

The crowd finally has a moment to catch up and are going nuts. Oddly enough, both teams seem happy with this turn of events. Koujin kneels down and crosses Raven's legs before planting a knee on them so he's unable to move. Raven is face down, unmoving; he seems to be knocked out. Koujin turns to the judges outside the ring and they begin a count. The numbers flash above the ArenaSphere holographically.

"LOOKS LIKE ANOTHER QUICK NIGHT AT THE OFFICE FOR KOUJIN!" the announcer blares over the loudspeaker.

10... 9... 8...He has to get up by the timer, or it's over that quick.

7... 6... 5... Koujin smiles confidently, nodding to his girlfriend. I look over to see the reaction on her face go from relief to shock. She wildly points behind him, but it's too late. With his legs still tied up, Raven somehow manages to completely twist around his upper torso at the waist. Something that shouldn't be possible for any human with a spine. There's no way he survives outside of that suit. He quickly wraps his claws around Koujin's neck and begins choking him from behind.

The crowd is just as shocked as me. This shouldn't be possible. I can see the confusion and fear on Koujin's face as he tries to break free. Raven flaps his wings and they both begin to lift into the air.

"LOOKS LIKE RAVENS GOT NEW TECH! HE COULD END IT HERE!" The loudspeaker screeches.

I can't imagine Koujin going out that easily, but his corner isn't showing the most confident poker face I've ever seen. Raven's torso slowly realigns to the correct orientation and soon, his legs are wrapped around Koujin, claws digging into his stomach. Koujin first tries to tear off the grip on the neck, but, after a while of struggling, he gets more desperate. He swings his legs back behind himself, then reverses direction and launches both feet above his own head and cracks Raven in the helmet again. Raven doesn't budge this time. Even after Koujin begins throwing wild punches behind his head, smashing into Raven's helmet, Raven only seems to tighten his grip. His claws crack and pierce into the MetiMetal armor as Koujin's punches start to become more labored and slow. He draws back one more punch and, swinging from his hip, puts everything into it. Damage. Raven's helmet has cracked open. Progress, but still no loosening of the grip. Raven is silent. Unnerving. Relentless. Koujin, for all his experience, surprises me. I thought he'd have more tricks up his sleeve, but he just continues punching. Over and over, he wails until Raven's helmet is hanging on by a thread. Another punch and Raven's head is fully exposed. As ugly as he was before he put on the helmet, he looks even worse now. But he's unprotected. One more punch should do it.

"Come on Koujin!" I scream out.

"Come on Koujin!" Migo yells, following my lead.

He cocks back his arm to throw one more, but the bag he

pulled it from was empty. The shot lands but with no relative impact. It's over. His arms drop to his side. Raven drops Koujin's limp body from the air and it hits with a dreadful thud. The crowd goes silent as they realize he might not ever get back up. There is no count. The announcer sends in a little android they use to test vitals. He lays still, a champion nevermore, while the Raven casts his shadow on the floor.

"THAT'S IT FOLKS! RAVEN IS THE WINNER!"

Shock and awe. The crowd can't believe it.

"Holy shit. I almost bet on that!" Migo says unsympathetically. A lot of people just lost a lot of money.

The former champion's team is devastated. Koujin's girlfriend is trying to force herself past security to get into the ArenaSphere. Raven slowly floats down and plants one leg over Koujin's body. Security rushes into the ring because the small Droid isn't able to get Raven off him. The crowd starts to boo. Raven won't let go of his talons' grip.

Koujin's girlfriend screams while Raven's manager tries to separate his talon. I can make out Raven's eyes. They're black and lifeless. The manager signals Raven to stop. Raven lifts his talon off of Koujin's body and they quickly remove his helmet. The Droid signals it is not able to find a pulse. It begins trying to resuscitate him using chest compressions and a tube for air. It seems like forever, but eventually, he is back on Earth, gasping for air.

"Allspirits man, I thought he was dead," Migo says.

"He *was* fucking dead," I correct him.

"WELL! A deal's a deal," Raven's manager says before Koujin can even catch his breath.

"Go fuck yourself!" his girl yells.

"Are we going to have a problem?" Raven's manager says, signaling to his wrist. Company credentials. The audacity. The Company is here testing new military-level mods in pro competition. Scum. Once Koujin gets a look at the credentials, his anger turns to fear. Even someone as tough as him isn't outside of the reach of the Company and its dominance. He knows what it would mean for him if he refuses.

It looks painful. Coming out of the Biosuit was something he probably hasn't done in decades. He sheds the skin-tight armor, and once it's fully removed, you can see he is completely emaciated. Weak and feeble, a stark contrast to what he was just minutes ago. He doesn't even have the strength to lift the suit once it hits the ground. He has his manager take it over to the Company manager. As soon as it is in his hands, the manager turns to the crowd, smiling devilishly.

"WHO WANTS A FREE BIOSUIT? MILITARY GRADE PALADIN ARMOR EDITION!" he yells before throwing it into the crowd. Before anyone can start a riot, I am smacked in the face by the helmet and suit, knocking me over. Migo immediately fights off the crowd of dangerously drunk MetiCitians.

"Let's get out of here!" Migo yells while dragging me away. I roll the suit up around the helmet as fast as I can, shoving it under my arm. The last thing I can see before turning away is Raven staring blankly at Koujin's withered body. He is in the arms of his girl, who is trying, unsuccessfully, to get him to his feet. He tries to push her away, but he isn't strong enough to resist the help. Nor is he strong enough to hold back the tears running down his face. Neither is she. A sad scene in a mad city.

We're out of there in a flash.

"Run a scan!" is the first thing Migo says to me when we get back to his place.

"On the suit?" I ask.

"No, on me." He says, falling dramatically onto his living room couch.

He has a sky-loft bachelor pad. It's not like his job doesn't pay well, but this place is above his pay grade. He'd never say, but my guess is it had something to do with inheritance. It honestly is amazing. The latest....everything. Above the city, the congestion, and best of all, the noise. "Yes, on the suit. Let's check it out! How did you get so lucky?" he asks, basically tearing it out of my hands to lay it under a light on the table.

"I don't even know what to do with it," I say, linking up to it.

"You can always sell it back to the poor guy," he says, laughing his way over to his seat.

"I could use the money. You don't want it?"

"Eh, that's the kind of thing you'd only use in an emergency, and I'm never in an emergency. Look at me," he says, kicking his feet up.

"I kind of feel bad for taking it, to be honest. Maybe I should just give it back to him?" I say.

"Why do you give a shit? Did you see his girl? If he can get it up without the Biosuit, I bet he's getting some good old-fashioned pity sex right as we speak."

"Yeah, you're probably right. I've never seen a Jardinera in person before. As a couple, they're sickening. Both could be MetiCity billboard models."

"I know, right? It's like they're both out of each other's league. In a modding war until one can be crowned prettiest plastic humanoid," he says, sipping a drink I never saw him make.

"She's not modded," I say sternly.

"What? She DEFINITELY has mods. No way she's natural," he says confidently.

"No, I could tell. She didn't have mods."

"Oh yeah? Why so confident? Did you get to cop a feel before I rescued you from that crazed crowd?" he says sarcastically. He is right, though. One thing I do remember is the switch that went off in people's heads when the armor flew at me. Not everyone in MetiCity is like Migo. Some of them would have given me a big fight for that thing. It wouldn't be the first night I got jacked for some gear in a crowded place like that.

"No. I can just tell." I say, wrapping up the Biosuit and joining him on the coach.

"So you were checking her out?" He says, poking at me.

"Nah, It isn't like that. She's just so...different."

We reminisce for a bit. It's been ages since I've been to his place. I start to tell him about the shape I found the Droid in, but I can see his eyes slowly start to close as I go on.

The Droid.

I can rig the Biosuit to the Droid. I mean, it's not impossible. I doubt anyone would be dumb enough to waste a suit on a Droid, but what else am I going to use it for?

I can hear the slow drone of the news anchor talk about more quelled protests drowned out slightly by Migo murmuring in his sleep. I begin going over protocols in my head and looking up any rules for Biosuit symbiosis with a Droid.

Nothing in the rules about putting a Droid in one. I'll have to do some coding to authenticate the link though. Not exactly my strongest field, but I don't see anything saying it's not possible. I also need to figure out if the prototype could still enter carry mode while wearing the armor. I'm not trying to have people looking my Droid up and down for its armor. Although, with it on, I doubt many people would try to run up on us. Once I link him to my credentials, he'll be able to protect me using minimal force if I'm under threat. Hell, he would even be able to travel to me if I'm in danger using location tracking. Something I could use if I'm ever caught scavenging in the wrong territory. This could be life-changing.

Shit, what time is it? I have to be at the stadium in the morning! I don't want to bother Migo with a ride, so I hop on the closest public transit to try and get back to the shop and sync the Droid to the Biosuit before I have to be back at the stadium. By now, the self-repair software should be finished, so I might have enough time.

CHAPTER SIX_

I work all night trying to get the Biosuit arrays attached to the spinal column of the Droid, but because of the extensive damage and wear, it takes forever. Because the suit is made for a human, I have to embed the connections into the Droid's internal circuitry. I'm literally threading a needle for each connection, and it's monotonous and mentally exhausting. The sun comes up, and I'm reminded of the bird chirps I used to hear when I was young. Animal sightings are rare now. We consider it a good omen to see one. I wish the same could be said for the insects who seem to have adjusted better than we have to the new climate.

Some time, long before me, there were decisions that should have been made on this planet that weren't. Now the birds are gone, and the sun reigns absolute in the sky above. Even in the morning, it burns its way down into the roots of everything. The beams cascading through the window of the shop hit my credentials and the light reflects into my eye. I look down and realize it is already 5:00 a.m. and I need to be at the stadium by 8:00 a.m.

Wait a minute. A slight sense of impending doom washes

over me like thundering storm clouds. Was I getting in over my head? I'd never even been to an O-Race. I'd seen them online but couldn't explain the rules if I had a knife to my throat. Why did I agree to this again?

"I thought I smelled you back here, stinking up the place. Ya dirty sandscav," Frank says, peeking out into the shop room I was in and scaring the shit out of me. How does he always get the jump on me like that? Sneaky old bastard. "How many times do I have to tell you, this ain't no mo—wait, IS THAT PALADIN ARMOR? Where did you get that? Ain't no way someone just threw away some Paladin armor!"

"That it is. I was at the HFL last night and the loser had his Biosuit thrown into the crowd," I explain.

"And an Outskirt caught it!? Well, I'll be damned."

"Kind of," I say, remembering the feeling of the helmet smacking my face as I watched Koujin writhe in pain. "The guy couldn't even stand up once it was off him. He was one of those guys you told me about. Scarring on the neck and everything."

"Poor bastard. It'll be a while before he's back to normal. I remember it took a whole battalion of rebels to take down one guy in an armored Biosuit. When we finally got him out of it, he begged for death. It's like separating them from the thing that leaves a hole in em'. Luckily, it was mostly Droids we was fighting back then," he says, peering back at the Droid. "They weren't much fun either though. I thought you were going to sell that thing?"

"Wait, did they put Biosuit armor on the Droids during the war?"

"Sure did. You plannin' on going to war with that thing?"

"No. It's just in bad shape. So I'm basically going to use the Biosuit to hold it together."

"So you're putting a Paladin armor Biosuit on that rusty old

Droid? Don't bother. It's probably a collector's item. You oughta sell both of em'. Or scrap 'em for the MetiMetal. I'll give you a good rate," he advises with a smile.

"You always say to sell it."

"I'm always right," he says, lifting his chin and walking over to a random workbench. He likes to act busy sometimes, but he hasn't fixed a thing in this place since I arrived. I'm unable to finish up the Droid in time, so I cover him up again and head out.

I arrive at the stadium fifteen minutes early. Luckily, the stadium is on all the public transport routes. I head through the long, empty parking lot to the front entrance. I can see two techs waiting outside to be let in as I get closer.

"A little early for an autograph, ain't you kid?" one of them says as I approach.

"Uh, Zander told me to be here at 8:00 a.m. Trying out for the new tech position?" As I speak, I barely recognize the words coming out of my mouth. They look as surprised as I feel.

"New tech position?" they say, looking at each other sternly. Clearly, they weren't told.

"Yup. New tech position. For the pit crew?"

The front doors swing open and out walks Zander in full racing gear.

"Hey Zander, who's the kid?" a tech asks.

"Ah, he showed. This is Ren Unkno. He was the one who figured out the prototype's heating coil was damaged. Any idea how that could have happened?" he says, questioning the two techs.

"You didn't check the heating coil?" one says to the other, and they burst into an argument.

"This kid here is the best mechanic in the Outskirtz. I'm going to be running him as backup to help with diagnostic tests and repair work. Be...welcoming," he says, walking back inside.

The two techs are still mumbling insults to each other as they follow him inside. I've never been in the stadium before, and I'm already getting behind-the-scenes access. If Migo were here, he'd glitch. Either that or try and stream it.

"Give him a tour, I'm going to finish getting ready for the prototype test run. Make sure you guys are at the pit in fifteen," Zander says, parting ways. The two grumble and begin to give the most half-ass tour ever. They point out the bathroom, Café, front desk, workshop, and the direction of the pit. All without taking more than three steps in either direction. They head in the direction of the Café without a single salutation.

"Thanks?" I say to the empty room.

I head to the workshop first to see what they're working with, and I almost shit a brick when I get there. This is a mechanic's dream. The newest analyzers, custom 3D printers they can use to craft body parts of the vehicles. They have every tool I've ever seen and more I haven't. It's intimidating but exciting. I pick up and test out gadget after gizmo until I stumble upon a wrench similar to mine. I feel its weight in my hand. Feels off.

"KID! What the hell are you doing? Let's go!" One of the techs yells from just outside the door. I break my concentration from the wrench and follow him over to the pit area. It's in the center of the stadium where the jets launch from. There isn't much of a track, as the actual racing is done in the surrounding air space. They still call it one anyway, but it's really more of a course. Just before each race starts, they magnetically lift an array of massive rings that float high above the 'track' that's just outside of the stadium. Racers have to fly through each ring in the correct order, but the way the track is set up, you're forced to make hairpin turns at breakneck speed. No rings can be skipped, and only a few jets can fit through one at once. One of the reasons it's so dangerous, and so watched. Luckily, the stadium is shielded, so fans can watch from a safe distance, using their credentials to access exclusive ticket holder tracking software. The software is essential if you want to have any idea what's going on. It lets you zoom in, gives in-time race stats, and tells you which direction to look for your favorite racer.

When I arrive at the pit, it's filled with a bunch of monitors and control panels. Odd to see a physical monitor in this day and age, but I can tell it's cutting-edge equipment, specifically made for this sport.

"But we only have two headsets," one of the techs says, talking to Zander via headset. The tech suddenly gets very angry and then snatches the headset from the other tech before tossing it to me.

"Here."

I barely catch it, but I'm able to get the volley under control after juggling for a bit.

"What are you doing?" the headsetless tech asks.

"He wants the kid to run the boards," the other scoffs.

Run the boards? I quickly put the headset on. It doesn't fit perfectly at first but adjusts to my odd ear shape. My scarring starts just past my left eye and runs just through the ear. I guess when it healed, it grew back at a sharp angle. Another reason I grow my hair out longer on that side.

"Can you hear me, Ren?" Zander says over the headset. Suddenly, I can hear his jet come blasting out of the launching area. It's even faster in person. "Listen up, I'm not going to repeat myself," he says before diving into detail about how the jet performs and what the most prominent issues are. He explains how the vitals for the jet are tracked on the monitors, and how it updates in lossless time. He says that by using the control boards, I can make instant changes as he requests them, or as they pop up on the monitor. As he explains, he's working his way through the course, cutting turns on a dime and flying through the rings so fast it causes them to shake slightly.

"Right now, I'm entering a stretch. While I accelerate to max speed, it's easier for the pit to loosen the air fins from there since my hands are on the gears and accelerator. The pit's job is to know these turns ahead of time to make these adjustments for me so I don't have to ask for them. The more in sync the pit becomes with the racer, the more easily the racer can focus on the race and not modifications or adjustments. This is an essential position for this crew. Everyone who works for me must know how to work the boards. Every second counts, and the quicker the pit is able to anticipate my maneuvers, the easier it will be for me to execute them. Understand?" I do. But it doesn't sound easy.

"It's almost as if the pit has to be psychic," I say over the headset.

"If they know what they are doing, they won't have to be," he says, making his final lap.

"This is the final lap coming up. I'm going to guide you at first, then I'll let you take it from there."

I approach the monitor and can see all the stats for the jet in real-time.

"Now, do you see how the tail wing is giving me drag? It should be flashing red on the monitor's diagram. All you have to do is level the angle and it'll lower the amount of drag," he explains as I try to follow. There are a million settings, but there is a blinking light highlighting the wing he is talking about. Using my finger, I press on the wing and glide it up until it's level. I can see an immediate increase of the speedometer.

"There you go!" he yells excitedly. "From here on out, it's going to get difficult. Watch the monitor, but don't take your eyes off me. I need you to watch where I am on the track to know what kind of maneuvers trigger alerts on the monitor data you're getting back." Did he just tell me to watch the monitor and him at the same time? Does he think I'm modded?

He isn't lying, though. There are blinking lights all over the monitor now, some only flashing for a moment and others flashing continuously. I try to keep up, but it's like killing ants. There's always more. After a while, one of the techs comes over and helps when he sees me panicking. Zander must be able to tell I'm falling behind. He calmly calls out over the headset, "Ren. Focus on what you can control. The usual setup is two techs to a monitor and one to keep eyes on me. But I need my techs to be able to do both simultaneously, especially if I need midrace repairs."

We run the track fifty times before he's had enough for the day. I'm steadily progressing, but I'm clearly not up to the techs' speed. As he comes around and hops out, he takes a swig of some water, gives me a thumbs up, and walks back into the stadium.

"See ya tomorrow kid," the techs say, cleaning up and heading the same way. Wait. That's it? Did I pass?

After he leaves, I take a second to walk through the stadium seats, watching as the track rings descend from the sky and lock back into position on the ground. I take a moment to soak it all in because I didn't have a chance to before we were off and running. By the time I make my way back in, the other techs have gone home and Zander is waiting for me in the lobby.

"You did good today," he says, reassuring me. "I saw you come here by public transport. You don't have your own ride?"

"Nope. Don't have enough social credit for that or a license," I say, eyes glued to the ground.

"Well, that's something we'll have to remedy, now, isn't it?" he says, walking towards the receptionist who is now present at the previously empty front desk. He mentions something to the receptionist before turning to me. "Give her your name and social credit ID. She'll get everything set for you." I am perplexed. Does he have that kind of pull? Can he actually get me the license that quickly? Even if he can, what am I going to drive?

"I can't have you coming in late with excuses about how public transit got lost trying to find you in the Outskirtz. And you're never going to really be able to anticipate how I drive without having driven one yourself. Once she gets you set up, I'll have her show you to the garage, where you can pick out one of the older units no one is using anymore. Just be careful."

A Droid. A Paladin armor Biosuit. And a fucking FlyBike. All three innovations in just as many days.

Is this real life?

I wait in the lobby, antsy as hell, until the receptionist calls me back over. She transfers me the license approval and upgrades my credentials with a wry, "congratulations."

"Your credentials are assigned to activate any of the previous generation transports. Sign here; this basically says it's a loaner and it's due back upon your termination. And it also says you're completely screwed if you wreck it, so be careful."

I confirm on my end, and she moves on to the next form, the contract. I almost forgot, to work for a MetiCity Company, you have to sign the contract. I take a long moment before confirming, weighing it over in my head. The document is broken into three sections: what MetiCorp provides, the rules it enforces, and the criteria for advancing in the social credit system. My excitement grows as I'm reminded of all the benefits that come with being a MetiCitian. I look up from my credentials screen after I hear her clear her throat. Oops. I must have forgotten about the line of thirty people behind me that doesn't exist. I hit "Confirm."

"Oh, and he wanted you to have these," she says, waving

over a massive file. "These are the track and vehicle schematics, previous races, and racer profiles."

She points me towards the elevator to get to the garage. It's filled with new prototypes, old race jets, shuttles, and stadium security backup cruisers. I walk up to what looks like the fastest and most impressive vehicle I can find. It's a jet, so it's something that probably isn't legal outside of racing.

"Access Denied," the credentials says as I scan over the jet.

"Just testing, just testing," I say, chuckling to myself. I can't take something like that back to the Outskirtz without raising a few eyebrows anyway. I look for something more middle of the road, but with enough similarity to the vehicle he is racing with so I can see what I would be working with. I find one that might work, but I'm distracted by a FlyBike. It's old but still in great condition. The jet, on the other hand, was some sort of a show vehicle modeled after one Zander probably used a few years back. It isn't as flashy as the one I was denied, so I can probably get away with bringing it home, but there is something about the FlyBike that catches my eye. How long has this thing been stowed away here? It doesn't seem to have been touched in years. It reminds me of the one Migo got as a loner and would probably fly fine with a little bit of love. Out of curiosity, I wave my credentials over it to take a look at the specs.

"Access granted, vehicle has been added to inventory. Please, drive safely," a calm voice recites.

What? Oh shit. I just wanted to check it out, not literally check it out. Welp, better than nothing.

I make my way out of the garage, slowly, as the multiple warnings to be careful ring through my head. Once I get cleared to ascend and a flight plan locked in, I am gone. I don't know how they got me clearance to drive without testing, but I'm not about to ask or pry too much. I've driven Migo home on his FlyBike a few times after he'd gotten drunk, but this thing is a different animal altogether. It has issues, probably from lack of use, but that only endears it to me even further.

Once I'm out of MetiCity-6, I really open up and get to test it without a speed limit and an automated flight path. I'm heading home to my apartment for the first time in three days when I realize I still haven't finished the Droid. My mind races with all the repairs I still need to make to the Droid and I change directions towards the shop. This thing handles like a dream.

When I get there, it's already closed down. Luckily, I have access codes. I hide the bike under some tarp in the back and make my way to the room with the Droid. The work is tedious, but I try to power through the night to complete the repairs.

CHAPTER SEVEN_

When I wake, there's a napkin under my head where I had been drooling and a blanket over me. In a state of confusion, I look around to see the Droid in what looks like a meditative state on the ground next to me.

Did I finish the Droid? I don't even remember doing that. It must have some sort of maid-like protocol that wanted to tuck me in. I guess this prototype was used as a household Droid of some kind. I'm lucky it didn't just walk out the front door.

"Hello there," I say to the Droid. It seems to wake and gestures a wave. Shit, that's right, I still need to order a voice modulator. I didn't have time to initiate a directive either, so it must be falling back to some base programming, as all I was able to do was establish myself as an owner.

I don't have much time left before needing to get to the stadium, so I do some basic strength, reliability, and volatility tests on him to make sure he isn't going to bug out while I'm away. He seems....happy. I can't explain it, but wherever he came from, it must not have been the happiest of homes. Now that I think about it, this thing is so old there's no way it's still being used in someone's home. I set him up with his directive, to clean the shop before Frank arrives so he can see he's up and functioning. The Droid should be able to take commands from him since I gave it his credentials. Frank just needs to accept the invite when he gets here. Either way, it's time to go.

When I get to the stadium, Zander is outside waiting for me.

"Follow me," is all he says. We end up in some sort of trophy room I hadn't noticed before.

"Have you studied the course?" he asks, staring into a glass case of what I can only assume are his accomplishments. Zander is one of the first from his city to place in a cup, so it's not like this city has had a storied history of victories, but it has photos of his various qualifying times and second place trophies. I can imagine how powerful a man might feel standing in a room full of his accolades and accomplishments.

"Yeah. I had a chance to look things over. Made me appreciate racers even more, considering you're not allowed to be modded and the acceleration you experience can get up to several Gs in a straightaway," I say, walking over to see what he's looking at.

"It's a lot more than speed you have to worry about. I could break a world record for this course if I didn't have a huge target on my back," he says without breaking focus. He isn't lying. In looking up his competition, it's basically all MetiCity royalty. All with lineages dating back to the original four Meti-Cities. Although, what's more surprising is that these wealthy families even let their kids participate in something so dangerous. No amount of rejuvenation is going to bring you back from wrecking a jet. At those speeds, you're like a bug hitting a windshield. And since cloning is still banned, it's not like they can scrape up some gunk and start over.

"I'm just impressed that any of the racers from the original cities are ballsy enough to get out there in the first place," I say, looking over the contents of the glass case. More trophies, photos, and some model versions of the vehicles he uses.

"It's not dangerous for them; it's dangerous for those who want to be them. Or at least beat them. They used to have agreements on who would win based on some stupid poll they took internally amongst heads of the original MetiCities. Ever since they opened the races to more cities, they've worked together to assure victory for those they've deemed worthy. Enemies compromising for a common purpose will always defeat those who can't do the same," he explains. "One of the things we need out there is trust. I need to be able to trust you. Can I trust you?"

"Uhh, yeah, of course!" I say, probably louder than is necessary.

"You see this here? This was taken after I placed last year." He points to a picture in the glass case. The picture is of Zander, Koujin, Koujin's girlfriend, and a girl that looks like her twin, but slightly younger.

"Koujin. Poor guy." My memory flashes to an image of him being resuscitated.

"Yeah, I saw he lost last night. It wasn't pretty, but at least he's okay," he says, finally breaking his gaze at the case.

"I was in the front row. He didn't look okay."

"He'll be fine. He's a tough one, but I'll talk to him and Zari about it tonight."

"Zari, is that her name?"

"Yeah. She and Elli are a good support system for him. They'll get him through this loss."

"I hope so. Once he was out of the Biosuit, he didn't look the same. I actually ended up winning the damn thing by way of bouquet tossing," I say, rubbing the back of my head.

"Wait, he took it off?" Zander asks sternly.

"Yeah, he bet his Paladin armor he'd win. When he lost,

they tossed it to the crowd. Who would have thought there'd be a noso like me in the front row?" I ask, but Zander seems to have stopped listening once I confirmed his question.

"I'll be out there in twenty," he yells, gesturing to open a com-link and stepping out. I look back at the picture. Zari. Not surprised to hear she has a 'Z' name. When they were growing up, Zelius was at the height of his brilliance, and Z names became popular for that generation. Must have been great times. She looks so happy in the picture. Hard to imagine it's the same person I saw the other night, crying over her fallen love. She has darker brown skin than most, even though nowadays everyone seems to have some color to them. Due to the climate thinning out the atmosphere, most people outside of the shaded cities end up tanned sooner or later. A lot of MetiCity's wealthy get 'work' done to modify their looks, so I thought she was modded when I first saw her. Zander looks modded too, but since it's banned for O-Racers, I ruled that out for him early. Zari has green eyes that don't quite seem to belong, which makes me feel like they serve some additional purpose. Like she could see through you or something.

I stop fawning over her and make my way to the pit area. Zander is late. The only reason we know he's even here is because we can see on the monitors that the jet has started up. Without warning, he comes blasting out of the launch zone and begins his ascent.

"HELLO?" He says over the headset.

"He's talking to you kid," the tech says, gesturing for me to approach the monitor. The screen is even more demanding than the day before. Or he is. Zander is blazing the course, but I can tell he's making some questionable maneuvers, considering his current speed.

"What did you do to piss him off?" the tech asks, trying to follow Zander.

"I ..." I say, trying to keep up with the monitor.

"You can do better than this kid," Zander calls over the headset. I am trying.

I notice out of my peripheral, a new warning has triggered. Some sort of system failure, but I'm not sure what it's referring to because the title of the error code is glitched.

"Uh, I've never seen this before?"

The techs ignore me.

"SHIT!" Zander exclaims and seems to lose control and spiral off course. I'm working as fast as I can, but I have to use a process of elimination to figure out which part of the error message it's referring to. He tries to regain his trajectory, but he can't seem to stabilize himself. The stabilizers. They're disabled! Why?

Zander tries to make a sharp turn to get back on track, but it sends him hurtling towards the stadium. I'm finally able to stabilize the jet and trigger the emergency parachute just before he slams into the stadium seats. He's able to regain control and glides the jet down into the ground, carving up the grass under it as it slides and settles. I exhale and sit back into one of the seats.

"Good job kid," the tech grumbles, running over to assist Zander. Does he sound...upset? At me?

Zander hops out of the jet and walks through the stands, kicking one of the seats up and disappearing into the back.

"I think we're going to call it a day. Go home," the tech says over the headset.

It's still early, so after getting some food, I stop to see how the jet looks before I leave. The techs have gone home, but the jet's still here. It looks pristine, so it must have been cleaned and inspected already. Why would the rear stabilizers malfunction like that? It's like they had been turned off manually, but that could only be done from the boards. Did I accidentally disable them? Unless it was set to disable beforehand. But the techs are supposed to do full diagnostic tests before it ever leaves lockup, so it should have come up when they ran them. Are they that incompetent?

"Still here?" Zander says, leaning in the doorway.

"Yeah. You okay?" I ask, rolling out from under the vehicle.

"You hungry?" he asks.

"Uhhh, actually...." I say, rubbing my stomach that I had just stuffed full of stadium food.

"Come have a drink with me. I want you to meet someone," he says, walking out of sight, so I follow. Shit, is he going to have Koujin shake me down to get his armor back? Is it Zari? Is she the one that's going to shake me down? A perverted person, unlike myself, could be into that.

We each take our own bikes, but because his is barely air-legal, I'm struggling to keep up. The bar he's taking me to is near the stadium, so it's not a long trip. When I finally land, he's waiting for me beside his bike.

"What took so long?" he asks with a cocky smile.

"Just doing a little sightseeing."

We step into the bar and I'm surprised, not the kind of place I would think someone like Zander would lower himself into. It's basically empty, aside from the bartender and the sound of some broadcast droning on about protests. It stands out in contrast to the beautiful and sterilized MetiCity standard. It feels kinda like home.

"I'll have the usual, Tony," Zander says, before sitting down at a table near the bar.

"And you?" the barkeep says to me.

"I'll have a beer," I respond, taking my seat across from Zander at the table. I look around, and the walls are empty. No sports heroes, no gorgeous women, nothing but the TV.

"He's waiting for you to specify, kid," Zander says, chuckling.

"You have Nopins?"

"Must not come to MetiCity too often," Tony says as he heads back to the counter.

"How can you tell?" I ask.

"Most sandscavs come to MetiCity and ask for the only beer they've ever tasted. Can't ask for something you've never heard of." He begins pouring our drinks, "You expecting company, Zan'?"

"They'll have their usuals as well," Zander replies, leaning back in his seat and sighing. We wait in silence for a bit, sipping our drinks periodically. I go to take another sip but stop the glass just before it hits my lips; someone is coming through the door. It's her, and just her.

"Hey! There she is. Where's Koujin?" he says, getting up to greet her.

"He uh...couldn't make it..." she says solemnly. "You?" She adds, puzzled.

"I believe you already know Ren Unkno," Zander says, "Ren, this is Zari." I wave awkwardly.

"Yeah, I know him. Koujin gave him some free tickets to the fight, and after Koujin lost, he took off with his armor."

Tony brings over her drink.

"Yeah, I feel really bad...I'm sorry about-" I begin.

"Keep it," she says, downing her drink. I'm relieved, but it doesn't quell the guilt.

"So, how is he? For real?" Zander asks, concerned.

"He's...not good. He doesn't want my help. He doesn't want to see anyone. I keep trying to bring him food and call to check up, but he won't answer," she says, looking down at her reflection on the table.

"He only needed two more wins, and now it all resets. It

can't be easy, especially losing to MetiCorp tech. It's just so convenient. They'll do anything to protect their status, and we were so close."

"We?" I say, confused. They both exchange glances for a moment.

"We're a team kid. We've known each other since ranking, and when one of us loses, we all lose," he says, glancing at her again. Something is off, but I can't quite put my finger on it. I don't want to pry and overstay my welcome.

"I'm not so sure it's just the reset. It's the suit, 'From us, nobody can be removed, nor can a body be added; once you have taken the Paladin oath, the body is one.' You know how seriously he takes that stuff."

"He hasn't been out of that thing since his first deployment. You and Elli shou-"

"I've tried Zander. We've tried," she says before taking a long swig of her drink. Her eyes raise from the cup and meet mine. "What's he doing here anyway?"

"Well, I was hoping you'd bring Koujin, since you're all so well acquainted. But he's extremely capable, Zari. You saw it yourself."

"So?"

"So I think I'm going to keep him around. The kid saved my life today."

"He did?" She sounds impressed.

"Yeah, another 'malfunction.' Luckily, the kid's a natural on the boards. I'm thinking about starting him for next week's Cup to shake things up," Zander says.

"You are?" Zari and I both question in unison.

"Sure, why not? I trust you. This city hasn't corrupted you yet. But be careful, you're a quick learner, and that's a dangerous talent to have," he explains.

"So what are you going to do with the Biosuit? Sell it?" Zari says, turning to me. I feel as if any answer I give will be the wrong one.

"If my boss had his way, that would be the move. But I came across an old prototype Droid the other day, and I thought maybe I'd put it on him. He was in a pretty rough state, and I thought it might help to cover up his loose wire situation. It worked too; he can even fully utilize the Paladin armor."

"Paladin armor, on a Droid? I don't know how you pulled that off, but I'm more curious about why. You looking to cause some trouble?" She raises an eyebrow.

"No, quite the opposite. I think he would be helpful around my shop, and maybe he could also be programmed to run security around the perimeter. Especially now that I'm going to be in the city more often. Unfortunately, I've been having some trouble getting him back to full functionality. He's got this weird base code I'm having trouble with, and it's not letting me sync and replace the part he needs."

This caught their attention as if I'd said something beyond the words I spoke.

"How old is it?" Zari asks.

"I'm not sure. I think maybe it's an original prototype, but I've never seen one, so I wouldn't know," I explain as they both share glances.

"What does he need?" she continues her questioning.

"Well, right now I think it's just the chipset responsible for his voice."

"That's an easy fix. You should bring it by sometime. We can take a look."

Is she...inviting me over?

"That would be amazing! Maybe you could find out what it's running on?" I ask.

"Oh, Zari specializes in coding languages. She'd never brag about it herself, but she's won awards, teaches seminars, and is a highly sought-after expert in the field. Have you seen the new little sanitation Droids around the city? Zari wrote the code for them. An eighty percent increase in efficiency," he holds his chin up almost as if the accomplishments are his own.

"Zander, I think he gets the point," Zari says, clearly uncomfortable being the center of attention.

"Can I ask you a question, Zari?" I try and change the subject.

"Hmm?" Zari asks.

"Are you Jardinera?" I'd been curious the entire time.

"Is it that obvious?" she says, running her fingers through the tips of her hair.

"Sorry, I've never met one before."

"Well, there aren't many of us left. My sister and I hold that legacy between us."

"Sister?" I wonder.

"Yeah, she was in the picture I showed you earlier. Elli." Zander speaks after setting his drink down.

"She's in her early twenties. I would assume you're around the same age?" Zari asks.

"Yeah. First time I saw you, I thought you were in your twenties too, until I realized you had a 'Z' name," I explain and they both laugh.

"You thought I was in my twenties? We've got a charmer, Zander," she says, nudging him.

"Ren, I didn't know you were into older women," he chuckles.

"Double it, and you'd be in the ballpark. And not a mod on us." Zari smiles, opening her arms as if to say, 'I have nothing to hide.'

I wouldn't have known if not for the name. Something I've not gotten used to about MetiCity. The advancements in rejuvenation and life-extension technology over the last fifty years make it difficult to place the age of someone with the naked eye. Even Frank is still in decent shape as a centenarian, aside from his rusty leg.

Zander carries on, talking about some of the more bizarre things he's seen people do with modifications.

I catch myself staring at Zari and try to reboot and catch back up.

"Why would someone replace their perfectly good arm with a robotic one?" he continues, "Anyway, it's getting late. We've got practice in the morning. Tell Koujin to give me a call, okay?"

"I will," Zari says, retreating back to the more solemn tone she had when she first arrived.

"It was nice meeting you. Officially."

CHAPTER EIGHT_

The next morning, I walk into the stadium shop to find the mechanics running analysis and prepping the jet for the runs we will do today. Zander is watching them and turns when he notices me. He shoots me a wistful smile.

"What's wrong?" I ask.

"Nothing. I'm just worried about Zari. We still haven't heard from Koujin; it's not like him," he says, leaning up against the wall with his shoulder. He seemed so confident Koujin would be fine last night. Was it a false front?

"Like you said, he'll be fine, right?"

"Right. He'll be fine," he says before placing a hand on my shoulder and walking towards his locker room. I'm left alone with the techs.

"Morning," I say, raising my hand for a slight wave.

"You're still here?" one of the techs grumbles without looking up from his credentials.

"Yeah, I'm as surprised as you." No, Zander fired me after I saved his life yesterday. Domehead. "You guys running scans?"

"What does it look like?" The tech says, pointing to the scan currently running.

"Can I see?" I ignore the sarcasm.

"Eh, it's done anyway. Time to get out there," he says, closing the unfinished scan.

The mechanics get to moving the jet to the launching zone, so I walk behind them, trying to get a better look at it. Something Zander said last night makes me think I should keep my eye on them. Nothing blatantly out of order as far as I can tell, but I can feel something is off. I speed up to walk past them so I can be the first to the monitor. Once there, I grab a headset and initialize the interface.

"Can you hear me, Zander?" I say over coms.

"Yeah, just waiting for them to bring it over so we can get started. You ready?" he asks.

"Yeah, before you get started though, I wanted to run a quick scan, if that's okay with you."

"Fine with me," he says. I can already see the issue as soon as the jet syncs up. These guys aren't even clever; they removed the kinetic impulse module, so it won't appear on screen until it hits a critical failure. By then, it would be too late. This is more than negligence. I need to fix it before they get back because I don't know how intentional this is.

"Zander. Do me a favor before you get going; run it in neutral for about ten seconds," I say.

They arrive back at the pit just as I'm fixing the settings. I drop a wrench and go to pick it up when my head slams into the monitor keyboard.

"Watch it, you clumsy slomper," the tech says as they make their way back to the pit. "This equipment is expensive!"

"Ha, sorry. I am pretty clumsy. Looks like I hit a bunch of commands accidentally. But everything looks fine now." Was that good enough? It was the best I could think of to draw attention away from the fact that I had just thwarted their kill-

Zander trap of the day. They shrug it off and sit down, awaiting Zander's launch.

"Hey, why are you in neutral? You know the clock is just starting, right?" the tech says over the open com.

"Just giving myself a handicap," Zander says before switching it into gear and blazing through the opening stretch. "You've done really well so far, kid; now I'm going to show you what a real run looks like," he says before taking the first turn. The monitor lights up again, and I get to work adjusting the parameters and trying to recall the track steps. It helps to know which parts I'm actually modifying, and that's where my years of experience come in. Every part, every system, every issue, I have seen all of it before in one form or another. These jets are state-of-the-art though, so at first it's hard to tell exactly which settings make the biggest difference. Once you know what to adjust and when, then it's all about reaction time. It's like some holoshooter; you're constantly trying to anticipate and adapt.

"Keep it up! One more lap!" he yells, coming up on the final lap. He sounds excited. It makes me smile thinking about what it will be like for this to happen with a stadium packed full of people. The race is only about a week away, and I've only just started to figure this out. But I can see why Zander says he needs someone he can trust.

"I've got you covered, Zander! I'm going to release all the filters as soon as you take this last turn so you can gun it as hard as you want," I explain while the techs begin checking the clock. He's probably slightly ahead of time, and by now, the trap they had laid for him should have come to pass. I can feel their anticipation as he draws nearer to the finish line.

"Wooo!" Zander whoops as he finishes the last lap.

I've learned that while he likes to push limits, he's always in control. It makes my job easier, knowing he's so good at what he does. Besides his looks, I think that's why he's so admired. His fandom extends far beyond MetiCity-6. Since only eight of the twelve MetiCities can participate, those without a star O-Racer have flocked to him. He's the only one, not from the four original cities, who has a chance at taking a win home. He holds the hopes of so many on his back. It's amazing how level-headed he is with all the pressure he's under.

I turn to see both techs staring at me.

"What?" I ask.

"Nothing, you...he started late, but this is one of the fastest laps on record," one tech says, showing the other the lap times.

"Not bad," the other says out loud, almost as if by mistake.

"I'm impressed," Zander says, cooling the jet engines and taking a slow lap to soak it in. "We may just be ready to shock the world."

"Yeah, even the techs looked impressed. I think I'm starting to get the hang of this."

Maybe they thought it was a fluke the first time, but I'm only getting better. All while cleaning up their mess.

"Hey, hang on, got an incoming from Zari," Zander says, switching over coms. Will we be meeting up with her again? I wouldn't mind seeing her...so she can check out the Droid's code, of course.

Suddenly, out of the corner of my eye, I can see Zander jump out of the jet and begin sprinting towards me. When he gets closer, I can see tears in his eyes.

"We have to go. Something happened to Koujin," he says. Me?

"Um, are you okay?" I ask, concerned.

"Yeah. No. I don't know. I need you to drive," he says, hurrying me back into the stadium. He doesn't even change; he just takes off his jacket and helmet and hands me credential permission to drive his cruiser. His hands are shaking. When we get in, he scrolls through locations until he sees Koujin's name. He clicks it and then buries his head in his legs, keeled over, sobbing. I don't know what to do or what happened. A cruiser like this has an automatic mode, so I'm not sure exactly why he asked me to come, but I'm not about to be selfish at a time like this. I follow the guided map and get us airborne towards what looks like the high-rise apartments, which are closer to the inner MetiCity infrastructure. I want to ask more questions, to ask if Koujin is okay, but I'm not sure if he even knows himself.

We arrive at a docking zone full of controller cruisers. Not a good sign. When I park, Zander immediately gets out. I can see Zari standing outside, speaking with the controllers. Once I lock up his ride, I make my way over and find her in his arms, wailing.

"This is a closed crime scene. Do you live here?" a controller asks, walking in between my view of them.

"No, I'm with him." I point to Zander.

"Well, if you don't live here, you're going to have to wait," the controller says.

"That's fine," I respond and step back. I find a nearby bench where I can still see them. I can't make out any of the conversation, so I just wait quietly, watching the controllers come in and out of the apartment. After a while, Zander and Zari walk over along with a Company controller.

"Now, I know it's a bit soon, but we would appreciate it if you could come in to answer some basic questions. Once you're ready, of course," the officer says to Zari, swiping over what was probably contact information.

"Okay," she says softly, sniffling. She glances over at me. I'm not sure if I should wave, so I just stare back, pinching my lips into a smile to show I'm aware of how things look and I don't want to be intruding. At least, that's what I am trying to convey.

"Do you want us to take you home first?" Zander asks her. I get up, anticipating he might need me to grab the vehicle.

"I...I don't know...I don't know how I'm going to tell Elli. I told her I would meet her at Tony's after stopping to check on him. But I don't...I can't..." She bursts into tears again. Zander must have been playing strong for her, but this new outburst causes streams of tears to roll down his face as well.

"It's okay. Take a second to breathe," he comforts her between shaky breaths. "Ren, grab the jet. Let's head to the same place from last night. I'm gonna need a drink," he says slowly, his loss evident. I run. I don't know why, but I feel like the request is urgent. I don't particularly think I belong here, but as long as I am, I will help in any way I can. Whilst on my way back, I receive a message from Zander.

'Koujin committed suicide. Please stay for a while if you can.'

Shit. Flashes of Koujin struggling out of his bionic suit distort my vision. This is why he wasn't answering his coms. It must have broken him psychologically to lose that part of himself. I pull up and they both get in, Zari in the front and Zander cramped in the back. It's mostly silent until we reach the bar, aside from some sniffling.

"Shit," Zari's voice cracks.

She turns her head away from the entrance as a fat tear rolls down her cheek onto her coat.

"What's wrong?" Zander says, turning his head to the entrance. "Shit," he repeats. "Elli's here already."

If she wasn't beside me bawling, I'd think that was Zari standing waiting for us in front of the bar. How is it that they're twenty years apart and look so similar? Elli throws up a peace sign and smiles at us. Zari opens the door and Elli runs to her, then she sees her sister's face.

"I knew something was wrong. What happened sis?" Elli asks. Zari closes the door and their voices become muffled.

"Give them a minute," Zander says, signaling to go park. As I start the engine back up, Zari wraps her arms around Elli. Elli embraces her back, but after a moment, falls to her knees. Zari follows her to the ground. There's no strength left in her to hold her sister up.

"Koujin was more of a brother than a friend to Elli. She was always telling Koujin that he needed to marry Zari, but neither of them believed in the old practice. And now..." Zander says, trailing off into a cold silence. After I park the cruiser, it takes Zander a moment to get out after me, but eventually he steps out, trying to fix his hair in the window reflection. My guess is that he feels that he needs to be strong for the girls, and that takes a little prep time. I hope when all is said and done, he gets time to mourn, because the most important race of his life is coming up and something like this can really bury someone.

We all walk inside together, and Tony strolls out from behind the bar to greet us.

"Looks like almost the whole gang's here!" he says jovially. "Where's Koujin? I just got some new Sake in." He winks at Zari, who has just seemed to compose herself, and she loses control once more. Tony's face drops. "Sorry, I didn't mean... whatever I said," he starts, compassion etched on his face.

"It's okay, Tony," Zander says, pulling Tony aside, and whispering something that makes him gasp. We take our seats as he does so. "Just give us four waters and my regular," he says afterwards, walking back and sitting next to me at the table.

"No. We'll all take our regulars," Zari says, correcting Zander. He puts his hands up as if to say, 'Whatever you want.'

"It's on the house," Tony says, bringing the drinks over. He pauses for a moment to scan each of our faces. It looks as though he wants to say something but holds back, smiling briefly before heading back behind the bar.

Elli finally lifts her head enough to notice me.

"Is this...the Ren?" Elli says to her sister.

"Yup," Zari responds, taking a swig and leaning back. Elli stares at me for a moment, her green eyes glistening.

"Thank you," she says. I look around. Is she talking to me?

"I heard you saved Zander's life. Thank you," she says again, sniffling and wiping her face. I don't know what to say.

"Yeah, I'm...I'm sorry...for your loss," I say, as her glance drops from me down to the table. We sit for a while in complete silence. Every once in a while, someone takes a swig from their drink and then returns to their leaned-back slump. Should I try and take their mind off things, maybe change the subject to the Droid? Luckily, my nervous and incoherent train of thought is cut off by Zander.

"So, was it MetiCorp?" Zander whispers out of nowhere. Why would MetiCorp...?

"I...I don't think so. He left a note. Carved in Kanji on the wall beside him, 'Keizoku wa chikara nari,' which translates to 'Continuation is power.' It's an old Japanese proverb meaning 'don't give up,'" Zari explains.

"That ironic son of a bitch. Clearly left that for us and ignored it for himself. Selfish bastard. Did he think this was some joke? A game he could just tap-out of!?" Zander says, breaking his cool and slamming his fist against the table. "He's lost before, I don't get it. What did he say when you took him home after the fight?"

"Nothing," she sniffs. "We rode home in silence. I tried to reassure him. I tried to tell him that I still loved him and that we could come back from this. I... I swear I tried," she breaks down while Elli tries to comfort her, rubbing her back.

"I know. It's not your fault. Sometimes I wonder if he loved anything more than that damn armor," Zander says, his jaw tight with frustration.

"I would have given it back. To be honest... I wanted to, but when they threw it, the crowd was after me, and we had to run before we were torn to shreds...I had no way to contact you. I didn't know what to do... I'm sorry," I say, trying to make sense of what, if anything, I should be saying.

"I told you to keep it, hoping he would spend some time out of it. He hasn't taken that thing off since he came back from active duty. I never expected him to gamble with something so important, but he's been different since he won the title last year. I was just hoping...eventually...things would get better. He'd be... happier. But I guess I didn't do enough." She closes her eyes, her bottom lip trembling. "Maybe it was the thought of working himself back up to where he'd climbed...all over again."

"He could have. If the Company hadn't stepped in to test out new tech. That Raven freak should be banned. Body modifications like that shouldn't even be allowed in the same sphere as real human beings. But they do as they please. They hold the power, and with it, they will always hold us back." Zander spits through gritted teeth. Silence again befalls the table. I scan their faces as I think back to Koujin's message: Don't give up.

CHAPTER NINE_

"You know, the sky looks different here than it does in the
Outskirtz," I start, and the three of them look over, giving me
more attention than I had anticipated. I clear my throat and
continue, "The lights in the city drown out the stars, but back
home, they shine like burning effigies. Sandscavengers believe
you can give the stars memories to hold for you. So when you
look out and see them again, they can remind you of the friend-
ships forged and those that we've lost. I think if you look hard
enough, you might still see one you can use to hold your memories of him. One that will inspire you to keep going, to not give
up," I pause again, but the table stares silently, so I try to finish
the thought, "We never know what burdens someone is carrying. Koujin must have felt he could rest now, knowing the
bonds you shared are strong enough to shoulder the burden he
no longer could. Even in this dark time, I envy you all. You
knew someone worth truly caring for and created memories
that will burn for eons, just like those stars," I say, the words
spilling out one after another like someone had said them
for me.

They continue to stare at me, absorbing my words, staying silent for what feels like an eternity.

"I hope I've caused no offense," I say, trying to salvage the moment.

"No I...I think you're right," Zari says with watery eyes. "Thank you...for that, and for saving Zander's life the other day. I can't lose anyone else. You two have to be careful. These 'malfunctions' are getting more and more dangerous."

"How common are they?" I ask. "These malfunctions? I noticed one earlier today, and the stabilizers weren't damaged. They were disabled. Almost like..."

"Almost like it was done intentionally?" Elli butts in, taking an angry swig of her drink.

"Yeah," I reply, concerned.

"I'm going to be honest with you, kid. I brought..." Zander starts.

"Zander...are you sure?" Zari says, cutting him off. He pauses for a moment, nods, then continues.

"I brought you in because I think the other two techs are trying to get me killed."

I guessed they were sabotaging him, but I didn't think they were actually trying to kill him.

"What? What are you talking about!? Why?" I say, confused.

"I've already fired one, as I thought it was just him, but now I'm sure they're all in on it. I've been noticing random malfunctions throughout this off-season, and it's not the first time I almost died running practice laps."

"Are you sure? I mean, you were really breaking things in today. Maybe it's a coincidence?" I ask.

"It's well beyond coincidence at this point, kid. When the real racing starts, maneuvers like today are par for the course. I was going easy on you so you could work your way up to the real thing. You passed with flying colors, I'd say, because if you didn't, I wouldn't be here to tell you this." He shakes his head. I sit silently, trying to process everything he's telling me. I know MetiCity can be a cutthroat place if you cross the wrong person, but this is beyond what I had imagined.

"But...why? Why would they try to kill their own driver?" I'm still confused.

"Doesn't matter. They work for MetiCorp. They'll follow orders no matter how deeply it indebts them to the devil. The Company isn't what you think it is."

"I know the history," I say confidently.

"No. You don't," Zari butts in. "The Company will argue that they've raised life expectancy, lowered crime, and are providing for everyone. But in order to get here, a lot of people had to die. Our people had to die."

Elli takes a sip of her drink, then pours the rest into Zari's empty glass.

"Drink up, sis," she smiles, trying to cheer her up.

"Have you heard of the ICON Status?" Zander continues, getting back to his point.

"Icon? Like Michael Jackson?"

He shakes his head.

"No. It's a secret social credit status bestowed upon those who meet a very specific set of requirements."

"What kind of requirements?" I ask.

"Well, you have credentials, and you signed the contract, so you know how the social credit system works, right?" Zander asks.

"I know enough." At least, I think I do?

"Well, you at least read the contract, right?"

"Well...some of it." Maybe not.

"Allspirits..." he sighs. "Let me just start from the beginning. Your social credit score is impacted by literally every aspect of your life: your score in ranking, your consumption, your work, the art you create, your notoriety. Basically, anything you do to contribute to MetiCity society, positively or negatively. It's all saved in the system and an algorithm takes that information and accumulates your social credit score. The higher the score, the more you can consume, the more space you can occupy, and the more access you have to resources. However, wasting those resources or disrupting the system is penalized. On the other hand, any contribution to the three innovations is highly rewarded. You do know what the three innovations are, right?" he says with a sidelong glance.

"Of course. Transport, Bionics, and Robotics. How we move through space, how we take care of ourselves, and how we take care of the world."

"Impressive. Like you read it out of a text file." I seem to have restored his faith a little. "Once your score is high enough, you qualify for mastery status in one of the three innovations. Once you reach mastery status, which is no easy task, you can become an ICON."

"You're simplifying that a lot, Zander," Zari cuts in.

"Yes, and thanks to you, I can afford to. Zari and Elli have been working towards breaking the ICON status criteria down to a science. This way, we know what moves to make in order to progress towards achieving it for ourselves. We didn't find out about it until we were well into our careers, so our paths were less malleable. I was already O-Racing by the time Zari discovered the status, so my innovation specialty is centered around transport. Specifically, being the first O-Racer from outside an original MetiCity to win a Cup," Zander explains.

"Because I work on updating various system code, my innovation specialty is robotics. My criteria stipulates I must develop the programming language for the next system update. Something that hasn't happened in over thirty years." She rolls her eyes before speaking softly once more, "Koujin...was part of a special military unit that was approved to use Paladin armor. He was so completely devoted to that bionic suit that his innovation mastery tier qualification required him to win an HFL title wearing it..." Zari trails off, focusing intently on a drip of beer rolling down her glass. I want to change the subject away from him, but I can't.

"So...Koujin became an ICON when he won the title, right? Why would MetiCorp kill him for a status? What does becoming an ICON give you that you can't already get?" I ask, thinking back to his high-rise apartment.

"An audience with the MetiCorp board, who are obligated to grant any single request that falls within the scope of their power. You get two choices, though," he adds, holding up two fingers. "The second being access to the MetiCorp Compendium. A digital record of every MetiCorp event."

"The real events," Elli says, with disgust on her face.

"Every order followed, every secret hidden, and every life taken," Zari continues.

"So, what did Koujin pick?" I ask, trying to follow.

An uncomfortable silence creeps over the table as Zander looks over to Zari.

"He chose the meeting," Zari says in a mix of anger and regret.

"What did he ask for?" I ask, trying to watch my step.

"His family decided that they wanted an island. One in a newly discovered habitable zone. They got exclusive MetiCorp contracts to build out the entire place into some mini MetiCity. It's going to be a tourist attraction. That's where they are now, overseeing construction," Zari explains.

"Instead of attending their only son's funeral," Elli snipes.

"Koujin's family doesn't see the value in attending. They

see everything in terms of hindering or furthering their family's wealth," Zari explains.

"So you would have rather he had taken the Compendium?"

"That was always the plan. So, I wasn't very happy when he decided to throw away everything we worked for. Maybe it's my fault after all...maybe I pushed him away," she says, slumping further back into her seat.

"No, Zari. It was selfish of him...of them. But they made their decision. You never left him. Never condemned him for it," Zander says, trying to look her in the eyes as she stares into her still-full glass. "It's hard to blame him for not wanting the Compendium. Koujin's family has deep ties with the board. Releasing it could have meant unsettling that relationship. Dishonoring his family."

"What will you do if you get it? The Compendium," I ask.

"We're going to publish it and expose MetiCorp for what they've done!" Elli yells, nodding her head determinedly.

It's starting to make sense. Why I've never heard of this status, and why MetiCorp would want to kill Zander or anyone who tries to reach it.

"How exactly did you figure this out?" I ask.

"I was working on a new programming language and during my research for it, I started to notice some odd code in the original proto-language the Engineer used in his innovations. I was curious what this code was used for, so I tried to find similar strings in the current social credit system. Turns out these coding strings are still present. By compiling them, I was able to decipher the purpose, an algorithm designed to designate the ICON status to those who earn it."

"Why wouldn't the Company just remove it?" I ask.

"The code itself is embedded, so MetiCorp would need to

rewrite everything in order to get rid of it. They may be working on a way to purge it from the system, but for now, there's nothing they can do about it. Well, other than trying to stop those who get too close. All we know is that the more original prototypes we can find, the more we will understand the algorithm, and the easier it will be to reach ICON status. That's why I was hoping you'd bring your prototype by. We don't want to lose our window for this. We promised we would each pursue our paths until one of us made it."

"With Zari potentially decades away from meeting her criteria and Koujin gone, it all falls on me," Zander explains.

"And me!" Elli says, feeling left out.

"Wait, what are your criteria, Elli?" I ask, realizing we haven't discussed it.

"Zari said I haven't met the initial requirements to trigger the algorithm, but when I do, I'll be ready!" she says resolutely.

"For now, she and Zari spend their time hunting down original prototypes and digging through code. Until then, I need your help, Ren. More now than ever," Zander pleads.

I have no idea how I feel. These guys are basically on a suicide mission, trying to dismantle the entire system. I definitely didn't sign up for this. Or did I? Maybe I should have read that contract.

"Hey, it's getting late. I know it's a lot, so you don't have to make any decisions right now. Just think it over. If you're scared that you're putting yourself at risk, you don't have to come back to work tomorrow. I'll completely understand your decision," Zander says, getting up from the table.

Zari and Elli decide to call a ride while Zander and I head back to the stadium to pick up my FlyBike. Barely two words are spoken between us on the way. Once we land, he gives me a nod before taking off once again. Feels like he's giving me space. It's welcome.

As I ride home, my brain is whirring. Is this 'algorithm'

something the Engineer coded? Or was it some rogue programmer who slipped it in under the radar? I get the sudden urge to tell Migo, but that would just endanger him. Not that he'd believe it. Or understand it.

When I get back to the shop, I can hear Frank yelling over loud music.

"WHERE THE HELL IS IT!?" Frank yells gruffly, rifling through storage units.

"Where is what?" I ask, walking into the back of the shop. The Droid looks up at me from the corner he's huddled in. The place looks amazing, other than the storage units Frank is ransacking.

"REN! Finally! Will you tell him to turn off the music? And tell me where the thirty gauge wire is! I can't find anything. Damn Droid ruined my entire organizational system!" he barks.

"What organizational system?" I laugh while bringing up the Droid's diagnostics. I cut the music which he had initiated himself, oddly enough. I notice he isn't completely registering the Biosuit properly. Shoddy work fusing the Paladin armor. That was my mistake, but in all fairness, I think I fell asleep halfway through. I should be able to get him all synced, but the vocal system is going to be an issue until I can take him to Zari's. I don't know how long that will be considering Koujin's passing, so for now, he'll have to wait.

"Can you hear me?" I ask. The Droid nods. "Can you show me where the thirty gauge wire is?"

He walks over to a storage container on the opposite side of where Frank was looking. He opens the unit, and Frank comes over and snatches some out.

"I came in to do one thing and leave, and this guy screwed up my whole night," he says, fussing with some repair. "You're here late; you coming from work?"

"Went to get drinks with Zander," I say, continuing to analyze the android. I wonder if there are any hidden secrets in this guy that Zari can find.

"Ah, so it's going well? That's great news. Haven't missed you at all," Frank says unconvincingly.

"Yeah. But it's definitely not what I expected."

"What do I always say? The best expectations are no expectations. Keep at it. I'm proud of you. Don't forget to lock up before you leave. And would you fix that damn Droid?" he says, grumbling something under his breath. Funny how he can go from sweet, endearing centennial to hard-nosed war veteran in the span of seconds.

I spend the rest of the night repairing the Droid, reinforcing his spinal connections, combing through his settings to confirm which ones are responsive. I try to figure out why he chose the song he did or if I can figure out a user history, but I'm not able to. I'm not familiar with the language he's written in, at least not to the level of someone like Zari. I also have a hard time concentrating. I keep thinking about what I was told tonight. MetiCorp has always prided itself on its ability to address societal grievances without the need for a legislative body. They lord their sophisticated AI which handles arbitration and updates protocols. So, the ICON status is something they would normally brag about. Something they would encourage people to strive for. Instead, it's hidden like they're afraid of its potential. Does this old Droid really hold such powerful secrets? Secrets so monumental that people are willing to die for them? Am I willing to die for them? If I'm going to continue working for Zander, I need to know the answer to that question.

CHAPTER TEN_

A call from Zander wakes me up from the brief moment of sleep I had gotten. I'm worried I might be late, panicking as I open the com-link.

"What time is it? Am I late?" I mumble, half awake.

"It's early. No, sorry. I can't sleep, and I wanted to see if you'd had time to come to a decision. But it sounds like you planned to come?" he asks.

"Yes. I'll be there. I got 'chu," I say confidently.

"Good. I wasn't sure which path you'd take, but I'm glad to hear you've made your mind up. Bring the Droid tonight. We're going to drop it off at Zari and Elli's."

"Yeah? Are you sure they are ready for that?" I ask.

"Yes. We're not giving up. And I think they need to get their mind off things. So bring the Droid, and Zari can get to work finding out what's in it after practice."

"Okay...but I don't know if it's going to take her mind off things. He's wearing Koujin's armor, remember?"

"Shit. I forgot. Well...still bring it. If it's too much, we can always abort the mission, okay?"

I try to put some normal clothing on the Droid, so it won't

be Koujin's Paladin armor staring her in the face. He looks ridiculous, but for some reason, I can tell he's enjoying being dressed up in human clothes. It won't be the first time a Droid has worn human clothes, but usually, they just wear a basic tracksuit or nothing at all. Unfortunately, all I have is some stuff Frank has left around the shop and an old poncho. Until I have Zari take a look at him, I don't think I'm going to be able to figure out any of the adaptable modes for travel.

"You ready?" I ask the Droid. He nods.

The stadium has gotten more crowded now that we're edging closer to the Cup. In order to qualify, we have to make sure we clock a good lap time. We'll soon be preparing for our own qualifying run. More techs, more fans, more cameras, and more noise. The two techs we have been working with are long-time Company members who were sent ahead of the rest to make sure everything was ready to go. Or rather, to make sure things didn't get off the ground. Zander bringing me in probably raised enough eyebrows, and since they were unsuccessful so far, I can only imagine what they have planned next. I sit the Droid on a bench in the locker room and head out to the pit.

"This is Ren. He's the best mechanic in the Outskirtz and has been steadily decreasing my time on the track. He's going to be lead on the board, and I want everyone to support him in any way possible. Does anyone have a problem with that?" Zander announces to what is now a full team. If they have something to say, they don't say it. I can't be sure if the original two techs are all I have to worry about, but I make sure that I'm now part of the pre-run inspections and try to pay close attention to each of them. Luckily, these new team members are way more personable than the original techs. By the time Zander has begun his test runs, they're more amazed than upset.

"You're kidding? You've only been doing this for three

days?" one of the new team members asks as I proceed to operate the monitor.

"Yeah. It took some time to understand feedback and response times, but really, Zander does all the hard work," I say, trying to be humble. I am a quick learner, for sure, but it is more than that. Sometimes, I feel like I'm anticipating adjustments before they even happen. I'm not sure if it's muscle memory, but I'm much more comfortable at this point, and it shows. Zander has subtracted three entire seconds from his lap time since I joined the team, and it makes the rest of the team excited. Aside from the two techs, who are keeping mostly to themselves, everyone else is cheering by the time Zander makes it to the final stretch.

"Hey. I noticed the coils were at maximum temp. Aren't you afraid they might overheat at this pace?" one of the techs says as I give a grin.

"I figured out that if I flick back and forth between the coils periodically, I can push them harder. It all comes down to timing. We had an issue recently..." I glanced at one of the original techs from the corner of my eye. "...with the coils, and I made sure to keep an eye on them."

The new tech is eager to share he's responsible for getting the jet from prototype status to ready for race day. A designer. Not many changes will take place internally, but the look of the jet might change before we get to the Cup. He knows enough to notice it's running better, but not enough to see any of the small modifications I made, which is what I wanted. Before practice, I grabbed some parts from the shop and made some small alterations to some of the systems we've had issues with in the past. It's hard to know what they might be planning next, but I made sure that anything that they tried before wouldn't work again. Besides, with things ramping up here and more and more people showing up every day, it is going to be a lot harder for them to pull anything off.

After the test runs, we have a meeting with the team in the stadium to discuss scheduling. We'll have a test run here tomorrow, then over the weekend, they'll complete exterior modifications. Monday is the opening media day, alongside our qualifying race in MetiCity-10. The actual race is on Tuesday. The times we've been clocking have been enough to get us into the Cup, but Zander warns that, since the test run won't be at our stadium, the times we get there won't quite be the same, so we have to be prepared.

There's a very wealthy team owner who shows up for a video chat and expresses his excitement for the times we're getting. Most owners are more hands-on, but the MetiCity-6 team owner takes a hands-off approach. I can see a woman swimming behind him in the video as he has his brunch on what is probably his private compound. Hard to say if he's the one giving the orders to the techs, as he does have a very super-villain vibe, but, to be honest, I feel that way about most people I meet with that kind of wealth. After the owner ends the call, we walk over to a monitor to watch a report on the competitors. There are a lot of the same names as last year, except for the new cities that have joined in on the race this year.

There are twelve MetiCities currently, and the race originated among the inner four. In the last three years, they opened the race up to a total of eight cities, and this year, they would increase that to ten. Zander isn't so concerned with the new racers, as they will be the target of the original four cities, just like we will. If anything, they'll be helpful in taking some of the heat off him during the race. They mention a young prodigy from MetiCity-10 who has the leading qualifying score, but Zander says he'll have a rude awakening once he gets in front of a couple hundred thousand people and has to share the track with other pros. He explains to me that being fast is only one part of the race; that you have to know how to attack and defend your position, as well. Things seem to be moving fast now, and it'll only be a matter of time before I'm sitting in the middle of a stadium full of crazed fans, trying to keep up the momentum we've had.

On my way out for the night, Zander is waiting for me by the exit.

"How are you feeling?" he says, smiling.

"Nervous. Excited. Overwhelmed. In control," I say.

"Those...don't align at all. But your hard work has really paid off. Now, let's head over to the girls and have a look at that Droid. I really need this to be something big," Zander says as we head to Zari's place.

"Something big?" I ask.

"Yeah. Sometimes, Zari finds a big piece of code that gives us a ton of information, and sometimes, we get a little bit of code that makes no sense until it's paired with a bunch of other pieces. Problem is, we've collected code from so many proto-types around here that we're running out of them," he explains.

After cruising for a while, Zander begins an ascent to the heights of the dome. A high-rise apartment this far outside of the city center? A structure comes into view, and I struggle to process it. It looks like...a castle? It's breathtaking, raised up on a circular platform, suspended above the city below. It looks ancient, as if it's been plucked from history and placed here, undisturbed. Gigantic spires punctuate the stone walls, topped with old but enduring stonework, blanketed in moss and foliage. Elaborate arches are spotted throughout, leading to lush gardens filled with flowers. There are balconies around all of the upper levels, and I can't help but wonder how the city looks from up there. I should have known the girls are wealthy, considering Zari went to a prestigious ranking institution, but this type of thing takes more than just wealth; it takes coordination on another level.

The girls are out in the front courtyard waiting near the landing pad we're lowering onto. Elli waves to us as we descend. She's sitting cross-legged, perched on a wall. Zari stands beside her, empty eyes staring through us as we finally land. We exit the cruiser, and Zander starts toward them as I hold the door open for the Droid to get out.

"Hey ladies! You eat anything today?" he asks.

"Too much," Elli says, hugging Zander.

"Koujin's parents have been forwarding all the flowers and condolences here...which means too much food," Zari explains.

"Anything good?" Zander asks, smiling and walking towards Zari before hugging her too.

"Well, someone ate all the Algae steak, but there's a bunch of stuff left; feel free to help yourself. You too, Ren," Elli says, turning to me and smiling.

"It's good to see you both again," I say, joining them. Zander and Zari share pleasantries, and I can make out that he's checking on her and making sure she's eating.

"You as well, Ren. Is this the prototype?" Zari points to the Droid standing behind me.

"See that, Droid? You're famous," I say to the Droid, who has been gazing up at the castle towers. He points to himself as if to say 'me?'

"Droid? You haven't given him a name?" Elli chastises.

"He's got a serial number, but I thought K-2405812 was a mouthful." I laugh.

"Let's get him to my workroom; we'll get him talking again. Maybe he already has a name," Zari says. The girls seem as out of place as their castle. They're so sincere and genuine, not a common MetiCity vibe, aside from Zander.

I follow them inside and into the grand kitchen. It's bigger than Frank's shop. Zander and I fill plates for ourselves. I have no idea what half of the food is, so I steer clear of the riskier-looking options.

"This place is amazing, guys," I say, trying not to talk with my mouth full. "It's like magic, like you brought this place from somewhere else."

"That's because we did. This castle has been in our family for centuries. We grew up in it. When we had to move to Meti-City for ranking, we missed it so much. I hated only being able to visit during a break. When our parents passed, they left it to us, and we couldn't bear to sell it. We heard about this Company that could transport the house and learned that it would be cheaper than building one of these new MetiCity houses. I saved up for years and was able to have it moved here just after graduation," Zari explains.

"*We* saved up for years," Elli points out.

"Yes, Elli helped," Zari says, rolling her eyes, which are red and swollen.

"Sorry to hear about your parents' passing. Best part about being an orphan is you never have to miss anyone when they leave," I say.

"You're an orphan?" Elli asks.

"Yeah. When I was old enough to be on my own, I was. The closest thing I have to a parent is my boss, Frank. But I honestly don't think about it much."

"And now he's working pit crew for the soon-to-be winner of the O-Race Cup," Zander interjects.

"You ready to get to work?" Zari says. "The castle itself has had some major renovations, so I could reroute enough power to work on the various Droids I've had over the years. Most of the place is exactly the same, but this was a must," she says, leading us into another room and flicking on the lights. This shop would make Frank shed a tear. Zero violations, zero clutter, but every tool I could think of somehow fits into the shop and is properly organized.

"It's...beautiful," I say genuinely, looking around.

"Isn't it!?" Elli replies excitedly.

She begins work, showing off the random machines they've acquired throughout the years. Prototypes are spread out around the shop depending on their purpose and designation. They've acquired quite a few already, possibly all the prototypes that are in MetiCity-6. They're dead serious about this, and it makes me much more confident about my decision to join them. I smile as Elli goes on rambling, articulately, but rambling nonetheless. She turns to me smiling, pauses, and says, "What?"

"Nothing. It's just that not many girls in the Outskirtz are tech freaks like you. It's refreshing; I feel like I'm amongst my people," I say, smiling.

"Let's take a look at him then," Zander says, taking a seat.

Zari makes her way over to the bench to grab a scanner and then back to the Droid, who is now sitting in the middle of the shop, meditating. She grabs the poncho he's wearing and pulls it off, freezing mid-movement.

"So you fused the Paladin armor after all..."

"Yeah, he was in pretty bad shape, so..." I begin.

Her eyes glaze over as she skates her fingers across the armor's surface, as though tracing the memories that lie within. Maybe it is too soon after all.

"Hey Zari, is it normal for a Droid to meditate?" Zander jumps in to cut the silence.

"No. I've never seen that before in any of the Droids I've come across. Any human-like behavior was rooted out pretty early," she says, recomposing herself. She hovers the scanner over him to start diagnostics.

"Hmm," she hums from time to time. Elli is standing behind her, tapping on the holographic screen. They're speaking to each other in English, but the terminology is above even my head.

"Right there!" Elli exclaims, eventually.

"What?" Zander asks.

"This doesn't belong, but it goes deeper than that. It's a polymorphic code, extra code that mimics the previous one until it's singled out. Then the variables change, and the code can mean something completely different," Elli explains.

"In other words, it's another puzzle piece," Zari explains, sounding frustrated.

"Is that bad?" I ask.

"No. It's not necessarily bad; it's just that I've been finding piece after piece lately, and none of them seem to connect in any way. I'll have to take a look and see if it fits in with the code I've already compiled."

"Sorry Zari. I was hoping for some progress, too," Zander says, trying to console her.

"Wait a minute," Zari says as Elli's eyes open wide. She adjusts her credentials to project out her screen so we can all see what she found. It's a message:

'Find 42. Blood alone moves the wheels of history.'

"Allspirits! There's a message?" Zander exclaims.

"What does that mean? Is this the first message you've found?" I ask.

"Yeah, it looks like someone is leading us to something. But I don't think it's related to the ICON status. This is something...new," Zari thinks aloud.

"42? What does that mean? And exactly whose blood?" Elli asks, looking a little queasy, but that could be from all the food.

"A quick search shows that the quote is actually from Martin Luther," Zari explains.

"The million man march guy, right? Twentieth century civil rights leader? What does he have to do with this?" Elli asks.

"Not Martin Luther King, Martin Luther, the priest. But they misattributed it, digging further, it says that the quote was actually said by Mussolini. The dictator," Zari says with a look of concern.

"The dictator? That's not a good sign," Zander says, sharing her concern.

"What if it means blood as in family?" Elli asks, trying to solve the riddle.

"I don't think the Engineer had any family," Zari says, entering in a search string. "It says he had a wife but no children," she continues.

"Yeah, I think if the guy had forty-two children, someone would have noticed," I proclaim.

"Damn...I really thought we were onto something. But now I'm more confused than when we started. Is that all there is?" Zander asks.

"I'm sorry..." Zari says defeatedly.

"You're doing your best, Zari. This is still a big deal," Zander comforts her.

"Maybe there's more here than just that message. Let's keep looking, Zari," Elli says, trying to pull her back.

We sit for hours, watching the girls scour the Droid's code for more answers. For something, anything.

"They could be at this all night, and it's getting late. We have to be at the stadium early," Zander says.

"Do you mind if I keep the Droid overnight? I haven't had a chance to go over all the code here, and I still need to fix his voice modulator," Zari asks.

It's one of the first times I've ever handed something over for someone else to fix. It feels weird not being able to do it myself, but she has better equipment and a better grasp of the code, so I let her. Maybe it will help her occupy her mind for a bit. A welcome distraction, I'm sure. They have been trusting of me so far; why not return the favor?

CHAPTER ELEVEN_

"Today, we have MetiCorp coming to watch our practice and perform their inspections, so make sure you're in full uniform," Zander says, skipping the normal pleasantries.

I hadn't had a chance to shower in days and only had a quick moment to wash my face in the bathroom before suiting up. Usually, the team is pretty lax about the uniform, but as we get closer to the qualifier, more and more people have been showing up every day. The parking lot is no longer sprawling empty asphalt and instead has been filled with rows of vehicles for stadium workers and, I guess, these MetiCorp officials. The security has beefed up as well. I was stopped at the entrance by some guy with a badge, so I'm running even further behind. I hurry out and head to the conference room, where I can hear someone has already started speaking. I sneak in and stand slightly behind Zander.

"This year, of all years, is the most important one in this team's history," an older, heavy-set man in a tailored suit says, standing at the front of a table where we are seated.

"He says that every year," Zander whispers, leaning over to me.

"This year, there are more racers than there have ever been, which means more eyes than there have ever been and more at stake than there has ever been. We need to show the world MetiCity-6 is worthy of competing. Do you know what happens to a team when they place last in an O-Race?"

"They race in the minor leagues?" one of the techs asks sincerely.

"What's your name?"

"Gary?"

"Gary. Get out," the MetiCorp businessman says. He stares at the tech until Gary realizes he isn't joking and quietly leaves the room, hiding the tears that had gathered in his eyes. "Speaking of techs. Is it my understanding that you hired a new tech that's going to be running the monitors? Are you nuts, kid?" It's weird to hear Zander called a kid by someone, but for all I know, this guy is a centenarian himself.

"I don't know if you know this, but this is the best tech in the Outskirtz," Zander nods to me. "Surely we aren't discriminating against the Outskirtz, are we?" he asks.

"Well...no, but running the monitors with no experience? It's unheard of." The man seems to be flustered, which is something I didn't expect. Maybe there's a history there I'm not aware of.

"Well, at first, I just wanted to train him as a backup, as I assumed giving him a basic understanding of how to run the boards would help him to assess issues with the jet, but after a few days, he was cutting time off my lap. Can't deny the kid has talent," Zander says, gesturing to me again. I gulp. The man looks me over, mumbling to himself before addressing Zander again.

"Well, I'll just have to see for myself," he says before storming off with a Droid of his own, which I assume he uses as a secretary.

"Don't sweat him, kid, he's just nervous. If we don't win, he'll have to look for a place near you. He's originally from the Outskirtz too, but to him, it's an insult to mention it. He doesn't seem to remember where he came from," Zander explains.

The rest of the techs and I make our way to the monitors. I'm worried, considering I haven't had a moment to check the jet today, but I must assume the other techs wouldn't try something on such an important day. There isn't much time for anyone to do much, considering the early meeting, anyway.

As soon as I get the headset on, I can hear Zander asking for me.

"Hey, kid. Can you hear me?"

"Yeah. Getting set up now. Everything good?"

"This is going to be great practice for the real thing. It's one thing doing these runs in an empty stadium, but when there are thousands of fans cheering to a deafening roar, and everything is on the line, it's a whole different run."

"So uh...no pressure huh?" I smirk.

"No pressure," he says as I hear the engine come online.

The countdown clock to the lap start is nearing thirty seconds and everything looks fine on the monitors, so at least that's one less thing I have to worry about. Twenty seconds on the clock and the techs jokingly advise me not to screw this up. Ten seconds down, and I can feel my palms starting to sweat. Am I in over my head? I've only had a few days of training. No time at all. Welp.

The buzzer sounds and Zander explodes into the opening stretch. The screens light up immediately and I get right to work. His thrusters are near max going into the first turn. Is he expecting me to adjust for him, or is he comfortable making the turn at that speed?

"Uh... Zander," I say, worried.

"I trust you," he says, assuringly. As he approaches the turn, he would usually slow slightly so I could adjust the angle of the trajectory, but he isn't about to lose a second on this lap. Just before he hits the turn, I dampen the thruster slightly. As he turns, I let off and turn around for a moment to watch him come blazing out of the turn. We had never done that before, but now that I think of it, he's never had to give me much direction. He's trusted me from the get-go.

"Again!" He says excitedly. Now that I know what he needs, I'm able to slightly adjust the trajectory before each turn and have to dampen less. It almost feels like I'm driving for a moment. He shoots out of the next turn, and one of the techs comes over to review the monitor.

"The hell did you just do, kid?" He seems surprised. No. He seems...impressed.

"Damped ten on the incline thruster gate after adjusting the fin ratio eighty percent," I say while trying to keep my focus. The tech takes his hat off to scratch his head. After all of these laps, I've progressively been getting better at not just understanding the limits of each individual adjustment toggle, but also Zander. As a person and as a racer, he's confident to all hell. Right on the verge of being cocky, but every ounce of this guy is born out of trials I can't imagine. He's the one who put this city on his back and has carried it. To trust me after just a few days? It gives me an overwhelming sense of responsibility but also increasing confidence.

We're nearing the final lap when the techs point out the time, not just a personal best, but potentially a world record. It would smash the new prodigy's time and make news going into the trials. One more lap.

"Hey, kid, can you figure out what's going on with all this vibration? It's getting harder to steer," Zander says.

"On it." I hate making real-time repairs because I have to run a diagnostic on top of everything else I'm adjusting, but luckily, the tool is able to find a loose connection that's shorting out some of the steering assist. I can't manually adjust from here. I'll have to take care of it after the lap. This isn't good news.

"Hey, Zander," I say.

"You figure it out?" he asks.

"I trust you." I reassure Zander.

The tech looks over at me in confusion. I disable the system, which cuts out the vibration, but also means he'll have to manually adjust the steering on his end. It isn't impossible, but it will take a ton more strength and coordination when steering. I wouldn't do this at the start of the race, but since it's his last lap, he'll have to take it home himself. If he's going to break the record, he'll have to do it with his bare hands. I allow extra airflow as he comes into the final straightway, which will max out the jet's speed and send him into a critical zone of performance. Extremely dangerous for anyone but him.

"After this turn, I'm going to release the dampeners and force the air through, but that means you're going to have to-"

"-Adjust in a downwind leg," he says, completing my sentence. "You little shit." I can tell he is smirking.

As he gets around to the final turn, I hear him grunting as he adjusts the angle. Once he makes it through the turn, my job is done. It is all up to him now. I turn around to see the final sprint and catch a glimpse of the team manager jumping up and down in the stadium seats. His Droid struggles to stay standing as he swings his arms in triumph.

"Aaaaaargh!" Zander is now yelling as the Gs hit him and he pushes everything to the limit.

He zips past the finish line, and everyone runs over to the monitor to check the time.

"WELL!?" Zander yells over the com.

"Close," I say.

"How close? Seconds?"

"Nope. Point one second behind. You matched him and are just behind the world record."

"That kid must be some kind of psycho," one of the techs says to another.

"Not a psycho. Just using assisted steering, unlike Zander," I say, sighing heavily and taking a seat.

"Wait, he did that run manually!?" one of the techs asks.

"Yup. Had to cut assistance around the final lap because he was getting too much vibration from a loose circuit. Probably could have beat it if not for that," I say, leaning back, frustrated.

"Quick thinking, kid, but next time…just tell me you cut the assist. I almost missed that last turn," Zander says before hopping out of the vehicle and landing right behind me. He pats me on the back, smiling.

The manager runs to the pit area with his Droid, trying to keep up. He's panting, hard.

"The kid stays! Holy shit, the kid stays!" he gasps when he gets close enough.

"I know," Zander says nonchalantly.

"You guys keep improving like this, and I'm going to drown myself in champagne and women, I swear it!"

"That's all for today. We don't want to overrun her the week before the qualifiers," Zander says, patting the jet's nose. "Let's get her back in the shop and make sure we find that loose connection, okay?" he says to the other techs.

Zander finds me waiting in the lobby for him and greets me with a pat on the back.

"Glacious board work, my friend," he congratulates me.

"Thanks," I smile, feeling recognized. "And thanks for what you said in the meeting today."

"Was it not true?" he asks.

"Either way, I appreciate everything you've done for me. A

few days ago, I was digging out some scrap metal from the burning sand, which turned out to be a toilet snake. Now I'm working for the fastest O-Racer alive."

"You have snakes in your toilets?" he cuts me off. "Made of metal? The Outskirtz certainly are a wild place," he laughs.

"No. A snake auger, it's like a long metal tool the old world used to unclog toilets."

"Oh!" he laughs. "So, not your best day?"

"Nope. But the best days are always ahead, eh?" I chuckle.

"Right, you are, and today isn't over. Zari said she was able to fix your Droid. Ready to head over and check it out?"

"Yeah!" I say, lifting my fists up to my face in excitement. Zander winces and steps back.

"Didn't have time to hit the showers, huh?" he asks.

"No, you said to meet you at the front entrance. I didn't think I had the time?"

"Zeesh, kid. Don't worry about it; you can shower at the sisters' place," he says before leading the way to his cruiser.

CHAPTER TWELVE

As we arrive at the castle, I look out over the massive landscape and see only Elli is there to greet us this time.

"Hey, you two..." she says, her nose wrinkling as she hugs me. "Ugh, no offense, Ren, but you stink."

"Yeah, sorry, Zander's last lap made me break a sweat. He really had me worried," I exaggerate to hide my embarrassment.

"Hey, I thought you said you trusted me?" Zander says, punching me in the shoulder playfully.

"I see you two are getting along quite famously," she says, pinching her nose.

"Yeah, can you do us both a favor and show him where the shower is?" Zander asks Elli.

"With pleasure," she says, pushing me from behind into the house.

"Oh, and Elli?"

"Yeah?"

"Your 3DCP still working?" Zander asks, yelling down the hallway.

"Yup! On it." She continues to push me along. A 3D clothing printer? Migo has one, but he won't let me near it. Says it's a very delicate instrument and doesn't like to use it unless he has to. Which is apparently once a month when the new fashion drops. That noso hasn't printed me so much as a sock since he got it.

The hot water and pressure of the shower washes over me, and for a moment, I can finally relax and zone out. I tilt my head against the glass as the water hits my face. Sometimes, it's the simplest thing, like taking a shower, that can make you remember where you came from. The showers in my settlement have timers and low pressure. The water there is sprayed out in small incremental bursts as a way to conserve what water we have. After some treasuring the moment, I finally step out, wiping the water from my eyes. When my vision clears, I can see Elli placing some clothes and a towel on the counter.

"Shit. Sorry. Fuck. Uh, Sorry!" she says, panicking.

"Oh fuck sorry, I-" I slip back, hitting my head on the wall of the shower.

"Oh shit! Are you okay!?"

"No, yes. I'm fine! You're good! You can leave!" I yell, trying to gather myself.

"Oh! Fuck. Okay, sorry! Towel and clothes. Let me know if they fit!" She says, running out the door.

She definitely saw my dick.

As I pick up the clothes, I can't help but notice the lack of... well, everything. There's no hems, buttons or seams, and the material feels incredibly soft in my hands. I get dressed before the red in my face clears up, but I'm able to muster the confidence to head toward the sisters' shop. The first thing I notice is Zander's face, barely able to contain a smile. Zari faces away from me, working on the Droid.

"You have a nice shower?" Zander chuckles.

"Yeah...why?" I say, knowing damn well Elli must have already spilled the beans.

"Well, since Elli has come back, she hasn't stopped doing... well, that," he says, pointing at Elli, who is in a corner crouched under what looks like a towel.

"I should have sent the damn Droid!" Elli yells from under the towel.

"Anyway," Zari says, butting in, "I found something you guys might want to see." She is not amused by our little mishap. She projects her credentials, and it shows three bleeping dots on a map.

"And those are?" Zander asks.

"Within the Droid's memory banks, I was able to find code that, when run, locates the position of three objects. This dot here is where we are, or more specifically, where he is," Zari says, pointing to the screen and then to the Droid. "The other two signals are coming from within MetiCity-10, and MetiCity-4. There's no information on which signal is what, but using simple deduction, I can assume one is a transport and the other a Biosuit," she says, looking back at us.

"Holy shit! You were able to get that from my Droid?" I exclaim, impressed.

"Yup," she says. It's the first time I've seen her smile since Koujin's death.

"Good work, Zari," Zander says, placing a hand on her shoulder.

"And Elli!" Elli yells from under her towel.

"Elli did help. But if it wasn't for Ren, who knows if we would have ever gotten here at all," she says, looking over at me. I'm not sure how to react. I kneel down in front of the Droid, surveying him.

"Destiny then, isn't it?" The Droid speaks. I almost fall back out of shock.

"You fixed his voice!" I say excitedly.

"She did," he responds.

"Yup. Ordered a part in overnight. It was nothing," Zari says, coming over. "He's fully functional now. I woke up to him cleaning the shop, so I'm assuming he was some sort of house Droid prototype. Still not sure how he survived this long without being scrapped or destroyed."

"I nearly was destroyed. Until Ren saved me," the Droid says.

"Don't mention it," I say, rubbing the back of my head.

"Elli, you can't stay under there all night. Grow up," Zari says to her sister. Elli doesn't move. "Unless you don't want to burn with us."

"Coming!" Elli says, jumping up to her feet.

"Greesha? You guys burn?" I ask.

"From time to time, but we don't abuse it. We see it as a medicine," Zari says, putting various tools away. "That's actually where my family made most of their fortune. The plant grows native to the island where my ancestors settled and they were the first to cultivate it. Have you ever tried it?"

"Yeah, my boss Frank uses it; I can usually smell it on him when he comes in. I used to think it was like marijuana when I first heard about it. One time, I asked him for a burn and found out it's nothing like it. Thought it was glacious until he told me how much he spent on it. Didn't seem worth it, considering the stories I've heard about people losing their minds on it."

"Well, likely whatever he burned was not what we grow. We grow a few plants at a time using the soil we lifted from our island. It doesn't have the same side effects, and you need to burn a ton more to get anywhere near an overdose like that," she says, finally finishing up and walking over to me.

"So they changed the formula or something?" I ask.

"Yeah. A few generations back, MetiCorp decided they wanted to regulate and distribute everything themselves. I suspect they killed anyone who fought that decision, considering there aren't many indigenous people left alive from that island but us. They did pay off our family for the land and formula, but it hasn't been the same since. Whenever I asked my parents about how that went down, they said they sold it, but I don't think they had much of a choice in the end. A few years later, when they passed, they left us this place and the inheritance. But I wish they had never left us at all," she says, looking down.

"What do you remember about them?" I ask sincerely.

She looks up at me. "They were amazing singers. I can remember them singing us to sleep at night, and I've never heard anything like it since," she says.

"You guys coming or not?" Elli says, popping her head into the shop. She and Zander were waiting in the hallway.

"Yes, Elli, I was just telling him about Mom and Dad. Do you remember how they used to sing you to sleep?" she asks.

Elli looks surprised, her eyes shifting down to the right before answering, "Hmmm, nope. C'mon!"

We make our way into the kitchen, where they show me the food printer Zander is using to make his dinner while he sips away on a beer.

"There you guys are. Elli started without you." He points over at Elli, who is already tearing into pancakes.

"Elli, I will never understand why you insist on eating pancakes for dinner," Zari says, shaking her head as a stuffed-mouthed Elli hands her the remaining greesha bundle. The plant burns extremely fast, so the idea is to hold a rolled bundle of it under your nose in order to catch a whiff of it before it dissipates. There's probably around six burns to the average bundle, so it's more of a communal event.

"They're not JUST pancakes. They're blueberry multi-grain protein pancakes, infused with a tasteless OMEGA-3 and probiotic complex!" Elli vehemently declares.

Zari burns a little of the bundle before grabbing a fork and stealing one of Elli's pancakes.

"Hey!" Elli yells.

"What?" Zari responds. "You act like we can't just print another."

"You mind if I try?" I ask.

"No!" Elli says, setting up a defense perimeter around her pancakes with her arms, half a pancake falling out of her mouth.

"Oh, I actually mean the greesha," I say, laughing.

"Sure, don't mind her," Zari says, handing me the bundle and swiping another pancake for me from Elli's plate. "I will warn you Ren, our greesha can be a little more intense your first time. It doesn't last long. But just be ready," Zari cautions.

I've had greesha before; how different can it be? I burn the bundle and inhale. The lines of reality slowly peel away into an oblique mixture of colors swirling about in front of me. Somehow, both intense and calming. Am I dreaming or awake? I'm too calm to be in shock. Too...peaceful. The colors start to organize into a pattern that slowly inches toward something recognizable. Categorizable. Blues and greens gather towards the bottom of my line of vision, while yellows, reds, and oranges gather toward the top like a light spectrum. So colorful and brilliant. I can see it now, the setting sun over the open ocean. But there's movement. Time and distance. Like being in a jet flying overhead looking down, but moving at twice the speed. Over the horizon appears a small landmass filled so densely with trees that it didn't reveal itself to be an island until flying directly over top of it. The motion stops. I focus in on the trees, slowly zooming in over long intervals. The groves of massive old-growth trees stretched into the sky.

I let out a soft "Whoa" as I snap back to the usual euphoric feeling on a normal burn.

"Yup. Now you know why I don't touch the stuff. I don't trust anything that makes you feel that good," Zander says, bringing over what looks like a banquet on a plate.

"Don't worry," Zari laughs, "the onset can be a little overwhelming the first time, but the body processes it quickly and you're left with the comedown, which is much more mellow. Like I said, nothing like what the Company sells. They water it down to the point where you need to burn a ton to get even close to the same high. Before you know it, you've burned too much."

"Maybe I burned too much," I say, still finding my place. A few bites into my pancake, I'm starting to find a baseline. "Can I have some more?" I say, looking at Elli.

"Slow down there, trooper. You shouldn't need more than one hit for a bit," she laughs.

"Oh, no. This time, I was actually talking about the pancakes," I say, smiling. Elli grabs her plate of pancakes and runs to a corner of the kitchen. "Make your own!"

She's always full of chaotic energy, a stark contrast to her sister, whose calm demeanor can come off as stern, but she's actually really sweet and caring. Maybe it's because she had to take over the parental role to Elli, who seems to be hard to handle. They get along better than most siblings, from what I can tell. They complement each other, like yin and yang.

"I've never used one before, but I'll try and figure it out," I say, tapping the screen on the printer.

"You guys don't have food printers in the Outskirtz?" Elli asks.

"Nope. And they rarely break, so I never see them come through the shop."

"Well, they come standard in all MetiCity housing. Why not just move to the City?"

I struggle to give a reason why not. I could still work at the shop, and the FlyBike Zander gave me makes the trip even easier.

"It's not like you can't afford it now," Zander reminds me.

"Yeah, I guess I could..." I hadn't given it thought, but they're right.

"I know the best little neighborhood! It's not far from here. I could show you!" Elli yells from the corner she's huddled in.

"That's a great idea, Elli. We have to be at the MetiCity-10 stadium early Monday morning. That trip would be a lot shorter if you were coming from the City," Zander says, then stops to think. "Speaking of MetiCity-10, since one of the prototypes is there, we should check it out after our media day on Monday."

"I was thinking the same thing," Zari agrees.

After eating, we return to the shop where Zari demonstrates how to get the Droid into what's called 'Carry Mode,' which enables it to compact itself into the size of a suitcase for easy transport.

"With this mode activated, you, Elli, and the Droid should be able to fit on the FlyBike."

"Can I drive?" Elli asks.

"No!" Zander and Zari speak in unison.

"Ren, you should give him a name," Zari says, turning to me.

"I was thinking Proto?"

"It's a bit on the nose, no?" Zari asks.

"Wait, what was the serial number again?" Elli asks.

"K-2405..." I start.

"K-2!" Elli says excitedly.

"K-2?" I wonder out loud.

"Well, he is wearing Koujin's armor, right Zari?" she asks.

"That he is," she says, not solemnly but approvingly.

"Then it's settled. Come on, K-2, we're going house shopping!" Elli says as she adjusts the navigation on my FlyBike to something called the MetiCity-6 estates. She explains she used to pass this place on her way to ranking every morning and loved the building designs and neighborhood layout. It's only a few minutes by FlyBike, and when we arrive, I'm able to see what she was talking about. The unique design of the neighborhood is eye-catching, full of various walking paths through gardens and social areas. It's quiet and peaceful and everything the Outskirtz isn't.

"It's beautiful Elli," I say, getting off the FlyBike and letting the Droid out of carry mode.

We walk for a while, and Elli comments on the different houses, eliminating each one for a different trivial reason. Towards the end of the street, Elli stops and gasps.

"Ahhh, but this one! Look at it! Isn't it perfect?"

"Sure. Although it looks very similar to the last three we just passed."

"No, this is the one. Let's check it out!"

As we enter the house, we're greeted by an overly friendly house Droid.

"Hello! And welcome to MetiCity-6 Estates. Please swipe your credentials and have a look around. Let me know if you have any questions."

"Thanks," I answer, walking past the Droid and swiping my credentials. I wasn't sure what exactly I was even looking for.

"Okay! First, you need to jump on the bed. It's the best way to confirm it has enough support. I'll take care of that part. You check out the kitchen and make sure the food printer is working," Elli says, already halfway to the bedroom.

I'm still trying to figure out if the food printer is working when Elli comes into the kitchen, followed by the house Droid.

"The bed is a dream!" Elli says before nudging me out of

the way and pressing a few buttons on the printer's screen. It generates a pancake and Elli takes a bite before giving me a thumbs up.

"And how are you finding the kitchen, sir?" the Droid asks.

"He'll take it!" Elli cuts me off.

"Wonderful! You have reserved this home for eighteen months. Your credentials will be automatically updated. Would you like me to put your antique away? This prototype seems to be quite a few generations old. I wouldn't want you to think you have to rely on such outdated technology."

K-2 looks at me, then at him, then back at me as if he wants me to speak up for him.

"Just leave him be. Treat him as you would any guest," I instruct.

"I see. Is there anything you need at the moment? I could prepare a meal?" the Droid asks, looking at Elli, who has now completely inhaled her pancake.

"No, thank you. I'm exhausted. I'm going to be heading to sleep soon. Elli, are you staying?"

"Me?" Elli asks, puzzled.

"I just wanted to know if you were going to use the bed?"

"You want me to sleep here...with you?" she replies, raising her eyebrow.

"No, I mean, I was just saying, I don't mind sleeping on the couch," I answer, stuttering my way through the sentence.

"I knew what you meant, 'scav. I'll grab a transport."

"Not a problem, miss! I've already scheduled one and it shall arrive promptly. Would you like me to see you out?

"Nope! I'm going to go test your sprinkler system!"

"What?" the Droid and I say at the same time.

"I think I'll need to accompany you, miss," the house Droid says, following her out of the kitchen. "Welcome to your new home, sir!" he says while bowing slightly, then exits the room.

"Great pick, Ren! Look after him, K-2," Elli shouts from the front door before it closes.

"It is my prime objective, Elli," K-2 informs her.

As soon as I hit the bed, I feel the tension in my shoulders and back slipping away. The bed is indeed a dream. Before I know it, I drift off to sleep without much time for my mind to race for once.

CHAPTER THIRTEEN_

Around midnight, I am awoken by a knock on the door and murmurs of an argument.

"Sir, may I speak with you?" K-2 asks. The house Droid is behind him, going on and on about protocol and not disturbing the homeowner.

"Uh, sure?" I say, wiping the sleep from my eyes. K-2 closes the door, pushing the house Droid out into the hallway.

"What is it?" I ask, sitting up in bed.

"There is something I need to discuss with you regarding your true origin."

"My true origin?" I ask.

"You see, I've been looking for you for quite some time. It took some investigation and many miles walked, so I'm quite relieved to have finally found you. I was assaulted, vandalized, and scheduled to be decommissioned. Each time, I escaped and marched further. Just to make it to you. To deliver a message...from your creator," he says, pausing a moment.

"My creator? Is this some kind of religious indoctrination protocol?" I start.

"No. You are your creator. And mine. I belong to you, Zelius Metihand."

I stand stunned for a long moment. My brain has shut down.

"Zelius Metihand...THE Zelius Metihand? Is this a prank? Did the house Droid try to alter you or something?" I finally snap out of my trance.

"No. My programming does not allow for 'pranks.' The only person to ever see my code was my creator, Zelius Metihand, until your friend Zari Jardinera fixed me."

"What are you saying?"

"Let me start from the beginning. Before he died, Zelius and his wife had attempted to have children several times but failed. They began to drift apart and he continued trying without her," K-2 explains.

"Without her? Like with someone else?"

"No, alone. Zelius began attempting to use his own DNA to produce offspring asexually. After many failed attempts, he was able to produce a direct copy," he says, pausing again.

"You're saying I'm a clone of Zelius?"

"Yes. As his primary Droid, he had grown close to me over the years, often confiding in me with his troubles, especially when his wife left. One night, he came to me, with you, barely days old. He instructed me to leave you at an orphanage in the Outskirtz with the same credentials you're still using even now," he pauses. I look down at my credentials. I always thought they were given by the orphanage or as a gift from my foster parents.

"It's the only night I was not there to protect him," he sounds remorseful. "After I delivered you to the orphanage, I returned to what was left of his home, and saw controllers already investigating his death. From there, I was sent back to the Outskirtz for processing. But for some reason, no one ever came. I was forgotten. I spent years deactivated in the basement of a recycling facility before some curious sandscavenger found me. He wanted to sell me but couldn't when he realized my ownership status was locked. By the time I found my way back to you, you had already left the orphanage and were placed with a family. For years I tried to find anything I could about a Ren Unkno, but the Outskirtz isn't a very forthcoming place. So I waited. I didn't know what else to do. Until one day, I heard a story about a mechanic with a scar on his face who could fix anything. You found me the very next day on my way to find you. The only one I can answer to. Like I said, it was destiny." The room falls silent. A plethora of reactions storm over me, but I settle on disbelief.

"Enter admin mode," I command him.

He jolts straight up, standing tall and completely still.

"Can you confirm the information provided is accurate?"

"The information is accurate," K-2 responds.

"Who was your previous owner?"

"Zelius Metihand," he responds immediately. This can't be.

I open my credentials and enter a search for 'Zelius Metihand + Young'. I'm able to find college graduation pictures. It says he was an award winner and number one in his graduating class. I can't find him in the class picture, but there's an option to view the technology club for that year, so I press it.

Suddenly, I can feel my heart beating out of my chest. I find myself struggling to get enough air in my lungs and my vision begins to blur. Even through my blurry vision, there's no mistaking it; there he is... there I am...a slightly different haircut, no scar, dressed in a graduation cloak. Me. Looking back at myself.

"How is this possible? Cloning is illegal because of its

failure rate. It rarely produces a living organism that lasts longer than a few hours. It would have taken him for-"

"Forty-two attempts," K-2 says softly.

I look at K-2, then back at my credentials, 'Find 42. Blood alone moves the wheels of history.'

So it was about his family, in a way.

I sit quietly for a while on the edge of my bed. It feels like I'm dangling off the edge of a cliff. I've always been curious about my parents, but I figured if they didn't want me, I didn't want them. Though, if he's right, I didn't have parents at all.

"Exit admin mode. You can sit..." I say after taking a moment. "So what about the stuff Zari found? In your code. You're tracking more innovations?"

"Yes. Zelius altered the code of three original prototypes. As Zari postulated, they are indeed the three innovations. I believe he wanted you to find them." His posture returns to normal and he takes a seat on the other edge of the bed. "What is in them, I could only speculate on. Perhaps it's related to the ICON system Zari found. Although I believe that was developed by Hypatia as well," he explains.

"Can you tell me about her? My mother...I mean, his wife?"

"Technically, you don't share any genetic information with her, but I guess you could consider her your mother. I do. Hypatia is the one who wrote my code," K-2 replies.

"I had always assumed Zelius did everything himself?" Information on her was always limited, and it never said anything about her writing code.

"It's hard to know now, as almost all information on her has been wiped clean from any database I have access to. But if I remember correctly, they met in college, and it must have been their shared work ethic that drew them to each other. I was only ever able to see her for short moments on the rare occasions they would share a dinner or when she would stroll through the enormous garden she had grown on the premises. Both Zelius and Hypatia worked tirelessly but were rarely together," he explains.

"She was a genius too?" I ask.

"She's the one responsible for the original programming language. Her code is the very basis for the social credit system. As wise as Zelius was, he could never quite master programming to the level of Hypatia. Her aptitude for such things was unparalleled. She kept to herself but was constantly monitored by guards. I remember one of them mentioning how lucky he was to get to be her security detail because he found her astonishingly attractive."

"What happened to her?" I ask, changing the subject.

"I was told she bought a small island and disappeared. Eventually, records indicated she was deceased, but I have no information on how or when exactly," he answers sincerely.

"Does anyone else know about this? About me?" I ask.

"I don't believe so. As I mentioned, the facility used to assemble you was destroyed along with his home shortly after I left to drop you off," he says as I nudge him to elaborate.

"Destroyed, how?"

"When I went back, there was nothing left, so it's hard to be sure. Zelius had grown suspicious of the board in the years before his death, so I have my theories, but they are all just speculation."

I fall back into bed and sigh deeply. All evidence of my origin has been completely erased, along with anyone who could attest to it except a Droid no one would believe. There's no point in trying to claim some sort of inheritance, considering I'm not even technically his son, and even if I did, it would cause an uproar. People would either see me as a miracle or a charlatan. The process of comparing my DNA would put a target on my back and probably get me killed before I could get the results public. The only way, if I even did want this known, would be through attaining the Compendium.

Should I tell Migo? Should I tell Zander? Should I tell anyone? What good would it do? Although it might help to tell someone in case something happens to me.

"What else do you know?" I ask.

"Other than the location of the other original prototypes, probably nothing you couldn't find searching the internet," he explains.

I get out of bed and begin digging while K-2 watches silently. Unlike Hypatia, everything about Zelius is written in one place or another online. By the time he was my age, he had already started MetiCorp, a small computer component business that made its money developing high-tech quantum chipsets. It wasn't long after that he designed and manufactured the first android, catapulting the small start-up into a major corporation almost overnight. By the time he was Zander's age, he was the first to successfully mine an asteroid. He almost bankrupted the Company doing it, but it paid off. The asteroid contained more rare earth metals in concentrated amounts than anywhere on Earth.

It wasn't the gold and platinum that made his mining mission lucrative, though. It was the discovery of MetiMetal. A superconducting material. It can hold a vast amount of energy without causing any harm upon physical contact. When the energy packs too tightly within, it causes the material to glow, discharging the excess. It meant an end to traditional batteries and all fuels became obsolete almost instantly. The insanely high impact strength, tensile strength, and melting points were just icing on the cake.

In the 2040s, the carnage caused by the rapid change in climate forced millions to migrate, looking for a habitable home.

Zelius invited all to join him in the original MetiCity. MetiC-ity-1. A gesture seen by the crumbling world governments as a direct attack. Politics became an inevitable arena. And in the arena of politics, arguments are settled in games of war. This, too, was something the Engineer found success at. As a general, he rallied millions behind his cause. He famously waved his "NO MORE KINGS" flag after winning The Last War. Growing up in the Outskirtz, I got used to seeing that flag inside people's homes, but it was rare to see it out and about nowadays except at protests. Most people, especially in MetiC-ity, are quite content and don't like to be reminded of the sacri-fices it took to achieve the peace they enjoy.

By the end of the war, the Engineer had no choice but to implement the society he and his people fought so hard for. He had promised all that had joined him food, shelter, education, medical care, and basic income. So, he developed the social credit system to encompass all of those needs. Although, if what K-2 is saying is true, it's Hypatia who designed it. Another reminder that not everything I read on here is going to be true.

The system worked well for the next forty years until there were public disagreements between Zelius and the rest of the board regarding new articles banning cloning, life extension beyond two hundred years, and limiting inheritance. The situa-tion only worsened when MetiCorp decided to close off its cities from the rest of the world, leading to the rebellion that Frank and his faction waged. After the rebellion was quelled, Zelius became extremely reclusive and secretive about his work, leaving the board to deal with the MetiCorp affairs. Most information on him in the years preceding slowed to small drips. Scholars would call it his dark period. He had become the King, the very thing he fought to destroy. This led to a public obsession with him and his potential offspring. The more he remained absent, the more they wanted an heir. I can't seem to find much about him after this, but ten years later, he was dead. His death was ruled as an accident, and it was reported that he was working on a highly dangerous experiment that went wrong.

The sun has risen long before I notice it. The house Droid offers me breakfast, and I can't resist. After sitting silently for a while, adrift in my thoughts, I begin to feel lost and decide to return to a familiar place: the shop. I take my time and cruise, looking at everything from a new perspective. From the impressive architecture of the MetiCity neighborhoods to the complex intertwining transportation systems built for land, rail, and air. Even after all my research, I still find it hard to believe that one man created all this. Would I have been able to accomplish all of this with just a change of scenery? Is that the only difference between a mechanic and an engineer?

Just before hitting the ground, I can make out several people coming in and out of the shop carrying boxes.

"Hey! Where are you going with that?" I ask a man carrying the front register.

"Mind your own business, kid."

"Where is the owner? I work here!" I say, looking around.

"Not anymore you don't. If you need a job, there's a shop a few miles down the road."

"Rogers Innovation Depot? Gross," I say, trying to reach Frank on com.

"Hey! If it isn't the big shot city boy!" Frank says, answering the invite.

"Hey, I'm at the shop; what happened? Are you okay?"

"Okay? Look at me!" He sends over a holo request, which I grant, going heads up to answer. As the holo appears, I can see Frank wearing odd clothing and taking a swig from a long, skinny glass.

"Where are you?" I ask, puzzled.

"I'm at the beach! I told you I was going to sell the place! It's just not the same without you in the shop to fix everything. You know I'm approaching the cap, so I'm going to enjoy my last few years!" he says, smiling drunkenly.

"You didn't have to sell! I could have still come by and hel-"

"Oh, shut the hell up, boy. You've been wasting away in my old shop for years. It's time for you to make your mark on this damn world. As soon as you left, I pulled the trigger. I didn't have time to wait around for you to get it through your thick skull," he says, pointing to his head.

"What are you talking about?" I ask sincerely.

"You have the gift, boy! I've never seen anything like it! Do you think everyone walks into a body shop like mine at ten years old and starts replacing engine frames and repairing electrical circuits for fun? I should have kicked you out a long time ago! As a matter of fact, get the hell out of there. The Outskirtz are a dead end! I'll talk to you in a year when you're sitting on the Company Board!"

"But-" I start.

"Aloha! It means hello and goodbye! But this time, it means piss off!" He says, closing the com-link before I can even say goodbye.

CHAPTER FOURTEEN_

I spent most of yesterday sleeping, waking up periodically to research more or study the maps for the race tomorrow. Wasting away the day in bed while the world continued to revolve the same as it always has. I had only my thoughts and two bickering Droids to fill the empty space in my new home. Even with them there, I can't help but feel alone. Who can I trust?

Frank fought against Zelius, so he's out, and I won't tell Migo because he can't keep a secret to save his life. I know for sure I don't want the sisters to know. They've lost enough at the hands of Zelius and MetiCorp.

Would Zander understand? I do trust him. His cause is noble, and in this short time I've known him, he's become someone I really admire. If this all works out and he wins, he'll get the Compendium and find out anyway. But I don't want him to be distracted now. I'll tell him after the race when there's a break long enough for him to process. It took me two days to come to my senses. Hopefully, it'll take him less.

I wake up before the sun and watch it rise while I get myself ready for a busy day. I ask K-2 to enter carry mode so I can bring him with me, a decision the house Droid is elated to hear. MetiCity-6 was the only MetiCity I had ever been to, so part of me is excited to see another.

Oddly, the heat outside the city doesn't dissipate once I cross the dock checkpoint. I had read about the temperature fluctuations during my research. Being newer, MetiCity-10 hasn't had time to regulate its water and air cycle within the dome. It feels familiar. I close my eyes and relish the heat, a comforting contrast to the cold air-conditioned MetiCity-6. My first stop is to check in at a hotel located just outside the stadium. I drop K-2 off in my assigned room and make sure he is out of sight.

The stadium and track are bigger than ours, and even though I'm here early, there's plenty of media and foot traffic here already. It's the first time in history ten cities are gathering for an O-Race Cup, so it's a big test for the emerging city. Roads are blocked off and Company presence is scattered all around the stadium at various checkpoints. I'm asked for my credentials and sign in next to a behemoth of a stadium guard. His words are more a series of grumbles than anything pronounced fully. I get the impression that he has been here for far longer than his body has approved of.

"Hey, kid!" Zander calls out as I enter the building. I merely wave. "Whoa, you don't look so good. Don't be nervous, kid; it doesn't look good on you. Besides, it won't be a packed stadium just yet, limited audience, mostly just other teams scoping out their competition."

"I'm fine. I'm not nervous," I say, looking down.

"Good. Get dressed, maybe fix your hair. We've got a ton of media to do before it's go time," he explains as I follow him through one of the back hallways.

"What kind of stuff do we have to do for the media anyway?" I ask.

"Interviews, photo-ops, stuff like that. The audience eats this shit up. It has almost the same viewership numbers as the race itself. You've never been to a bar during the pre-show?" he asks.

"Nope. I usually just watch it at the shop and don't catch the qualifying lap."

"Well, even the qualifying laps are huge with betting. People gather around drunkenly telling stories about how their old buddy 'used to race.'" He chuckles. He isn't usually an arrogant guy, but I have a feeling he doesn't really see it as a team, so much as us being his backup dancers. Although, at the end of the day, it's him taking all the risk. There's only so much we can do from the sidelines.

I change into a new uniform that hangs in the locker room. Some of the crew have already arrived and are changing. I head to the bathroom, run my fingers through my hair, and wash my face, but it doesn't seem to do much for the bags under my eyes or the clear bewilderment at the scale of the occasion.

There's a woman doing PR who directs us through the row of media getting prepped and shooting live news segments. The first stop for us is an event room they have designated for photos. High-end Company drones circle me, scanning me, taking in every detail pixel by pixel. I can't remember the last time someone took a picture of me. In fact, this might be the only picture to exist of me up until this point.

Afterward, I'm guided to a different room where Zander is currently being interviewed. The woman doing PR advises me to be quiet as we take our seats, waiting silently while they finish up.

"...So you're saying an outer city is going to win this year? Considering you've failed in your last three outings, you'll have to forgive my lack of confidence," the interviewer asks with a wry grin on his face.

"If it's a fair race, I win it every time," he says, smirking.

"Thank you, Zander, for your time, and best of luck," he says, outstretching his hand to shake Zander's. "Who's next?" he calls out to the woman standing next to me. As Zander passes, he merely smirks and pats me on the back before he leaves.

"Ren Unkno," she says, pushing me ahead.

"Unkno? Well, it's getting interesting already." He shakes my hand as I sit down in front of him, his stylus tumbling between his fingers back and forth. "So you're the new board operator for MetiCity-6?"

"Yes, sir," I reply, barely able to make eye contact. I glance over to the woman near the door and she is miming lifting my head up, so I do.

"And how did someone so young end up operating boards? Clearly, you don't know if you have racing in the blood. So what makes you so special?" What an asshole. Unkno is a name given to orphans from the Outskirtz.

"No, no racing in the blood, and I never said I was special. Zander just wanted somebody who didn't mind getting their hands dirty, and the only place to find someone like that is the Outskirtz," I explain.

"Where did you learn to operate the boards if you're from the Outskirtz, of all places?" he presses.

"I learned on the job."

"I didn't see you listed on last year's roster; how long have you been on the team?" he says, looking at his notes.

"About a week?" I say, trying to remember.

"A week!?" He drops his stylus. "You mean to tell me you've been on the boards for a week and are going to be operating for the Cup?" he exclaims.

"Yes, sir."

"So an orphan from the Outskirtz, with zero history in

racing and no experience on the boards, is going to have his first race be the biggest race in the history of this sport?"

"Yes, sir."

"Why would Zander make such a... shortsighted decision?" he asks, and I'm not sure if it is rhetorical. I hesitate a moment before I notice he wants an answer.

"Because. Well, I guess because he trusts me," I say, thinking back to our last run.

"He might regret that. But I guess we'll see now, won't we?" he says, regaining his composure a bit and turning to the camera. "Quite the story coming out of MetiCity-6! Will their decision to trust in Unkno be their undoing? Or will he break Zander's losing streak?" he says, chuckling to himself. He turns back to me after a brief pause. "Thanks, kid. Great stuff. I don't know if it's a lie for the publicity or if you're serious, but you've got my attention."

"Thank you?" I almost feel as if I am asking.

I'm rushed out of the room, where I meet with the team for group photos. Zander's jet is parked near us and we're positioned to pose around it. As the shortest, I'm placed in the front, next to him. He's the star of the show, holding his chin high and staring directly into the cameras. It's clear that he was looking forward to this. It must be intoxicating to be able to show himself to the world. He wears a look of 'come at me' and zero regret. The two original techs are there as well, but they're basically along for the ride at this point, so I feel more at ease around them. I shake my head, making sure my long bangs are covering my scar as the camera flashes.

Once Zander is done modeling, we can see that another team has gathered and are awaiting their turn. Most of them are older, but one in particular looks to be even younger than me.

"Wessin, correct?" I hear Zander say to him.

So this is the kid everyone is talking about, the fastest test lap in all ten cities, the youngest ever pilot. He's shorter than me and very well groomed, with the confident aura of someone who has already won.

"Zander," he responds, glaring up at him. There's an energy in the air, a momentary pause, and I can tell his team is beginning to become uncomfortable.

"I heard you're pretty fast," Zander says, extending his hand to shake Wessin's.

"I heard the same thing about you, Zander. About four years ago," he says, chuckling.

"And, thankfully, not much has changed," he replies, gripping Wessin's hand. They stand again for a moment, eyes locked, neither breaking a glance. "Best of luck. And be careful. It can get pretty dangerous out there."

"I know. I'm not worried," Wessin says, breaking the handshake and brushing past him.

"You should be..." Zander says softly under his breath as their team piles into the room. "I like him," he says, turning to me.

"Could have fooled me. Sounded like you were threatening him," I say, looking back into the room.

"I wasn't threatening him. I was warning him."

After a short lunch, we take some time to run a full systems check. The team manager walks in with his secretary Droid, to have a word with Zander. He doesn't look particularly happy about whatever he is saying, but I can't make out the words over the techs' conversation.

"What was that about?" I ask Zander.

"Nothing. He was just saying he loved your interview," he says sarcastically.

"Should I have lied about how long I'd been learning the boards?" Now that I think about it, that couldn't have been the best thing for the betting lines.

"Don't worry about it. He's just not used to people telling the truth," he says, slapping me on the back.

"I know. I'm not worried," I say, mimicking Wessin's tone from earlier. Zander laughs.

After the systems check, we take the vehicle towards the launching zone. We set up while MetiCity-4 is going through their qualifier ahead of us. His name is Lionnel Pricsus and he's good, top-level. He placed first in the last cup, but Zander says the original cities like to rotate winners, so he's not someone we need to worry about. As he finishes his lap, he makes his way over to his team that is set up next to ours.

"Beat that, you piss ant," he says before spitting in our direction. We all see it and choose to ignore his childlike behavior. He walks off in a huff, disappointed at our lack of response.

There's no tact in how those from the original cities flaunt their sense of superiority. They act like by merely existing in those cities, they're owed some kind of inherent respect.

Zander is up next and it isn't long after the start of his lap I notice something is...off. All the equipment is working fine and there are no adjustments to make. But that's the problem. He's moving fast, but he isn't pushing for a record-breaking lap.

"Everything okay, Zander?" I reach out over the headset.

"Just trust me. It isn't purposeless," he says. I don't know what he means, but I'm relieved he isn't suddenly overcome with anxiety.

"I do. Just checking," I reply.

Zander finishes his lap behind his best time but comfortably ahead of the Metifuck that went before us.

When Zander gets back towards us, he's met by the team manager, who is having a less-than-private conversation this time.

"What the hell was that?" he yells, waving his arms outward and almost hitting his secretary in the face.

"It's fine. Relax. It was a solid time," Zander replies calmly.

"Fine!? That was nothing like the lap I saw you hit back at home! Was it the kid? If he's not up to it, we can have him replaced. It's not too late," he says, glaring over at me.

"Ren did exactly as I told him. The only one behind the wheel is me, and I say it's a solid lap," Zander says calmly.

"You're going to end up starting from the back!" He continues.

"No one is going to beat that time. Well, nobody except him," he says, focusing his gaze on Wessin, whose team has just arrived to go next.

"Okay, Zander. You're the fucking King. But if you don't win, you'll be the King of the fucking Outskirtz when I'm done with you," the manager says, storming off.

"He could use some of the sisters' greesha, eh?" Zander says, smiling.

"He doesn't deserve it," I reply.

We pack up and clear the area to make room for Wessin's team, but I notice Zander is sticking around, so I decide to hang back with him. We exchange a glance before standing silently, staring at the entryway to the track. Wessin's team is oddly quiet and orderly, all business. The countdown begins, and immediately after launch, I can see what all the fuss is about. The kid handles like a veteran: no hesitation, no fear. He makes dangerous choices that push his jet to the limit. When I glance over, I'm struck by how calmly and slowly his board operator attends to the jet adjustments. At the speed Wessin is taking these turns, I imagine it would put a lot of stress on the operator, but the guy isn't struggling at all. Maybe he's been doing it so long that he's gotten used to it. Or maybe the kid is just so good they barely need to make adjustments.

Wessin finishes his lap time well ahead of Zander's, but

there is no excitement from his team or manager. As he makes his way back and hops out of his jet, he glances over to Zander.

"Not bad, kid," Zander congratulates Wessin.

"Yeah, I know. I thought about slowing down, but honestly? You can have the slipstream. I don't think it'll make any difference. I'll be too far ahead for it to matter," Wessin taunts.

"It'll matter," Zander says, turning and leaving the loading area.

"The slipstream?" I ask him once I catch up.

"I told you I like that kid. You know, in his interview today, he said he denied his family's inheritance, even though the new articles said he was entitled to it?" Zander says, ignoring my question.

"I didn't know you could even do that. Why would anyone do that?"

"He wants it to be his."

"Wants what to be his?"

"The win. He wants to earn it himself. He must have heard about my lap time and figured me out. I ran a slower lap so I could start in the back and draft off him. It's funny. Last cup, I did the same thing he's planning to do. I knew I was so much faster than the original cities that I placed my best time thinking if I got out in front to start, no one would be able to catch me anyway. Unfortunately, the faster you go, the easier it becomes for them to catch up when they're riding your slipstream," he explains.

It makes sense now. Racers start in order of their qualifying lap times, so having the best lap time isn't necessarily the smartest move. At the same time, you don't want to be stuck in the middle, trying to maneuver around other racers. There's so much more to it than just speed. When you break it down, it's a game of inches, and whatever opportunity you can take to get ahead, you do. This is Zander's third Cup. At this point, not even he can avoid playing the game.

Once we get everything accounted for, we go to see the final lap times. Wessin will be in front, as predicted, but Zander will start third. He was probably aiming for second, but clearly, he took it too easy, and Lionnel Pricsus placed ahead of him. He doesn't seem upset when he sees the times, though. He is his usual calm and collected self.

"I'm going to check in with Zari and Elli and see where they want to meet tonight. Why don't you meet me out front?" Zander says while signing autographs for the line of fans that were waiting for him.

CHAPTER FIFTEEN_

We meet the sisters down the street from where the beacon signal is guiding us. It's located at the outer edges of the city near their docks. While MetiCity-10 is fairly new, this area shows its wear, as if the sanitation Droids haven't been deployed in some time.

"Zander!" Elli calls out as we approach, waving and smiling.

"Elli. Zari. What do we know?" Zander says, getting right to business.

"We asked around and apparently, this is UG territory," Zari says, looking again at her surroundings. "That explains why this area looks so squalid; probably thought they could find a better use for the parts in a sanitation Droid."

"When you get this far from the original cities, you can see that the hands of MetiCorp only stretch so far. Any info on the signal location?" Zander asks.

"From the looks of it, I would think it was abandoned. But apparently, it's some sort of repair and pawn shop. The sign is written in some weird graffiti. I needed a translator to decode. I couldn't even see it until I used my credentials," Zari answers.

"It's unlisted in the registry, so it's probably just a front to resell stolen tech."

"Zander? No fucking way! Dude, can I get your autograph?" a passerby stops after recognizing him. This time, Zander's not as excited about adoration. He obliges begrudgingly, faking a smile.

"Hey! The Outskirtz kid, right?" the stranger says, punching my shoulder harder than I would have preferred.

"Is that what they're calling me?" I say, looking down and scratching my head.

"Don't listen to what people are saying, man! Make em' choke on their words!" he says, clenching his fist.

"...what words?" I ask.

"You know anything about the pawn shop down the street?" Zander says, changing the subject.

"Overpriced. And the girl who runs it, Taxia, she's stubborn as hell. Unless you're UG, chances are she's going to charge you double what she'd charge them. Although, who knows, the famous Zander from MetiCity-6 might get a discount. You're a fucking hero, man."

"Yeah? Here, take a free ticket for tomorrow's race," Zanders says to the now elated stranger. After ten too many thank yous, he runs off excitedly.

"You're a fucking hero," Elli says, mimicking the stranger as he gets out of earshot.

"Elli," Zari says, silencing Elli's teasing. "...don't forget to bow in his presence," she says, bowing in front of Zander. Elli giggles and follows suit.

"Cute. Really cute," Zander says, walking in the direction of the pawn shop. "Come on, we don't have all day. Me and Ren actually have jobs to get to in the morning." He pulls off his credentials and smashes it against one of the buildings we passed by.

"Zander, we were just messin'!" Elli says, gripping his arm to stop him.

"I know," Zander says, stepping through the entrance.

We can hear someone yelling on the inside, "YOU PIECE OF SHIT!"

The voice is coming from a girl about my age. Her shoulder length locs sway in front of her face as she hammers away on whatever she's working on.

"Everything is priced with AR. No haggling," she says without looking up.

"Are you Taxia?" Zander responds.

"So what if I am? What do you want...Zander? What the hell are you doing in a place like this?" she says, jolting up, her eyes now wide. They match the color of her skin perfectly, a warm, deep brown. This isn't the same reaction of the guy from the street. She isn't impressed or overjoyed; she seems more confused and perturbed than anything.

"Well, I need a repair, and I was told your prices are fair."

"No, you weren't, or whoever said that lied," she says, looking at him suspiciously.

"That's too bad. I was hoping to have this repaired by someone who actually knows what they're doing," he says, handing over his shattered credentials.

"Buy a new one. I've got a section towards that wall," she says, pointing.

"I've got a bit of sentimental attachment to this one in particular. How long would it take you?"

"Depends on your definition of long. I heard guys like you only last one lap. This'll take me at least a day," she quips.

"I'm quite busy tomorrow. Any chance you could do it now?"

"Oh Allspirits! You're busy? Well, why don't I just drop

everything I'm doing because Zander Thorne is in a big hurry," she says, smiling.

"Time is precious," he says, pulling off the championship ring on his finger. "Hold on to this for collateral, and when it's fixed, I'll make sure you're paid fairly for your time," he says, handing the ring to her.

"What's fair?" she asks, slipping the ring into her pocket.

"More than that ring's worth."

"Give me about thirty minutes," she says, heading back towards a workbench behind the front desk.

"Well?" Zander whispers to Zari.

"We're right on top of it, but I can't pinpoint where it's coming from," she responds, looking at the beacon signal.

"Ok, you and Elli, check out the Biosuits and I'll check out the transports in the lot," he instructs. "I'm going to take a look at your vehicles," he continues, calling to Taxia.

"Be my guest! Not much to look at, though," Taxia says as she begins work on his credentials.

I follow behind Zari and Elli as they make their way through the aisles. Pawn shops in my settlement take it as an insult to look at the code of something they're selling, always claiming it's illegal. Ironically, it's usually stolen Company tech they're selling in the first place.

"You don't think she'll notice you looking at the code right out in the open?" I ask Zari.

"She'll probably just think we're checking the product, but just in case, why don't you go over there and distract her. Give us a signal if she starts to get too curious," she says.

Distract her? How?

I roam around the shop while keeping an eye on her. Her repair skills are pretty impressive. I can tell she has done major modifications to whatever scrap she could get her hands on. I guess if you're going to be selling to UG, you don't want to have them coming back complaining about a shoddy product. I circle around right in front of her work area and catch her glancing over at me before I straighten my gaze on an assortment of visors Zander could have easily replaced his with.

"They say you're inexperienced, and you're going to crack under the pressure, that Zander is crazy for putting an Outskirt on his team," she says and I turn back around to see her staring directly at me. It takes a moment for me to even realize she's talking to me. "Ironic, isn't it? As if we don't know about pressure," she says through a soft smile.

"You're from the Outskirtz?" I ask.

"No, I'm actually from Meticity-2. I just like to cosplay as a sandscav." She's very, very sarcastic.

"Me too," I say, chuckling. She smirks, starting up a small soldering laser. "What were you yelling about when we came in?" I say, walking over to the counter.

"Oh, it was nothing. Was just trying to help out a friend," she says, her eyes glancing over the object she had hidden poorly as we walked in.

"Odd. You don't seem the type to have friends from the Company," I say. Her hands pause. "Besides, don't MetiCorp disruptors have to be repaired by Company tech?" Disruptors are expressly forbidden for use by anyone but control officers.

"Are you trying to start some trouble, you little shit?" She says with an annoyed glare.

"No, no!" I say, reassuring her. "I was just wondering if you were having trouble branching the auxiliary power after the locator was removed."

"How did you know?"

"I'm cosplaying as a psychic. Mind if I take a look?"

"Now that I think about it, they did say in your interview you were a mechanic in the Outskirtz before joining Zander's team." She picks up the disruptor and lays it on the counter after taking a look at the door.

Once it's in my hands, I can tell that there are more issues than just powering it by auxiliary. She has fried some capacitors and part of the outer shell is damaged from her forced entry. MetiCorp has so many fail safes laced into their tech it makes working on them next to impossible. Even if you can get past all of that, there's the code, which has its own protocols for alarming the Company when stolen. Luckily, she's already dealt with that, but the hardware has clearly given her grief. I have to apply pressure and twist to release the outer shell. She looks frustrated at the ease with which I remove it but continues watching closely nonetheless.

"Do you mind?" I say, pointing to the soldering laser she was using on Zander's credentials. She looks down at it and then up at me before handing it over. I quickly repair the auxiliary and reattach the shell. "There you go."

"Are you fucking kidding me? I've been working on this thing for days!" She says, holding it up and examining it. "How the hell did you–" she grabs the disruptor and quickly shoves it under the desk. The front entrance opens and two men come in.

"Allspirits, guys. You scared the shit out of me," she says, looking relieved.

"Hey Taxia! How's our little project going? We're really coming down to the wire now," the bigger of the two says.

"Of course, Anarki, I just finished it up!" she says, smiling at me. "Once I repair this cred, I'll grab it for you."

I catch the other walking toward the Biosuit section and it sparks my memory. I'm supposed to signal if I see anyone coming. I jump to push it out through coms, but it's too late.

"Hey Taxia! Looks like these customers don't know how to respect your establishment," the smaller one says, pushing Elli and Zari towards the front. Shit. Elli just looks annoyed, but I can tell Zari is smart enough to be worried. "They were linking up to a suit, checking code. The disrespect. Want me to see them out?" he says, grabbing both of them, a fistful of hair in each hand holding them in place.

"Hey! Get your hands off me!" Elli says, trying to push the man off her and having very little luck.

"They're with me," Zander says, making his way back into the shop. Both men turn to see Zander and unhand the girls.

"I don't give a shit who you are, get the hell out," Anarki says, pointing to the door.

"I'll leave when I'm ready," Zander says defiantly. The two men now circle Zander, locking eyes, none of them giving any ground. I reach for my wrench when Taxia speaks up.

"Everybody relax, and no one touch nothing. I'm almost done, then they can leave."

After a moment of tinkering, she walks over and stands between them, handing Zander his fixed credentials and his ring. "Now go," she says, pushing at him. Zander doesn't budge. He looks over at the sisters. Zari shoots him a quick nod. He swipes his credentials for payment as Taxia continues to usher him out. Zander and the sisters turn to leave and I follow. I glance back at Taxia, who makes eye contact with me. She mouths the word "thanks" and then nods her head towards the door.

"Did you get it?" Zander says to Zari.

"Nope. I got it," Elli says, smirking. "She was trying to download the entire set of code!"

"Elli was able to single out the code we needed and saved it just as we were spotted."

"Good job, Elli," Zander says, rubbing the top of her head. "Thought I was going to have to fight my way out of there."

"So did I. And something about the pristine nature of your

face tells me you haven't been in many fistfights," I say to Zander.

"Maybe that's because I've never lost," Zander smirks.

"I don't know, that guy Anarki looked pretty tough."

"That guy Anarki? Which one? Anarki is what they call each other. It's just a term of endearment amongst the UG," Zander explains.

"Why Anarki?"

"The term is derived from the word Aniki, meaning big brother in Japanese, and the word Anarchy, which means... well...I think you get it."

"I do now."

Zari looks up at the sun and releases the valve on her jacket that controls the temperature. It must have risen twenty degrees since we were inside. The other two follow her lead and adjust their valves as well. I can feel the cool air coming from them, but I want to appreciate this heat before we have to leave.

"Let's head back to the hotel," Zander guides.

CHAPTER SIXTEEN_

The sisters have gotten a room at the hotel on the same floor as us, so after we get back and change, we meet them in their room. As we walk in, they're hunched over their displays in deep concentration.

"Found anything yet?" Zander says, leaning against a wall beside them. They don't respond.

I take a seat on the bed as they work through the code, trying to assimilate it with what they already have put together. I think about how Hypatia was the one who had actually written the code. I wonder if she knew about the ICON status. Was it her way of putting her mark on things? A signature?

Elli plops down on the bed next to the one I am sitting on. She huffs, grumbles, and then falls onto her back. As I look over, I can see Zari's head droop down as Zander puts his hand on her shoulder.

"It's okay. You couldn't have expected to get it that quickly, right?" Zander says, trying to comfort her.

"I'm going to burn and then try again. Elli?" She says to her sister.

"On it," Elli responds. She proceeds to dig through their

bags and pull out a pen-like device. "For travel," she says, smirking as she takes a hit. She throws it over to Zari, who also takes a hit. They shiver and then relax.

"I wonder what my specialty is?" I ask, randomly blurting it out. Zander shoots me a curious glance and Elli pops her head up from the bed.

"I... didn't want to be rude, but... no one from the Outskirtz qualifies. Living within MetiCity is like the first qualification and you-" Zari says, trying to be soft.

"But I do. Well, now," I say, shrugging. Zari glances to the side as she realizes she hadn't thought of that.

"Well then... let's just see," she says, turning back around to her display.

"How exactly do you determine someone's specialization?" I ask.

"Basically, I put your credentials through a review algorithm I've created that checks everything from your social credit score to your blood type...even the location of the stars in the sky when you first got your social credit ID. The algorithm I've created mirrors the one hidden within the code running the credential system. From there, I just run another algorithm that changes the credentials to various sets of attributes to figure out which set triggers the ICON status."

I wait patiently while she inputs my information into her setup.

"Wait, this can't be right," Zari says out loud, prompting Elli to rise from the bed and rush over to her display.

"Droid specialty? It's just like you, Zari; what's wrong with that?" Elli says, tilting her head.

"Elli. Look at his place in the Droid path." Zari points at the screen.

"Holy shit! Top tier?! How is that possible? He's so young!" Elli looks at me, her eyes wide.

"I don't know. I've never seen this before..."

"What does this mean?" I ask, looking at Zari.

"Well, usually, at your age, you're much further from ICON status, having multiple paths with varying degrees of completion...Wait...wait...multiple paths..." Zari says, returning to her display and navigating through the code.

"Huh?" Elli says, trying to catch up. She passes me the greesha and sits down next to Zari, looking lost. I take a hit and there's no vision of some far-off land, just the euphoria I felt the last time. I welcome it. The thought of this revealing who I am is replaced by the thrill of excavating the hidden secrets of the code. If they keep up this pace, they'll find out eventually, and I'd rather have that burden off my chest.

"Droid path...hmm, but I've only just gotten a Droid, and only recently signed the contract. How can I be top-tier? I don't get it," I think out loud.

"Have you ever worked on a droid before?" Elli asks. I nod my head. "And did you have those credentials when you did?" she questions. I nod again. "Then I'm guessing your rank has to do with the work you've done repairing Droids. Once you signed the contract, it applied all past work to your social credit score. Like she said, there are multiple pathways. I've seen a set of credentials that could reach ICON status with a mastery in Bionics by making a major biomedical discovery. It's different for everyone. Sometimes, for fun, I'll look up successful people with the algorithm to see how close they are. There was even a singer who modified his credentials, wore them on his neck to improve his singing, and he was getting really close, but just as he touched the threshold..."

"He ended up dead," Zander jumps in.

"How did you know?" Elli asks.

"They all end up dead," he says solemnly.

I think back to Koujin. I wonder if he was the only ICON they knew. I want to ask, but I can't muster the words.

"I got it!" Zari exclaims almost out of nowhere. "See Elli? Multiple pathways." She says, pointing to the screen.

"Oh! You ran additional code paths!" Elli yells excitedly. I am tempted to ask for a follow-up, but it would be buried in so much technobabble I wouldn't understand.

"And?" Zander says eagerly.

"It's asking for the code," Zari replies.

I know the answer before they even speak.

"Try forty-two," Zander responds immediately. Shit, here we go.

"A two-digit code? There's no way that's gonna'-" Elli starts.

"It worked!" Zari exclaims excitedly.

The screen flickers to all black and there is a toggle switch displayed in the middle. It simply says "ON" or "OFF" and is defaulted to the "OFF" option.

"Ewww, it's asking you to turn it on. What kind of perv wrote this?" Elli chuckles.

"Anyone have an idea as to what exactly it's for?" Zander asks, looking at the sisters.

"Maybe we should wait until we find the other prototype? Maybe it has more information we need?" Zari asks. She looks worried.

"Aww, we got this far and you guys want to stop right at the best part?" Elli complains.

"It could be a trap. Some failsafe to make sure the ones who find this give away their location. Could be some kind of alarm sent directly to the Company," Zander thinks aloud. He falls silent as he contemplates the options. "I... I don't know what to do." The usually confident Zander is at a loss.

"Maybe Zari is right. Maybe we should wait until we find the last prototype?" I say.

"Yeah, maybe it has another on or off switch like this? Maybe they both need to be turned on at the same time?" Zander reasons.

"OOPS," I can hear Elli say as she clicks the toggle on.

"ELLI, NO WAIT!" Zari says, trying to stop her, but it is too late.

"ELLI!? WHAT WERE YOU THINKING!?" Zander says angrily.

"I wasn't," she says with a joyful smile. Greesha has a way of making people impulsive, down for anything. It isn't the kind of thing you'd want to burn anywhere, with just anyone. Part of removing the anxiety and worry makes it easier to just go where your instincts take you.

"Nothing happened. Should I turn it off?" She asks.

"Yeah. No, wait...wait a second," Zander says, opening his credentials and scrolling through the latest news. I guess he thinks if it is something major, it will come up fairly quickly. Problem is, it could be anything. He walks over and pulls open the blinds a bit. Probably checking to see if the Company pulled up outside or if anything looks off.

"Nothing," he sighs. "Turn it off. That was not funny, Elli."

"Aww, c'mon! You know you wanted to press it, too! We were all thinking it," Elli says.

"...maybe a little," he smirks. Zari is not as amused.

"See! And look. No explosions. No Company controllers kicking in our door," Elli argues.

"Let's try again when we have the third prototype," Zander says, looking down at Zari, who has turned the toggle off and closed the screen. "I should get back to reviewing the run for tomorrow before I go to sleep. Don't stay up too late, kid. If anything happens, you know where to find me," he says to me, then heads to his room, leaving just me and the sisters.

They're going back and forth, exchanging unintelligible coding jargon. I can only understand a word here or there. I should probably rest as well. I have a lot to think about, and tomorrow is going to be really important for Zander...for us.

I take another hit.

"Ren, you okay?" Elli asks.

"Yeah, what's this you've put on?"

"It's an RFL match! I need a breather."

"Do you watch it much?" I ask.

"OF COURSE! Zari thinks it's a waste of good Droids, but I think it's fun! The previous champion had this pilotless mech he converted. He was getting close to ICON status himself. But it turns out he had been cheating by using a device to pilot it remotely. Strictly against the rules. There's actually a vacancy for the title right now."

Elli goes on for a while about RFL history, the rules, and some of her favorite Droids. At one point, Zari shoots me a smile to acknowledge how long Elli has been going on without pausing to breathe. After a while, I doze off, and when I wake up, I'm lying next to Elli in bed. She passed out with her credentials open, playing some old match. I look over to Zari, who is still sitting at the desk, looking through the code.

"Anything new?" I say, regaining consciousness.

She's startled, then she realizes it's me. She replies, "Nothing yet. You scared me. I thought you were both asleep."

"Yeah, that was one hell of a bedtime story. Sorry, I'll get to my room," I say, standing up.

"You're fine. You know...I caught Elli singing the other night? The songs my parents used to sing?" she says, smiling. "I haven't heard her sing in years; bringing it up the other day must have reminded her. Would you like to hear?"

"Of course!"

"Shhh," she says, pointing to a now drooling Elli. She comes over and sits next to me on the bed and begins scrolling through her credentials. "Here, listen."

She hits play and I can see it was filmed from a doorway. Elli is sitting in the room, staring out the window. She has an amazing voice. It's delicate and calming. I'm so entranced I don't even notice Zari has rested her head on my shoulder as she watches. Every second feels like days as I sink into the moment and forget about everything else. I think about what it must feel like for her to have something from her parents as a reminder. Then, I realize I am constantly surrounded by reminders of my 'father.'

Suddenly, the song ends and I snap back to see Zari staring at me, inches from my face. "Did you like it?"

"I loved it," I say, almost stuttering. She smiles and for a moment, it is just us, staring at each other's faces, lit by the light of her credential screen. She brushes the hair away from my face to see me. She draws closer, and at first, I think she is going to kiss me as her eyes begin to close. She squints a bit while pushing the hair away from my face.

"You know, this scar really gives you character...and you're actually kind of cute under all that dirt...you look...familiar," she says, tilting her head to try and understand where she has seen my face. I get up abruptly.

"Yeah? Um. Anyway, I should get to bed," I say, hurrying to the door. "Goodnight." I leave without looking back. As soon as the door closes, I press my back against it and take a deep breath. What the hell was that? Was she flirting with me? Did she figure it out? Well, if she didn't, I sure gave her a reason to be suspicious.

When I get back to my room, I notice that Migo has sent me a video message with him, his girl Tovah, and Lucy standing with the guy I briefly had met that night in the bar. They're yelling "Good luck!" in the background. They seem excited and really drunk. He mentions seeing my interview and is rambling about how they better not doubt someone from the Outskirtz. He tells me to take care of Zander. Just as I start to feel like I'm getting a truly sincere moment from him, he slips in a question about Zari, asking whether or not I had sex with her. Some people never change.

I check on K-2 to make sure he's not been messed with by any of the cleaning Droids. Just as all the thoughts stop racing through my head and the anxiety clears, I feel myself drifting off to sleep.

CHAPTER SEVENTEEN_

"Hey, kid! Get up! We're going to be late," I can hear Zander yell from outside my door before knocking. It sounds like he's been out there for a bit.

"I'm coming!" I yell through the door. I only have enough time to jump into my uniform before I'm out the door. "I'm ready!" I proclaim, brushing my hair out of my face and adjusting my outfit.

"Jeez, kid. I thought you might be dead or something. You had me worried," he says, smiling and heading down the hallway. I fasten my boots and follow behind him. As we pass by the girls' room, he mentions they had already made their way down for breakfast. We see them on our way through the lobby and wave through the window to the dining hall. They break away from their food for long enough to cheer us on. Zari seems in good spirits, so I don't think she suspects me. Yet.

As soon as we step outside, it's like another planet. Crowds as far as the eye can see are working their way up and down the street to various vendors and attractions. I don't think I've ever seen this many people in one place before. I go heads up, and the sky fills to the brim with even more transports and FlyBikers. Tailgaters. I can see the stadium is partitioned off and there's an empty sky all around and above it. The Company makes sure to clear the sky above the race area, whether it's online or off. We make our way to the other techs who are already waiting for us by the shuttle.

"Hey! You guys too cool for food?" I can hear Elli yelling as we start to get into the shuttle. She throws us two heavy white paper bags. Zander catches the first and the other hits me in the chest. I catch it before it hits the ground. He flashes a quick smile before getting in. I wave and Elli smiles big. When driving away, I can see Zari coming up behind Elli and they both wave us off. The excitement hits us all in different ways, but Zander hides his best. I, on the other hand, am smiling like Migo picked my drink for me.

Once we hit the stadium, camera crews are scattered all around, taking pictures and conducting interviews with stars and high-ranking Company members. Race fans are crowded outside watching the drivers and crew all arrive, but they aren't allowed in yet. As we pass the entrance, I spot a crowd of UG members holding up signs that read "NO MORE KINGS." A reminder to the board and whoever else watching the coverage that they haven't forgotten the Engineer, and they haven't forgotten his promise to end tyranny.

Once I get inside, we're swarmed by reporters asking questions, taking photos, and scattered fans hoping to see someone important. When I find a moment, I sneak past most of the chaos while they swarm Zander. In the shop, I find the other techs and jump right in to help with diagnostics on the jet. The techs are mostly silent, besides a few grumbles and some heavy breathing while working. I enjoy the calm over the chaos and I'm able to get a really deep analysis done. Perfect condition, no tampering, even double-checked the individual connections. I hope it looks this beautiful when the race is over.

Finally, one of the techs speaks up.

"Take one final look at 'er, boys," he says, dusting his hands off. Everyone else stops what they're doing to soak in the jet in its most pristine shape.

"You make it sound like he's not a safe driver," I snark.

"It's not him I'm worried about, kid," he says, patting me on the shoulder. It's the first time one of the techs has shown any emotion other than anger, so I can't tell if it's sincere.

There's a large opening ceremony soon after, which is led by a pop singer I've never heard of singing some drivel I never want to hear again. The song revolves around some pink popcorn they're selling in the stands. The crowds almost overwhelm the attendants selling it. But the fireworks, now that's something I don't see every day. The boom and crack of the sparkling lights burn out across the sky. It's followed by a drone storm that begins projecting geometrical patterns behind the ongoing fireworks. It's a way different experience in person. I go heads up to see the full show. Projections show portraits of previous racers, trophies, burnouts, and victory celebrations drenched in alcohol. As soon as things calm down, a board member takes to the middle of the stage to grand applause. The platform sits in the middle of the stadium, just outside the racer launch zones.

"Hello MetiCity-10! Hello World! Are we not honoring the contract today? Are we not living in truly the golden era of human civilization?" He loudly professes into the microphone to more thunderous applause. Zander doesn't look very impressed.

"Who is that?" I've done all the research on the Engineer, but never looked much into the board.

"Gideon Stein. The highest ranking and oldest member of the board," he says, continuing to gear up instead of listening. "We start after this 'roided out neanderthal is done flexin'."

"For years, this race has been the pride of MetiCity's ingenuity and achievement. Now, we continue the tradition of sharing it with the world. Last year, we allowed cities seven and eight to join. Who could forget such a riveting race? Won by MetiCity-4's own Lionnel Pricsus!" Another large applause. "This year, we have invited MetiCities nine and ten. Please, give the new entries a round of applause!" Yet another round of applause. "One of the racers is only sixteen years old! Can you imagine if he won? I would sure be impressed. Might have to give that kid a seat on the board!" The crowd laughs in unison.

"Please, everyone, be safe. And never forget, it's only being streamed to billions of people simultaneously," he says, chuckling, waving, and walking off. He doesn't seem like an evil villain; he seems jovial and relaxed. I guess that comes from being one of the most socially credited individuals on the planet. The rings begin to rise up from their locked positions, high enough for me to see from where I'm standing. They're slightly more polished than the ones at our stadium, probably specially for this event.

Migo sends me across a com-link. While walking to the vehicle to begin strapping in Zander, the com-link opens up to Migo and others who are in the background of the video are screaming.

"REN IS IN THE ROOM!" he yells. "REN, SAY WHAT'S UP TO MY STREAM!"

I shrug, "Yo," dryly, yet they all scream excitedly anyway.

"GOOD LUCK MAN! Show us Zander!" He says and I can see user after user suddenly joining.

"Ah, the real reason for the call," I say, allowing the com-link to see through the cam on my credentials. I can hear them go wild once more before I say, "See ya!" and exit the livestream. I guess he thinks having someone on the inside will boost his numbers. Not today, Migo.

Zander is all strapped in and we run the coms test, check diagnostics again, power everything on, and then comes the calm before the storm. We wait as all the racers are named, along with their corresponding city. Each racer is housed in their own walled-off launch zone. When the buzzer sounds, they'll get a green light, signifying it's their turn to go, in the order of their qualifying time. Once they announce the last racer, Zander revs the engine and gives us a thumbs up.

"RACERS, YOU READY?...3...2...1...GO!" we can hear over the speakers, but just barely. The roaring crowd drowns out everything else.

The first out of his launch zone is Wessin, who takes off at what looks like top speed, even though he knows he's going to have to maneuver sharply at the first ring. I'm so focused on watching him that I don't even notice that Lionnel Pricsus has already headed out. A loud buzzer sounds and Zander comes burning out of his gate. He's just behind Lionnel as they approach the first ring, and he's already giving the guy a run for his money. Unfortunately, Wessin is way out ahead as they battle for second. Just as they whip past the first turn, Zander takes his chance and accelerates just enough to slice past. Lionnel tries to adjust and cut Zander off, but he's too slow. Pricsus isn't slick. That highcred, spoonfed fucker knows exactly what he just tried to do.

"Kid's fast!" Zander yells out over coms, noticing the lead Wessin has.

"He'll make a mistake," I say. His speed is insane, but there's no way he can keep this up long-term. He has to break at some point, or his momentum will get so overwhelming it'll make the mistake for him.

"I know," Zander replies as he blasts through the second ring. The rest of the racers have struggled to find an agreement on positioning and are losing time for it. There are now three groups moving together: Wessin is out front, Zander is followed closely by the next three racers. Then, a pile of five drivers trail behind as they battle for control of the flight lanes. This is great for Zander, who is now starting to break away from the rest of the pack behind him. As they approach the next ring, the groups begin converging. Not because Zander or Wessin are slowing down, but because they've started to get their footing and there are only a mere few seconds between any of them. As the jets pass by the various sections of the stadium, the crowd below them screams in excitement.

One hundred miles, ten at a time, for ten laps total. Unfortunately, I'm only afforded a few moments to look up before I have to concentrate on the monitor that's firing up on what feels like every screen simultaneously. It's nothing I haven't done before, but the pressure is palpable. I can feel the roar of the crowd even with my headset on.

"There!" Zander yells suddenly over the com. He speeds up even more.

"What!?" I yell back, trying not to fuck up the board as it starts to overwhelm me.

"The mistake!" he yells. "Gonna take a second off of him. Get ready." Before I can even process what's happening, the alerts start piling up. I bite down, clenching my jaw, and zone into the work. He needs more adjustments than ever before, and it's taking me time to find the rhythm in this uncharted territory. He's focused on catching Wessin and is hoping I'll be able to pick up the slack.

I am, barely. As they round the second lap, I can see him gaining on Wessin, but it looks like the rest of them are, too. Everyone is drawing closer together, and it's starting to look dangerous. They slipstream off Zander as he drifts off Wessin, and I'm not sure how many more shots we're going to get to take the lead. I continue to work the board while Zander tries to help me prioritize adjustments.

"Focus on maintaining speed. I'll take care of the turns so you can keep the fins on the back burner until you catch up!" he yells.

It isn't going to be easy to take the turns if we keep his speed as it is. I have to trust Zander to handle his end if I handle mine. I can hear him take the sharp turn, gritting his teeth and breathing heavily as his body takes the brunt of the g-force needed for his current pace. Wessin hasn't slipped up since, but one of the hardest turns is coming up before the straightaway. That might be a good place for Zander to accelerate and take over, as the prodigy worries more about the turn than losing speed. Just then, I hear the techs grumbling about something they see in the formation of the other racers. They've filed directly behind one another and are syncing their movements, all gaining speed. I look up just in time to see them start to gain on Wessin and Zander.

"Here we go with this bullshit!" Zander says angrily over the com.

"They didn't even wait til the third lap," one of the newer techs says.

I've seen this before in one of the races I had time to watch. They'll basically slingshot for one of the racers to gain speed before the turn. This means that clearly, these cities have agreed to work together against Zander and Wessin. Coming out of the turn, the racer from MetiCity-1 is slung past Zander and up towards Wessin. Zander moves out of the way just in time; otherwise, he would have gone straight through him.

"SHIT!" one of the techs shouts just as the fourth-place driver from MetiCity-2 comes barreling towards Zander. The racer speeds up, clearly aiming for Zander. I adjust the fins as

I'm finally caught up, and he's able to tilt ever so slightly out of the way.

"NICE JOB KID!" Zander says over the coms.

Or so I thought. The wing of the jet takes a snipping slice out of Zander's tail end and the jet begins to wobble from the impact. Unfortunately, the delay is just enough for Lionnel to snake his way back in front of him. Even small collisions are enough to throw me out of my flow of precise adjustments.

"I got it from here!" Zander yells over the com, taking the vehicle under full control. I look up at the sky to see the MetiCity-2 racer has lost complete control and is forced to stop just before hitting the wall. He must have pissed himself. But it's over for him now. At these speeds, coming to a complete stop gives racers virtually no way to win. He opens the cockpit canopy to his jet and gives a shrug as the crowd laughs it off. As if it wasn't dangerous, stupid, and cheating. Unfortunately, as far as rules go, there isn't anything against stuff like that. No way to prove it was coordinated.

As the turn comes up at the start of lap three, it looks like Wessin is starting to feel the pressure and has lost a bit of speed. Lionnel takes it in perfect timing, gaining on Wessin as he further separates from Zander. There's no one in front of us now besides those two, and Zander is breaking from the pack as well. Just before the next turn, the MetiCity-1 racer decides to max his vehicle speed to catch up, and breaks the sound barrier. The crowd cheers until the racer suddenly ejects from his cockpit and his jet slams into the side of the ring, exploding on impact. The ring barely budges.

"Well, at least that's two less problems I have to worry about," Zander says. I can hear him smiling.

"Just worry about the problems in front of you," I reply, trying to catch back up on the boards.

"The kid's really good," Zander says.

"Yeah," I say back without thinking.

"You're supposed to say, 'You're better,'" he chuckles.

"Are you?"

"Can you keep up?"

"I'm waiting on you," I reply, feeling cocky as hell.

"THEN LET'S GO!" Zander yells, and the screens light up.

CHAPTER EIGHTEEN_

The straightaway gives him the opportunity to gain on Lionnel and Wessin, who are now neck and neck. Zander drifts further from the rest of the pack as they struggle to find a suitable formation again. They're probably bickering back and forth, too prideful to let the other speak. Much of lap three is me struggling to keep up, but as Zander starts to feel more comfortable with the turns, my workload lessens and he's able to take much of the work off my shoulders. Having time to rest, I make some quick assessments of positioning.

"Zander, coming out of this next turn, I want you to take a break; it's where Wessin lost positioning last lap and I want to hit this one hard."

"I was thinking the same thing," he replies.

As they come up on the turn, Wessin loses traction and Lionnel hits the turn harshly.

"Perfect," Zander declares. The screen lights up like before, but I'm able to time it better. I hit the rotation on the fin just right and Zander corrects his pitch, drifting right through the turn. He's gaining on them.

"NICE!" I shout. The first turn continues to be the most

difficult to maneuver, and similarly to the opening stretch of the last lap, more racers struggle to stay in the race. The racers from behind get into a bullet-like formation and start to accelerate. This makes Zander push even harder, hitting the turn too quickly for my taste.

"IT'S GOING TO BE TIGHT!" he yells over the coms.

"I know that!" I yell back.

Just up ahead, Wessin takes the turn at the beginning of the fourth lap perfectly and Lionnel can't keep up. He's losing speed, just what we need. Zander hits the turn the fastest I've seen, and I can't lie; I'm starting to feel scared. Sweat drips down from my forehead into my eyes as I try to focus on the boards. It burns as I blink it away. I can hear Zander gritting his teeth again through the coms as he takes the brunt of the force himself. If I had eased his turn, I'd have cost him time.

Suddenly, I hear a loud crash. I look up to see that the MetiCity-3 racer has lost control and spins backward towards the rest of the drivers. Zander breaks away from the collision as their parachutes deploy. The competitors from MetiCity-3, 5 and 7 eject from their jets, slowly making their way to the ground crew, who are awaiting their landing. The crowd must be genuinely concerned about their wellbeing, as they're quieter than normal.

"Five left. Two in front of you. Two behind you. MetiCity-8 and MetiCity-9. And they didn't make it out of that turn too well, either. I doubt they'll be trying that again. Looks like it's a three-person race." I comment.

"So you're saying I'm last?" Zander gasps.

"If you're not first, then..." I don't finish.

Since he made it out of the turn so well, he's able to gain on Wessin and Lionnel, but only by so much. We'll have to work if we're going to catch up now.

The fourth lap finishes without anyone taking too many

risks. Even Wessin has slowed slightly and is giving ground to Zander and Lionnel. Does he feel that unthreatened, or is his endurance fading?

The three of them are closely situated, making conservative decisions around each turn. Taking every straightaway by the book. We'll need someone to fuck up or slow down to catch their breath. Propelling at these speeds for a prolonged period, along with the bursts of acceleration they'll take around some of these turns, can cause racers to pass out if they aren't focused.

"You okay up there?" I ask after not hearing from him for a while.

I hear nothing back.

"Hey, Zander! Can you hear me?"

Silence.

"Techs, can I get a com check!?"

"It's not yours, it's his. Must have happened when he got swiped," the tech figures.

"Fuck!" I yell. There is no bypass. There's nothing we can do.

Five laps to go and I have no com-link with my racer. All I can do now is monitor the boards to the best of my ability, but I can't strategize or coordinate this way. As the fifth lap commences, I'm trying to keep up, but without coms he'll have to play it by the book and keep speed without trying anything drastic. But we aren't going to win the race that way, and If I know that, then he does too. I watch the movement of Wessin and Lionnel to see if I can find any decelerations we can take advantage of.

"I don't know if you can hear me or not, but I'm going to go when I spot the opportunity, so just be patient," I say. I don't know if it's the right decision to plan something without him, but I don't have much choice.

Through the sixth and seventh laps, all of the racers try to maintain their speed. Now that they're separated slightly from each other, there's no way to drift or slice through anyone using angles. From here on out, it's all about saving up the energy for the last two laps and not losing any ground in the meantime.

At the beginning of the eighth lap, however, Wessin makes another mistake. It's a small one, but big enough. He hits the turn fine but doesn't accelerate immediately after. A moment too long, and he doesn't hit his full speed coming into the straightaway.

"NOW!" I yell into the broken com as Zander hits the turn. I adjust everything for a breakaway. All he has to do is punch it. I can see the acceleration on the monitor rev up enough to burst through the sound barrier and there's a loud crack. Maybe he can hear me?

No one can maintain that kind of speed though, so he'll have to slow down before the next turn. But that last burst allowed him to catch up to Lionnel in second place. They're now milliseconds apart and jockeying for position; Zander coming in close but not wildly; he's fully in control.

The crowd is getting hyped as we finalize lap eight. Zander is tailing close behind, and the young prodigy is starting to show signs of panic. He keeps on the attack, and the opening turn for the ninth lap will be highly contested. As each racer approaches the ring, they bear down on one another, Zander and Lionnel gaining on Wessin. He makes it through the ring first, and I look up just in time to see Zander come ripping through the ring with Lionnel at the same time. Usually, two jets can't fit through the ring at once, but Zander pulls a move that almost takes Lionnel's cockpit straight off. They angle perfectly and come through the turn, swirling around one another from the momentum. Lionnel was clearly not prepared for this. Neither was I, for that matter. As he tries to regain control, he loses just enough time for Zander to steal second place back. The crowd cheers a roaring applause as he gains on Wessin coming into the opening stretch of the ninth lap.

"Nice Job, Zander!" I yell into the non-working com.

Lionnel is now in third, and although he's given up ground, he's still fighting for position. Zander is keeping calm, and I have a lot less stress on the boards. He's getting stronger as the race progresses. Handling more of the work, steering insanely well, and not letting the lack of coms deter him. Two more laps.

This lap, there's more urgency, each racer accelerating to their jet's speed thresholds. They're taking riskier maneuvers and burning caution in their exhausts. Even with the struggle between second and third, they continue to push closer and closer to Wessin on each turn. He's struggling to keep his position. It's not that he's making mistakes; he just isn't keeping pace. The intense focus is starting to wear on him. He just can't make the split-second decisions needed to stay ahead. Zander is now pacing for the best lap time he has ever run on this track, far outpacing his qualifier, but we always knew that wasn't the best he could do.

Towards the end of the ninth lap, I realize they're too close. There's no way they can take the opening turn all at once. Someone is going to have to speed up, risking an overshot of the turn, or slow down and let the others pass through first. If they all fight for it, someone is going to get hurt. This is it.

The three racers edge closer to the large floating ring. None of them have slowed; none of them have given any ground. They're side by side, fighting for positioning for who gets through the ring first. Once close enough, Lionnel shifts to attack Wessin. I can tell this is going to be a fight, and my heart is racing, trying to focus on the boards. I have a bad feeling about this.

I glance back up at the ring and suddenly feel like I'm losing my balance. My vision shifts as I adjust my head and try not to fall. Fuck. My heart sinks. I'm not falling...it is.

"ZANDER! BE CAREFUL! THE RING IS COMING DOWN!" I scream as soon as I realize.

The magnetic levitation system that keeps the rings afloat has lost power somehow, and I don't think they can restart it before the racers hit it head-first. I don't understand. How is this happening?!

The coms are completely quiet.

"Zander, please! Look out! It's coming down!" I try again, my voice cracking.

The audience finally notices, some of them screaming while the rest stare in complete disbelief.

"There seems to be an issue with the opening ring! Allspirits, they're going to be crushed!" the announcer yells through the stadium speakers.

As the falling ring gains momentum, so do the racers. Regardless of the danger, they want this too badly to stop. They adjust their trajectories and aim to get through the ring as it falls. I'm tempted to drop the fins and slow Zander down whether he likes it or not, but against my better judgment, I trust him. He can make it. I just have to believe.

"Zander! Don't do it! It's over!" I yell into the com.

It's obvious not all of them will make it in time. The MetiCity-4 star and the prodigy are slightly ahead of Zander, if only by inches. Lionnel pushes up against Wessin until they become entangled in each other. Any slight mistake and they'll all be killed trying to play this stupid fucking game.

This is the longest few seconds of my life. My world shifts to slow motion. Zander speeds up, detangling Wessin from Lionnel's jet, and pushing him back into the lead. He chose to defend the kid instead of taking the lead? Everything speeds back up, and before I can blink, the ring comes down atop them. There's no explosion; they just disappear. Gone. No, wait...

Wessin zooms out the other side. Wessin, and only Wessin.

"ZANDER!! ZANDER!? CAN YOU HEAR ME!?" I yell into the com.

"ZANDER!?" I yell again.

Tears come streaming down my face and onto the board.

"ZANDER!?" I scream into the oblivion of the open com.

Looking down at the board, I can see everything I need to. The jet is completely offline. He's gone.

"Zander..." I say one more time, quiet enough for nobody but the Allspirits to hear. The fight has left me. I stand there for a moment, watching the screen. Wessin has slowed down but is, for some reason, still going moving through the track. The last two racers slowly approach, stopping just above where the falling ring had been. To them, it is over.

The screams of the audience start to die down until a loud thump rocks the entire ground with shockwaves. The ring lands hard and slowly rolls towards the stadium. Panic ensues. The screaming intensifies. People are running to get out as fast as they can, and the audience breaks into pandemonium. So many people begin to get trampled that when I look into the crowds, it's like there are two layers of people: those who can run and those being run over. I look away. I can't stand to watch how quickly they turn into animals just trying to survive. There's a commotion coming from the back of the hangar where all the team's gates are housed. UG thugs have come charging through the door, plowing through security in a hurry. Is that...

Taxia? She's with them. I don't know why, but I can sense it. Even though they have Anti-Facial Recognition Masks on, there's something about the way she moves. Before I'm a hundred percent certain, they're out of another door and gone in the blink of an eye. Security scramble to figure out what just happened, but it's too late.

"Kid! We gotta get out of here!" One of the techs says, grabbing me by the arm.

My mind shifts from Zander. Oh fuck, Migo...the sisters, are they okay?

I'm dragged to the exit as the stadium begins to clear. Once we're outside, we watch as the ring hurtles toward the stadium. The impact shields are designed to withstand a jet collision, not...this. The large ring collides with the side of the stadium, rolling up over the impact shield, and for a second, it teeters on top. The remaining crowd below it tries to escape, but the shield can't bear the weight and begins to fracture before shattering into thousands of pieces. The ring plummets down, crushing whichever unfortunate souls didn't make it out in time. The only solace is that it was a quick death.

Migo. He was streaming! I open up my credentials to his broadcast. He's still there, consoling Tovah. I breathe a sigh of relief.

"Are you okay?! Where did Lucy go?! LUCY!" He yells. To be honest, I'm not as concerned about Lucy. I'm just glad Migo is okay.

I swipe off the stream and send a com-link invite to Zari. No answer. Same for Elli. I'm worried sick and I can feel the panic rising again. I'm surrounded by mayhem. I notice out of the corner of my eye, amongst the swarm of fleeing vehicles, that the UG crew is just lifting off. A few of them have taken off their masks, and I spot her. Taxia. I knew it was her. The security drones around the stadium won't be able to track them amongst all this commotion. Someone has got to do something.

I break away from the crowd and sprint for the garage as one of the techs screams, "Kid, where are you going!?"

All I can think of is vengeance. Revenge.

CHAPTER NINETEEN_

In the garage, I rev up my FlyBike and waste no time heading for her shop. Even if it's UG territory, it won't be a safe haven from me. On the way there, I turn on the feed again to find Migo reunited with Lucy and her boyfriend, crying incoherently into the camera, trying to figure out what just happened.

"How could this happen?!" he yells to the Allspirits. That's what I want to know.

I tune in to a news feed talking about the accident. I'm surprised to see they're not covering the race, or Zander's death, not even the tragedy of the casualties in the crowd. Instead, the headline reads "Board Member, Gideon Stein, Assassinated." Apparently, during all the commotion, the board member who gave the opening ceremony speech was beheaded by an unknown assailant. It's crazy to think, after all the progress we've made in technology, the best way to make sure someone stays dead is to take their head. Which is exactly what I plan to do. They won't get away with this.

I land down the street from the shop, surveying the empty streets as I head over on foot. Anyone this close to the race would be at the stadium, or fleeing it. I go heads up on my credentials and scan the building. It has a graphic saying, 'Closed for the race, see you there!' I spit on it.

The door is locked via encryption. I could try and decode using my backdoor login generator, but that would take forever and possibly trip an alarm. Lucky for me, I always carry a master key. I pull out my wrench and take a huge swing at the handle to the front door, knocking it off. The door clicks and glides open. No alarm? I slow the opening door so I can take a peek before I'm fully exposed. They're huddled behind the front desk.

"Oh fuck, man! FUCK! We're totally fucked!" The smaller of the two UG guys shouts. They didn't hear me breaking in over their own shouting, and they're exposed.

I sprint and vault over the front desk before they even know what's going on. Using all my momentum, I take to the air, slamming the heel of my foot into the larger UG goon's jaw. The one who was shouting stops and, as soon as he realizes what happened, begins to swing on me. I duck a wide hook, bob back up, and jab my wrench forward, aiming for his nose. He had already begun winding up his left, but my wrench beat him to the punch. The wrench lands right on target, the metal thudding against his nose as I drive it into his skull. His head snaps back and his hands rush up to meet his face, blood dripping down between his fingers. He attempts to regain himself while I take a swing at the side of his knee. It buckles him and he keels over to one side. I drop my wrench, grab Taxia by the wrists, and slam her against the back wall.

"WHY!?" I scream into her face.

"It wasn't supposed to..." she says softly, looking down, not fighting back at all.

"KILL ANYONE!?" I rage.

"No... it was just supposed to fall over onto the track once we set off the disruptor," she responds, looking away from me.

"The disruptor? The disruptor I helped you repair!?" I yell again, my skin crawling.

"Yes..." she looks directly at me now, eyes full of tears.

"He's dead, Taxia! He's fucking dead! Because of..." I say, coming to the realization it was my fault. I killed him. I killed Zander.

Next thing I know, I'm looking up at her from the ground. The UG punk I kicked in the face had gotten up and hit me with what I assume was my own wrench. As my vision returns, I notice he isn't holding my wrench. He used his bare hands. The guy just really hits that hard. Taxia had slid down the wall and was now sitting, staring into nothingness. The UG bastard towers over me while rubbing his jaw, so I scoot backward until I hit what I think is the front workbench. It is not.

"We should go," I hear the voice of K-2 announce. He tries helping me to my feet.

"No! I'm not finished!" I yell, trying to break free from his grip.

"Please, reconsider," the Droid responds. Wait, when the hell did he even get here?

"How did you even find me!?" I yell, turning to look at the Droid.

"You're my owner. Due to your vitals and the terrorist attack, my protocol allows me to-." before K-2 can finish his sentence, he grabs me and pulls me back just as a fist goes rushing past my head. The UG member goes for another swing and K-2 pushes my head down, causing him to miss again. The guy's fist slams right into K-2's head. K-2 is unphased.

"Arrrgh! Fuck!" He screams, wincing as he cradles his own hand.

The other UG member is finally up, limping towards us. He throws out a labored punch at me, and this time, K-2 grabs my shoulder, urging me to kneel. I duck the punch, causing the guy to spin 180 degrees. I push his back, launching him forward, and he hits the front desk face-first. He lets out a groan, once again covering his face with his hands. The blood begins to flow again.

"These damn things aren't supposed to fight!" He says, picking up the wrench I dropped. He turns his focus to the Droid and begins wildly swinging the wrench at him. K-2 ducks, dodges, bobs and weaves his way through the assault while calmly explaining to them that his directive says he can't harm humans. He can however attempt to remove himself from imminent danger. As he's explaining, he dodges a heavy swipe of the wrench and uses the momentum to grip the wrench at the end of the swing. K-2 easily yanks it out of his hand, disarming him. Frustrated now, both UG circle the Droid and let out matching punches aimed at his head. K-2 slightly adjusts the angle of his head and their fists catch each other. They both fall to their knees, grasping their hands in pain.

"Perhaps we should take this moment to leave this imminent danger?" K-2 says to me, pointing to the front door.

"Who said we'd let you leave?" the bigger UG member says, pulling himself up from the ground.

"Stop it! Let them leave..." Taxia says, tears streaming down her face. The two turn back to see her standing now. They look back at us as we start to make our way towards the door.

I don't want to leave. I want to make them pay. I've never been so angry in my life; I find it hard to regain my senses. I can hear the blood rushing in my ears. Part of me knows I should have stayed at the stadium. I left so suddenly that I never confirmed if the sisters were okay. K-2 feels my hesitation and starts pulling at me towards the exit. I reluctantly follow him until suddenly, he stops.

"No, you're right. Let's go. I'll deal with these scumbags later," I hiss.

"Unfortunately, I cannot proceed. Shutting down," he says before powering down.

The front door opens and a figure walks through, completely cloaked, wearing a mask. I can only tell it's a person because of the slight fluctuations of light as they pass through the entrance. It's not the same mask the UG wore to throw off the camera in the stadium; this one is faceless. The cloak looks like it's made from crystal, but somehow flowing and silky. It refracts light off the walls as they move. The figure is somewhat transparent, like a ghost, blending with the environment. Do I have a concussion? The UG begin to whisper behind me.

"Our songs have been heard!" one of them says in complete astonishment. The figure walks right up to me. They lift their arms, and I wince a little as they caress my jaw.

"Zelius..." It's a woman's voice. She lifts up the mask to reveal the most beautiful woman I have ever seen... and I mean ever.

"What have you done, Zelius?" she soothes, her voice sad and confused.

"Zelius?... Did she say Zelius?" one of the UG whispers again, a little too loudly.

The hurt and sorrow on her face turns stern as she glares in their direction. She lifts her hand, and without warning, a dart of light shoots right through him. Before he even realizes where the hole she left in him is, he hits the ground. Taxia looks terrified. I'm sure I do too.

"What the hell did you just do!?" I yell, jarred at the whole situation.

"I'm sorry. I meant to speak at a level only you could hear, but it seems my shock forced me above my normal volume for private conversation," she says, looking me up and down.

"The Queen lives," the other UG member says. "I can't believe it. This changes everything. Don't worry, my Queen. I will take your secret to my grave." He rushes to her feet and kneels before her. She sighs. Queen? As in Hypatia?

"Please..." she begins. "...Take a couple steps back so as not to sully my clothing," she continues, waving him back a few feet. He awkwardly gets up, and moves back a couple feet.

"Thank you," she nods to him before raising her hand again and wiping him from existence in the middle of the shop. "As for you," she says, looking towards the back of the shop at a terrified Taxia, "come forward. Running will only make it worse."

"NO!" I yell, seemingly out of nowhere. "STOP! Not like this. Are you really Hypatia? You were known to be kind and elegant! And you're just killing people indiscriminately? For what? I mean, it's not like I don't think they deserve it, but...this feels wrong."

"Did it feel wrong for those two? Or just this one...do you know her?" Her voice is oddly sweet, and she seems almost intrigued.

"Not really, but..."

"What's your name, young lady?"

"Uh, Taxia?" she says, completely unsure of what to do. You can tell by her body language the idea of running is not far from her mind.

"Taxia...it seems that you will be joining us for dinner. Follow me," Hypatia says, leading us out onto the still-empty road. K-2 powers up again and is able to move freely as he follows us closely, mumbling about how he hates not being in control.

"Please, get in. We don't have much time before this entire city is locked down."

"Get...into what?" Taxia asks.

"I'm certainly not uncloaking in a wretched place like this. Follow your Droid," she says, signaling the Droid to enter the cloaked cruiser.

"Not again," he says, apparently being compelled to move but not under his own volition.

We enter the cloaked cruiser together, and Hypatia inputs coordinates before taking off. It's not exactly like she took us at gunpoint, but I get the feeling we didn't have any choice in the matter. I knew what she had in her sleeve as soon as I saw the beam of light. MetiMetal blaster. A weapon that utilizes the charge MetiMetal can hold, rapidly pushing it through a barrel via magnets, into a temporary beam. Frank had one in the back of the shop that he showed me for shits and giggles, but it wasn't able to fire multiple shots and was nowhere near that powerful. Usually, the first shot will pull out all the energy at once and often hurt the user more than anyone else. But the one she has is highly concealed, potent, and doesn't seem to have any drawbacks for the user. Everything on her is next level. It was intimidating enough to keep me from running.

"Where are you taking us?" I ask, still fighting back the rising anger inside me.

"To be honest, I should have killed you both. Unfortunately, I did not anticipate having this level of emotional reaction upon seeing your face," she says, turning back to us while the autopilot takes over. "As for the girl, I guess I'm just curious as to why you thought she was worth dying for. Considering your...potential."

"My potential?"

"Don't be coy. If you didn't know who you were, you would have been shocked to be called Zelius. But you didn't look shocked; you looked scared. Like the secret you were holding onto was leaking through your fingers. I'm guessing this rusty antique is the one who educated you?" She says, looking at K-2.

"And why in the world is he wearing Paladin armor?" She looks at him, confused.

"He wasn't... Wait, so you knew I was alive?" I ask angrily.

"I didn't have the slightest of clues. That was until someone tripped the alarm. The signal came from this city, so I decided to see who might have tripped it. In my research, I came across this 'O-Race' event and a video of a young Zelius working the pit crew for MetiCity-6. How beneath you, Zelius." She rolls her eyes.

"My name is Unkno. Ren Unkno."

"That's not a name; that's a designation. But I'm assuming it was you who tripped the signal? How did you find it? What was it?" She questions me.

I think back to the toggle switch Elli had turned on momentarily. Elli. Zari. I still haven't heard from them. I open my credentials to a scrambled screen.

"Oh, that's not going to work here. Or where we're going, for that matter."

"And where is that exactly?" I demand once again.

"So hostile. As I said, I've cordially invited you both to dinner. You know, some would simply die for this opportunity," she says matter-of-factly.

"Some have," Taxia finally speaks up. She doesn't look directly at Hypatia. Her head hangs down, locs hiding her face.

"Indeed they have. What a pity," she says, turning back around to review her dashboard control panel.

"YOU BITCH!" Suddenly, Taxia winds her fist and swings at the back of Hypatia's head. Just before landing, K-2 grabs her by the wrist, preventing any contact.

"I see the girl's got some spunk. I was expecting nothing less. Keep still; we'll be arriving soon."

"How are you doing that to my Droid? And where have you been this whole time? And where are we go-"

"In due time," Hypatia cuts me off.

She doesn't answer any more questions. Or even acknowledge us.

We're able to slip past the security checkpoint to get out of the city surprisingly easily due to the cruiser's cloak. We're flying over open water, so I'm not exactly sure where we're headed, but if she wanted us dead, she would have dealt with us back in the shop. I feel safe for the moment, so I try to calm down and think. Anger bubbles in my throat as the image of Zander's jet flying towards the ring flashes into my head. I glance over at Taxia, who is completely silent. She looks scared and lost. It's hard to hold anger at someone who looks so helpless. I know she didn't plan for things to happen this way, but that doesn't change what she did. What we did. The guilt rips my stomach apart as I think back to fixing the disruptor in her shop. Her shop, where her friends were just brutally killed in front of her. We both just lost people close to us, have no idea where we're going, and are traveling with a ghost. I can't help but try to reach out.

"Are you okay?" I ask. She's rubbing her wrist where K-2 had grabbed her.

"What do you care?" she says under her breath.

Well, I tried.

I gaze out the window and notice we've descended just over the open ocean. Now, it's easier to see the intense speed we're moving at. It looks like time traveling, we should be melting into our seats but we don't seem to be affected inside the cruiser. We slow down before plunging straight into the water. I jump slightly as we hit, thinking it would be a rougher impact, but her cruiser slips right through the ocean surface. I have never ridden in anything like this: extremely fast, undetectable by radar, nearly invisible to the naked eye, submersible, and as much as I hate to admit...

It's very comfortable.

There isn't much sea life around; hasn't been in quite some time. The chalky coral reefs are a reminder of the world that was here before I existed. They say the ocean's sudden ecological collapse caught scientists off guard. Even when all their data pointed to it, year after year. We slow down more and I'm able to see a small school of fish swimming by, a rare sight. I accidentally let out a low "whoa" when I see them. I notice Taxia looking over, but when I turn to see her, she quickly turns to look out her own window.

We come upon a low-lying rock formation that gradually splits in half, revealing a tubelike chamber embedded inside. We enter the chamber and the rocks close behind, sealing us away from the ocean. The water drains out just enough so that the vehicle can float next to a walkway that's rotating toward us. It feels like I've just made my way into an evil villain's lair. Light spills into the room as the doors open in front of us. Inside, I can make out what looks like a high-rise apartment.

"Please, follow the Droid," she gestures towards the entrance.

We step inside, and I gasp at the sheer size of the place. Casting my eyes into the room, I can't help but fix them onto an imposing crystal chandelier hanging from the ceiling. A huge glass table reflects the chandelier, causing splashes of light to dance across the colossal walls. That chandelier alone could probably cover my rent in the MetiCity until I'm 200. How could someone build something like this discreetly? It's magnificent.

Massive columns embellish the corners of the room, framing it as though it were a piece of art. In the center, a cream-colored velvet sofa with matching silk pillows and furnishings that look soft to the touch. The all-white kitchen to the left is a modern contrast to the luxurious living room. The place barely looks as if it's been touched, let alone held host to guests. There are matching double doors to the far right of the living room and another set in the back. Hypatia glides inside and stops about halfway in to turn around and face us. She looks like she belongs, extravagant but cold. K-2 quickly follows in an awkward shuffle, taking a seat on the sofa next to her. His Biosuit is far too industrial for this place, and he looks ridiculous trying to get comfortable on the couch.

CHAPTER TWENTY_

"Welcome to my lovely abode," Hypatia says, bowing. "There's the kitchen if you need water; the bathroom is through those doors, down the hall, on the right. Your bedroom is on the left," she says, pointing to the doors where I was expecting some sort of three-headed dragon. "Further down the hall are another set of doors, which for now are off-limits to proceed through. Also off-limits, is my room, where I'll be changing out of this." She gestures to her outfit. "But first, I'll get dinner started." She smiles, heading over to the kitchen area. She proceeds to hit a few buttons on the food printer interface before turning around again. "There! Now, I expect to see you both at the table ready to eat shortly." She says before disappearing behind the doors of her bedroom.

"Umm...Room? Are we guests? Or prisoners?" I say to the now-closed bedroom door.

"Are you asking me? I'm still trying to figure out how she's even alive. Or why she called you Zelius," Taxia says, surveying the living room.

"I'm not."

"Not asking me?"

"Not Zelius. Not really…" I try to explain.

"That's a shame. Because if you were Zelius, maybe you could engineer our way out of this mess," she sighs. "So if you're not Zelius, who are you, really?"

"I'm…"

"Hungry, right?" Hypatia says, coming back through the doors from her room.

She's dressed in a high fashion gown, custom printed to fit her figure perfectly. It hugs her curves closely, making it nearly impossible not to stare. She is brilliantly stunning, in an ethereal otherworldly-being way. Even Taxia stops for a moment.

"Wait. No. I'm not hungry. I want to know why you have taken us here! Why you killed those men! And I want to know when we can leave." The confidence in my voice dwindles as I get further into my questioning.

"You're here because I don't know what else to do with you. You can leave whenever you'd like, but I doubt you'll get very far this deep underwater. Might as well make yourself at home for the time being. I have some questions, and I'll need time to assess the situation," Hypatia replies while making her way over to the kitchen. "Dinner is almost ready. Can I offer anyone something to drink? I have wine, juice, and water."

"I'm not thirsty," I say, frustrated with her answer. "What do you mean to assess the situation?"

"I'll take some wine," Taxia says after examining the exit. Even the best swimmers would have trouble making it to the surface, and if they did, where would they swim to? We're too far from land, and MetiCity shipping vessels are all fully automated.

"Lovely. Are you sure you wouldn't like a drink, Zelius? It's your favorite," she says, holding up the bottle, showing off its label and smiling as if I am supposed to know what it is.

"My name isn't Zelius," I get up and head to the bar, sitting two seats down from Taxia, who is already downing her glass.

"It's a Roussanne, Viognier, and Chardonnay blend that's going to pair quite nicely with the rich fish that's coming out in a moment," she explains once she notices I haven't recognized the bottle. "It's been sitting out for a day or two. Ever since I found out you were alive, I've been so nostalgic for something less bitter," she explains, pouring a bit more into Taxia's glass. Taxia, having laid her face in her arm, looks up to down the rest of her glass. I take a sip myself and I'm blown away by the taste. It's delicious, and... familiar. I take another sip and the liquid warms my chest, calming me. It's strong, but pleasant. I guess if she wanted to poison us, this would be the opportune moment. I don't even care if she does. I take another sip as Hypatia continues.

"Zelius and I would often share a bottle, burning greesha together while working in near silence for hours, completely content," she drifts focus for a moment before being caught by the buzzing of the food printer. "Ah, it's ready." She hands us our plates and awaits our response. The sick pit of anxiety in my stomach turns to gnawing hunger as the smell drifts up, so I dig in. Taxia, however, pushes the plate aside and shoves her glass towards Hypatia for another drink, to which she is obliged.

"Do you know how he died?" My question catches Taxia's attention. People have devoted their entire lives to solving this mystery and I'm finally going to.

"I do not. I doubt anyone alive truly does." She sighs. Taxia downs her glass and plops her head back into the fold of her arm. "I left him years before he passed."

"You left him? Why?" I ask.

"Because of you."

"Me?"

"Towards the end, he became insistent that we have a child. When we realized that wasn't a possibility, he became obsessed with the science of cloning. I was against it from the beginning. I often had to remind him of the duality of his creations. How the food printer could so easily be manipulated into a catastrophic weapon without the proper precautions in place. How his AI could not be allowed to progress uninhibited. He was usually willing to budge when I pushed, but with cloning, each failed attempt drove him further into his obsession. Like an itch he couldn't scratch. He became a recluse. Started to miss deadlines, wasn't showing up to meetings, and rarely spoke a word to me. It was like being married to a ghost. Eventually, I had enough and left. In fact, the Droid over there probably knows more than I do." She gestures towards K-2 with her glass, who looks over from the sofa, almost excited to be mentioned.

"How did you know it was his Droid?" I ask.

"He was always with that Droid. Paladin armor or not, I'd recognize it anywhere. If he wasn't in the lab working beside it, he was in the shop working on it. He felt all his creations were, as he put it, 'infinitely stumbling towards perfection,'" she says, smiling, looking down into her glass. "You know, after the tenth or so attempt, I really thought it was a problem even the great Engineer couldn't solve. Seems like he wasn't that far off if you're in your what...early twenties?" she asks, looking me up and down.

I pause for a moment and, without thinking, mutter, "Forty-two."

"Forty-two?" Taxia slurs.

"Forty-two? But how? I left roughly twenty-five years ago," Hypatia asks, perplexed.

"No. I'm twenty-one years old. The Droid said I'm the

forty-second clone attempt. But he doesn't know what happened after Zelius sent him off with me."

"Well, congratulations, Zelius, you did it. But that doesn't change the fact that I fundamentally disagree with your..." She struggles to find the words. "...entire existence."

My expression is disgust. That's what she landed on?

"Fortunately for you, I can't help but feel like killing you would be a waste. It's possible that your lack of accomplishments is just a clear example of nurture over nature. Perhaps you just need the right environment to grow in," she ponders flagrantly.

"Lack of accomplishments?" It's like she can't help but insult me. "You don't know me or where I come from! I grew out of ash and sand. Maybe if you actually spent any time out in the world you created, you'd understand what an accomplishment that is. Instead, you hide down here, printing food and drinking wine." I throw my fork onto the plate in anger. Taxia sits silently, but the way she's looking at me, it's almost like she's proud.

"You think I'm down here by choice?" she says, glaring at me. "The board didn't let me just walk away. Zelius warned me that if I left, they would come after me, but I assumed it was just one of his paranoid rants. Sure enough, they tracked me, ambushed me, and tried to kill me. I spent much of the last twenty years looking over my shoulder, never knowing if I was being pursued, never knowing if the next glass of wine I drank would be poisoned." She downs the rest of her glass before continuing. "You have no IDEA what I've been through, child!"

Taxia and I sit wide-eyed as the once regal and calm Hypatia loses her cool. She realizes this and calms down after a deep breath. "I was always on the move. I inhabited the uninhabitable. Constantly changed my appearance. I even wore garments unbefitting for someone my stature. But they still came for me. And believe me, if they find out who you are, and they will, they'll come for you too. And when that happens, you'll be looking for a hole to crawl into yourself."

"How would they know? It's like you said: I have no accomplishments. I'm nobody. I could go back, and they would never know the difference," I explain.

"They may not now, but when you are actually forty-two, you'll be virtually indistinguishable. I'm surprised no one noticed sooner. You're the spitting image of him from his early college days. Aside from this unruly hair and that scar," she says with a repulsive wince.

"But-" I start.

"You don't get it. You are Zelius. Eventually, you're going to fix something that wasn't supposed to be able to be fixed. Build something that wasn't supposed to be able to be built. Besides, as much as you've been able to keep a low profile up until now, you won't be able to do that anymore. I recorded this broadcast on the way here," she says, gesturing towards the wall where she begins projecting her credential screen. The volume on the newscaster increases as a picture of me next to Zander appears on the screen.

"Among the missing is also this technician who worked for MetiCity-6 O-Racer, Zander, who tragically passed earlier today." The pictures they had of Zander and I slowly fade from the screen as they continue to display more of the race aftermath. "The UnderGround organization is being blamed, although they have not taken credit for the attack as of yet. The perpetrators are still at large as bodies are being dug out from amongst the rubble. It's hard, at this point, to know exactly who is missing and who is still hoping to be found. Graphic videos of the tragic event are being shared senselessly, so we thought it might be more appropriate to show the families who have come to mourn the passing of, what now is confirmed to be, over three hundred casualties and climbing." The feed changes to the on-site reporter standing in front of a memorial board which cycles through pictures of the deceased. I turn away to stop myself from breaking down, and notice Taxia has already crumbled into tears again, staring at the screen in disbelief.

"It seems you had something to do with this, didn't you, Taxia girl?" Hypatia says, looking over at Taxia. "I know that look. The look of someone with innocent blood on their hands. The UG have been very careful not to sully their reputation with murderous acts. They will want those responsible to pay just as much as MetiCorp, so I can't imagine it's much safer for you out there now than it is for him," she says, putting her hand on Taxia's shoulder. I expect Taxia to smack her hand away, but I'm sure it's hard to get angry at the truth.

"Elli?"

The camera pans over to a young girl singing with a candle. The camera stops and fixates on her.

"Elli? Was that the girl from-" Taxia begins to question before I shush her.

Elli is singing through tears, voice cracking slightly with the overwhelming emotion. Is she there for Zander? Or Zari? Both? The crowd surrounds her, and I don't think she even notices them starting to gather. Her voice carries, captivating the crowd, drawing them in close.

"Never forgotten like dreams so surreal, moments that blossom forever instilled, I'll hold on your line until you let go... I know, my love, I know." She ends her song now at a near whimper, laying her candle down beside the rest and walking out of the frame. When the feed transitions back to the newscaster, he's wiping his eyes with his sleeve, barely able to get ahold of himself.

"That was just... beautiful," he says, choking on his words. "We'll be right back." They cut the feed.

"She has quite the voice. Is this another friend of yours?" Hypatia asks.

"She's the one who set off your signal," I choke, "Elli and her sister... her sister who may be..."

"It wasn't you?" she asks.

"No."

"What was the trigger?"

"Elli and her sister Zari had been finding hidden code fragments in the system, and when they dug deeper, they found the ICON designation."

"The ICON designation? You mean it's running on the current system iteration?"

"Yes. You didn't know? I thought you designed the entire system?"

"She did?" Taxia sniffs.

"I did. The ICON designation was something I was working on before I left, but the board wouldn't approve it. Zelius said it was pointless to pursue it any further. He must have finished my work and implemented it before he died. I'm impressed, Zelius. You were always so terrible at coding," Hypatia thinks out loud. "So, does the ICON status still grant a meeting with the board?"

"It does. As one option."

"He added a second?" Hypatia's curiosity is piqued.

"The second option is the MetiCorp Compendium," I explain.

"The what?" Taxia asks.

"Elli and Zari thought maybe they could use it to expose what happened to their people. The Jardinera," I say, thinking back to the girls.

"Very sad indeed. This Compendium was something

Zelius had kept under lock and key. When he died, I assumed no one would be able to access it. So he left a back door. Absolutely genius. Has no one gained access?" she asks.

"I've only known one ICON. And he chose the meeting. Unfortunately, anyone who achieves it or even gets close usually ends up dead. He wasn't an exception to that rule," I explain.

"So, how did you end up triggering my signal?"

"When looking through that prototype Droid's code," I say, nodding to K-2, "Zari found instructions to build a separate user interface that displayed only the message 'Find 42. Blood alone moves the wheels of history.' Also, in his memory was the location of two additional prototypes. Three in total: a Droid, a Biosuit, and a vehi-"

"Vehicle? Transport, Bionics, and Robotics," Taxia finishes my sentence. It's not surprising that the words are now second nature for all of us. The three innovations.

"Yeah. We found the Biosuit prototype at her shop," I signal to Taxia.

"That's what those girls were doing back there?" Taxia questions, clearly unhappy to be used like that.

"Using the password '42', we were able to find the toggle switch that must have been your signal," I finish.

"Zelius had told me before I left that if he ever truly needed me, he would contact me using that signal. But really, it sounds like he wanted me to vet whoever found the code. And with such a simple password, he assumed there would only be a few to find it, if at all. What was in the third prototype?"

"Not sure... we never found it."

"Well, now I've got to find it before someone else does. If I know Zelius, that third prototype was probably a failsafe for if I was no longer alive. He had a backup plan for just about everything. I just didn't think his plan would be me cleaning up his mess," she says in a huff.

"Um... How do you get this ICON designation?" Taxia asks.

"Well, I designed it as a complex algorithm to honor those in our society who contributed greatly, accomplished low-probability feats, did not overuse resources, and had huge public favor. It was supposed to give people something to strive for, to inspire those who would otherwise feel no obligation to struggle and break boundaries," Hypatia explains.

"I can't help but feel that's a bit...ambiguous?" Taxia was as lost as me the first time it was explained.

"Because it's not a simple answer. It's different for everyone," I chime in. "And it's constantly changing. The sisters found a way to narrow down each person's pathway to ICON status, but it varies widely depending on what you've accomplished so far. But once you reach a certain level of social credit, you then need to master one of the three innovations. Mastery means you are number one in your field and have gained great fame and notoriety for it. For Zander, this current race cycle was his shot. If he had won, he would have been the first outer MetiCity Racer to win a Cup. He would have been an ICON. For Elli's sister Zari, it was creating a new programming language for Droids. That's how she even learned about the ICON system in the first place. She had been working on a way to innovate the system for years, but she never..."

"What was yours?" Taxia asks.

"Well...if I ever got a high enough social credit score, my mastery would have been Droids," I say.

"Is that common? To know your mastery before you have the social credit? Could you find out what mine is?"

"No."

"To which question?"

"Both."

"So the board must have some way of recognizing who is on the verge of ICON status and then take them out when they get too close. Self-preservation," Hypatia adds. "Well, I'm going to do some digging and see if I can figure out where the transport prototype is. I'll head out tomorrow morning, first light... alone. I'll also have to clean up the mess that was left in the shop. In the meantime, make yourselves at home. Once I'm back, we can begin to assess what use you might be of."

"To who? You?" I ask.

"To the world."

"Wait, are there two beds?" Taxia asks.

"No," Hypatia says before walking over to K-2 and leading him into her bedroom.

"Well-" Taxia starts.

"I'll sleep on the couch; it's fine," I say, heading over to the couch. "What are you going to do with my Droid?"

"This isn't your Droid, silly. This is Zelius's Droid. And you're not Zelius, are you?" Hypatia smiles and walks away, K-2 following close behind. The door closes behind her, and me and Taxia are left in the room alone. Taxia takes a deep breath and groans while haphazardly sliding her palms down her face from her eyes.

"Okay! Great. I'll take the room, and you keep an ear out to make sure she doesn't try anything funny with the Droid," she says with a sarcastic tone.

"Funny? Funny like what?" I ask.

"That's probably the closest thing to a man she's had in there for years," Taxia slurs through her words, seemingly giving up on composing herself.

"Gross."

Before lying down, I go to use the bathroom and take a peek at the guest room. It's surprisingly barren compared to the rest of the apartment. Taxia has gotten down to her underwear already and is closing the door when I walk by. I do my best not to make eye contact, but I can't help myself. When I do, she's looking at me and simply mouths "thank you," like she did in the shop.

I go to say, "you're welcome," but the door shuts before I have a chance. The intrusive thought of smothering her with a pillow wanders through the back of my head.

Much of the night is spent listening to Hypatia yelling at K-2 or loud thuds I hope aren't her hitting him...or worse. The couch is surprisingly comfortable. Unfortunately, because of everything going on, I can't keep my thoughts from racing.

Zander. He was always calm and always knew what to do next. He was a leader to all of us. I keep thinking of how we lost coms before he crashed and I can't help but wish I had said something more. Maybe I could have convinced him to stop. Maybe I could have stalled out everything on the console to keep him from moving. Even though I know he could always have manually overridden it, it doesn't stop the thought from festering. He must have really liked Wessin. He gave his life so some kid he barely knew could make it out safely.

Elli. She was all alone. I hope she's okay. Why wasn't Zari there with her? I could hear it in her singing that she was in pain, and I'm powerless to stop it. Instead, I'm here with the girl who killed Zander, and even worse, I'm technically an accomplice to the murder. Why did I stand up when Hypatia went to kill her? Was it because I wanted to do it myself? If so, here's my chance. She's just down the hall. In the room I let her take.

Part of me was excited to finally meet Hypatia. We didn't share any DNA, but for some reason, I can't stop thinking about her as a mother. Not what I expected at all. Graceful but ungracious. Enthusiastic but sharp and discourteous. To be honest, I have a hard time figuring her out. I thought, for some strange reason, that she might be excited to see me.

"I fundamentally disagree with your entire existence."

What does someone say to that? I didn't choose this. But she is right. My existence is problematic, to say the least.

"We will assess your usefulness."

I've never had my worth as a living being questioned so flippantly. Maybe she has a plan? A way for me to get back to my friends? I must be dreaming...

CHAPTER TWENTY-ONE_

I was dreaming...but not deeply enough to miss Hypatia coming out of her room with K-2. My credentials work enough to tell the time, at least. 5:00 a.m.

"Did you find it?"

"OH! You scared me. I see someone was a proper gentleman last night. But yes. Obviously. I should be back by afternoon," she says, opening the door to the chamber containing her cruiser. "Stay put," she says, closing the door behind her.

K-2 comes over and sits down on the ground next to me, entering his meditative state.

"You okay?" I ask.

"I am functioning at optimal parameters. Hypatia made a few alterations, repairing the work you performed on my Biosuit," he says before returning to his meditation.

"Really? I thought I did a pretty good job. Let me see." I get up to examine his back, where she has adjusted the alignment slightly to better synthesize with the Droid's hardware. It is impressive. I had a lot of trouble attaching it myself. I wonder if she made any alterations to his code? Though I'm not sure why she would need to, she can already take control of him at will. "Do you know how she's able to control you like that?"

"It would seem she has some sort of master key that enables her to control anything running on the code. It's not something I'm able to resist, so I do apologize for being unable to comply with you during her presence," he says sadly.

"It's okay. Like you said, she designed you; it makes sense she would have some sort of back door. I wonder if Elli could write something to stop you from being overridden," I say.

"Or Zari?" he asks.

"I'm not sure if she's going to be able to work on you anymore..." I say, withdrawing into myself.

"Oh, that's too bad. She was very gentle. Unlike Hypatia. She's not how I remember her at all."

"Yeah." Not how I imagined her either.

Taxia comes out a while later, ventures into the kitchen, grabs the bottle we were drinking from last night, and makes her way back into the guest room without so much as a word. Has she been in there drinking all night?

No way I'm getting back to sleep, so I take some time to explore the lock systems Hypatia uses for the front door and her room. There's nothing visible; not a doorknob, keypad, nothing. It must be controlled by Hypatia directly, which is what I had feared.

It means that if she gets herself killed out there, we're going to die down here. There's no way to communicate with the outside world. There is food, but I'm not sure how long two people will last on whatever she has in the kitchen. I open the cabinets to see what kind of timeline I'm working with should she disappear, and find she has enough atomized food to last a few years. I'm pretty surprised she has so much, but I guess it makes sense, considering she's been living down here for over twenty years. If it wasn't for the food printer and running water, I'm not entirely sure how she would survive... or us. Let's hope neither breaks anytime soon.

I decided to set it to print some pancakes. For some reason, I'm in the mood for them. While it's printing, I check out a bookshelf she has against the furthest wall. It's filled to the brim with books of all kinds. Engineering, history, blueprints, many of Zelius's books, and some classics, like *Moby Dick* and *A Tale of Two Cities*. One that catches my eye is *One Hundred Years of Solitude*. How fitting.

The monitor on the wall picks up pretty much every station I've never heard of, most of which are covering the O-Race Cup disaster. The toll is now five hundred people confirmed dead and many more injured. If I had any kind of signal, I'd be able to check the list to confirm which side of the coin Zari landed on. Unfortunately, I don't need to check for Zander. The image of his vehicle being crushed is burned into my memory. The newscaster is going on about how the Company is working as hard as it can to take down those responsible for this tragedy. Another anchor says the Company has revived several people who had been found dead before they suffered major brain injuries.

"Can you turn that down?" I hear Taxia mumble from the hallway. She's clearly been crying, is drunk, and from the looks of her, must have been wrestling some sort of wild animal. Her coveralls are tied loosely around her waist, exposing a white, wine-stained tank top. She tries half-heartedly to cover the stain with her hair. "Wait...are those pancakes?" she says, sniffing the air.

"Yeah," I say, lowering the volume on the monitor.

"Mmm, I could go for some-" she cuts herself off and quickly runs to the bathroom to puke.

"I'll save you some!" I yell. She sticks her hand out and gives me a thumbs up.

After the retching stops, I walk over to take a peek and she's passed out over the toilet seat, sleeping like a hungover angel. I go to take a step back towards the kitchen, but the door Hypatia had told us was off-limits catches my eye. Same thing: no knob, no keypad. I think back to the bookshelf suddenly and remember there is a portfolio named 'Blueprints.' The food printer goes off as I grab the book. It's beeping, so I run over to shut it off before it wakes up Taxia.

"URGGHHHHH!" I hear her groan from the bathroom.

"Sorry, I got it," I say, stopping the beeping.

I open the blueprint portfolio and see the layout for this apartment...base...hideout. Whatever it is. It has detailed schematics for the docking bay, the cruiser, and a layout of the entire place. Odd she would leave something like this out in the open, but maybe she just forgot about it? Even more odd is this place is about five times bigger than I thought. The area we occupy is just the front entrance. While it doesn't specify what the additional space is for, it's about the size of an O-Race course. Just past where the off-limits door is, there's another hallway with three doors at the end, each leading to different areas. If there's another guest room back there and she's letting me sleep on the couch, I'm going to be pissed. Flipping further, I find schematics for the doors, and it seems there's a mechanism above the door that receives a signal and controls the entry.

"What's that?" Taxia says, suddenly appearing in front of me and grabbing a pancake off my plate.

"Blueprints for this place."

"What? Let me see!" She says, coming around the countertop to stand in front of me. "Whoa! This is some heavy-duty shit. The back doors all seem to work on the same mechanism, but the front door is different. Damnit." She says frustratingly.

"Wait...what's this?" She points to a symbol noted above each of the doorways.

"I'm not sure. I was wondering the same thing."

"Let's find out!" She grabs the blueprints and heads towards the back door.

She starts to feel around above the door, looking back and forth between the wall and the blueprints.

"It should be right about here, but I'll need something that can tear through this to get to it..."

We search around the rooms and then the kitchen. But Hypatia was smart enough to only leave forks and spoons, nothing sharp enough to get through the wall.

"Wait a minute," she says, looking over at K-2. "Why don't you get him to do it?"

He looks back over at us and kind of tilts his head like a confused dog.

"Hey, can you help us out?" I say, ushering him to the door and pointing out the spot.

"Sir, are you sure? I'm not sure Hypatia would be happy with this kind of property damage," he questions.

"In case you haven't noticed, she's got us trapped in here. So if she's not happy, she can kill us," Taxia explains.

I nod, and K-2 proceeds to tear a hole in the wall by stabbing through it with his fingers, and spinning his hand extremely fast.

"Nice!" Taxia says before getting to work, disabling the mechanism controlling the door.

After a few minutes, the door opens to a long hallway. There are three doors on the other side. The floor, walls, and ceiling are all white, illuminated by scattered lights built into the walls. Modern, but Hypatia's touch is evident in the gold trimmings.

"Which door should we try first?" Taxia says, looking at us.

"I don't know. I've got a bad feeling about this. Almost feels like a trap," I say, rubbing the back of my neck.

"Door number two it is!" She exclaims. It's the closest one to us. K-2 looks at me for approval. I nod, and he proceeds to do the same thing above the door. Taxia again disables the mechanism without hesitation. I can still smell the alcohol on her as she fumbles around. She is pretty handy; I guess that's why she had a reputation in her area, even if she only served UG.

When the door opens, what's revealed is some kind of boiler room filled with mechanical equipment.

"Pretty anti-climatic, huh?" she says. "What is this, a hot water heater?"

"Not just that," I say, looking behind the large cylinder and various tubing for pumps. "This one over here is the atmosphere control. Behind that is the desalination machine, which explains where she's getting the clean water from. The last looks to be the atomizer. She must be pumping in ocean water, minerals, and microscopic organisms to collect enough atoms to get consistent amounts of biomatter for the food printer. It's actually genius. With this setup, she's completely self-sustainable," I explain, geeking out on the cool tech.

"So you're saying we're eating sea scum pancakes? Maybe that's why the smell made me throw up," she turns pale. "But where's the power coming from?"

"There's a backup generator here, too, but I can't get it to turn on. Power is probably collected elsewhere and has direct lines in."

"Right...next!" She yells before exiting the boiler room to presumably check out the other doors. "Door number one."

I stop investigating the monitor long enough to catch the first door open to an empty room. Well, it isn't exactly empty...

"Is this what I think it is?" she asks, walking into the room.

The room is bigger than the two front sections of the apartment combined. The walls are all a light gray, squared off into roughly four-foot sections.

"Full holo?" she asks, sliding her hand across the wall and feeling in between the grooves.

"Yup. But it's not just that. I'm seeing slots for cybernetics to mimic the environment and sensors all over the place. Fully glacious. A friend of mine has a full holo, but it's much smaller and doesn't have anywhere near this amount of complexity. You could do anything in here. This is probably how she's passed these last few decades so easily. It's got to be lonely being down here by yourself..."

"Oh, poor Hypatia," she says, continuing to look around. "She probably uses it as a dating simulator," she huffs.

"Why waste it on that...with this thing, you could jump into the Grand Canyon. Swim with blue whales. Explore the galaxy," I say, looking at the ceiling.

"You and I got a different idea of fun," she says dryly.

"And what would you do?" I ask.

"I'd burn a kingdom down and rule as Queen," she says, snickering.

"You know, I experienced that one first hand... It's not quite as fun as one might think." We turn to see Hypatia standing in the doorway.

"Shit," Taxia says under her breath.

CHAPTER TWENTY-TWO_

"I thought I'd come back to one of you dead or you both in bed. This, I had not predicted. Maybe I underestimated you, boy," she says, looking up at the damaged doorway. "I had planned to show you both this section of my home when I had returned, but alas, it's true what they say, sandscavengers never stop moving. Come, I'll show you the last room before you break something else." She ushers us into the hallway. Taxia and I give each other nervous glances before I shrug and follow Hypatia.

"So, did you find it?" I ask.

"Of course," she says matter-of-factly.

"What was in the code?"

"Well, I'd be finding that out right now if you hadn't insisted on rummaging through my things," she says, standing before the last door. After a moment, the door opens to a brightly-lit room roughly the size of the holoroom. Unlike the holoroom, though, this one is full of plants.

"It's a garden, just like the one you used to tend to!" K-2 exclaims excitedly.

"You remember it? I've worked many years to try and get it

to the quality of my last garden. I can't help but be elated that the Droid is able to make the correlation."

"It's...beautiful," Taxia says unexpectedly. She walks ahead of us to inspect some pansies that are in full bloom.

"I find this room especially calming. It reminds me of days gone by. Also, it makes me feel like a samurai," she smiles to herself. "At least that's what Zelius used to call me...his little samurai. I always liked that," she says, sniffing a flower with her eyes closed.

"Weren't samurai like...warriors? What does that have to do with a garden?" I ask.

"The samurai followed a code of Zen Buddhism. When they weren't at war, this code emphasized the value of meditation and a disdain for the opulence of the imperial court's lavish standards. The garden you see here resembles the aesthetic of the ancient Japanese gardens of the samurai during the Kamakura period: simple and clean. Often, Zelius would find me in my garden, meditating," she says, sitting on a stone bench. "Just like this."

She closes her eyes and crosses her legs.

"The point of meditation is to clear your mind of all thoughts and be present in the moment. When putting your brain at rest, it allows for the memories you've made to be properly stored. Without this, you're basically shutting down a computer before it is saved. All progress is lost," she says calmly, eyes still closed like some guru spouting Confucianism.

"I never could meditate. The UG was all about it. But I've got too many thoughts going on in my head to quiet," Taxia says, coming over.

"That is how it is for all in the beginning. Eventually, you learn to identify these thoughts, accept them, and let them phase through you like all the rest of the hundred trillion neutrinos that pass through our bodies every second," she says, getting up now and dusting herself off.

"Or like the beam of light you sent through my friends. But then I guess that's the other side of being a samurai, huh? Killing with no emotion?" Taxia scoffs.

"Yes. Unlike you, they saw it as a privilege. You weren't so accepting. Why?" Hypatia replies calmly.

Taxia looks shocked. I'm not sure why she decided to pick a fight right now, and I'm not sure she knows either. It's the first peaceful moment I've had since I got here. Maybe that's the issue. She snapped back to reality and remembered what happened to her friends. That we're being held captive.

"I...I wasn't UG, like them. The UG, they worship Zelius like a god. Seeing you must have been a sign to them. Some kind of honor... But I couldn't have imagined they would be almost... eager to die," she says, looking down.

"I wasn't surprised. The UG has long used prophecies of Zelius's return to proselytize and spread their influence. They foretell that upon his return, he would usher in a new era of freedom and prosperity. A technological revolution that will return the planet to us. And us to it. They see any action by me as preordained and a sign of this future to come. Something they would be willing to die for, clearly."

"But you didn't have to. You had a choice," Taxia says sternly.

"It couldn't be avoided. Word of Zelius's resurrection would send ripples through the fabric of the entirety of human civilization, potentially altering it irreparably. Keeping his identity a secret is a valuable advantage I will not lose," she explains.

"It's not a resurrection," I correct her.

"Again, you deny the very blood in your veins. You just don't comprehend what you're capable of. A fact I cannot blame you for in your current state: you aren't capable of much. The problem is you have no direction. What is it that you want?" she asks me directly.

"I want to go home."

"Impossible. I've already decided. I'm not going to let you leave here until you can convince me that I should. Zelius would have a plan," she explains, walking out of the garden room.

"A plan?" Taxia and I exclaim, chasing after her.

"A plan for what?" I ask.

"You have the body of the world's most prolific scientist and military commander. Unrivaled genius and physical prowess. The promise to lead the entirety of civilization to salvation, the power to claim the throne of the Last King. I'm not going to sit idly by while you piss that away. I made the decision a long time ago that I would never tell Zelius what to do. He would just know," she says, closing the door to the third room behind us and sauntering down the hallway.

"Didn't Zelius come from a wealthy family? Educated at the best schools by the best teachers? Ren is from the Outskirtz. It's not the same," Taxia retorts.

"Zelius was educating his teachers by the time he was old enough to attend any of those schools. What Zelius had was inherent. But he did work hard to accomplish the things he set out to do. Which is why I'm surprised to see that you've made so little of yourself. If you can't find your purpose, you're just a failed experiment," she says, stopping in the living room area and looking at me again.

I don't know what to say. Yesterday, I had a purpose. Today, that purpose seems meaningless. I don't have a plan. I don't feel like someone who has it all figured out. I don't feel like I can conquer the world. I feel cornered. Trapped. Not just underwater but boxed in as well. What's even worse is that something inside tells me that she is right. Maybe it is inevitable that people will find out. Expect great things from me. Treat me differently. Even those I would consider close.

"Can I at least see if my friends are ok?" I ask sincerely.

"If you're wondering about the singing girl from the news announcement, I saw her today. She seemed quite well. In fact, it was her newfound fame that allowed me to so easily retrieve the remaining code. The code itself was located in a vehicle that was on display at a retro transport conference. Even cloaked, it was difficult to sneak through the crowd without anyone accidentally bumping into me. But once Elli showed up, everyone rushed her for photos. Her singing must have made quite an impression on those watching. Clever girl, too. She was able to download the code before I even could. Did it right in front of them," Hypatia explains. "Now I'm going to see what Zelius left on this thing. When I come back, I expect that my doors will be fixed. You are both mechanics, are you not?" She doesn't give us time to answer before disappearing into her room again.

We do our best to patch door overheads, but with limited materials, it isn't the prettiest job I've ever worked on. It is eerily quiet; Taxia's usually quippy attitude is completely missing. The only noise echoing through the halls is the sound of the Droid using his fingers to solder the holes closed. After we finish, Taxia heads back towards the bedroom.

"Hey Taxia..." I say softly. She stops just before entering. "I don't know what to do. I don't have a plan."

"I know..." she says solemnly before disappearing into her room as well.

That isn't very helpful.

After lying down on the couch, I realize why she's so quiet. I'm her ticket out of this place. In order for her to leave, I need to come up with a plan, and I don't have the first clue what

Hypatia is expecting me to do from here. I almost wish she had said, "Well, think of one!" at the least. I feel helpless and lost, and sitting here staring at the ceiling of my prison cell is only making it worse.

"Zelius, you relentless bastard!" I hear Hypatia yell from her room, even with the door closed. Hours have passed, I didn't even notice. The door to her room opens suddenly. She storms out in a huff, but composes herself.

"Not everything is meant to be known," she finally says, looking at me.

I return a puzzled glance.

"What does that mean? What did you find?" I ask.

"Proof. I didn't doubt him, but...now I know it's true. You really are a carbon copy. Zelius left the cloning process in great detail inside that vehicle. He assumed once the Droid found you, he would tell you to find the other prototypes. And once you found the other prototypes, you'd signal me, if I was still alive, because he knew I would help. Or at least stop anyone else who shouldn't see this information. And even though he was wrong about the exact circumstances, some-how, he was still 'right.' He wanted you to know. Wanted us to know."

"Does this mean you're going to help?" I ask.

"You don't understand what that could mean for you. For everyone."

"You can't just let me rot down here," I plead, looking around the grand living room.

"You'd break."

"All I know is how to put things back together," I say as she heads toward the hallway, beckoning me to follow her. She leads me back down the hallway until we hit the door before the rooms.

"I see the doors were repaired as requested," she says under her breath. She opens the doors in what she calls the "civilized way" and leads me to the holoroom.

"What's going on?" I ask nervously.

"Do you know your history, boy?" she asks with a stern glare.

"Yes?" Why does everyone keep asking me that?

"This Compendium you're after. If released, it could cause wars." With a flick of her hand, suddenly, we are in the middle of a chaotic warzone. A nearby explosion is loud and sudden enough to make me lose balance and fall. "The things we had to do." With another flick of her wrist, we're in the middle of a hospital that is overflowing with patients, screaming cries of pain, coughing, and gurgling noises.

As I get to my feet to look around, I can see the people there are suffering from some kind of disease that causes huge boils and discoloration of the skin. Nurses and doctors dressed in hazmat suits try frantically to keep up.

"The accomplishments that we all stand on." Another flick, this time, we sit in the middle of an enormous factory, watching machines creating millions of Droids, as other robots whizz around handling random tasks. These are older Droids, in what I assume is the original facility from a century ago.

"Queen Hypatia," she says, disgusted. We're in an empty room again, other than a holo image of Hypatia, but younger. Not that she looks much older now, but side by side, it's much easier to see the differences. "And King Zelius," she says as a holo of Zelius appears, he being much younger as well.

She stares for a moment at the two figures longingly. I study them as well, taking them in as if they are real. I can see myself in Zelius. But he was just...different. He seems so confident and regal. They both do.

"You may think you and he are different, but I assure you, you and he are one and the same. Whatever noble cause, whatever heroic aspirations you have, know that he had them too. He fought so hard for this world you see today. And you cannot change this world that significantly without getting blood on your hands. You have to understand..." she starts, before turning to the open doorway where Taxia now stands, listening quietly, making no particular expression, just watching.

"Go on..." she says after a few moments.

"You see, Ren, if you expose the Company, you expose yourself. Some may blame you for what Zelius did," she sighs.

"Then what is the point of him creating the Compendium?" I ask.

"That was the point. Full transparency," she answers. "He must have developed this plan even before I left."

"So what was his plan?"

"You. He wants you to make the decision. He wants you to decide if you still want the Compendium, knowing it'll mean you have to answer for his actions. Knowing you're going to be persecuted."

"What do you think I should do?"

"You don't want to know what I think."

"Tell me."

"Kill yourself. So I don't have to. You're an abomination. Cloning is science taking a step too far. We are given one chance. Two hundred years, maximum. No person should be able to alter time any more than that. I thought we agreed to that once..." she says, looking away from me at what I assume is some fleeting memory that has burrowed its way into her periphery. She turns and walks towards the doorway as I catch a glimpse of Taxia. She looks almost like she feels sorry for me. As Hypatia makes her exit, she stops in the doorway. "I cannot decide this for you. If you choose to continue on this path, I will not let you leave unprepared. But if you don't follow it through, I'm ending every little piece of this scheme.

The clues. The code. The players," she says, looking over at Taxia.

"When the alternative is death, it isn't much of a choice."

"Death, for some, can be an escape," she says, fading out of sight.

It's hard to swallow, and I choke at the seriousness of her threat. Flashes of the two UG members' bodies appear and vanish suddenly. I can feel myself starting to breathe faster. I pull at the neck of my shirt and try to think. There's a soft ringing in my ear from the explosion earlier. It was so real. It was like I was there. I've never experienced anything like it, its ability to recreate reality to such a degree and so quickly. I look around the empty room that was once filled with so many dizzying environments, and I feel like I'm losing myself.

"You okay?" Taxia gently murmurs from the doorway. I forgot she was still there.

"Uh, yeah. I think...for now," I say, coming back to reality.

"Why don't you sleep in the guest room tonight? I'll take the couch," she says, offering what seems like a sympathetic gesture. I'm not about to turn it down. As lavish as the couch is, it doesn't have pillows. And I miss pillows.

"Yeah? You don't mind?" I confirm.

"It's fine. We can trade back and forth," she says. "You sure you're okay?" She seems sincere.

"I don't know what she expects me to say to that."

"Maybe you should stop thinking about what she expects from you and start thinking about what you expect from her? She's giving you an out. Minus the threat to kill us all, it was kind of sweet. It almost sounded like she said she would help you if you wanted it."

I sit silently for a moment as she turns back down the hallway, leaving me there in the room.

By the time I make my way back, something in the kitchen

smells amazing. She's lying on the couch watching television with K-2.

"I left a bowl of ramen on the counter if you want it. Couldn't think of anything else to make," she says without looking over at me.

"Thanks," I say curiously. I'm not sure why she's being so nice. I am starving, though, so I dig in. She flips through channels and eventually settles on the news. I'm not in the mood to be reminded, so I head back to the guest room to lie down.

I take a big slurp out of the remaining ramen broth in the bowl and set it on a side table next to the bed. Laying down, I can immediately smell her. It's a mix of the soap that was left in the shower and...her. Pheromones, I guess? It smells good, too. I burrow my way into the bed and sigh in relief as I let myself drift off into thought.

Would Hypatia really kill us now if she didn't before?

How can she make sure I'm prepared?

Even if she does help, how can I reach ICON status before they catch on to me?

If I say no, Zander dies for nothing. Zelius's plan is all for nothing. What a waste.

If I say yes, I might get to see Elli and Zari again. Migo. Frank.

"It's time for you to make your mark on this damn world," I hear Frank's words echoing in my head.

CHAPTER TWENTY-THREE_

I jump up from bed, charge out of my room, and make my way to the Hypatia's door. Taxia is passed out with the TV on, and K-2 is in the corner meditating again. Glancing at the glowing clock on the screen, I notice it's been a few hours. I knock on Hypatia's door, but I can't hear anything, so I try again, harder this time. I notice the Droid stop meditating and glance over at me.

"What are you doing?" Taxia asks, sitting up and wiping the sleep from her eyes. I don't answer.

I begin to draw back my hand to knock again when suddenly the door opens.

"It's late. Out with it," Hypatia says, clearly showing signs she has been sleeping as well.

"I want to do it," I say sternly.

"Do what, exactly?"

"I want you to help me become like Zelius. If I'm going to pick up his mantle, I at least deserve to stand on his shoulders. To see the world from his eyes. That holoroom is more than enough to help me walk in his shoes. I can do it. I can be Zelius.

No, I can be better," I say, swelling with sudden confidence. My answer clearly intrigues her.

"Are you sure? It's not going to be easy. You have quite the shoes to fill."

"I'm dead sure. If you help me, I'll get the Compendium, and I promise I'll make my mark on this world."

She pauses for a moment, thinking it over. What seems like a lifetime passes. I glance at Taxia and we trade glances before looking back to see what Hypatia will say.

"We start in the morning," she says before abruptly closing her door.

I can't help but smile. If we are the same person, there should be no issue accomplishing what he did. I've never wanted to be a leader. I never asked for this. But sometimes, the choices you want to make are hidden behind the decisions you don't. If I can just get out of here, maybe I can take control of my own destiny. Frank always said I'd be serving on the board one day. Maybe I will.

I walk back to my room, and can feel Taxia's gaze, but I never look back.

After getting some of the best sleep of my life on the auto-adjusting mattress, which felt like a cloud, I'm startled awake by Hypatia.

"Holoroom. Five minutes," she says abruptly before heading in that direction.

I'm able to grab a few quick pancakes in the kitchen and wash up before heading to the back. Taxia is still sleeping on the couch as I pass by.

Even before I arrive in the room, I can see large stalks of grass peering out from inside. Entering the room is like stepping deep into the jungle. Vines and branches block what little pathway I can make out. While it's not 'real,' something about seeing it and interacting with it makes it feel so, almost like the mind makes up all the little details. There's a clearing at the center, where I find Hypatia roasting something over a campfire.

"Sit," she commands. I walk over and sit next to her near the fire. She pulls a marshmallow from a stick she has sitting in the fire and hands it to me. "Taste it."

I take a bite out of it, and it burns my tongue. "Ow!" I exclaim. Hypatia smiles slyly.

"But how?" I ask.

"This holoroom is unlike any other. Not everything you perceive within these walls is the product of mere programming and projections, so it's essential to your survival that you approach it with respect rather than treating it as a mere game," she says, standing up. "I thought about your idea nearly all night. To be honest, I find it a bit ambitious. Luckily, you're coming to the right person. I know every intimate detail about Zelius. I thought back to what formed him as a person. What made him so special. And there's always been one consistent part of his routine that he would return to year after year. One of the few things Zelius actually enjoyed that people today seem to think is another dubious legend. But it was true. All of them were. And considering the leaps and bounds you'll need to improve, I need to know that your ambitions don't outweigh your abilities. So, you shall be tested," she says, making her way to the edge of the clearing. "Good luck," she says before disappearing into the wilderness.

"Hey, wait!" I call out to nothingness. A test on my first day. Perfect.

The longer I sit, lit by the glow of the artificial campfire, the more real it all feels. I can hear the tall grass bristling in the wind as they brush up against each other. It becomes clear very quickly how powerful this simulation is. The minor details of the bugs making their squeaking chirps and the ceiling lights that are indistinguishable from the night sky seen from the furthest reaches of the Outskirtz. If you let your mind relax even for a second, you might forget you're miles beneath the ocean in an underground bunker. I have this unsettling feeling I am being watched. I assume Hypatia will be nearby watching the footage in a separate room, grading me against some scale I wasn't shown. But this is different. It feels ominous. Close.

I turn to look over my shoulder, barely able to see much beyond the dancing shadows of the grass and tree branches. The campfire bounces its waves of light onto the verdant meadow. As I peer into the darkness, a flicker of the campfire catches something bright yellow. A small disk of light refracted back at me. As the disc moves, one becomes two, and I realize what they are. Eyes. But of what, I'm not sure. Here we fucking go. I get up from the log I'm sitting on and slowly take a step back as the eyes move closer, flashing as it passes behind the blades of grass. I use small, deliberate steps as it nears the edge of the clearing. Just before it peeks its head out of the brush, I notice something moving around my feet. I look down to find a huge snake hissing at me and jump back instinctively.

"Fuck!" I shout before tripping and stumbling to the ground. The creature in the brush stands up at my scream. The artificial moonlight illuminates the silhouette to reveal a large bear. I've never seen a bear in person, but it's hard to mistake one for anything else. Moving away from the snake as quickly as I can, I'm not paying attention enough to realize I planted my hand right into the campfire.

"FUCK!!" I scream. The bear comes back down to all fours, and the light from its eyes disappears behind the foliage. I look down at the snake just in time to see it strike head-first toward my legs. I roll back as quickly as I can and get to my feet, holding my burnt hand in my other. Looking back, I can see several snakes now coming towards me, chasing me into the brush. When I get close to the edge of the brush, suddenly, I can see the bear's eyes again.

"FUCK!!!!" I yell, pivoting quickly to the other side of the brush and running as fast as I can. "HYPATIA! WHAT THE HELL KIND OF TEST IS THIS!?" I yell, running into the brush now towards the direction of the door. No response. And it never ends. I run and run, but no matter how far I feel like I get, I never come any closer to any kind of exit or door. The trees I pass never seem to resemble the one before it exactly. This simulation isn't repeating footage; it's tracking me and adjusting accordingly. I assume there's some sort of rotation happening under my feet, making the already large room feel even bigger than it is. Every sound I can hear is something dangerous I have to pay attention to. When the growls, snarls, hisses, and buzzing stops, I take a second to catch my breath and try to think. As soon as I do, I'm surrounded by what I think is a flock of birds. I quickly realize it's a swarm of bats. I throw my hands around me, trying to ward them off, but one has attached itself to my back. I can feel its claws dig into my skin as I try to reach it to get it off. I take off my shirt and throw it at the rest of the swarm before breaking out into another run. I really can't sit still. Is this part of the test?

I can feel the hot blood running down my back, the searing pain of my hand, and my lungs starting to burn from pumping so much air. Still running, I try to reason my way out of this madness. Is there a point to this? Does she expect me to fight a bear? I was given no instructions. I was given no goals. I was given nothing. Keeping a decent pace, I try to battle with the thoughts in my head until it becomes clear to me. Is she laughing somewhere, watching me struggle? Some kind of sick torture? How long would this go on?

"FUCK!!!!!" I feel a sharp pain in my foot. I look down to find a trail of ants leading their way into my shoe. I was standing still too long. I quickly pull it off and throw it into the darkness. I get a running start by hopping a few steps, then take the other shoe off and toss it as well. Working my way into a sprint, running barefoot, I can start to feel the ground beneath me rotating and adjusting. I make more sporadic movements now, zigzagging through the forest, hoping to throw things off. I've completely lost sight of the campfire, if it is even still being rendered. Only the moon and stars light the forest now, and I've completely lost any reference point for where the exit might have been when I came in earlier. I can't run forever, but every time I stop, it seems to trigger some life-or-death scenario. I slow my pace. Maybe I just need to keep moving but not running. I slow to a brisk walk before I notice my steps have become harder to lift off the ground. I stop for a moment to look down at my feet, which are sinking into the ground. Are you kidding me? Quicksand? Isn't that a bit... cliche?

Before getting too far in, I take a few steps back and am able to change directions to avoid sinking any further. Once freed, I pick up the pace into a light jog. So, even moving slowly doesn't stop events from triggering. I need to get to higher ground. I make my way to the nearest tree and begin to climb. It feels so real. Is this part of the simulation? The feel of bark under my fingertips? I get up to a branch sturdy enough to hold my weight and begin trying to survey my surroundings. It's impossible to see the edges of the room. The walls are mimicking the depth of a full forest.

"WHO!" I hear behind me. An Owl? I turn to look and can see just the eyes above me in a burrowed-out hole in the tree. Was that there before? Suddenly, the owl leaps out towards me, its wingspan fully extended and talons drawn out. I just barely get my head out of the way in time to avoid it, then turn to see the owl circling around for another attack. I begin making my way down the tree and back into the tall grass.

This continues for what feels like days. Dodging randomly spawning attacks, trying to get a grasp of where I am in the room. Looking for a door. With no directions, I have no idea what this test even is. A game of escape? A survival game? All I know is that it isn't fun. It's one panic attack after the next. My lungs are burning, my legs are cramping, and my stomach is grumbling. The thought crosses my mind to try and eat the next thing that attacks me. What was once a forest has slowly become an unforgiving jungle. I desperately search for some kind of opening, some pathway out of it all. After a while, I can start to see the sun rising in the distance. Moving now solely on fumes, I head for the rising sun as it shines through the heavy jungle brush. I can hear the rumbling growls of an animal I don't have the heart to look at, so I ignore it and all the other sounds until I'm met with an open clearing. On the other side of the clearing, I can see rustling in the grass. Again, the large figure from this morning appears, this time lit by the rising sun. I can now confirm it is, in fact, a bear. I can either keep moving forward or head back into the jungle. The bear doesn't give me any time to think and growls as it charges at me. I stumble back again, lightheaded, starving, out of energy, and on my ass. I barely have enough energy to hold out my hands in some feeble attempt to stop the bear in his tracks. Right as the bear reaches me, I brace for the impact and close my eyes. This is it. This is how I die. Fuck.

No highlight reel of my life plays. I don't see any bright light. There's...nothing.

I slowly open my eyes to find myself a few steps away from the door to the holoroom. The door opens and Taxia comes bursting through, Hypatia slowly following behind.

CHAPTER TWENTY-FOUR_

"ARE YOU OKAY?" Taxia yells to me, running over. I fall onto my back, out of breath, feeling utterly wrecked. I'm relieved, though, that the nightmare is over. "Ren, are you ok?" Taxia repeats. "I heard screams, and Hypatia wouldn't tell me anything! You look terrible! What's going on? And what happened to your shoes?" she says, looking at my torn, bare bloody feet.

Hypatia tosses my shoes over and they land beside me. "Here. So you don't track blood through the house. By the way, you passed the test."

"Some test!" I squeak out. "What was the point of that? How is being left alone in a jungle full of every old-world predator from the northern hemisphere going to teach me how to become Zelius?"

"It's called a stress test for a reason, boy. Zelius is the one who created this program as a training simulation for the military. He used to run through it himself when he wanted a taste of...reality. It's been long retired now due to psychological trauma, but we always felt it was quite effective at both evaluating and strengthening one's mental and physical state. Or breaking it," she smirks.

"This isn't what I had in mind when I..." I start before she cuts me off.

"I needed the data. I now have your heart rate variability, V_{O2} max, and a blood sample, which gave me a comprehensive metabolic panel and hormone panel. I also got a detailed reading of your brain activity that I used for a preliminary mental evaluation, which you passed as well. The full mental examination will take place after you recover. But for now, we will proceed as I have planned," she explains.

I'm stun-locked. Passing is the last thing on my mind. The worst night of my life was a playful game for Zelius? Something he used to do for his routine checkups? Did I pass because I'm not... dead?

"Now, Taxia, help him to the guest room, will you, darling?" she says, then vanishes out of the holoroom.

"Darling?" Taxia questions under her breath. She helps me to my feet, and we make our way to the guest room. K-2 is waiting in the hallway, somehow looking concerned.

"I was getting the most dreadful readings from your biosignature. Are you okay?" he says worriedly.

"He's fine," Hypatia cuts in as we walk by.

"I'm fine, thanks," I say to the Droid, partially held up by Taxia.

Once in the guest room, Hypatia waves her hand in front of one of the walls and out comes a full medical tank. Something that wasn't in the blueprints, as far as I could tell.

"You'll spend an hour in the tank, and then you will complete the assessments I've left within this tablet. They aren't easy. Don't procrastinate, as they will be part of the discussion before tomorrow's test."

"Another test? You know you can just kill me now, right? I

thought I was going to learn about his life and how he became who he is? So I can figure out a plan?"

"Trust the process. The assessments will detail his political and scholastic accomplishments, decorated history of military service, and his personal historical perspective. It's all in there. There are people who would kill for these Zelius manuscripts. So study well. I'll see you in the morning," she stops by the doorway before leaving. "Well done."

"Well done? Is she being sarcastic? You're a few small steps from death. What the hell happened in there? You were attacked by animals?" Taxia says, helping me into the tank.

"Lions...tigers...and bears. The usual assortment of hair-raising creatures of the night," I respond, struggling through the words. I'm growing faint and have probably lost more blood than I realized. Another scar to add to the lovely one across my face.

The tank is a large pod filled with nano-creatures that penetrate any wounds, disinfect by eating any harmful bacteria, and shit out the building blocks your body needs for recovery. I lay down in the tub as Taxia closes the clear bubble-like enclosure. Once sealed, the tub begins to fill with the water solution. These things are considered highly luxurious. Anyone who has one needs to be granted consent and state a specific reason for having one. Even though I know it's meant to heal me, I can't help but feel a bit claustrophobic. Regardless, I grab the mask that is now floating in the water and hit the button on the side to seal it around my face. The solution is the same temperature as the human body, so it feels like floating. Once I give in and relax, it slowly becomes the most comfortable I've ever been. I can feel the tingling of my wounds as the nano-creatures start their dinner. I'm starving but dead tired. I begin to copy the Droid's meditative state, and before fully closing my eyes, I can see Taxia eating food on the end of the bed, watching me.

I'm not quite sleeping, not quite awake. In some trance-like state, I can completely evaluate my performance. I'm no longer so concerned with the fear. Instead, I'm fascinated, slowly and methodically, working out each little individual piece that would have to fall into place to make something as complex as a jungle feel so real.

I wasn't tapped-in or even heads up; there was no indication anything was being projected, and everything seemed to have the right weight and feel. The texture of the bark was rough on my skin and left little smudges of broken particles on my fingertips. At a minimum, the room felt like it had quadrupled in size. I had run miles in any given direction and the room couldn't possibly have grown, so it must be a rotating system of some kind. Unless the room appears smaller than it really is? How massive is this compound? Then there were the animals and insects. The life. Some kind of robotic structure combined with a synthetic exo-layer, with the holographic projections used to round out the aesthetics, maybe? It was hard to know if every animal I was physically in contact with was real, as I had only been attacked by a fraction of the animals I saw. And what kind of device was she using to pick up my brain waves at a distance?

I go on like this for longer than I realize because, before I know it, the beeping of the machine snaps me out of my daze. The water begins to empty through holes that have opened in the bottom of the tub until there's enough room for me to take off my mask. Taxia is no longer in the room, and the door is closed, so I assume she's gone to the couch to let me have the space. There's a tracksuit on the bed, sweatpants and a hoodie. They must be from a 3DCP because they're seamless, like the ones Elli gave me. I get out of the tub and take off the only article of clothing I have left on, which is my soaked boxers.

The door flings open.

"I know you love pancakes, so I made-" she stops mid-sentence, stunned to find what looks like an empty room. I'm not about to have a repeat of Elli, so I quickly dove behind the bed. I groan slightly at the impact of hitting the ground shoulder first.

"Ren?" she calls out.

"Yup, just changing!"

"Oop. Um. Okay, I'll just wait outside," she says, turning around and shutting the door by pressing her elbow to the button. The door slides closed, and I grab the clothes, quickly wrestling them on.

"All clear," I say through the door.

"Glacious," she says, walking back in. "As I was saying, I wasn't sure which you'd like, so I got banana, chocolate, and blueberry pancakes."

"Oh... thanks! I usually just eat it plain, with some protein added," I say. She looks disappointed. "But I'm starving, so hand them over," I smile, grabbing the platter of pancakes.

I place the platter on the bed and sit down next to it. I make it through three pancakes, each one a different flavor, before I realize Taxia is still standing in the doorway, my mouth still full of bits of breakfast, or lunch—is it dinner? I have completely lost my sense of time.

"Don't you want any?"

"Oh no, those are for you!"

"I'm obviously not going to eat all that myself. Have some," I say, ushering her onto the bed next to me.

"Ummm.... Okay, sure," she says semi-reluctantly. She takes one of the blueberry-flavored pancakes and begins eating. Her head down, she stares at her knees. "Are you feeling any better?" she says, not looking up from her knees.

"Well, I'm still in a somewhat of a mental fog. Not sure if this is breakfast or dinner that I'm eating. But physically, I feel great. More than great. I feel...better? Like I used to have this kink in my back from leaning over in the workshop. It's not bothering me at all anymore. I mean, that tank is one of those things you hear about in whispers in the Outskirtz. You ever come across one at your shop?" I say in between bites.

"Me?" She chuckles. "You've been to my shop. A meditank is not exactly something someone would throw away. You know you don't have to put yourself through this, right? Isn't there another way?" she asks.

"Nice! I was hoping you had a plan! I'm all ears!" I say, leaning forward.

"Oh, well... I don't have a plan..." she says, looking at me sadly before she realizes I have a smile on my face. "Funny!" she nudges my shoulder.

"Well, then, I guess this is the only way. If I can put myself in his shoes, maybe we can walk right out of here," I explain.

"Last time you tried that, you ended up shoeless and daringly close to death," she points out.

"You either get busy living, or get busy dying," I chuckle.

"Huh?"

"Nothing. Something my boss Frank used to say."

It hasn't hit me until now, but Taxia is acting completely differently. Fuck. I look down at the pancakes and back at her.

"What?" she says, questioning my stare.

"You didn't... poison me, did you?"

"What? No, why?"

"You're being... nice."

"I...I guess I've just had time to think about it all, and if It wasn't for you, I'd be dead. Now that you're my only way out of here, I've got to make sure you stay alive. I mean, if you die, you think Hypatia will keep me around for my looks?"

"Have you seen my face? I don't think that's a qualifying factor," I say, lifting a piece of my hair to reveal my scar.

"It's not so bad," she says, reaching over and lifting my hair herself to look over the scar. "How did it happen?"

"Actually, that's my fault." K-2 is standing in the open doorway. It's odd. It's such a small room, but I don't notice a nearly six-foot robot entering the room? Must have been distracted.

"How long have you been standing there, K-2?" I ask, startled.

"39 seconds…40 seconds…41 seconds…" he begins.

"Okay buddy, I got 'chu," I say, trying to calm him.

"I'm sorry to disturb you. I was waiting for a moment to attain visual confirmation that you are fully recovered," he says while seeming to perform a digital scan of some kind.

"I'm fine. Thanks. Think I've been scanned enough for one day. Sorry, I don't have more for you to do."

"Oh. Well, actually, I quite enjoyed cleaning the kitchen just now. Taxia left multiple messes. Thank you, Taxia," he says in a tone that sounds like sincere joy.

"You're welcome," Taxia says, smiling with embarrassment.

"What were you saying about my scar?" I ask.

"Yes. The blast radius of the explosion that killed Zelius was quite… large. Since we were still relatively close, some pieces of burning debris…well. I tried to protect you, but, as you can see…some got through," he says, gesturing to my scar.

I feel the scar across my head. So I almost died along with Zelius.

"Well, I can barely even see it," Taxia says, cutting the silence with a comforting smile, which I return.

"It is located on the upper right portion of his head right here," the Droid says, getting closer and pointing directly at it.

"OH, THAT? WHAT IS THAT?" she says, then chuckles to herself.

"Thanks, *Droid*. What time is it anyway?" I ask.

"8:00 p.m.," K-2 Responds.

"I don't know how long it's going to take, so I need to get started on this assessment," I say, looking over at the tablet Hypatia gave me.

"Understood, Sir. Well, good luck with the assessment. It would be nice to have Zelius back," he says before exiting the room.

"Taxia... Taxia..." Taxia starts in a spooky voice. "Do you hear that? It's the couch calling my name. Taxia..." she continues.

"Out of principle, I would advise against following spooky voices calling your name," I say as she gets up from the bed and stops at the door.

"It's fine; she gets like every channel in here somehow. You can have the bedroom for now. Besides, it's not like I'd get much sleep in here," she says and pauses a moment. "Hypatia seems to enjoy waking you up at the break of dawn, and if I'm going to be a prisoner, I'm at least going to sleep in. Good luck," she says, smiling slightly before heading out.

CHAPTER TWENTY-FIVE_

The tablet is filled with various folders, each with a specific topic. I navigate through the individual ones to understand the scope of what has been assigned. It's an intimidating amount of work and it's been ages since I've done anything academic. The test comes with a required reading beforehand called a historical overview, which I view as an almost merciful act until I realize how long it is. I guess I should have expected tough assignments, but there is no way I'm going to be able to complete this all before morning if I sleep. She knows that.

I never had any issues in ranking; I just got bored after rank twelve. Plus, it's bad luck to stop at rank thirteen, so I quit while I was ahead. In the Outskirtz, most people stop at rank ten anyway. I wonder what level Zari was? I've heard of people hitting rank twenty, so I bet she had to be even higher than that, considering her mastery. I'm procrastinating. I regain control over the crippling anxiety holding me back and begin to dig into the historical overview.

It starts, "Once there was silence, now, there is music." I expect to be hit over the head with the methodically dull passages of typical MetiCorp academic literature, but even after just a few sentences, I'm spellbound. In it, Zelius writes with more authority, coherence, and logic than I have seen in any other text of his. It's somehow succinct and, at the same time, dense. I am enthralled. Zelius takes on the perspective of the universe as he provides an overview covering the history of the cosmos, the Earth, the fauna, biodiversity, and human achievement. It somehow reads like a novel, telling little connected stories as it flows seamlessly through the various subject matter.

I am careful to try and sus out any embellishments when Zelius discusses his own innovations, but it's free from bias, almost to the point of being emotionless. He makes astute observations about complex concepts and draws upon their correlations in order to bind them in your mind. He advises the reader that all knowledge flows from matter's vibrational frequencies, which he calls music. Zelius views anything that is affected by entropy as data, arguing that all matter is data when viewed through the proper lens. Using this framework, he's able to simplify nature's most prominent algorithms, providing small equations he says are the most efficient ways to view, interpret, and calculate data.

I finished the overview by noon, but I was so captivated by the words that I decided to go back and reread bits of it because it's hard to pull myself away. When I'm finally able to, I move on to the first subject: mathematics. Gone are the sprawling walls of text filled with flowery literary language in a potent stream-of-consciousness style. Instead, this section is strictly high-level mathematical concepts and formulaic equations. The questions aren't multiple choice, just a box big enough to submit your answer. I feel confident, though, as this was one of the areas I excelled at in ranking. My anxiety comes down a notch as I realize the test really just wants to confirm if you understand the basic concepts, not throwing any curveballs off the bat.

The chemistry section is harder to feel confident about, but even with my unfamiliarity, I find myself breezing through it as easily as the math section. It isn't because I have some photographic image saved in the archives of my sleep-deprived brain; instead, it's the overview. What Zelius wrote, I now realize, are essential fundamental truths that are ubiquitous throughout all systems. They are all causal and linked. This test seems to be trying to prove the point that the answers are all clear once you fully adopt his perspective.

"Yo!" I hear suddenly. I look up and Taxia is standing by the doorway. I can see K-2 peering out from behind her, again, looking concerned. I never quite understand how he is so able to convey human emotions without a face. Taxia's expression is one of concern as well. Her brow is furrowed and her nose is crinkled. I find myself staring. It's oddly endearing, and I'm confused by the comfort her sudden presence gives me.

"You okay? You look...out of it? Did Hypatia plant some mind-numbing virus in there?" she says jokingly.

I chuckle, breaking myself out of the stare. "No, it's actually...really interesting. It's got this overview Zelius wrote and it's the size of a novel."

"A novel? Like the ones of his we read in ranking? I mean, he clearly was an intelligent man, but I was never blown away by any of it," Taxia explains.

"Yeah, neither was I. This is...entirely different. It makes me wonder if what we read from him was really him or some highly edited and watered-down version," I say, once again wandering into thought.

"Interesting. I'll be reading that when you're done, obviously. Anyway, I didn't want to bother you, but it's been dead silent in here for hours and you haven't come out to eat once. I made extra if you're hungry," she says, handing me a plate I hadn't even noticed she was holding. It's filled with a dozen or so pastries, each with intricately carved flower-shaped tops glistening in sugar or butter.

"Thanks! ...what are they?" I say, picking one up and smelling it. It smells sweet and savory but unfamiliar.

"Never had one? We just call them meat pies where I'm from. I've had to cook for myself since I was fourteen, so I made it a priority to get a food printer as soon as I could find one. I found and repaired my very own food printer a few months later. So you could say I've had some practice. In fact, this is my specific recipe. Let me know what you think," she says with a smile, watching for my reaction.

"Sounds amazing. I'm actually starving," I say, looking down at it. How bad could it be? I take a bite through a flakey crust, with some of the top slightly crunchy in texture. I sink my teeth in and can immediately taste the savory protein inside. I had to take a second bite to try and confirm what animal signature she used, but I knew immediately it was quite possibly the best thing I've tasted since pancakes. It's hearty yet light. It is crunchy and flakey, but soft. Surprisingly delicious. I've cleaned the plate before I even look up again. I can see Taxia's bottom lip pushing up as she lets out an audible, "aww."

"So you liked it, huh?" she chuckles. I can see K-2's shoulder shaking with laughter as he peeks out from around the corner, trying to hide and failing miserably.

"Yeah! I'm stuffed! Wait... was that meant to be shared?" I say, squinting and rubbing the back of my head.

"Well, it'd be a damn shame if it was, wouldn't it?" she asks jokingly. "No, I just wanted to drop it off. The RFL reruns are on soon, so I'm going to catch that."

"Robot Fight League..." I say, looking down. It was all Elli could talk about the night before...

"Don't tell me you haven't heard of that either? As a mechanic from the Outskirtz? It's like the sandscav official sport," she asks, puzzled.

"I used to watch it as a kid but felt like it became too theatrical as it progressed," I shrug.

"That's the best part." She smiles. "And just like the O-Races, it's opened up to all cities and made it easier for amateurs to participate. The current champion is actually from your city, MetiCity-6, and he's so unstoppable. Lately, there have been a lot more creative bots. We should watch it sometime."

"We should," I confirm.

"We should. Okay, I'm going to go before I miss out on any of the THEATRICAL walkouts." She giggles, heading out of my line of sight.

"Hey Taxia?" I say, almost without thinking.

"Yes?" She says, only sticking her head around the corner.

"I'm going to figure this all out. And I'm going to get us out of here," I say sternly.

"I know," she says back sternly as well before smiling again. "Why do you think I've been making sure you don't starve to death? You're my ticket out of here. So get back to work," she commands sarcastically. So I do just that.

The biotech, physics, and engineering sections go by with a breeze. I'm worried the break might have slowed down my momentum, but the food seems to have invigorated me. She really knows her way around a printer, which is something that is brought up in the historical overview. It was first theorized by someone named Watson Hudson, who sent the designs to Zelius to create. Slowly, the story of Zelius being the sole innovator of

MetiCity life is peeled back as these and the revelations of Hypatia are put into focus. The technology utilized by the food printers is mentioned again in the engineering section. It asks an interesting question about the difference between molecularly assembled food vs. organically grown produce. The answer is, in fact, none. Something that is considered blasphemous among the sandscavengers. And while the answer was confirmed correct, it was hard to submit, considering I know in my heart I disagreed. Regardless of the source, in the right hands, assembled food is better.

I look at the clock and notice I have worked my way into the night. I stroll into the kitchen area to grab some water and find Taxia passed out on the couch, half her body hanging uncomfortably over the edge. K-2 is in the corner meditating again when I notice his sensor come on. I put my index finger over my mouth to signal to be quiet, and the Droid nods slightly. The light in his face dims back down as he returns to meditation.

Back in the room, I complete the philosophy section and move on to the art section. I'm surprised to find another passage by Zelius at the end of it. It's a continuation of the overview. However, this time, he slowly and meticulously translates the various vibrational frequencies of matter into individual musical notes. He then combines them to form simple harmonies which represent different states of matter. Zelius says that he, the universe, is but one string. Affected by the strings that surround him. He says in order to explain the quantum fluctuations that perplexed twenty-first-century scholars, you must first understand the resonant frequency of the other strings. I spend longer pondering this section than I anticipated, and before I know it, it's morning. I have an hour left before Hypatia will likely come barging into my room, ready to drag me back into the jungle. I can't help but read it again before completing the final section. I finish it up in a rush and am done with time to spare.

I think it might be a good idea to eat before this next test, so I grab some leftover pies. I don't see Taxia or K-2 in the living room area or the kitchen. The worry surprised me at first; how quickly I went from wanting her to suffer to wanting to make sure she wasn't.

Apparently, I finished the tests in the nick of time because I can hear a loud knock right after I sit down to eat. The synchronicity of it spooks me a little, but I'm up and on my feet. I meet Hypatia at the door. She doesn't make eye contact but simply holds her hand out. I hand her the tablet. She grabs it and begins walking down the hallway, muttering things under her breath.

"Mmm hmmm...hmmmm," she whispers as I try to keep pace.

"Where is Taxia?" I ask.

"In the garden," she quickly responds.

"Oh." I guess it's not the worst place to be. It is a gorgeous garden, and the artificial sunlight is set up in a way that feels just like the sun on a cool summer day, breeze and all. Those are so rare nowadays. "How did I do?"

"Interesting. Well, it isn't bad, but not perfect. And music scores. Abysmal. Which is odd considering..." She stops mid-sentence.

"Considering what? I've never even played an instrument," I ask.

"Hmm, that might be why. I shall have to adjust your training accordingly."

"Sounds like I did pretty good, though, right?"

"Pretty good? Have you stopped to consider you might have done better if you had never gone through ranking at all?"

To be honest, I had. A lot of the questions were phrased in a way that had me pushing back against some of my common thoughts and perceptions. That being said, it didn't leave the questions weighing any less on my mind.

"Exactly. I will add music to your training regimen," she advises.

"Music? Is that relevant?" I ask.

"Ren. 'Once you know the way broadly, you will see it in everything.'" She seems to be quoting someone. I can't tell; I haven't heard it before. "Enter." She guides me.

CHAPTER TWENTY-SIX_

I step into the empty holoroom and nothing is being projected. The system is completely off. It's strange looking at it again at this size, considering how endless it felt last night. Wait, no. The day before yesterday. Time, like sleep, has been escaping me as of late.

"You've got quite the shoes to fill today. Zelius was extremely adamant he be involved in nearly every aspect of governing. He lived through times of war and times of peace. I've designed this test to exemplify what would be considered a "typical" day for him. This test will be scored on a sixty-point 'must' system, as in, you must make it through with at least sixty points. The more like Zelius you are, the less likely you are to lose points. Once you fall below sixty points, the test restarts. You have three attempts. Now, begin," she says abruptly before the holoroom's doors close. Right in front of my eyes, I can see the door disappear and I find myself looking down a long, empty hallway.

"Sir?" I hear a voice call from behind me. "We're going to be late," he says as I turn back around. I can see it is someone in the classic uniform of Zelius's standing army. There is no longer a standing army now, so seeing the uniform in such pristine condition is jarring. I must have lost track of timing trying to assess the situation because the man is now staring at me with a grave look on his face. Almost like he's never seen Zelius look confused before. "Are you feeling alright, sir?" he asks, concerned.

"I'm fine," I respond, trying to get my bearings. I look down and notice my clothing has changed as well. The odd thing is that my uniform feels real. The capabilities of this holoroom are constantly astonishing.

BRRRRRt. The sound shocks me at first, some kind of buzzer.

"Ten-point deduction. Ninety points remaining," a soft voice says. I can't tell if it's a speaker or something being beamed directly into my head.

I can hear it loud and clear, but from the look on the guy in front of me, it seems I'm the only one who can. I must have gotten the deduction for taking too long and arriving at the meeting behind schedule. Now this I can deal with. Rules. Parameters. It's certainly better than spending the night being hunted, slowly descending into the madness of the jungle. I adjust my posture and try to assume the role I was given.

"Ahem. Shall we?" I usher the man forward and follow closely behind him. As we walk down the hallway and approach the door at the end of it, he begins preparing me for what sounds like a possible board meeting. The thought alone has me reeling. How accurate can she make this? Most people would kill to sit in on a board meeting.

"Yes, sir. All members are present and accounted for. We've got your briefing here with the most recent numbers from the front lines as well as the most up-to-date satellite imagery." He hands me a tablet very similar to the one Hypatia had given me for the assessment. The door opens to a room with a large table sitting in the middle. It's modern, yet grand and circular, like it once sat the Knights of the Round. The exterior wall has a large window that brings in the light from the rising sun. I step in and the door shuts behind me. I walk towards the only empty chair left in the room, trying not to make eye contact or seem too curious. I'm still able to sneak glances at each of the seated individuals without raising any flags. All four of the original city's board members are present, and since there is a fifth person, I can narrow the time to the 2080s. That was around the time they began adding members to govern the additional cities they had recently built.

Directly to my left is Shinzo Takamatsu, nicknamed "the Shogun." He was instrumental in bringing the classically Eastern Powers aboard the MetiCorp banner. Asia was one of the first to be heavily impacted by the climate catastrophe and the people of those nations had to relocate en masse. Zelius promised to provide shelter by building a MetiCity there. Shinzo, having control of the Eastern Powers coalition's army, committed his forces to Zelius early on in a backroom deal. On the board, Shinzo mostly specialized in war strategy and also led a highly secretive espionage team they code-named 'Ninja.' Shinzo sent them into various societies years before full war broke out, and using the most advanced mods of the time, they were able to topple world powers and recruit from within them.

Sitting across from me is Mobi Kantu. He was from Africa, Nigeria, to be precise. He was known for being one of the earliest adopters of MetiCity. He was able to speak every African language, over two hundred and fifty, and was also an Oxford-educated citizen of Britain. His utilization of advanced guerilla tactics combined with the aura of being a holy man allowed him to unite the various clans and nations of Africa. He declared himself the next prophet in the line of Krishna, Buddha, and Jesus, lumping all the previous deities and prophets into one who we now call the Allspirits. At a time when the population of religious adherents in the world was plummeting, Mobi sparked a religious revolution. Zelius adapted the holy man's beliefs into his own in order to secure his growing population of followers. When Zelius died, Mobi released a series of cryptic texts about the future. The texts are responsible for the establishment of the UnderGround, and to this day, they still fuel their wild conspiracies. The prophecy included in the text says if humans can live in harmony for long enough, the Allspirits will send us a savior. It is said he will 'join our songs, harmonizing as he welcomes us to everlasting enlightenment.' Whatever that means.

On Mobi's right is Iara Costa. Iara was born to the indigenous Ticuna people of Brazil. Her claim to fame is leading the expedition that discovered the Jardinera. She was a Naval Architect who served as Brazil's Minister of the Environment. As the foremost expert on offshore engineering, Zelius himself even consulted her when designing the original cities. Her political life focused on creating a committee to draft conservation legislation aimed at protecting indigenous land. When treaty after treaty was broken, she orchestrated a protest so massive it turned into a full-scale riot. By the end, the governments of all South American Countries were dismantled. Part of her agreement for coming on as a board member was that she would get to design the planned additional cities. With her help, Zelius was able to build further out into the Atlantic Ocean, connecting South America and Africa.

On Mobi's left is Joseph Hunter, nicknamed 'The Last President,' a play on one of Zelius's many titles, 'The Last King.' He was the one who negotiated the surrender of the United States, but only after their currency had completely collapsed. He's somewhat of a folk hero to his people, though, having survived an assassination attempt by a militant fundamentalist Christian organization. What's lesser known is he was a member of that organization before he became president. The story is he fought his way out, guns blazing, using his secret service members as body shields. They even made a movie about it. In the reading, it was said that Joseph was the perfect embodiment of keeping your enemies close.

Lastly, there is the face I had seen in person, sitting to the right of me. Gideon Stein. A totally menacing figure, muscles full of the old mods, towering in height. He gave the speech at the opening ceremony of the race. The reading from last night barely references him other than to say he was a friend and right-hand man to Zelius. That he was responsible for creating the controller force regulations and training, so I'd guess he has some sort of law enforcement history. After Zelius's death, he remained relatively unseen until his last appearance. I think back to the newscasters prioritizing his death over the hundreds of others. I know that if he is in this room, it means his contributions were at least equal to the others. Though, I'm still not sure how anyone was able to get the upper hand on him now that I've seen him up close.

Either way, I'm astonished. Ren Ukno, sitting in front of the creators of the world as we see it today. Everything we have now is directly related to the accomplishments of this group of people. As bloody as their hands may be, it's easy to see I'm sitting at the table with some of the most strategically fearless people the world has ever seen.

"May our songs be heard, Anarki," Mobi says first, bowing slightly towards me. I bow back and say thank you.

BRRRRRt. A buzzer sounds.

"Ten-point deduction. Eighty points remaining."

Mobi and the rest look at me oddly. Allspirits. Points are already falling and the meeting has barely gotten off the ground. The pressure is mounting and I only have what seems like three mistakes left. I'm slow to remember the greeting. It was written in the overview and I've heard the phrase before.

"May harmony guide us to peace," I say, having finally found the words.

DING! A chime sounds.

"Correction, eighty-five points remaining," the voice again notifies me.

What? I can earn points, too?

Everyone is staring at me again, this time not confused but more...expectant. I need to have them lead this as much as possible. That way, I can avoid having to say too much.

"Well?" I say, putting my palms up towards them.

"Ahem. I'll go first," Joseph speaks first. He has some sort of cigar-like vaping device he hits before beginning. Smells so much like one, I wonder why not just burn the real thing. "I'm sure you've seen the casualties from the front lines, and I just want to make sure you don't go calling in Gideon to go all biblical. To solve this, it's going to take a more...democratic approach."

I hear audible groans from some of the board members. I'm not sure if it is a subtle prod at me or a bad joke, but he continues nonetheless. He goes on to describe the situation on the ground near the post-American border. He says there were protests regarding a new tax he was trying to implement. He had earmarked it within their surrender agreement, and they weren't happy about it.

"What new tax?" I ask, cutting him off. Zelius made it clear there would be no taxes in all of his writing. Even now, years later, the board hasn't been able to implement any taxation within the social credit system. Any changes to the system are seen as traitorous, and even the mention of them could lead to mass riots.

"Was I not clear?" I ask. I know I have some leeway in the amount of dominance I assert.

"Yes! Of course. This was meant to be a gift! To be used as a patronage to the great Zelius!" He smiles. Iara puts her face in her hand for a moment. They aren't shy about showing their disdain for him. He can't possibly be stupid enough to think I will go for this. "Say the word, I'll tell the rebels there will be no such tax, and all further negotiation will include the stipulation that the contract must be signed. I just thought we might exhaust all the options at our disposal," he continues.

"And I'm sure the people of your city won't be confused as to whose idea this tax was when you tell them it wasn't Zelius's," Gideon says calmly to Joseph. Suddenly, the smile disappears from Joseph's face.

"Of course! Of course! I shall have this taken care of at the soonest opportunity. I'm sure you all have more important business to take care of then; that's all from me," he says, shrinking back into his seat.

"As a matter of fact, we do," Iara suddenly begins, "conditions at the mining colony have been deteriorating since their supply lines were attacked. There are whispers of a major strike if things aren't improved. Zelius, we cannot continue to spread ourselves so close to the margins. We need to begin to rebuild and stop focusing so much on these tiny factions of dissidents."

"I remember we were once a small faction of dissidents ourselves, Iara," Mobi speaks now. It seems like a sincere compliment to cut the tension.

"Yes, but if we don't improve their conditions first, we're going to see even bigger numbers joining their cause. We must show them that our way is a peaceful way, a way of abundance," Iara continues.

"Yeah, I'm not sure PR is our problem," Joseph cuts in.

"He is correct," Shinzo chimes in. "Those who are left will not be conquered by advertisements of us living peacefully. It will only strengthen their cause. We should keep advancing and allow the enemy no safe haven. Push them to the Outskirtz. Then, we can work on fixing the miners' conditions. I've seen the bases; the concessions are not necessities and will take a large portion of manpower to execute. To lose focus now would give them time to think. I have nightmares about giving them time to think," he confesses. "And there is actionable intelligence backing up those nightmares," he adds, his eyes hidden beneath the Japanese kasa he wears. "Any leniency we give could lead to drastic changes in their strategy's effectiveness."

"It's hard for me to say, from my perspective. As one of the first cities, I am forced to agree with Iara." Mobi gestures towards her. "We must support the workers to ensure steady shipments of MetiMetal continue. If we lose the miners at this critical time, the ripple effects could interfere with the sincerity of our intentions to provide shelter to surrendering forces. We must show them that those who have signed the contract are living in harmony," Mobi adds.

So Iara and Mobi want to focus on the miners, while Shinzo and Joseph want to continue the fight.

"Gideon?" I look over his way to get his opinion. He looks shocked to have heard his name.

BRRRRRt. The buzzer sounds.

"Ten-point deduction. Seventy-five points remaining."

What did I do this time?

"You honor me, Zelius, but I will always defer to you on such matters," Gideon replies almost nervously. Strange coming from someone towering over Zelius horizontally and vertically.

He sits on the board but doesn't have a say? Do I not need to hear all their opinions first?

"Ahem." I sit forward, trying to retain any last bit of composure I have.

"It would seem that both matters are urgent. However, after reviewing the casualties on the front line, I'm inclined to pull back before any more lives are senselessly lost. Shinzo, have your Ninja already infiltrated the rebelling factions?"

"Hai. However, information travels slowly as the encrypted messages take time to decipher. They use a system of private, in-person handoffs where the messages come in the form of a song. Once the message is received, it must be repeated for verification. For those of my men who are not musically trained, a wrong note has often come with a death sentence," Shinzo explains.

On a typical day, Zelius decides the fate of millions of people. I think deeply about this decision as I assume an unworthy response will come with another deduction. Scanning briefly through the information provided on the tablet, I noticed there was recently an armory robbery where confiscated weapons were stolen before they could be destroyed. I don't recall any strikes on the mining base, but I do remember there were attacks up until just before Zelius died in the 2090s. Solving the theft would be his priority and keep Shinzo's agents busy while we provide the much-needed aid to our miners. Joseph's complicated relationship with the rebelling factions also pushes me further into Mobi and Iara's corner.

"We will await the intel from your agents so we can find out how the weaponry was stolen from the armories. If they were able to access those facilities, it means it's possible we've been infiltrated as well. If so, we need to stop this hemorrhaging immediately. Meanwhile, we cannot lose sight of the important role our supply chain plays in the-"

BOOM!

Before I finish my sentence, the window behind us explodes, throwing us back against the opposite wall. The deafening ringing in my ears reverberates as guards run in. They are yelling my name and trying to help me to my feet. The area just inches away from where I was sitting is now a huge hole of smoldering rubble. Shinzo runs towards the hole to see where the explosion had come from.

"Rebels. Using rocket launchers. Archaic," Shinzo yells back to us. "I'll show you old weapons!" He screams, then pulls out a sword with a glowing edge before jumping down about thirty floors with zero hesitation. Gideon runs over to survey the area below and begins speaking to a team on coms. I can hear gunfire and yelling below, but my security is pulling me towards the exit. I look back at the rest of the board who watch as I am pulled out of the room and see them all head towards the large hole in the wall to watch Shinzo fight.

BRRRRRt. A buzzer sounds.

"Ten-point deduction. Sixty-five points remaining."

On a typical day, Zelius survives assassination attempts? It's utterly unbelievable. How am I supposed to know what to do or say in this situation? I was almost just blown to pieces! I can still feel the singed hairs on the back of my neck sizzling from the extreme heat.

"Sir, we have to get you to a secure location; please follow us!" The gentleman who had shown me into the boardroom pleads with me. I follow his men down an emergency stairway and barely get two steps before...

BRRRRRt.

"Ten-point deduction. Game Over."

CHAPTER TWENTY-SEVEN_

The entire façade quickly fades, and I find myself back in the hallway with the same assistant as before.

"Sir?" I hear a voice call from behind me.

There is no delay in the restarts, and I only have two more chances. I start to get nervous. Would Hypatia kill me if I don't pass? She said it was a 'typical' day for Zelius. I guess he just survived random terrorist attacks on a regular basis. Why not?

"Is everyone ready to proceed?" I ask, trying to avoid the deduction for being late.

"Yes, sir. All members are present and accounted for. We've got your briefing here with the most recent numbers from the front lines as well as the most up-to-date satellite imagery," he explains, handing me the tablet once again.

I make my way over to my chair without surveying faces this time. Before sitting down, I take a glimpse out the window that had exploded before. If I change seats, that might be awkward, considering a bomb is about to go off. I can't say anything about it either, or it'll raise suspicion, possibly causing a deduction. Am I really going to have to go through that again?

As I sit, my mind stirs, trying to think of every possible scenario and how to avoid the literal sting of defeat.

"May our songs be heard, Anarki," Mobi says.

"May harmony guide us to peace," I respond quickly to avoid any deductions.

The meeting continues much the same as I try to evaluate where I went wrong. Was it leaving the room? Was I supposed to follow Shinzo? Should I have stopped Shinzo?

The audible groan from the board members snaps me back to the holo reality of the moment. Joseph continues on describing the surrender agreement he was negotiating. The first time, I had cut him off, but this time, I allowed him to continue speaking to understand his reasoning for the tax.

"Perhaps if we exempted them from signing the contract, we could allow them into the nearby MetiCity. The act might show them how gracious you are. Then they would surrender without a fuss and we wouldn't need to tax them for entry. We could all move forward and welcome them into the harmonious MetiCorp family," he finishes.

Silence. Gideon looks to me for my response.

BRRRRRt.

"Ten-point deduction. Ninety points remaining." says the calm voice that is becoming increasingly frustrating to hear.

As I thought, Gideon does not speak unless I do. And my delayed response must have been perceived as me weighing over his non-starter of an idea.

"I believe that I have made my position on taxation clear. We are here to provide, not take," I instruct, taking a slightly different approach to my answer than last time.

"Yes! Of course! This was meant to be a gift! To be used as patronage to the great Zelius!" He smiles again, repeating the response he gave the first time. "Say the word, I'll tell the rebels there will be no such tax and all further negotiation will include the stipulation that the contract must be signed. I just thought we might exhaust all the options at our disposal," he continues.

"You will continue negotiations as we try to further infiltrate their forces. It's my understanding that Shinzo is awaiting intel that should give us insight into their operations. Until we have that information, we need to focus on repairing the supply lines to the mining colony," I order, trying to speed the meeting up to give me more time to think.

"Yes, but," Shinzo starts, caught off guard slightly.

"And if I find out negotiations have stalled because of another bright idea from you, I'll gladly send Gideon in to sort this out," I say to him sternly. This draws sly smirks from Iara, Mobi, and Gideon.

"Of course not," he says with a fake smile.

Hmm, no correction of points. I thought that by not allowing Gideon to speak and coming to a well-informed decision quickly, I could potentially boost my score. Instead, the dread of what's coming next slowly creeps in.

"I'm glad to hear you've made your decision," Iara begins. "There are whispers about a strike due to deteriorating conditions. Even though your Droids have taken the brunt of the work, without supplies, the stability of the colony won't last long."

"I'm well aware of the deteriorating situation at the colonies and I've also been watching the front lines closely. I was happy to see a decline in casualties and would like to see these numbers continue to fall, Shinzo." I begin, trying to avoid deductions while anticipating the impending explosion. "For now, we will lower the amount of active combatants and relocate them to assist in rebuilding the colony supply lines. This will help to reduce any interruptions the rebel faction might-"

BOOM!

I was trying to anticipate the explosion but was too busy searching for the right words. As the ringing in my ears returns, I find myself on the opposite wall of the explosion, lying next to the rest of the board members. Shinzo is first to his feet and wastes no time getting to the other side of the room.

"Rebels. Using rocket launchers. Archaic. I'll show you an old weapon!" Shinzo screams, leaping down through the burning hole in the wall. Gideon calls for backup while he watches Shinzo fight below. It's all happening so fast. The security guards and assistant are pulling at me once again and I'm dragged towards the door again.

BRRRRRt.

"Ten-point deduction. Eighty points remaining."

WHAT AM I DOING WRONG!?

"Sir, we have to get you to a secure location. Please follow us!" I hear security say.

"UNHAND ME!" I say, shaking them off.

I walk to the edge of the room where the hole is to see if maybe there's something I'm supposed to see. I see a few armored vehicles trying to pull off as Shinzo gives chase.

BRRRRRt.

"Ten-point deduction. Seventy points remaining."

The rebels begin firing at Shinzo, who is only able to stay elusive for so long. The bullets rain through his body, knocking him back through the air, the shots still catching flesh on the way down.

"SHINZO!" I hear Iara scream as she watches in horror.

BRRRRRt.

"Ten-point deduction. Sixty points remaining."

"LOOK OUT!" Gideon yells while tackling me to the ground seconds before another loud explosion. The sound it makes is slightly different this time and as I look up, I can see the board members being engulfed in a bright white light. Even with Gidon blocking some of the impact, I could still feel the heat burning my skin to the bone. I close my eyes due to the blinding brightness and every cell in my body sends its own excruciating pain signal to my brain.

"AHHHHHHHHHHHHHHHHHHHHHHHHH" I want to beg to be killed. The sensation is unbearable and the only thing bringing me relief is what I assume is the release of chemicals meant to shield someone from the pain of death. A natural process. I feel the last breath of air leave my lungs before everything fades to nothingness.

Am I going to die?

BRRRRRt.

"Ten-point deduction. Game Over."

"Sir?" I hear a voice call from behind me. Again, there is no delay, but the pain is still there. I can't tell if I'm still literally on fire or if it's phantom pain, but I can't escape it. I grunt it out until I can't take it anymore and cough, placing my hands on my knees. I gasp for breath, but it feels like my lungs never get filled.

"Are you feeling alright, Zelius?" he asks, concerned. "Do you need medical attention?"

BRRRRRt.

"Ten-point deduction. Ninety points remaining."

The pain slowly subsides enough for me to grumble out an "I'm fine."

"Of course, sir. All members are present and accounted for. We've got your briefing here with the most recent numbers from the front lines as well as the most up-to-date satellite imagery."

He opens the door to the room full of ghosts. People I'd just watched burn alive in what felt like slow motion. I can't interrupt the meeting, can I? Knowing what's about to happen? Would that drop my score?

Working through the pain, I am able to follow the same pattern as the first meeting without screwing up Mobi's greeting or making too many delayed responses, but it is difficult. I am still in pain and having trouble forming the words. Joseph drones on again about his stupid tax proposal like the scheming noso he is.

"What...tax?" I say.

After following the same dialog tree I used in the first meeting, Gideon cuts in again, warning him about misinformation regarding who suggested the tax. I can't help but feel like it is all irrelevant now. I try to listen closely but keep anticipating the attack like a wounded veteran with PTSD. My leg shakes as my breathing starts to increase in pace. My heart is racing as fast as my mind, trying to figure out a way out of this.

I once again question Shinzo about his intel, knowing my decision is coming next. I'm not sure if the timing was different the second time, but it felt longer. I pause for a moment after he finishes before beginning the explanation behind my decision to prioritize the colony.

"We will await the intel from your agents so we can find out how the weaponry was stolen from the armories. If they were able to access those facilities, it means it's possible we've been infiltrated as well. If so, we need to stop this hemorrhaging immediately. Meanwhile, we cannot lose sight of the important role our supply chain plays in the-"

BOOM!

I must get this right! I won't fail! NEVER. AGAIN.

"EVERYONE! FOLLOW ME!" I yell out to the disoriented room. Shinzo, who was running towards the open wall, stopped and looked back at me.

"NOW!" I yell, leading them out of the room as security pours in. Shinzo and Gideon, who were about to open their com-links, turned and followed us out.

We are in the stairwell when the second explosion hits, rocking the building and throwing us slightly off balance.

"Well, I guess now we know what happened to the weapons stolen from the armories," Gideon says almost jokingly.

No one laughs. All eyes are on me.

"Are you sure you don't want us to go after them?" Shinzo asks. He wants heads to roll.

Gideon is on coms, telling his security forces to track them. Iara works to calm her breath as Mobi recites his prayers in whispers. He's not quite afraid, but he seems to be trying to calm himself down by telling us over and over to not be afraid. That the Allspirits are with us.

"I'm sure they are, holy man," Joseph quips.

"Score: Ninety. You Win."

Zelius always found some way to take the higher ground. Even the last of the fighting nations eventually would succumb not to war but to economic pressure. He wasn't enticed by the idea of war and spilling blood. Like me, he was happier building than destroying.

The game's façade fades for a moment, then I see grass growing and trees springing up.

NO. NOT THIS.

Suddenly, I can feel warmth and light coming from behind me.

"Good job. You had me worried for a second."

Hypatia.

"ARE YOU INSANE? I THOUGHT I DIED!" I yell, walking over to her sitting at the campfire.

"Well, to be completely honest, technically, you did die," she says nonchalantly.

"I, what!?"

"If it doesn't feel real, you won't understand the consequences of your decisions. In this place, it's nothing to alter brain waves or even stop one's heart...or restart it," she explains.

"YOU KILLED ME?"

"Oh, calm down. You did excellent. In fact, Zelius was never able to stop Shinzo before he engaged the enemy. He died that day, just as you saw it. But you lived!" she sounded almost excited, like she wasn't sure if I would. "Besides, you're fine now, aren't you?" she says, smirking.

"Well, I guess that depends. Why are we back here?" I say, looking around.

"We're here because this place is part of your curriculum. And I've added an additional stipulation for tonight," she says, pointing behind me.

"A piano?" I say, confused.

"Correct. Your understanding of musical theory is abysmal, and it's the linchpin of Zelius's theories. You cannot understand the workings of atomic waves without understanding resonance. And you cannot truly understand resonance until you have a better understanding of music theory. There's a piece of sheet music laid out for you to play. If you can play the piece before sunrise, you will be allowed to return to your room early. If not, you can try again tomorrow," she says, getting up and walking towards the now visible door just at the treeline.

"Wait!" I don't have a moment to breathe or think. The door closes behind her, and I am left listening to the subtle crackling of the campfire.

CHAPTER TWENTY-EIGHT_

I have never played an instrument and only have a basic understanding of how to read music. So before anything has a chance to assemble itself into something formidable, I run over to the piano and start pressing around on random keys. I have no intention of getting anything right, and I'm getting nowhere fast. Sliding my finger across the keys in frustration, I hit my first correct note. It lights up as I strike it anyway, so I assume it must be the correct one. With this little bit of information, I should be able to try the keys in either direction to find the next correct note. Once I figure out the sequence, I'll have to memorize it and play it out completely. This isn't going to be easy.

The sun has completely set by the time I make it to the second note. I can just barely make out a massive paw before it takes a swipe at my head and I fall backward off the chair.

"Shit!" I exclaim, trying to get to my feet. The fucking bear is back. "Nice to see you again too," I joke.

Running back towards the campfire, I take cover behind the logs placed around it. As I peer over them, I can see the bear sitting beside the piano. With him guarding it, getting in and out quickly will be the only way to explore the keys in between decapitation attempts. Either that or I need to somehow lure him away... or kill him. It hits me that I might be able to go full commando and fashion some spears out of sticks. Not sure it will be enough to take down the bear, but it might help protect me from whatever else is waiting in the darkness.

Making my way over to the tree line opposite the campfire, I try to recall in my head what the opening notes are. Etching my way to success, one note at a time seems an insurmountable task. I will ideally need to be as quiet as possible, but even if I sneak up, as soon as I hit a key, I'm going to make enough noise to alarm the bear. How is anyone supposed to learn like this?

Working my way up the closest tree, I pass several branches too small or weak to use. I pause for a moment. Is that... buzzing? I've climbed far enough. I reach out and grab the nearest branch I can find, yanking at it to force it to snap. Shaking the branch vigorously, it starts to crack. The buzzing gets louder. The sound starts circling around me, but I can barely see anything as the tree top shades the light coming from the night sky. The only illumination is the dim glow from the campfire nearby.

The first sting isn't so bad. Not that it doesn't hurt, but it's the second and third stings that almost make me lose my grip on the tree. The fall from here wouldn't be great for my ankles, to say the least. Tugging on the branch harder, it begins to crack more, but the buzzing is only getting louder. I am not a bug expert, but I'm assuming by the sting and them being hard to see, they are wasps. A swarm of them, and if I could spot the nest anywhere nearby, I might have a word with the Queen myself. Is this any way to welcome a guest? The pain is getting worse, and the branch isn't budging. I feel like they've stung me with enough venom to take down a wooly mammoth.

"ARRRGHH!" I let out a scream. One of them stung me in the ear. It's the most painful one so far. I can't take much more.

I have to get down. Allspirits! Another sting on my already swollen hand forces me to abort the mission. I leap off the tree, landing on the branch I was trying to take off. I get a grip of it and they begin to follow. Suddenly, the branch snaps and I plummet, hitting more branches that slow my fall and break some of the impact. I hit the ground hard and try to roll to brace my fall, but it doesn't matter. From the sole of my foot, into my ankles, and up to my knees is just pure, unfiltered pain. I lay there on the ground, wincing in pain, afraid to put any weight on my legs. At least there's no more buzzing.

Bzzzzzzzz.

I spoke too soon. I look over and see that one of the branches I had taken down on my descent had their nest attached. It's broken into pieces, and the wasps are frantically swarming, looking for revenge.

Getting to my feet as quickly as I can, I grab the branch with the most leaves and stagger my way back to the campfire. The noise fades into the distance. All that for a slompin' stick. I stop by the campfire to catch my breath before looking over to where the piano is. After squinting a bit, I can make out the figure of the bear crouched behind the piano, waiting. Frustration is building. This task seems unnecessary, trivial, and pointless. What is the point of learning music, anyway? And why do I have to do it under threat of bear mauling? Once again, I feel as if I can sense Hypatia laughing while she watches from some secret observation room. Does she enjoy this? Punishing me for the sins of my father? How is anyone supposed to fill these shoes?

Am I going to die? The question again stumbles into my thoughts like an intrusive neighbor inviting themselves in, sitting on your couch, and demanding tea. I look back over at the branch glowing in the campfire and come to a realization. Fuck it. My motivation comes not from inspiration but spite. I pick up the branch and hold it over the fire, glaring at the shadow of the bear. I grip the branch tightly in my hand as the leaves burst aflame.

"ENOUGH!" I yell barbarically. I have gotten to a place I haven't been since storming into Taxia's shop. But this is somehow worse. I am a secluded, trapped prisoner, locked away by a tyrannical teacher who is probably somewhere eagerly waiting for me to give up. *Keizoku Wa Chikara Nari.* I won't let her win.

Fighting through the pain, I walk towards the piano with my flaming branch of leaves and march myself into oblivion on what feels like a suicide mission. I make it a few feet before I notice the ground moving below me. Small rodents squeak as they pass. Fucking rats? And a ton of them. They flood in from both directions and form a blockade in front of me, preventing me from moving forward. Their little squeaks communicate with one another, probably targeting the crazy guy with the bright stick. They begin to close the distance, and as they get within a foot or so, I take a step back before leaping forward into the air, landing behind the swarm of them. They turn around and follow me as I try to pick up speed. They are surprisingly fast. As they catch up, they begin nipping at my feet. I try to outrun them, but they begin climbing my leg and I shake it wildly to get them off. I will not be slowed. I give up, trying to shake them off and fight through the pain as I pick up speed again. Gritting my teeth and closing my eyes, I keep running in the direction of the piano, trying to get clear from them. As I near the piano, I notice they are no longer nipping. Have I outrun them? I stop to look down to find them scurrying away, hopping off my legs and fading into the darkness. That's weird.

ROAR!

I hadn't realized it, but I'm mere feet from the piano now. The bear has stepped right in front of it, blocking my path.

"ROAR!!!" I scream back. A guttural scream. The bear looks perplexed. I swing around the fire in between us, and it pauses, taking a step back. YES.

"BACK! BACK BEAR! GO!!" I yell to the bear, who is not a fan of my loud noises. It takes a faint swipe at the fire before I push it into its face, forcing the animal back. "Don't like fire, do you? It burns, doesn't it?" I think back to the explosion at the board meeting. I can still feel the sensation of my flesh burning as I erratically wave the ignited tree branch.

The bear lets out another frustrated roar, this time not as loud, before backing off and slowly trotting into the darkness. I waste no time, sitting back at the piano, pressing keys, trying to get back to where I had started. Barely a drop in the bucket. The few notes starting the piece are used several times throughout, so I can go back to them when needed.

I keep watch for the grizzly or any other random spawning animals, but it seems eerily quiet. I try to get a grip on what I'm reading as I've been ignoring the sheet music. It all breaks down to math, and that is something I can wrap my head around. It gets easier as I get further into the song. I start to feel the melody boiling up to the surface after lighting up the correct keys in a rhythm that suits the phrase. It's a very simple, somewhat familiar melody, thank the Allspirits.

I get about halfway through the piece before I can hear what sounds like horse hooves clopping. I stop playing to listen closer. I realize they are coming from behind me. I attempt to spin around to face it as something slams into my back, throwing me forward. My head bounces off the top of the piano stand where the music sheet had been, and I can hear the pages flutter before they hit the ground. My nose feels like it's broken, and I am only able to breathe through my mouth, which is quickly filling with the blood dripping from my nose. My vision is blurred, but I can make out what looks like a... goat? No, not a goat. A ram. Its horns curled backward.

It dips its head down, almost egging me on, before hopping up onto its hind legs. Once it comes back down onto all fours, it bursts forward, heading straight at me for a second charge. I step back and bump into the piano, hitting a few keys, which make the random sounds a horror movie might use for a jump scare. Panicking as it gets closer, I look down in front of me to see the bench I had been sitting on. Right before the ram gets in range, I grab the bench, pick it up, and swing it like a baseball bat at the ram's head. I swing so hard that I fall to the ground just as I see the bench break into two. Thousands of what look like diamonds glittering in the moonlight come streaming from the bench. This must be the true reality. Whatever nanotechnology this place is made up of hadn't rendered the inside of the bench in time, and for a moment, I am reminded that this isn't my real reality.

The ram takes a moment to get back to its feet. Shaking its head, it seems to be trying to regain its balance. Once it does, It huffs air through its nostrils and walks off.

"Thanks! Appreciate it!" I yell at it while it fades into the darkness, just like the others.

I look back over at the bench and it's fully rendered again. It's surrounded by scattered splinters of wood, which were crystalline nanoparticles seconds ago. I work myself up to my feet and limp back over to the piano. I dust the sheet music off and put it back in place. Where was I again?

I've played the first half so many times that my fingers find their way to the keys much faster, lighting them up as I press the correct notes. Scanning through the second half, the melody seems to be the same, just a step up in key. The rhythm and patterns remain the same, too. I'm going to make it. I can see the sunrise starting at the horizon as I continue to etch away, progressing steadily but perhaps too slowly.

The last bit isn't so hard. But playing it all flawlessly without making any mistakes is. There are no chords. One note at a time, I methodically press the keys in the order I remember them. I'm so close. I don't even stop playing when I hear a loud screech coming from above me. Stabbing pain shoots through my shoulder and into my neck. I can't feel my left hand anymore. Large wings flap at my ear and hit me in the back of the head. It's trying to take off with me, but I weigh too much, so its talons are ripping open the wounds it made. It must be a scene for Hypatia as I take a deep breath and zone out the pain. I don't know what comes over me. Maybe I am over all of it. Or maybe I am too determined. Since the hand I had been using has lost all feeling, I switch to the other and continue playing over the loud screeching bird. Hawk. Eagle. Falcon. Pterodactyl? Could be anything. I refuse to look. It's way more difficult with my right hand, but I've gotten to the end of the song, so I won't stop now. The bird finally rips free from my shoulder, almost causing me to hit the wrong key. I pause a moment to find the right one as blood from my nose drips onto the white ivory keys. The melody is so clear now, but I still can't place where I have heard it before. Perhaps some children's nursery rhyme. It doesn't matter. Once I hit the last key, the piano makes a clicking sound and plays the whole song in its entirety once more. I fall backward to the ground as the sun rises in my peripheral vision.

"EAT THAT, YOU STUPID BIRD!" I yell as it circles above.

CHAPTER TWENTY-NINE_

The holoroom doors open and in comes Taxia. She doesn't seem as worried this time but shakes her head as she approaches.

"We've really gotta stop meeting each other like this," she says, helping me to my feet.

"Tell that to her," I say, looking at Hypatia, who is now standing in the doorway.

"Ay, at least you've got your shoes on! But man, that piano really beat your ass," Taxia jokes, then her face turns cold as she shifts her focus to the blood-soaked piano.

"What do you mean?" I ask sarcastically, leaning my weight onto her to avoid putting any on my ankle.

As we get closer to the doorway, Hypatia steps aside, not even looking up from her tablet.

"Well done, boy. You can rest for the remainder of the morning. Combat training will be in the afternoon. You'll need to be fully recovered by then," Hypatia says.

"Fun," I say dryly.

"For me, it will be," She says hauntingly as she walks past us over to the piano.

"Well, if you keep me alive, maybe I can tell you why your system is having trouble rendering," I smirk.

Hypatia stops and looks back at me with what is either shock, intrigue, or both.

"Okay, tough guy. You're bleeding all over me; let's go," Taxia says.

We walk past K-2 on the way back to the guest room and he doesn't seem too excited to see my condition.

"I'm okay," I say to calm him. It seems to work. He is always so concerned for me. The newer Droids don't tend to show this kind of emotional reaction. Something was clearly lost between Zelius's death and the new Droids. It wasn't apparent immediately, but K-2's social intellect seems to be more...advanced.

After a good nap in the tank, I wake to Taxia once again bringing me food. Each day, she becomes progressively more friendly and supportive. It's nice to not have to come out of these tests into a contentious environment. Even if it is a prison, at least I've got a cellmate.

"When did you become so domesticated?" I say, taking one of the bowls of food from her hand.

"I've always had to take care of myself. It's only recently that I've had to learn to take care of someone else," she says, nodding to me. "Plus, there's not much else to do in this place other than watch TV, get high in the garden, or meditate with Hypatia."

"Meditate with Hypatia?" I ask, puzzled.

"Yeah. She's been showing me this meditation technique that has really helped to clear my head. She insisted, and when she did, she didn't give the impression that she was asking. I think it's because I was smoking all her greesha," she says, laughing before taking a spoonful of her bowl.

"Maybe I could use a lesson myself. My head is all over the place," I say, taking a spoonful from my own bowl. It is a mix of vegetables, gravy, and what I think might be artificial beef. It tastes amazing. I think she can see it on my face.

"Good?" she asks. "It's called mush. We always picked the most appetizing names, don't you think?"

"This another dish from back home?" I ask.

"Yeah. It's funny that this printer can make anything in the world, but if you don't know what to ask for, it's pretty useless. Can't make caviar if you've never heard of it. You have to know good food, and me? I know mush," she says, going for another spoonful.

She sits beside me on the bed while K-2 comes in, finding his little spot near the corner to listen.

"So how does a girl from the Outskirtz end up with a Meti-City shop of her own anyway?"

"I got the money for the shop from my parents' inheritance."

"Since when do us sandscavengers have an inheritance to give?"

"We weren't always sandscavs. They were originally from MetiCity-10 but ended up deadcreds with a designer drug addiction and got kicked out. They were saving up to get back when they died. I wanted to get out so bad after they passed. Everything there reminded me of them, and they were terrible people. So they weren't fond memories. You know, you're kind of lucky in that way. Not having parents. Sometimes they can be the fucking worst. I was basically raised by the nanny."

"I can actually relate. My foster parents only got me for the social credit," I explain.

"I was too old for a foster home when my parents passed. Were yours sandscavs?" she asks.

"Nope. Just some deadcreds looking for a way back. Just like your parents. Luckily, they mostly left me alone. I was gone as soon as I could afford a small place of my own."

"That shop was the first place I could call 'my own.' Don't tell anyone, but I used to sleep there too," she says, looking embarrassed.

"I think we have more in common than you realize," I comment, thinking back to when we first met. "How did someone like you get mixed up with UG anyway? I don't see any tattoos, and you didn't throw yourself at Hypatia's feet like they did," I say, digging into more details than I had the chance to before now.

"Because I'm not UG...yet. Not officially, anyway. It wasn't easy for someone like me, coming back from the Outskirtz, to open a shop in a MetiCity. I didn't even know it was UG territory when I signed the contract. My parents would have loved that. Business was slow at first and I wasn't meeting the minimum for commercial credit income, so I had to try some sort of customer base. Those guys had been coming to my shop for years and in the beginning, it wasn't so bad. They bought a ton of gear, and they protected me and the shop. They got me customers in other MetiCities and secured travel for me. Unfortunately, they also scared a ton of people away, too. They slowly became the only ones selling and the only ones buying. I was forced to hang out with them, and while that could be fun sometimes, at their heart, they're all fanatics. They talked in deep conspiracies about how everyone is just a zombie under the control of MetiCorp. How their morning worship was the only way to break out of this cycle of suffering. Once they started to trust me, they would tell me all about their grand plans and try to justify their public acts of disobedience. They just seemed like taking swings at the beehive, not making political statements. They tried recruiting me for a while, but I refused. I didn't believe as they did. Eventually, they stopped asking and started giving ultimatums. I put it off as long as I could, but they told me if I joined them on this one job, they would consider me UG."

"The race," I cut in.

"I couldn't afford to lose their business, so I went." She pauses, "It wasn't supposed to go that way...you gotta understand. The UG has never targeted civilians. Their protests and demonstrations are supposed to be acts of resilience, not violence. I'm sorry, Ren. I'm so sorry. I didn't mean for this to happen. That wasn't the plan," she says, pulling her knees up into herself and wrapping her arms around them.

"It's okay, Taxia. It's not your fault," I say solemnly. She looks puzzled. "It's mine. If it wasn't for me, the plan never would have gotten off the ground in the first place."

"Are you saying I wouldn't have figured out that disruptor?" she says angrily.

"No, I-" I begin, then notice her frown breaks into a smile. "Funny," I say, rolling my eyes.

"That's what I thought," she says before standing up with her bowl now empty. "I'm going to burn some more greesha in the garden if you wanna come. I could show you the meditation technique Hypatia showed me?" Taxia asks, now standing at the doorway awaiting my response.

"Um. Is there more of this?" I say, pointing to my empty bowl.

"Yeah, there's some in the kitchen on the counter."

"Good. I'll meet you there."

After I finish up, I head to the garden, where I find Taxia. She's laid out amongst the flowers, taking an inhale of the greesha she rolled. Her eyes are closed, and I can't help but take a moment to look at her. The light is diffused through the leaves, illuminating her soft features. Her face is relaxed, and the corners of her mouth turn up into a smile punctuated by a deep dimple. I've never noticed it before. You'd be surprised how unattractive someone can be the day they accidentally killed your friend. She looks different now in the tracksuit Hypatia gave us. Wearing the arms around her waist, the only thing she's got on is her tank top. The room feels warmer, maybe because of the grow lights? Not that either of us mind the heat. I snap myself out of the stare before it gets weird.

"Work out much?" I ask jokingly, failing miserably at switching gears.

"Are you hitting on me?" she counters, sitting up and raising an eyebrow.

"No. I uh, um, sorry I-" I start to mumble out.

"I'm kidding, relax. It's not mods either, in case you were wondering. A lady must keep herself in good shape if she's to fight off the kind of slompers who can't take a hint. It only took one time for me to learn that lesson," she says, looking down, almost in shame. "You give them everything they need to survive. Give them access to all the VRporn anyone could ever want. Brothels. Escorts. And still, they want what they can't have," she says before taking a deep breath. "Anyway, sit there."

I sit down, cross-legged, mirroring her posture. She passes me the greesha. I inhale and I brace for the blast off. But there's no mystic vision, no melting away of reality, just calm, euphoric waves of positive vibes. I can see her watching for my reaction, and she nods when I don't lose myself in it.

"Not your first time?" she asks as I pass it back.

"Elli... that girl singing on TV? Her family used to grow this stuff, and they were Jardinera so you know they knew what they were doing. This stuff is similar to theirs. Not as strong, but also not that synthetic MetiCorp crap they burn in the cities," I explain. She chuckles.

"I noticed that. I was surprised the first time I burned it how intense the come-up was. But the mellow side is glacious," she says, breathing it in before passing it back to me. "So this Elli girl. Were you two a thing?"

"No. Elli and her sister were friends of Zander's. Now Zander and possibly her sister are dead, so she's all alone. I wish I could let her know I'm okay. That someone survived. Even if it's the last person she would have wanted to survive out of the three of us."

"I'm sure she'd be happy to know you're okay."

"What about you? Is there someone you wish could tell that you're okay?" I ask before taking a hit.

"Nope. Was hard to make friends with UG always hanging around. Like I said, everyone in UG is a little...off. Plus, I never had any time. I just want to get back to my shop. If I don't make the payment at the first of the month, they'll lower my social credit score and I won't be able to do business in the commercial area. Which means back to the Outskirtz. I'd almost rather stay here than go back to the Outskirtz."

We talk for some time about the best and worst parts of the Outskirtz. Her experience is slightly different from mine, but she knows the difference between a settler and a sandscavenger, which is more than I can say for most MetiCitians. Even though our stories started in different places, we both seemed to end up doing the same thing: fixing other people's shit.

"Oh, shit. I'm supposed to be showing you the technique!" she suddenly remembers mid-story.

"Oh, yeah," I laugh. The greesha had long gone out. I hadn't realized it, but K-2 had slipped into the room, quietly listening to us. "Hey, when did you get in here?" I ask.

"I'm sorry to disturb you. Would you like me to leave you two alone? I quite enjoyed that," K-2 replies. 'Enjoyed?' Not the typical Droid at all.

"No, you're fine, buddy. Maybe you'll get a laugh out of this." I turn back to Taxia. "Okay, what do I do?"

CHAPTER THIRTY_

"First, close your eyes," she instructs. I close my eyes. Only her voice is left. "Now, I want you to take a deep breath, but don't blow it out!"

I draw in a deep breath through my nostrils until my lungs are at full capacity.

"Give it a few seconds," she adds as I continue to hold the breath of air. Her version of seconds feels like minutes. "Now release."

I release the air, exhaling from my mouth.

"Good. Now breathe normally, but focus on your breathing," she speaks slowly and confidently as if she's an instructor leading a class. "You're going to start to feel thoughts come to you. Let them come, acknowledge them, but when you've done that, release them. Let them phase through you and into the nothingness of forever. Then, once again, focus on your breathing."

She's right. As I sit quietly, I try to focus on my breathing, but thoughts keep popping into my head. What's the going price for a capacitor? Is Taxia sure those aren't mods? Is Elli okay? Is Frank okay? A flash of Zander flying towards the O-Race ring as it falls. Hypatia's evil glare.

"Accept the thought. Then let it pass. Do not dwell. Focus on your breathing," she says. After about a minute longer, she says it again. The same cadence. It was calming.

"You will start to notice the thoughts come less. If they increase, just take your time. They will pass."

It takes another minute before she's proven correct. The issue I always have with meditation: too many thoughts, flashes of images, random quandaries. But slowly, as she said, they come less and less.

"When the thoughts calm down and you can immerse yourself in the silence, I want you to try and maintain it. Hold onto it as long as you can until you forget you're holding onto anything at all," she calmly instructs.

Like a dimming light, I continue to get sporadic flashes of every last thought until I approach the silence she spoke of. Each time I get close, I remember where I am and they all come fluttering back in.

"Accept the thought. Then let it pass. Do not dwell. Focus on your breathing," she repeats. "Find your silence."

A few moments later, I can almost grab it, but it slowly slips through my hands. I'm able to sustain it for a long period, but again, the thoughts come fluttering back in. I'm getting frustrated as she speaks again, almost as if she can sense it.

"You're so close now, don't force it. When you find it, I want you to build walls around yourself. Four walls until no thoughts can get to you anymore. Protect the silence."

It takes a little time to find the silence again, but once I settle in, her voice echoes in my head like a distant memory. 'Protect the silence.' In my mind, I try to imagine myself surrounded by four walls. Every time I feel secure, I try to picture the wall itself, and I lose focus. But I can feel myself getting closer.

She hasn't spoken in a while, but I keep at it and try not to focus on the walls so much as the feeling of being surrounded and protected. It feels safe. It's comforting. I'm starting to feel the walls begin to solidify in my mind when she finally speaks again.

"When the walls are secure, I want you to put in a window. In this window, you can see whatever you like. When you look through it, you will find all the answers you need. Everything in the window is clear. Everything in the window is real," she explains. "Focus on your breathing, and build your window."

Her explanation takes me out of it for a moment, but it is easier to find the silence this time. The walls are still tough to create, though. I struggle to create the visual imagery without thinking about the act of creating the visual imagery. I focus on my breathing.

"Build your window," I suddenly hear echoing in the dark infinity of nothingness before me.

I finish the walls and begin to picture a window in the one I've created in front of me. I feel a warm, calming light shining down through the window after it appears. Slowly, it fades until the image inside is darkened and barely visible. A dim light appears. Then another. I realize they're candles. The light from them is hitting the face of a young girl. Elli, she's singing. It's the broadcast from the TV, but there are no news banners or reporters' voice-overs. It feels like I'm there. I can hear her singing so clearly now. Tears are streaming down her face and into her mouth as she opens it to sing the next line. Everyone is fixated on her. There's something so nostalgic about her singing, and I'm lost in it. I feel like crying and smiling at the same time. I'm so focused I can almost feel the warmth from the candles and the cold wind blowing through the hot night. I can feel the vibrations of her voice resonating in my ears. I want to run to her. Tell her I'm okay. I lean in closer towards the window and feel myself pour through it to the other side. Closer. She's all alone. I need to find a way to help her. I reach out for her, trying to step out in front of the crowd of people. I grab her arm and stand in front of her, looking her directly in the eyes. I lean in to hug her and to my surprise, I feel lips pressing against mine. It's so soft it feels real.

I open my eyes to see Taxia, who is leaning over with her lips pressed to mine. She pushes me away and plops back down, as shocked as me.

"Dude! Are you okay!?" she exclaims.

"Huh? Wait? What? What just happened? Did you just kiss me?" I panic. My face must be as red as blood on piano keys. I look over at K-2, who quickly turns his head as if he hasn't seen anything.

"Bro, you were deep! I tried to nudge you, but you weren't responding. I thought you were kidding around, so I..."

"So you kissed me?" I ask, confused.

"I was trying to see if you were breathing, ya slomper! You're the one that leaned into me!" She says. "Where did you go anyway?"

"Go? What do you mean?"

"I tried to end the meditation like twenty minutes ago, but you were just sitting there. I was starting to panic, I'm not going to lie," she explains.

Twenty minutes? Could I really not hear her?

"Where were you, man?"

"I was..." I pause for a second. I don't want to say I thought Elli was kissing me.

"So it worked? On your first try?" she presses on.

"You sound surprised," I say, glad to have left the subject.

"It took me until the next day, and I practiced for hours!"

she exclaims, frustrated. "Hypatia said I picked it up quickly. Bullshit."

"I don't think she's the type to give out compliments for no reason," I reassure her. "Besides, I don't think I completely got it. It felt more like watching a memory."

"You saw what you wanted to see. Hypatia said once you get the hang of it, you can control what you see. Use it to break things down and think things through. Or remember things in better detail," she explains.

"Hmm. I'm going to try again."

"Are you sure?" she asks.

"Yeah. Hey K-2! Make sure she doesn't make any sneaky moves, okay?" He nods eagerly, then glares at her.

"What? HEY!" she yells, almost embarrassed.

I lay down to get into a more comfortable position. I can't think of the last time I stared up at the sun from a grassy earth. The lights warm me and the room smells pleasantly of flowers and various plants. They help me further relax as I close my eyes and dig my way back to where I was.

I want to try and see if I can control what appears in the window this time. Specifically, I want to see what is really going on within the holoroom. Figure out how it works and why, for just a split second, it didn't. If I can, maybe there will be a way to fight back in the jungle. Or maybe Hypatia will be impressed enough to give me a little leniency. Each test I've passed has come at a cost just short of death, and I don't know how much longer I can live up to her expectations.

Finding my way back to the silence comes easier each time I try. I'm quicker to accept and dismiss the fleeting thoughts as they appear, but the walls are still hard to form. After several attempts, I am able to stabilize them in my mind and I begin to try and construct the window. It's a frustrating process but also fascinating, like working a muscle you've never used before. At first, it's weak and unable to move small pebbles, then before long, it's moving mountains.

The window begins to solidify in my mind, enough to peer through, and I try to focus on the holoroom. It slowly comes into view, and I can start to see the infrastructure building from the ground up. All the various technologies necessary to create the realistic environments I've been thrown into. At its core, it seems no different than a normal holoroom in that it uses light to project images holographically from above. The difference here is that nanoparticles spontaneously form the physical structures underlying the projected image, giving the projections the ability to interact with the environment. This explains how the animals have been able to physically attack me, but it isn't enough to account for the vivid and lossless way in which it all appears. There is something missing.

As I look around, examining the room, a faint light starts to fill the gaps between the panels that make up the walls. The light increases in luminosity as the panels separate further from one another, and before long, it completely obscures my vision. I squint as it shines through the window and fills the small space I've created with its overwhelming intensity. I can no longer maintain my focus as the brilliant light breaks through the walls and into the silent darkness.

I open my eyes to find the much less abrasive artificial light beaming down on me from inside the garden. After a moment to gather myself, I roll over to see if Taxia stayed and almost end up on top of her. She is sleeping next to me, and luckily, bumping into her slightly didn't seem to disturb her slumber. I look over at K-2, who is intently staring at her. He must have been taking his command very seriously. I take another moment to look at her, studying her face.

"It's time. Wake sleeping beauty and bring the Droid to the holoroom," Hypatia says from the doorway. I only catch her for a brief moment before she disappears again. I don't know why Zelius called her his little samurai; he should have called her his psycho ninja. Why does she want Taxia and K-2 anyway? Does she want an audience to witness the ass-beating she's probably about to put on me?

We meet in the holoroom before it comes online or anything is projected. It's a cold and empty shell of what it was last night. Taxia's time spent here has only consisted of helping me up off the floor, so she doesn't quite fathom yet the menacing terror that it can produce.

"I forgot how enormous this room is," Taxia says, looking around the room.

"Indeed. Let's fix that." Hypatia says as she waves her hand. Suddenly, the room feels a lot smaller. We find ourselves on a raised white platform that has a slight give to it. A chorus of voices begin yelling and I look up to see a crowd of people cheering us on. Taxia is impressed. I'm not. I have a better idea of the horrors that await us.

"I can't lie, Ren, this is some sick tech," she says, looking over at the crowd.

"As I've explained to Ren, it's best to treat everything in here as real," Hypatia says, just as Taxia steps outside the plat-form. She pushes at one of the crowd members, testing to see if they're real. It's some drunk fool yelling incoherently, and he doesn't seem happy to be pushed. He takes the beer bottle he was drinking from and turns it upside down over her head. Instead of being upset, Taxia is more interested in why the drink feels 'wet' as it pours over her.

"As I was saying. So far, we have tested your physical apti-tude and your mental fortitude. Combat is the convergence of both of those things. The most capable fighters who ever lived knew of this duality to combat. At the top, there is no one without both, and Zelius is no exception to the rule. You cannot be a leader to the people without showing them you can protect them. And you can't protect them if you can't protect yourself. That goes for each of you," Hypatia explains. This gets Taxia's attention.

"Each of us? What do I have to do with this?"

"If you are to be freed, I must know that you will not become a liability during his ascension."

"A liability? I can protect myself."

"I anticipated that. That is why you are here. And why I didn't feel the need to put you through the same physical testing as him. My initial readings showed you were high above the average in terms of athletic ability. I assumed that 'physical prowess' is why Ren has so easily forgiven you. But perhaps there is still anger inside him. And that is what we are here to find out."

"Wait, what!? When did you scan me? And what did you mean by-" Taxia starts but is cut off.

"It's a complex algorithm based on resting heart rate, posture, musculature, height, and weight. All of which were gathered as soon as you stepped into this place the first time. Now. Don't go easy on him. Or I'll make his second and third opponents even worse," Hypatia threatens as she gets seated amongst the crowd. She sits upon a large throne of a chair, something quite contrary to the idea that she didn't like being called a queen. "You may begin!" she announces once comfortable. Is she serious? She wants me to fight Taxia? Is Taxia going to be okay with-

The air suddenly escapes from my lungs and I'm on my knees, gasping for it. When I look up toward Taxia, I can see her smiling, slowly lowering the leg she just used to drive her foot into my stomach.

"What was that!? Is Hypatia controlling you?" I force out, in between coughs.

"Um, no. She said to begin? Get up. I didn't hit you that hard. Besides, this is a test, isn't it?" She turns to the crowd. "Hypatia, I'm assuming if I refuse to fight, he fails the test?" she asks.

"Very perceptive young lady!" Hypatia answers over the roaring crowd, who are spurred on by the action.

"See? Come on, it'll be fun!"

"Fine with me." I smile, thinking back to the times Migo and I used to spar before he decided his face was too valuable an asset to him. I think the real reason was that, eventually, I started to get the upper hand and it wasn't fun for him anymore.

CHAPTER THIRTY-ONE_

Taxia and I lock eyes as we loosen into our respective stances. She has her hands low down by her waist and her knees slightly bent. I bend my knees slightly, too, bringing my elbows up to chest level, with my forearms guarding my head.

"There are other opponents to get to. Let's not take all day," Hypatia commands from the crowd of belligerent onlookers.

We maintain eye contact, but our smiles drop into serious expressions. I inch closer to her and throw out a flicking, jab-like kick towards her midsection. She adjusts by shifting her hips back and arching forwards. Her head is in range now, so I throw out a light jab, but she snaps back upright, narrowly avoiding it. I inch closer and aim another kick to her midsection, this time forcing her to step back in order to avoid it. I gauge her speed and range and estimate distance with a number of feints. Once she settles, I dash forward, chambering a right hook. She tilts her head back in anticipation, so I adjust my hips to throw her off with another body kick. Her feet are planted, so there's no way she can dodge at this range. As the kick approaches her, she leans forward, crouching slightly and catches it, grabbing me by the knee. She continues her forward momentum, slamming her forehead into my right rib and pressing her body weight down on my knee. My back hits the platform hard, but I immediately pull my legs up into my chest and then push my heels into her hips, throwing her off of me and keeping her from following me to the ground. I roll back and hop up to my feet, hoping to keep things standing.

"I guess you don't like being on the bottom?" she snickers with a cheeky smile before running at me, this time throwing full punching combinations that I can barely avoid. I try to use footwork to escape, but she is overwhelming me, and I keep finding the edge of the platform. Hypatia didn't explicitly say we can't fall off the platform, but then again, she never really explains anything completely.

I'm able to land a few leg kicks while keeping my distance, but I get the feeling they're hurting me more than her. I circle to find openings, but her stamina is relentless, and her fast twitch movements make her extremely elusive. After nearly having my head taken off several times, I find an opening and time a quick jab to her body. When it lands, she stops and looks down where I hit her.

"Come on, Ren, what was that?" she says, brushing it off. She's fierce. Her onslaught continues, and I realize I won't be able to put her down after tiring her out like I had originally planned. My stamina has increased since I got to this place. I'm moving more agilely than I could before, so I thought I could use that as a weapon. If I had known the secret to elite athleticism was running for your life in a jungle, I would have started doing it a long time ago. But that's what I'm doing here, running for my life. She finally gets through my guard, hitting me right at the temple where my scar is. The shot jars me, and for a moment, I lose balance. Most of the punches she has landed so far have been on my shoulders and forearms, but she has slowly broken me down, whittling away at my ability to defend my head. I recover in time to land another jab to her stomach to create space as she pressures. She grunts, unphased. Aiming for the body or legs and circling aren't having the effect I hoped they would on her cardio. I need to try something else.

"Are you...purposely trying not to hit my face?" Taxia sounds angry now. She's onto me. I just...can't. I was hoping to gas her out and take advantage once she slowed. But she isn't slowing; she's getting faster. Like she's being awoken from a long slumber and stretching her legs. My guard is slowly falling apart, and I don't know if I can do this without throwing back. I don't even know if I can do this, even if I do throw back. Her leg kicks hurt, and at first, they weren't as crisp as mine. But the more she throws them, the more dangerous they become. Almost as if...she's learning it from me as we fight. The next leg kick is almost crippling. I wince, struggling to keep my pain from surfacing, and she moves in to take advantage of my weakness. She fires through a right straight that shakes my foundations. I drop to one knee and spit out the blood that has gathered in my mouth.

"Ren. If you don't fight back, you're going to fail. Put aside whatever outdated gender bias you've got stuck in that head of yours and just fucking hit m-" she starts. There it is. Finally, an opening. It's a disgustingly cheap shot, but I have to take it. And I do. Pushing off my knee and using my legs to rise from the crouching position, I chamber an uppercut that should put her down. It connects cleanly before she can finish her sentence, catching her completely off guard, but she doesn't drop. As she steps back, her back foot just misses the edge of the platform and she falls off. She lands with a huge thump but springs to her feet immediately. Taxia opens her mouth to scream something but stops, her face wearing confusion.

"Actually, you know what," she says, rubbing her cheek, "I

may have asked for that. But it was a cheap shot," she yells, pointing at me angrily.

"No, my dear, that was a win. However, you did learn a valuable lesson: we must protect ourselves at all times," Hypatia says.

"Round 1: Winner, Ren," a voice overhead announces. The crowd explodes into cheering.

"Whatever. Makes sense you got your ass kicked by a piano! I was totally winning," she jokes, still slightly frustrated, but unable to hide the slight smile she wears.

"You poor little thing, come let me see what wound the boy inflicted upon you," Hypatia says, walking over to her and placing a hand on Taxia's cheek.

"It's okay, I'm fine," Taxia says, clearly uncomfortable.

"Oh, but look at the bruising on your hands," Hypatia coos, holding Taxia's hand in hers.

"It doesn't really hurt that bad," Taxia responds, trying to slowly pull her hands back.

"That's too bad." Hypatia grabs Taxia's arm, locking it up and forcing her onto one knee, and then snaps it at the forearm. The sound alone is enough to make me want to gag. I can't imagine how it feels for Taxia. She screams out in pain.

"Are you two under the impression that this is a game!?" Hypatia yells. "Taxia, have you no remorse for the people who have died by your hands? I didn't think I would have to remind you what is at stake, the lives that will be impacted by your actions. Giggling and flirting while training for a cause of this importance is an insult. Have you no shame?"

Taxia's groans slowly fade to murmurs as she falls to her knees, holding her arm. I don't know what to say. I'm afraid to exit the platform, and I don't know that going over there would comfort her anyway. She's not looking up to make eye contact, so I'm stuck standing here while she suffers.

"You two need to understand that every victory you attain will be paid in blood. And blood alone moves the wheels of history," The familiar phrase echoes in my ears as Hypatia guides K-2 onto the platform, using just a flick of her wrist to get him moving. It almost looks as if he's resisting her commands but is unable to do more than slow his own movements.

"How am I supposed to fight a Droid in a Biosuit?" I ask as he makes his way onto the platform.

"This old thing? You shouldn't have any issues, especially after that dominating performance. But to make it fair, I will allow you one weapon of your choosing. Nothing pre-2100."

She means no projectiles. But I know something that would be much more capable in my hands.

"X8100 multi-tool wrench." I gesture like I'm carrying the one I lost in Taxia's shop.

As soon as the words leave my mouth, I feel a weight pushing down on my hands.

"You mean that?" Hypatia says as my exact wrench slowly renders in my hands. "There was one in Taxia's shop that I found when I was cleaning up, and it felt out of place, so I saved a schematic of it," she explains.

"It's perfect," I say, examining the weight and dimensions. "If only I could take it out of here when I leave."

"What makes you think you can't?" she asks.

I stand stunned for a moment. The sheer complexity of this room is baffling. The line between holographic and real matter is amorphous and constantly in question.

"Well, if that's all you needed. We shall begin. Now," she says, lifting her finger aimed at me.

K-2 kicks off into a full sprint.

"I'm sorry, sir!" he yells on his way over. His arms are dangling by his side and his running is awkward, slanting side to side as he runs. As he gets closer, though, he starts to reorient himself into a more natural-looking run. My assumption is that was his last little attempt to resist her commands.

Once he's in range, he unleashes a number of bewildering combinations, all aiming for my face. I think the warmup with Taxia helped because his strikes are easier to avoid. Perhaps he is still resisting, but either way, if I get hit, I'll be lucky if the meditank can revive me. My bare hands grip the wrench, and I use it to dull the blunt force of the strikes I can't dodge. Each one lands with enough force to unlevel my footing and knock me back. His movements are unpredictable. He doesn't move like a human. He rotates his entire torso around, throwing kicks by bending his leg at the knee in the opposite direction a human would be able to, and using his shoulders after punches to bump me away so I can't return fire to counter. Timing his next shot, I swing my wrench to intercept his hand, hoping it might break his rhythm. As it hits, he twists sideways and finds an opening to land a heavy body shot right to my liver. I fall onto my back, head hanging over the platform, body paralyzed. I can see Taxia upside down as I look out through blurry vision.

"LOOK OUT!" she yells, still holding her arm.

I look up to find the bottom of K-2's foot hurtling toward my face. I quickly roll out of the way, and when I look over, I can see K-2's foot has almost touched the ground outside the platform. He quickly pushes off the foot still on the platform and jumps back towards me. His balance is far superior to most consumer Droids. I get up to put some distance between us, and K-2 pauses for a moment, following me with just his head as I circle behind him. I can see the area of his spine where Hypatia had repaired my work, linking him way better than I ever could have. Perhaps, too well. I had reinforced my shoddy work because it was something I had never done before and I wanted to make sure it could withstand the kind of tampering that goes on in the Outskirtz. But when she repaired the spine, she was too proud of her work and didn't reinforce it. It was prettier, but it wasn't stronger.

K-2 takes his time turning his body to face me, but once I stop moving, he's quick to close the distance. I was trying to find some pattern in the way he was attacking so I could take advantage and get to his back. But everything is so spastic and nimble it's hard to understand what's coming next and from what direction. He wasn't giving me anything. There was no room for error, and my hands were forming blisters from taking the impact of his strikes on my wrench. I run, sprinting away from him, trying to get as much distance as I can between us. It's embarrassing, but I have a plan.

"If you continue running, I shall end the test as a failed attempt," Hypatia yells from the sideline.

When K-2 approaches again, I stop running and throw the wrench into the air with an ark, taking his focus off me for a moment. As soon as his eyes began to follow the wrench, I burst into a full sprint, heading towards him. He stops watching the wrench long enough to see me slide between his legs and end up behind him. He spins just his torso around, and before he can connect his fist with my face, the wrench lands, hitting him in the back of the head. It knocks him off balance, and I kick at his ankle, causing him to faceplant on the platform. I catch the wrench as it bounces into the air and immediately drive it in between his Paladin armor and Droid spine. He grips the wrench in his hands and begins to pull it out, exposing some loose wiring.

"Thanks!" I say as I reach down to the wires. I connect two wires you're never supposed to cross, says Frank, and sparks come shooting out of his chest. K-2 grabs me by my shirt, lifts me into the air like he's going to dunk me, and then stops.

"What...what just happened?" a puzzled Hypatia asks, continuing to move her hand to command the Droid, finding him unresponsive.

"Scav 101. There's always a full reset," I say as the Droid gently puts me down. "Right, Taxia?" I ask, looking over at Taxia, who has been watching silently but intently. She nods slightly, but she's glaring at Hypatia with a tense, piercing glare.

"I'm sorry, Ren. It wasn't me, I swear. I tried my best to resist!" K-2 implores me.

"I know K-2. If you didn't, I'd be dead," I say, reaching up and patting him on the shoulder.

"Well played, young Ren. Seeing as I can no longer control him, I guess I'll have to use my own Droid to defend myself. Ones like him are more common than you think," Hypatia says as a goop of nanobots rise up from the platform and organize themselves into a Droid identical to K-2.

"Wait, what? Don't I win?" I plead, still catching my breath, the taste of blood lingering now.

"Win? But your opponent is right here. K-2. Attack," she says.

CHAPTER THIRTY-TWO_

The K-2 clone is within range; before I can blink, wincing, I weakly hold up my wrench to block the oncoming onslaught. I hear the loud smack of metal on metal, and when I open my eyes, I find K-2 standing in front of me. The clone Droid is kneeling before him like he's about to be knighted. From their posture, I can tell K-2 had dropped him with something heavy and fast. Uninhibited by Hypatia's control, his speed has increased exponentially. He could have ended me in an instant if he wasn't fighting so hard not to.

Hypatia's Droid rises to its feet, focusing its attention on K-2, over at me, and then back to K-2 again.

"That was a warning. Any further threats made upon my owner will reduce my options to only those containing violence. Please proceed no further," K-2 cautions Hypatia's Droid. The warning falls on deaf audio inputs. Hypatia's Droid launches at me, completely ignoring K-2. I'm still trying to compose myself enough to stand upright when the clone Droid appears, hovering over me, fist cocked back, ready to strike me down. Again, K-2 intervenes. He flashes in between us and for a moment, he's standing face to face with me. Whipping around to face the clone Droid, K-2 elevates his leg, rotating it until it smashes into the attacking clone in mid-air. The impact causes the Droid to flip vertically before crash-landing on the platform.

"Proceed any further and I will be forced to disable you," K-2 threatens in a voice more aggressive than I've heard before.

"Those are confident words aimed at your equal," Hypatia retorts.

The clone K-2 Droid struggles to his feet, now fully focused on the real threat, K-2. There's a brief pause before they dash to one another, throwing attacks at a speed I can barely believe. They are so evenly matched it's like watching someone spar in the mirror. Neither can land a decisive shot. I can see Hypatia concentrating hard, trying to keep the Droid's movements up to par with K-2. Should I help somehow? I take a step forward instinctively.

"Sir, your assistance will not be required," K-2 says while dodging a blinding barrage of attacks.

"SCRAP HIS ASS, K-2!" Taxia unexpectedly screams from the sidelines, causing Hypatia to scowl. As disrespectful as she was, a smile was usually the mask she wore. Until now.

"Sir, do I have permission to 'scrap his ass'?" K-2 calls back to me.

"End it K-2," I say, sticking my hand out, thumb down.

Without delay, K-2 is on the offense, quickly overwhelming the imposter. The clone Droid resorts to staying defensive, blocking most of the more damaging shots. As it defends itself, I get a glimpse of his back and notice it is slightly damaged already. It wasn't something K-2 had done; it was something I had done to K-2. Hypatia must have cloned the version of K-2 after our fight, meaning with the same damage to his back.

"K-2! She cloned you after we fought! Every scratch, even dent, every opening," I hint.

"Great observation Sir," K-2 is quick to understand.

K-2 grasps the clone Droid, wrapping his arms around its waist and lifting it up into the air. The Droid begins slamming elbows into K-2's face. One of them stumbles K-2, but he's able to regain his balance and I can see his arms begin to shake as if he's pulling on something. A gut-wrenching metallic shriek sounds as K-2 tears at the Biosuit, severing the connection between it and the Droid. I can almost hear K-2 grunt as he pulls it off. Hypatia's Droid, still fighting to free himself, suddenly breaks down into nanoparticles that hit the ground with nothing more than a whisper.

"Well, how grotesque!" Hypatia scorns, disgusted.

"Woo! That's what I'm talking about!" Taxia yells from the sidelines.

"Thanks, K-2," I sigh, leaning in and putting my hand on his shoulder. He's supporting my weight now, but I don't think he minds.

"Thank you. Both," he says, nodding at me and then Taxia. "All within protocol."

"To be honest, I didn't anticipate the Droid having such a rich assortment of self-defense protocols. This must be why he was Zelius's favorite," Hypatia quips dismissively.

"Well, now he's my favorite, too," I proclaim, further congratulating him.

"Unfortunately, he will be unable to provide assistance in your next challenge. No one can."

"Next challenge? I thought that was three! Taxia, K-2, and the imposter Droid!" I scream, knowing I can't take on another challenger, especially without K-2.

"Naive boy," she says, avoiding the obvious math. "I must warn you, this next opponent is quite unpredictable, much like yourself. Once he is manifested in this holoroom, it's only a short matter of time before he becomes, well, sentient. Even without providing him with any memories, he's still able to regain them somehow. I've only replicated him here a handful of times, but he's always able to ascertain the state of things within moments. I don't know what he'll do when he sees you, but you must be prepared in the event he isn't satisfied with the results of his experiment."

Could she mean...

Taxia and I share looks of shock and anticipation.

"Because he is able to interact freely once he becomes sentient, we will need to leave the room. As not to be a distraction."

"Is it him?" my voice cracks, quaking with fear.

"Boy, don't you already know? It's you," Hypatia whispers and proceeds to push Taxia and K-2 to the exit.

"Can I stay?" Taxia asks.

"Not this time," Hypatia says in almost a comforting tone. They exit and I'm left alone on the platform.

The lights dim a bit and the crowd disappears. It's eerily quiet. A cold breeze brings in a gust of thick smoke. It pours through the platform and surrounding area. The silhouette of a dark figure slowly materializes as the smoke begins to clear. If the smoke was for effect, it wasn't necessary.

"Who are you?" The voice is low and gritty but calm, as if he already knew the answer.

"The name's Ren."

"Are you sure you are not me?" he speaks again.

"No. My name is Ren."

"And who is Ren?" he asks.

"The best mechanic in the MetiCity-6 Outskirtz."

"Good. So it worked. And I perished. As was the plan," he says, matter of fact. I can see the figure looking around at his surroundings for a moment. "This holoroom is something only I could have designed. So it must be Hypatia's. That means you found the clues I left and are now running simulations to train yourself in order to take over as rightful heir. So I ask again. Are you sure you are not me?"

She said he would be quick, but he figured it out in seconds. I guess seeing a younger version of himself might have tipped him off. Zelius Metihand is completely unfazed, his tone inquisitive and unperturbed.

"Speak," he commands.

"Well...no...well...kinda..." I stumble as his voice rumbles through the room.

"Maybe it didn't work. Why are you here?"

"I'm here to learn about you."

"To learn about me, or to become me?" he questions. Finally, the smoke clears as he steps into the dim light, revealing his features. He has a full beard with long silver-white hair. He still looks distinguished, but this version of Zelius depicts him in his twilight years.

"I don't want to become you. I want to expose you," I retort, trying to find some confidence.

"Expose me? You think the Compendium was created to expose me?" Zelius questions.

"Wasn't it?"

"So you haven't heard the true harmony? The hum of waves?" he says, lifting his chin, eyes closed as if he's smelled something pleasantly familiar.

"I don't know what you're talking about."

"You must meditate on this. When it's over," he says, stepping closer to me.

"When what's over?"

"This...game. This is a platform for combat, is it not? I am here to test you. That I am sure of. And because Hypatia will not let me continue to attack her system for too long, our time is limited. Let us proceed."

"Attack her sys-" I start before what feels like a sledge-hammer comes hurtling through my chest. I hit the ground so fast it almost feels like one impact.

"Slow," he mutters to himself. He had cleared nearly five yards in the blink of an eye. He was cloaked in a cape, so I can't tell if he has a Biosuit on, but I can't understand how he was able to accomplish such a feat without one. I pull myself up off the ground to stand before him. He isn't much taller than me, but it feels like he is towering over me. He draws his right hand back, and as I go to brace myself for the impact, I'm stunned by a quick jab that he throws with his other hand. It knocks me back a few feet and I take the silent victory of staying upright. My nose is gushing blood onto the platform and I can no longer breathe through it.

"Weak," he mutters in the same tone.

I notice my wrench is just a few feet to my right and reach out to grab it. As soon as I lock my fingers around it, his foot comes slamming down onto my hand, breaking my grip on the wrench.

"Arrrgghhh!" I scream out in pain, curling up on my knees, holding my hand in agony.

"And foolish." He seems to be talking to himself more than to me, disappointedly evaluating my existence.

"Were you not raised in the Outskirtz? Does this change in upbringing not make you equipped to handle such chal-lenges? Or did the process of cloning dull my cells, reverting me to a cowering-" I take advantage of his long-winded berating and throw a similar uppercut to the one I landed on Taxia earlier.

"Feeble-minded, child," he finishes without missing a beat, slightly tilting his head off-axis to avoid me. He grabs my wrist before I can reel it back in. "But you do have the hands of a craftsman," he says, examining my hand.

"I'm getting really tired of you ancient relics telling me what I'm worth!" I yell, throwing another shot with my free hand at his head, which is easily blocked. Immediately, I throw a knee up the middle aimed at his stomach, and it lands, but he is unfazed.

"And you do have grit," he responds, pulling my wrist down towards the ground until my chin crashes into his now-risen knee. My teeth snap together and my jaw rattles. "It is quite evident that you're not ready. Tell Hypatia to bring you before me one year from now. And If you are to appear in front of me again, and you haven't at least found the frequency of influence, I will consider this a failed experiment. Because until you do, nothing you see will be clear; nothing you do will be just."

I lay there in a state of almost euphoria. There is no pain; I'm numb. It's as if my brain has shut down my sensory perception and I can hear only the sound of Zelius walking away.

The lights return, filling up the room as Taxia and Hypatia's silhouettes appear in the corner of my eye. Still on the ground, I force myself up, and as my vision slowly returns, they come into focus.

"Well done, boy," Hypatia's comforting tone is anything but.

I sit silently, feeling a mix of relief and anger.

"I hope you are aware that the test was pass or die. Enjoy every breath you take from here on out. They are gifts. Speaking of gifts, I will allow you the use of the medical tank one last time. But only one of you," She says, looking over at Taxia.

"She can have it," I say, finally bringing myself to my feet.

"Oh, how noble," Hypatia remarks. Taxia looks shocked.

"K-2, please help Taxia to the meditank. I've got to take a look at something," I say sternly.

"No! I don't deserve it. K-2, your owner should take priority; check your protocols," Taxia argues.

"It does align. Ren. Come with me." K-2 grabs ahold of my shirt.

"Hey! No!" I try to plead, but I'm too weak to fight.

K-2 drags me forward and I'm forced to follow him out.

CHAPTER THIRTY-THREE_

I awake from the tank to find Taxia in bed sleeping. It's about 2:00 a.m., and while I'm healed, I'm still exhausted. I dress and head towards the door, trying to make as little noise as possible.

"Ugghh," a low murmur from Taxia. It stops me in my tracks. Her arm is wrapped up, but she looks to be breaking into a fever. Her skin is clammy and covered in cold sweat. I look back at the tank, which is slowly emptying, and quickly scoop some of the liquid into my hand. I slowly crawl into bed, trying my best not to wake her. Hovering my hand over the arm that's broken, I tilt it slightly, dripping little drops of liquid onto it. I know it won't be enough to heal the arm, but I want to prevent an infection if I can. As soon as the last drop hits her, she twitches in her sleep, her soft snoring slowing down. I pause for a moment, holding my breath before her chest begins to rise and fall again. Her eyes remain closed. Phew. I crawl up beside her on the bed and lay down, worried the weight of me leaving would wake her now. Drifting off into the dream world comes without warning.

They start as visions. Different from a normal dream. The

ring falling into the stadium, Elli singing her mournful song, Hypatia breaking Taxia's arm...Zelius's low, rumbling voice.

"The frequency of influence," Zelius speaks, standing firmly in the middle of the holoroom. I'm seeing it now as clearly as if I was meditating. It's serene and empty besides him.

CRASH!

The O-Racing ring comes crashing down through the holoroom. As it lands, large pinwheel-shaped metal spinning structures come flying out of the wreckage. My vision becomes overwhelmed by spinning pinwheels of vibrant colors and varying shapes. I awake as it becomes too much, too intense.

Taxia is still sleeping beside me on the bed, but this time, she's facing towards me. Did she notice I was here? I trace my eyes over her features, which are no longer contorted in pain, before I slowly climb out of bed and make my way towards the holoroom. When I walk inside, I see my wrench lying against the wall. I grab it, walk along the wall, and slowly glide my hand across the surface. I slam the wrench head into it and start to pry until a panel is revealed. Behind the panel is a complex system of wires, structural parts, and then another panel. I pry the smaller panel back to reveal its contents. A pinwheel mechanism, like the one from my dream. These things must be all over the place, under every panel. The mechanism must be a frequency regulator, which is used to remotely control the nanoparticles, but I've never seen one like it before. Perhaps one of these isn't functioning properly and that's why Hypatia is having random rendering issues? I find more, examining them, but I can't figure out how they work without turning on the holoroom. Something I don't think Hypatia would be happy to oblige, nor do I think she'd be happy to see me tearing apart these panels.

"What's that?" Taxia's voice softly fills the room, making me jump.

"Hey. You should be resting," I say, matching her tone.

"I can't sleep. What is that?" she asks.

"I'm not sure just yet, but I can't help but feel like it's important," I say, not looking away from the mechanism.

"It looks like the new frequency regulator they added to the last generation of credentials. It's what allows that new auto-translate feature that gives real-time vocalizations in your head," she explains.

"Mine was made beforehand, so I've always just learned the language if I needed to. Can I see yours?" I ask.

She holds out her hand, showing her credentials. "I can't take it off, but it's inside." I slide it off her wrist and begin separating the outer shell to get to the inner portions. Under the chamber, housing the rolled glass for the heads up display is another small compartment. I open it to find a similar-looking pinwheel device, except much smaller.

"It does look the same! I wonder why I've never seen one like this before," I ponder.

"Because most people who have the latest credentials don't often show up in the Outskirtz," she explains.

"How does it differ?" I ask.

"The upgrade was supposed to make the credentials more immersive. I think they called it 'neural syncing'. The few times I've had to repair that component, it was usually because the customer complained they felt 'off,'" Taxia explains.

"More immersive? Makes sense why they're used here in the holoroom. But I don't quite understand what emitting a frequency does to alter one's perception. To me, that sounds almost like brainwave synchronization."

"What's that?" she asks.

"So they categorize the types of electrical waves our brains produce into different 'states,' right? Beta, Alpha, Theta, and Delta, and so on. Like if we're active, we emit Beta waves. When we're asleep, we emit Delta waves. Brainwave sync is basically the process of manipulating someone's brain waves to another state."

"Can you tell what kind of waves this thing is emitting?" she asks.

"Yeah, the scan just finished. Looks like they transmit using Theta waves. Theta waves are what we emit when we're being creative, or meditating...or under hypnosis," I think out loud.

"Hypnosis? That explains why this room feels so real. It's almost as if you're in a state of hypnosis. Maybe that's why the headsets feel so immersive? It would make sense, but it's dangerous, right? I mean, what if the Company wanted to control the populace using this?"

"What if they already are?"

Once spoken, the silence creeps in, and we sit quietly thinking to ourselves. I remember the girls at the bar suddenly changing their drink. The strange obsession people had with the pink popcorn they were selling at the stadium. The uniformity of MetiCitians. The eerie loyalty to the Company.

"They're hypnotizing people!" I suddenly announce. "Even if just subtly enough to manipulate behavior, make them more passive. More accepting and compliant." I'm met with silence, but not disbelief.

"Maybe we can ask Hypatia? Do you think she already knows?" Taxia asks.

"I'm not sure. If she's been down here all this time, there's a chance she hasn't had a chance to inspect the new credentials up close. She'll be up soon, so we won't have to wait long to find out. Shit!"

"What?" Taxia asks.

"It's getting close to morning and I have to repair this

before she comes and wakes me for the last test. I'll finish up here; you get some rest." I say, turning to try and reattach the panels. Taxia hadn't moved.

"Go!" I command. It's a stern tone, but I wasn't going to take no for an answer.

"Fine, fine..." she says after a moment of shock.

I work for an hour or so repairing the panels and end up on the couch. I'm just falling asleep when Hypatia walks out of her bedroom door. Perfect timing.

"I know you're not sleeping, boy; I heard you hit the couch like a meteorite. Not a good idea to stay up before the day of a final," she instructs.

"If I pass, I can leave?" I ask.

"As I said, these tests are just to confirm you are able to complete the training you'll need to face Zelius again when the time comes."

"In one year."

"Yes. If you pass, that is. Come, let's get it over with."

She leads me back into the holoroom, where I just was no more than an hour ago, stops a few yards in and turns around.

"For your final test, I need to know that you are technologically adept. In order to walk in Zelius's shoes, you have to be highly proficient in understanding and navigating the technology that dominates society. Here, I have the three innovations. Fix them."

Between us appears a one-seater cruiser, an armorless military-grade Biosuit, and a Droid that looks eerily similar to my house Droid. I'm immediately relieved, finally, something in my wheelhouse.

"Why are you smiling?" Hypatia asks, seeing the joy beaming out of me.

"Because the alignment on the cruiser is out of rotation and the landing gear is stuck," I explain, crawling under the vehicle to adjust both.

"How did you-" Hypatia starts.

"And the Biosuit, it's too big. When it's taken off, it should return to a smaller frame. Because it hasn't, I'm guessing that it needs to be stretched out, then reset internally so it can return to form. I'll need tools for that, but do you really want me to go through the trouble?" I say, moving on to the Droid.

Hypatia looks at the Biosuit and then back at me. "Wait, but how-"

"And lastly, the Droid here is simply a coupling mismatch. The hips and shoulders need to be rearranged and most likely need to have the fittings redrilled. I can do that as well if you'd like," I offer.

"I don't understand." For the first time, I can see Hypatia's cool, calm demeanor turn to a bewildered confusion. She had clearly meant for this to be one of the harder tests. And perhaps it would be, to someone who didn't do this for a living, but her attempt at making the repairs hard to figure out just made them stand out more.

"Things like this are no trouble for me. But, what did give me some trouble last night was this holoroom. I've been trying to figure out exactly why you were having syncing issues, so I took off a panel."

"You did what!?" Hypatia exclaims, looking around the room to try and figure out which panel.

"When I took it off, I found something curious. A pinwheel-like frequency regulator. Are you aware there are thousands in this room?"

"Yes. Of course," she says, trying to return to a more collected tone.

"Do you know what they are for?" I ask.

"They are why this room feels so real. They enable the user

to more easily accept the illusion. It fills in all the little gaps that the holograms and nanobots cannot. Why?"

"Well, what if I were to tell you that they have added this frequency regulator to all the current credentials in use inside of MetiCity?" I ask.

"Those bastards...these regulators were never to be sold, and the technology behind them was supposed to have been lost along with Zelius and the rest of his prototypes. If that's true, then they could sync them up across entire cities, turning huge populations of people into living drones. They could influence public opinion on a massive scale. They could-"

"Control them?" I finished her sentence.

"Does Taxia have one in her credentials?" she asks.

"She does," I reply.

"I need to investigate this. Take the rest of the day off. You pass," she says, hurrying out of the room. So she didn't know. I should have been more excited. But Hypatia was right. It's not a game. I couldn't revel in the fact that these people were having choices made for them. That they were just puppets. That their freedom was an illusion.

I watch as the tests she had set up for me disassemble and pour back into the ground of the holoroom. I take a deep breath of relief. As I walk out of the room, my mind flashes to all the things I've survived here. The jungle, the board, K-2, and even Zelius. In a year from now, I will have to come before him again. But this time, I will be prepared. I will show him that his experiment wasn't a failure. That I can run with the torch he gave me and burn down his mistakes like a bundle of greesha. This is my story, not his.

CHAPTER THIRTY-FOUR_

After the test, I find Taxia in the kitchen cooking again. I sit down on one of the open stools, and as I look over, I can see K-2 sitting comfortably on the couch.

"Well, that was quick! So, I guess you passed?" Taxia asks wide-eyed as the food printer beeps. I nod.

"You talk to Hypatia?" she asks, walking up the island in the kitchen. I nod.

"Well, I wasn't going to make yours until you were done recovering from whatever nightmare Hypatia had set up, but since you're here do you want some?" she says, pointing to the printer.

"What are you making?"

"Just some French toast," she smiles.

"That's okay, I'll make some pancakes," I say, declaring my favoritism bluntly.

"If you say so. They're showing a rerun of last night's RFL fights. You want to watch?"

"Sure, why not," I shrug.

K-2 was already on the couch, so I sit down next to him.

"I'm excited to see this next match. Taxia and I have been

watching this sport as of late, and it's quite a spectacle," K-2 excitedly chirps.

Once Taxia is done, I start up the printer and grab a plate. As soon as Taxia hits play, I almost drop the plate, catching it just before it hits the ground.

"Raven!?" I exclaim.

"Hey, I thought you didn't watch?" Taxia asks.

"I've seen him before. Not in the RFL, but in the Human Fighting League," I explain.

"Oh yeah! This guy used to fight in the HFL, but after he killed some poor bastard, they ruled that he had too many body modifications to compete against normal humans. He's fairly new to the RFL, but he's already flying through the ranks," Taxia explains.

I watch as Raven walks through the ring, explaining to Taxia that the poor bastard was Koujin and that it's where K-2 got his Paladin armor. Raven is escorted in by the same manager from that night, but this time, he wore a long cloak adorned with black feathers. The bird theme was even more elaborate than before, and more menacing.

"Even his manager is in on the act," I point out.

"Exactly! You know how these things are. Everyone in the RFL has some kind of shtick. A lot of them do it to conceal their identity; some do it for the fans," Taxia explains.

"Conceal their identity? So you can enter into these competitions anonymously?" I ask.

"Yeah. Since the RFL, like the HFL, is a private company, they use an internal identification system. The league still requires credentials to enter, but that's kept completely separate from the MetiCorp system. The only time MetiCorp cares to check someone's identity is for those who become champions. Champions have their credentials linked to confirm they signed the contract. If not, they will need to. Even though those from the Outskirtz with credentials can enter, only citizens can win a belt."

I continue to watch, fixated on the screen, the wheels in my head full spin. The fight begins and Raven jumps into the air, hovers for a few seconds, then swoops down on his opponent, a robot with buzzsaws for hands. Raven's feet open up into massive talons just before driving them into the opponent's head, the buzzsaws sparking as they attempt to shield the victim from the inevitable. The match is quick and decisive. He's clearly had some upgrades since he fought Koujin.

"How does one enter this competition?"

"I mean, there are tons of ways. There's an amateur league you can fight through if you've got no experience or relevant battle data to provide. Sometimes, they do tournaments for a shot at becoming professional, so even those with only a little experience have a shot. It's really opened up in recent years. People from all over have been bringing some really amazing tech to the arena. Well, besides this buzzkill over here." She says, gesturing to the screen. "It's so popular now; I hear the waiting list takes forever."

"Over a year?"

"No, but months for sure," Taxia confirms.

"Perfect," I say as she glances over at me.

The door to Hypatia's room slides open and she saunters out sadly.

"Well, you were right. I've done some investigating and have picked up a frequency being emitted throughout each of the cities. The credentials of every single MetiCitian working to amplify the signal, causing a collaborative communication system. All of whom are blissfully ignorant to their fate as nothing more than mere ants, high on the hive's pheromone signal. Plainly, even if you find a way to release the

Compendium, I'm not sure anyone will give a damn," she says, looking defeated.

"We'll worry about that when the time comes. Until then, I've got a plan," I declare.

"A plan?" Hypatia and Taxia sync up.

"I'm going to enter K-2 in the RFL. I'll have to run a credential test, but due to my high Droid mastery level, I think if I can become champion in record time, I might be able to reach ICON status."

"RFL is popular, sure, but what makes you think you'll be granted ICON status from one title?" Hypatia inquires.

"Because K-2 is like nothing they've seen before. They're going to love him," I say, looking over at him.

"They will?" K-2 asks.

"Yes. They will. Are you up for it?"

"You mean I would compete like them?" He can't hide the excitement in his voice.

"As Taxia said, most competitors hide their identity when competing. So we wouldn't have to worry about raising too many red flags by signing up. I have no doubt, after seeing his competition in action, that he would rise through the ranks quickly. A title fight would put me on a massive stage where I might be able to speak to the people, long enough to tear them away from the frequency influence to digest the Compendium."

"Hmmm," Hypatia says, thinking for a long moment. We all watch her.

"This is...an acceptable plan. I should be able to find some benign credentials for you to use as cover, then you can use your actual credentials to sign up for the RFL. But once you're back in MetiCity, you're going to be on your own. You cannot contact old friends, you cannot reveal your identity. Not until you've secured the Compendium. And then there's Zelius. You still need to meet with him again before you leave."

"I can take care of myself." I wonder how that sounds coming from me, bruised and black-eyed, shaken to the core. Taxia and I trade glances. She's all wide-eyed and shocked. I smile, and the corners of her lips begin to curl.

"Then it appears we have reached a resolution. One could say you took your time, but it seems sometimes perfection and patience are close relatives. There is still work to do, but I do believe this calls for a celebration!" She exclaims.

"A celebration?" Taxia asks, confused as I am.

"Yes! I've always wanted to properly entertain guests in the garden. I'll make tea!" she says excitedly, making her way over to the kitchen. "You two head into the garden and I'll meet you there."

Taxia, K-2, and I are slow to react, but Hypatia gestures to us to get moving.

"Ren...what just happened? It's like she just rebooted. How did you do that!?" Taxia says as we make our way down the hall. I shrug and a shooting pain goes up my back. I could really use a nice bath and a nap, but it sounds like attendance is going to be required for this little tea party.

We arrive in the garden and Hypatia follows behind with a set of three elegant cups on a tea tray. She waves her hand over a random spot in the grass and up springs a table and chairs. So, the technology in the holoroom isn't limited to just that space.

"Please sit," Hypatia says with a friendly smile that's more unsettling than the one she usually wears. Is that because it's sincere? We sit down at the table and she begins pouring tea. "Initially, I had planned to celebrate Ren's little graduation, but I was so disheartened to hear how they had twisted Zelius's technology, I lost my appetite for it. But now that you have arrived at a logical plan, however low the probability of its success, I feel renewed."

Taxia and I begin sipping our tea as K-2 finds a seat near us to watch. Hypatia sits down across from us and takes a sip of her tea, smiling through the sips.

"So, do you already have a theme in mind, Ren?" Taxia breaks the awkward silence.

"A theme?" I ask.

"For the RFL. We're going to need something that stands out. You know, a shtick?"

"Oh yeah. When we win, and I get the Compendium, I'm going to go from an RFL professional to Zelius. So, I don't want the transition to be too far-fetched. But I also don't want to show up looking like Zelius. So I thought maybe a military theme? K-2's Paladin armor would already be quite fitting." I say, glancing over at K-2. Hypatia watches silently, smiling, listening closely.

"Eh, it's been done. We need something...grand. Something eye-catching," she explains.

"I see. Well, if we can't draw from his military experience to make the connection, maybe we feed into the rumors and give the people what they really want."

"What's that?" Taxia asks.

"They want their King back," I explain.

"Do they now? Haven't you ever heard the phrase 'No More Kings?'" Hypatia asks.

"No more kings? Sure. But the Last King? That's a different story," I proclaim to a skeptical-looking Hypatia.

"No, he actually makes a good point. Royalty. MetiCitians are obsessed with the aristocrats and dignitaries, so presenting yourself as such might draw some eyes."

"Presenting ourselves," I correct her. Hypatia takes another sip now, almost hiding behind her glass as she waits for Taxia's reaction.

"Presenting ourselves," Taxia echoes my sentiment. "Not only that, the UG are obsessed with the idea of Zelius's return, so mirroring him could win their favor as well. Plus, RFL is surprisingly popular in the Outskirtz, so those still loyal to him may also be drawn to us. It's actually quite genius." Taxia smiles at me before taking a sip.

"So, you do want to be King after all," Hypatia speaks softly, getting to her feed now and stepping over to me.

"Well..." I start but notice she has now dipped the tip of her thumb into her tea.

"Umm...what's happening?" Taxia says nervously. Hypatia takes her thumb and presses it against my face, smearing the tea across my brow.

"A King must be anointed Ren," Hypatia says, taking a step back. "Behold Ren, the anointed one, rightful heir to the throne of MetiCorp. In the likeness of Zelius, he is reborn, heralding the dawn of a new era as the Last King," she says in a tone that insinuates there is a crowd listening. There's an awkward silence for a moment that's broken by K-2 faintly clapping in excitement. Taxia cracks up and I can't help but to follow suit.

"Well, it's true," an unimpressed Hypatia says as she returns to her seat.

"Well, I hope the Queen doesn't have to go through the same ceremony," Taxia says through her continued laughter.

"She does not. They only ever care about the King, my dear. But don't forget it is the Queen who keeps the King in check," she nods to Taxia. "Oh! I almost forgot. I have a little present for you Ren."

"Allspirits, please tell me it's not another test," I groan.

"I've been keeping tabs on your friend, Elli. She recently released a song that is breaking all kinds of streaming records. I thought you might like to hear?" she asks, leaning in. Taxia looks over at me to get my reaction. I can't hide my shock.

"I thought so," Hypatia says while waving her hand slightly.

Overhead, I can hear violins and an assortment of other instruments building into a crescendo before stopping and letting the silence speak volumes. Elli's voice enchantingly emerges, radiantly transcendent; her song speaks of profound loss.

"Beautiful, isn't it?" Hypatia says, closing her eyes. Taxia's focused on her glass and it's hard to gauge her reaction, but it can't be helped; Elli's voice is entirely unique and entrancing. Hypatia goes to set her tea glass on the table and just as she sets it down, the table and tea cups drop, plummeting to the ground at our feet. We all share a stunned moment, puzzled as to what exactly just happened.

"I mean, I didn't think her singing was that bad, but zeesh!" Taxia jokes.

Hypatia and I stare at the shattered cups and tea, and then, slowly, our eyes meet. It's the second time today she's worn that confused look. The same look she gave me as I flew through her last test. She didn't know either.

CHAPTER THIRTY-FIVE:
TAXIA'S STORY_

"Ren?" I call out, my voice hoarse. Panic rises in me as I sprint after the cloaked figure. I round the corner, the door to my shop standing in front of me, lock broken and glass smashed. I step inside carefully, only to hear the squelch of something wet beneath my feet. Lifting my boot, thick red blood drips from it onto the floor. Dread courses through my veins as I follow the trail further inside. It ends as it meets two broken bodies lying in a heap on the floor. Anarki... I try to scream, but I'm unable to make a sound. I look up, and back in the shop, I see Ren through the darkness, holding Zander and Zari, both limp in his arms. His glare is piercing and full of hatred, and the mournful song of a grieving sister fills my head.

"Why!?" Ren questions me. I'm too stunned to speak. "WHY!?" he screams this time. He rests their bodies on the floor and stumbles his way over to me as I sit, knees covered in the blood of my friends. "WHY!?" he screams again before swinging his wrench at me, eyes full of tears.

I jolt upright, my heart thudding in my chest as I gasp for air. My body is coated in cold sweat, and my hands are shaking. I take a second to catch my breath before rolling over to the cool side of the bed, muffling my frustrated scream into the pillow. I thought the nightmares would lessen after almost a year. Apparently not. Flipping my arm up, I activate my credentials and the time projects from them. 2:10 a.m., less than four hours before my alarm will sound. Hypatia is making us wake up early to pack before Ren meets Zelius again. I'm sure she'll also force us into some last-minute combat training. I turn over once more to my back and stare at the ceiling. My stomach lurches. Am I ready to face the MetiCity again with only four hours of sleep? Am I ready to face the MetiCity at all?

So much has changed since the first day Hypatia dragged us down here. Ren hasn't shown me the kind of hatefulness I saw in my dream since then, so I'm not sure why my night-mares insist on playing it out for me. Maybe because I know the only reason he forgave me is that he blames himself instead of me. I've gone out of my way to help as much as possible and atone, though. I've been his chef, his training partner, his smoking buddy, and anything else I could be to alleviate the huge burden that's been placed on his shoulders. All of this time, the guilt still lingers, simmering beneath the surface until it boils over into these nightmares.

A sudden rush of air from the door sliding open makes me shiver.

"Ren?" I squeak, squinting into the dark to see his silhou-ette in the doorway.

"Sorry Taxia. Did I wake you? I couldn't sleep. I was looking for an extra blanket." His voice is soft and calm. It soothes me. "I'll let you rest. I'm sorry." He turns to leave.

"Wait." Did he hear the scream? "Please stay." I've said the words before I have time to think. Seconds of silence tick over into what feels like hours in my head. I pull the covers further up over my chest. I doubt he can see me in the dark, but I wonder if he can hear the thump of my heart through the blanket. He steps forward and the glow from the clock washes over his features. Climbing into the bed, he kicks my feet away from him.

"You ask me to stay and then you point those things at me?" he huffs. I smile into the darkness.

"Well, if you didn't eat so many pancakes, you might not take up so much room!" I quip. The bed shakes as he laughs. I turn my head to the right and watch him. He folds his hands over his chest and flips his bangs out of his eyes, a habit he has when he's thinking.

"How do you feel about meeting Zelius again?" I ask.

"I thought you had forgotten. I'm not worried. I was ready the day after meeting him, when we found the frequency of influence in the holoroom."

"He underestimated you," I say.

"I couldn't have done it without you. I underestimated you, Taxia," he replies.

I've always been stubborn about accepting compliments, so I change the subject. "I wonder how much control MetiCorp really has, using that frequency? If we release the Compendium..."

"When," he corrects me, "When we release the Compendium, the truth will be revealed, even to those with closed eyes."

Ren had become more confident as of late, perhaps because we had analyzed and planned every little detail. Our only concern now was how we could guarantee anyone would actually read the Compendium if the frequency told them not to. The pinwheel that produces the Theta waves can transmit from any one of a billion devices or all at the same time. There's no program we can run to stop it remotely, even if we had access to the entire credential database. The only way would be to manually disconnect every single MetiCitian's credentials, one by one. I suppose Ren is betting that there's only one person who could get them to listen, and he's becoming more and more like him every day.

He hasn't moved since I drifted off into thought. It's not the first time we've shared a bed; that would have been about a year ago when Hypatia broke my arm. Ren had begged me to use the meditank, but I refused to waste resources. Plus, I deserved the pain. Pain is definitely what I got, and a raging fever from my fracture. I remember drifting in and out of consciousness and catching glimpses of Ren. The feel of cool liquid splashing my arm, him passed out on the bed beside me. He was gone when I woke up, and my fever had broken. I don't think he meant for me to know he had been there.

I swallow my anxiety and open my mouth, but he speaks first.

"So, you ready to kick some Droid ass?"

I know winning the RFL is the most logical way to reach ICON status, but the thought of hiding in plain sight still scares me. My sole comfort comes from the amount of work we've put into our disguises. We can't risk being recognized at all, so we're covered from head to toe. Even K-2 has a set of exo-armor to cover up Koujin's Paladin Biosuit. We worked for three nights solid with Hypatia to design it for him. The main issue was weight, since he already had the Paladin armor on. In the end, a carbon fiber shell worked best. It's form-fitted over the existing Biosuit, so we didn't have to change too much. I even had fun with the airbrush, making it white and gold to match our capes and masks. All we have to do is win the tournament and release the Compendium. When I think about it that way, it doesn't sound so difficult. But as confident as we are, we both know it will be.

"Born ready. In ranking, they told stories predicting my future. Taxia, the Droid destroyer. They must have known I was going to be this smart and strong when I grew up," I boast sarcastically.

"Don't forget beautiful," he whispers. Heat rises in my cheeks.

"Lucky for you since you've had to look at this face for a year," I call his bluff by turning over to face him. You don't faze me Ren Unkno.

He turns to face me. Fuck, I didn't see that coming.

"Who said I was looking?" he says softly, staring at me. He's really changed over the past year. Not like a dam breaking, but slowly, day by day. The shy mechanic who couldn't look me in the eye has grown, mentally and physically. My gaze traces over his arms, but I catch myself and flick my eyes back up to his. He's smirking. Cocky fuck. I can see his scar from where his bangs have fallen away. I reach out my hand and trace my finger across it. He closes his eyes and leans into my touch, his breath catching in his throat. His lips instinctively brush across my palm as I bring my hand down his face.

"Fuck it," I growl. His eyes open wide and then close as I bring my other hand to his face, straddle my leg over him and press my lips against his. He pulls me in roughly, tangling his fingers in my hair and letting instinct take over.

BEEEEEP.

I blink my eyes open.

BEEEEEP.

"Alright, shut up!" I grumble as I slam my hand down on the alarm button. 6:00 a.m. I guess I fell asleep? I lay for a second, yawning, then stretch out all my limbs, which are weirdly aching. My hand hits something warm and I shriek. "Ren?" I whisper to myself.

One of his eyes opens and the corner of his mouth turns up in a sleepy smile. Oh fuck. I lift the covers to escape. I'm naked. His eyes crinkle. He's enjoying this way too much. I should ask where my clothes are, but the look on his face is pissing me off. I need to wipe off that smug smile. I throw the blanket off, stand up and stretch, arching my back and letting out a sleepy moan as I do. Glancing over my shoulder, his eyes are nearly falling out of his skull.

"Can't a girl get a little privacy?" I feign annoyance. He quickly turns away. Checkmate.

I walk back into the room after showering, and Ren is gone. I get dressed and triple-check the contents of the backpack Hypatia gave me before heading out to the kitchen. She's on the couch drinking a nauseous-looking smoothie. Ren's standing in the kitchen, inhaling pancakes like an animal. He looks up at me, and his expression is reassuring.

"I trust you slept well, Taxia dear? Considering the couch was empty when I woke up this morning." Hypatia gives me a look over the top of her glass. I could be mistaken for saying it's envy. Ren slows down his assault on the pancakes; he's listening for my response. Unfortunately, K-2 has entered the room and takes it upon himself to speak.

"I recall Miss Taxia and Master Ren having an in-depth conversation late into the night. It seemed to be surrounding the topic of religion," he recalls.

"Discussing God, were we?" Hypatia lets out a shrill, condescending laugh at her own joke. The only way to handle this is to pretend it never happened. I stroll over to the kitchen counter and steal a pancake from Ren's plate.

"That was quick. I guess it went well?" I whisper to Ren. His meeting with Zelius couldn't have lasted more than forty-five minutes. He must have even had time to shower since his hair is wet. It suits him.

"Like I said, I wasn't worried," he replies, his mouth full.

"He passed," Hypatia adds. I wonder what would happen

if he hadn't? I ponder this while picking at the edges of the pancake.

A few hours later, we're crammed into Hypatia's jet. Thankfully, I'm in the back with K-2, so I don't have to make small talk. My body is still aching. I tell myself it's from the self-defense drills she had us running after breakfast and not from last night. As awesome as Hypatia's place is, I missed this heat. I close my eyes and turn my face up to the sky. The cruiser is insanely fast, and soon, the glare from the domed MetiCity-6 heat shield is too bright for me to keep pretending to sleep. We zip through one of the docking panels, and the city atmosphere hits me. It's at least ten degrees cooler and way noisier.

Hypatia pulls the cruiser into a random space out the back of a QuickPick and activates the stealth button. Last time I saw her use it, the whole thing disappeared. This time, the silver paint becomes rusty. The shiny trim becomes mismatched shades of black, and one of the side wings disappears. It looks like something that would have pulled into my shop and never left. It's perfect. Not even a 'scav would try their luck with it now. I wish we had stealth buttons. I still worry if the costumes we have are enough to mask our identity. At least long enough to do what we need to. Hypatia looks us up and down after we step onto the asphalt of the parking lot.

"Remember the plan. Don't die," she says curtly, pulls up her hood, and walks off in the opposite direction. She mentioned earlier she had 'alternative business' in the city. Whatever that means. The lady is impossible to read.

"How inspirational," Ren mumbles. He turns towards me, and I can tell he's smiling through the mask. I shake my head in agreement. We move in silence under the leafy canopies that cover the MetiCity backstreets. Greenery was originally installed as a buffer for the heat, but it grew way faster than expected. Now, there are pockets of plants braided amongst almost all the white buildings. A city 'scaping bot rushes past us, fighting to keep the unruly vines perfect, and K-2 tilts his head at it.

"The landscapers are different now. More aesthetically pleasing," K-2 states. I forget he was stuck in the Outskirtz for so long. I wonder if he ever feels like outdated tech.

"Zari," Ren says, fiddling with his cape. "Her work on the maintenance Droids earned her some serious credit in ranking. She was the only one who could figure out how to introduce the plants to their cleanup cycle. Of course, she had to make them way cuter too." There's hurt in his voice. It's jarring to hear him mention her name; he never talks about her. Or Zander. My nightmare flashes back into my head, and I shake it away.

"Those girls are wicked smart," I reply.

"Will we get to see Elli soon?" K-2 asks.

"No. We can't risk her getting hurt, and we agreed not to contact anybody we know," Ren says coldly. I know he doesn't mean to be so harsh. I continue to pull K-2 towards the city center. He follows willingly, though I have to drag him away multiple times from the simplest of things that catch his eye.

"Come on pequeño," I praise.

"Who?" Ren asks.

"Remember the nanny I told you about? The one that raised me? That was her nickname for me. It means little one. She called my parents idiota. Bet you can guess what that means," I smirk.

He snorts at the nickname now. I guess calling a six-foot Droid 'little one' is ironic.

As we approach the RFL arena, there's a line of fans scanning their credentials for entry. The crowd looks bigger than it does on TV. Ren grabs my hand to pull me through, which makes my stomach flip. We push towards the competitor's entrance, and I notice him staring at a guy elbowing his way towards us. He's tall and toned, with slicked-back black hair. The outfit he's wearing screams highcred. He's filming himself, and a girl clings to his arm, desperate to be in the shot.

"Here comes another competitor! Hey man. Sick costume. It's based on those old Mexican luchadores, right?" he asks. He's met with silence. "So, new guy, what makes you think YOU can win this thing?" His tone is almost as arrogant as his demeanor. Further silence as Ren ushers me ahead of him. Hypatia had mentioned some interviews might boost our status among the other competitors, and I know Ren can change his voice with the mod I installed in his costume. That means there's a reason he's staying silent, and it makes me want to push forward even faster. The cocky voice follows us.

"What's your deal man? You some kind of first-city freak? Too good for an interview? Droid looks like shit anyway. Any noso could crush that thing," he says, dismissing us.

I can see a controller behind a barrier beam. I hold my breath as we pass through, and I turn back to see the guy has already cornered another competitor.

"Migo," Ren whispers loud enough for only me to hear, confirming my suspicion. I try to offer him a sympathetic gaze, forgetting my face is covered. I settle for squeezing his hand, he squeezes back. We're lucky that Raven decided to hold this invitational tournament, allowing the winner a shot at him. It makes our journey to a title fight much shorter, but it also means we have to fight in Ren's City. So, running into someone he knows was inevitable.

We continue inside and I spot a giant screen with the words 'Sign In' flashing in MetiCity white. I point it out to Ren and tap the credentials on my wrist to signal him to switch social credit ID. Hypatia had layered some bogus credentials over Ren's in order for us to get around the city, but in order to get ICON status, he'd have to use his own to check in. He scans in, and a message pops up:

'Operator Name: The Anointed. Arrival confirmed.'

He breezes through a few generic waivers as I look around.

"What the fuck?" Ren gasps. I turn to see 'Pre-Fight Scan' as the next step.

"I don't get it. We sent 'em the experience files. Why would they need to scan K-2?" I question as we read the details on the screen.

"As of the year 2120, by MetiCity law, all competitors are subject to pre-fight experience scans. This will include, but is not limited to, a download to verify the authenticity of your submitted documentation." A nearby voice recites. I spin around to see a security guard standing behind us. Where the fuck did he come from? Have they been listening the whole time? Ren flips on his voice alteration. His words come out low and distorted.

"And what does this download entail? My Droid is that of the highest caliber. I won't stand for any kind of interference in his code." He holds his head up and stares down the security from behind his mask.

"You must learn to speak like royalty," Hypatia had said one day in training. I'd rolled my eyes at the time, but I'm glad for it now. Outskirtz slang is way too recognizable. The guard zooms into the small print on the screen and begins to read:

1. Safety Scan - Prohibited modifications include firearms, explosives and projectiles.

. . .

2. Impact Absorption - How much damage can your Droid take?

3. Impact Causation - How much damage can your Droid cause?

4. Battle Experience - A rating of your Droids past battle experience.

He then gestures for us to read the fine print. You can choose a full or partial download, with an automatic point deduction for the partial.

"Very well," Ren agrees.

"Follow me through this gate," the guard says. I guess condescension is in his job description since there's an obvious arrow showing us the way. K-2 follows him, and Ren pauses to wait for me.

"We can't let them do a full scan. He'll score too high," he whispers.

"Ask them to scan his solo fights only, none with your face in," I reply. He nods, and we step into the next room. It's pristine, white and shining steel. A few competitors stand in the middle of the room. Scanners surround them, and battle footage is projecting onto a central monitor. Our uniformed friend from earlier is setting up K-2, his finger hovering over 'download all data.'

"Solo battles only," Ren interrupts. The guard looks up defiantly. "Solo, battles, only, *Sir*," Ren grits his teeth. The guard reverts the menu, rolls his eyes, and activates the partial download. He probably thinks we're embarrassed about our skills. The scan activates, and visions of the holoroom arena we used during training appear on the monitor. I see a few of the owners checking it out. Without Ren and me, K-2 looks competent but not hugely threatening. The scan finishes in about thirty seconds. The footage disappears and I notice a blurry figure watching us from a privacy tinted window above the room. I guess he's the one scoring us.

"Take your hands off my Droid," Ren says, through gritted teeth. I whip my head back around to see the guard shoving K-2 off the scanner. "Now," he hisses. The guard slinks away, and we rush to K-2.

"I was given no instruction to step off."

"I know pequeño," I say reassuringly.

"I'm very glad there was no interference in my high-caliber coding," he adds. On any other day, his blasé comment would have had us in fits of giggles. Today, we share a glance with laughing eyes and shake our heads in tandem.

CHAPTER THIRTY-SIX_

We find an empty area near the back wall and sit. A room off to the side is labeled 'friendly fights only'- the print beneath urging us to observe. I slip my credentials off my wrist and fit them to my ear, the screen sliding over my eyes as I activate them. My vision is filled with a replica sphere. I'm sitting in the front row, so close I can see the rust on the screws of the Droids competing. I feel Ren tap-in beside me, turning to my left to confirm his presence in the simulation. We focus in, and it looks like the smaller Droid has been underestimated, as usual. It slides directly under the control panel of the larger. One touch, and a current pulses through the opponent. Short Circuit. Rapid incapacitation and all the Droid's actions are now reversed. It stumbles, unsure of its next move, its gigantic mallet modification swinging up towards itself. The owner immediately calls for surrender to prevent its total destruction.

"That's it folks! The Hammer has forfeited! The electric touch of death was just too much for the giant Droid!" the announcer booms.

"Well, at least he went down swinging, Clint!" a second commentator jokes. A simulated laugh track rattles in my ear, and I tap-out. Cringe. Zoning back in on my actual surroundings, I look at Ren. I guess he tapped-out faster than I did, as his credentials are already back on his wrist.

"Should we enter him in a friendly?" I ask. He shakes his head. We never got to see any of this pre-fight stuff on TV, and I find myself curious about the minutiae of it all.

"Friendly matches are designed to fuck you over. Alliances competing to draw in unsuspecting rookie competitors. The less time they know our touch of death, the better," he says. I trust he knows what he's talking about. Night after night, I'd catch the light of him researching from under the bedroom door at Hypatia's. So instead, we sit and we wait, watching the competitors get scored one by one. An escort ushers out the non-qualifying teams through a back door. Occasionally, I tap back in to watch more of the friendlies, and I start to notice the alliances Ren mentioned. I count the teams as they pass through the scan.

"The Anointed?" A voice calls out over the speaker. I don't move until Ren steps forward, tapping me with his boot to remind me that's our name. The official gives us a judging glance. "Pass," he reads. I let out a sigh of relief. We came across respectable, not overly flashy. It's what we needed.

"Final competitor count: 16 qualifying teams. Please follow your assigned security to the briefing room."

"Great. That slomper wasn't just security. He's OUR security," I roll my eyes as the uniform from earlier saunters over. He looks as pleased about this as we are.

The briefing room is private, with a small white sofa and a big screen. A portable food printer sits on the table in the center of the room, accompanied by two crystal mugs. I set it to brew us some algae tea. The stuff tastes disgusting, but we're gonna need the energy.

"You will compete fourth. You may observe your competitors until it is your turn. Any vacating of this room or the adjoining restroom at any point will be classed as immediate disqualification. Place your belongings in this tray for scanning." The guard declares. I wonder if he even knows how to say please. I tip the pack off my back and place it in the tray. Ren does the same. The guard leaves and we settle onto the sofa and drink our tea. K-2 rests on the designated charging port against the far wall. I want to speak, but I know we're being watched. I have to be careful. I gesture to the screen to turn on, and Ren mirrors my action to turn it off. I look at him quizzically.

"A King has no use for the observation of events preceding ones he's already seen come to fruition," he says. He wants to learn about them in the fight. It's a power play. I trust him; he's more than demonstrated his competence over the past year. Plus, we've watched so much RFL that we know a lot of the common strategies. The usually comfortable silence that follows feels heavy. My head is filled with worry about the upcoming plan. What if we're somehow recognized? What if K-2 can't win? Even if we do win, how on earth are we going to defeat a creature like Raven? The gravity of the pressure on our shoulders sends me into a spiral. I look to Ren for comfort, and the thoughts are replaced by fleeting memories of last night. His lips on mine, his fingers gripping my hair...suddenly, I'm incredibly aware of my leg pressed against his. I shift in my seat and he presses his hand on my thigh.

"Sixteen qualifying teams...that's four fights in the tournament. We only have to win four fights." My attempted nonchalance comes across as strained.

"Relax Taxia. Close your eyes," he says softly. "Clear your mind, be present in this moment with me," he recites the words I've used before. We meditate for a short while, until the door opens. Our security drops our bags in a heap at my feet.

"HEY-" I start. Ren steps in front of me and cuts me off.

"In the future, I would appreciate it if you were more respectful of our belongings," he says. The guard stares him down. I clench my fist.

"Your opponent is Cal n' Crusher. Raise your arm so I can transfer their statistics," the guard says.

"I don't need it," Ren replies. He has already analyzed the fights a thousand times. Security doesn't argue, and turns to leave.

"My Queen. You must remember your royal tongue," Ren exclaims as he grips my wrist. I forgot to modulate my voice. That's why he cut me off.

"The Anointed to ArenaSphere door five please," a voice calls over the com-link.

The door is easy to find 'cus of the noise behind it. Taking one last look at each other, we push through it into the arena. It's so bright. Studio lights flood the room, glinting off the gold on K-2's exo-armor. Blaring music assaults my senses. MetiCity war anthem. Since the original cities are just about the only Metifucks dumb enough to play this shit, we thought it might be a good distraction for anyone trying to figure out our identity. I recite the plan in my head as we're lifted to the owner's box. Actually, it's more of a platform than a box. A slab of translucent perspex suspended ten feet up from the side of the sphere by cabling so the audience has an unobscured 360 view.

Our competitor, Cal, stands across from us on the platform with his arms folded and his chest puffed out. He's definitely old enough to be a rebel, and his vintage US flag shirt strains over his fat stomach. It's way hairier than his head, which at present is reminding me oddly of the MetiCity dome. A door on the platform opens into the sphere, and K-2 steps inside to meet Crusher, a huge, boxy-looking bot that towers over him. I kinda wish I had a chance to analyze the data they offered on this thing, but the anthem is slowing down and we have no time to spare. Slipping off my pack, I pull on the strap so the fabric flips inside out. Ren grabs my hand, and we tap our credentials to the packs in sync. Out pop the modded flatpack discs, and we move to stand in front of them. The bass of the music covers the sound, but I can feel the energy knitting together behind me. I focus on the music and tune out my surroundings. At the crescendo of the anthem, we sit. King and Queen, on our thrones. They were my idea, based on a portable holodisc Hypatia used for a tea party once, so I'm relieved we didn't fall on our asses.

"Quite an entrance from The Anointed there!" the announcer booms.

"You're telling me. Those thrones appeared from nowhere!" his partner replies. The mixed reactions from the stands demonstrate that our disguise and performance are working perfectly. Confusion and curiosity are the aim. I take a deep breath, happy for the seat keeping me grounded. The brief silence after the song is filled with yelling as onlookers begin to thrust their credentials at the gamesters. I wonder how many of the punters are taking a shot at the underdogs today. Looking over at our opponent, I can tell he's sickened by our act. He reeks of ego and has the aura of a career battler. He saunters over.

"Ah'd shake yer hand, but I 'magine Mr. and Mrs. high-and-mighty would pitch a hissy fit at the feel o' hard-workin' skin," he drawls. Ironic. I extend a single white and gilded glove in his direction.

"Charmed," I respond, batting my eyelashes as he shakes it limply. His nails are filthy and jagged, but I shake back anyway. Cal obviously isn't used to people engaging with his bullshit, as his eyes widen and his nostrils flare.

"Ah, dunno who you think you are, all gussied up, but I seen yer stats. That ancient hunk o' junk got no chance against my Crusher," he spits. I notice the crowd has hushed. They're waiting for our response.

"Silence. Your false confidence fills the air with a putrid stench that reeks of vanity and ignorance," Ren yawns, looking through Cal, uncaring. Cal picks up his dropped jaw and begins to stutter in response.

"Well...well, how 'bout this?" he taunts, flexing his flabby arms in a desperate attempt to provoke a reaction. Of course, his fans roar, and Cal wipes the sweat from his upper lip. He's making me queasy, so I turn my attention to the Droids. K-2 patiently waits on one side. I take a good look at his opponent. Besides the massive stature, the next thing I notice is the palette of red, white and blue coating its armor. Cal the patriot. Stats scroll through the holoprompter above. Crusher; 15 feet tall, 420lbs...10,000 NPI!? The math is not adding up on that mass. Those Newtons Per Impact make his damage almost twenty-five times his weight. I scan the Droid for a reason, and quickly spot it. His shoulders are bulked out with thousands of tightly coiled springs.

"The springs," Ren observes at the same time. "I bet they pack a punch. Bending the rules on projectiles, I'd say." Our eyes scan Crusher, looking for any exploitable weaknesses. His broad chest-plate is reinforced with MetiMetal, and steel struts encircle his neck. A face plate covers everything besides a thin red light in place of eyes. The legs are more carved MetiMetal, connected via thick discs, which are dripping lubricant. I can't imagine the suspension needed to keep its weight up. From here, Crusher looks airtight. An imposing monster of metal and spray paint. Cal may look and act stupid, but there's no doubt he's created a weapon.

"We know nothing about the speed," I say to Ren, "His

impulse momentum probably sucks," I add. He nods, but the look in his eye tells me he's spotted something else.

The noise tapers off as the room dims. Spotlights flicker and focus on a holoscreen, which displays an image of a short, wisened-looking old man.

"Welcome to the first ever Robot Fighting League invitational in MetiCity-6 history. We have some new competitors today, so just to reiterate, there are to be NO firearms, NO explosives, and absolutely NO projectiles. The fight is over when one of the Droids is unable to inflict damage, or through forfeit. No human contact. You may only communicate to your Droid through your com-link. Be civil, folks. Now, let the fight begin!" A bell rings. The screen disappears, and the lights focus on the sphere. Ren notices the look on my face.

"It will be okay. Don't worry."

"I wasn't worri-"

A sudden whooshing sound stops me mid-sentence. Crusher's fist rushes through the air. His springs are hyperextended, the distance of the sphere covered, it'll hit K-2 any second. I want to look away, but I don't even have time to react. His giant fist collides with the glass and an impact pulse ripples through the arena. Huh? K-2 stands five feet to the left of the collision, his head tilted in thought. Conversation explodes behind me.

"Holy fuck, that thing can move!"

"I blinked! What happened?!"

Security drones buzz around us. A wave of relief washes through me, coursing through my blood, and rapidly turns to adrenaline. Ren is hyperfocused on the sphere, where a barrage of smaller punches is taking place. Crusher's right arm takes a few seconds to spring back once it's hyperextended, but his left fist is busy putting in work. A series of shorter, faster jabs aimed at K-2's head. But he is fluid, side-stepping, ducking and backing out of connection from any of them. The pair are almost dizzying to watch, one strong and one quick, dancing a grotesque waltz of grinding metal and springs. Crusher's right arm is fully retracted now. I hear winding, but it's his left fist that jolts forward. K-2 steps to the right, anticipating the blow, but no springs uncoil. Instead, Crusher spins on his ankle axle, his foot speeding towards the place K-2 is about to step. At the last second, K-2 twists his back towards the ground, the kick breezing inches above his face. He stumbles. It missed, but the feint has thrown him off guard.

"Got 'cha, you slippery bastard!" Cal yells.

Winding. Uncoiling. K-2 is still trying to orient himself. A screeching, metal-on-metal sound pierces my ears. Our Droid is thrown through the air and slams into the sphere right in front of us. The breath escapes my lungs in a hiss as though the injury was mine. I lift my hand to the glass, K-2 resting in a heap on the other side, looking impossibly small and frail. Ren grabs my hand and brings it to rest on the arm of his throne beneath his. He squeezes it tightly. Somehow, I can feel him grin behind the mask, and I'm reassured. Crusher's arm begins to retract, and K-2 lays still. Seconds pass. Suddenly, he leaps forward and grips his fingers around a coil in the giant's wrist, locking them in place. The larger Droid is unable to punch whilst his mechanism is resetting, and K-2 is rapidly dragged towards him. Crusher may be quick to attack, but his other reactions are too slow to do anything to stop him. As the arm snaps back into place, K-2 unhooks his fingers. Using the momentum from the ascent, he flips himself over the bigger Droid's shoulder and grips onto his back. Crusher flails. Too bulky to reach his back and too slow to shake him off. I've never seen panic in a featureless face until now.

"T6 Thoracic Vertebrae," Ren says calmly into his com-link.

Cal looks bewildered. As Crusher spins, desperately trying

to remove his new parasite, I see the weak spot. His back is a series of exposed cables and twisted steel in the shape of a spine and ribs. Multiple rivets pin each rib to his lateral chest-plate, and one of them is loose. K-2 nods, chopping his hand down and slicing into the weak spot. Unfortunately, the jolt from the blow forces him upwards, and Crusher's meaty metal hands grip onto his head.

"Crush his slompin' head!" Cal screeches.

"TOUCH OF DEATH. TOUCH OF DEATH!" the rabble roars.

My heart is in my mouth. I turn to Ren and his eyes are glazing over. Again and again, K-2 slices into the rivet, sparks bouncing off his arms and chest. Yet still, his head is in a vice grip of a tonne weight, and getting tighter by the second. Pistons hiss and groan as the pressure is forced into the grip. A bolt pings out of K-2's exo-armor, whizzing through the air. My stomach churns with anxiety, sweat building up beneath my mask. White noise fills my ears, and my vision begins to blur. Suddenly, Crusher stops. A loud hiss, and his arms retract to his sides. The light in his eyes flickers, and then it's gone. The room is totally silenced, but my ears are still ringing. K-2 climbs down the giant's back and walks towards us. I stand as he does so, hearing Ren sigh in relief behind me. Rushing to the glass once more, I raise my hand. He does the same. Pushing on my voice module, I try to comfort him in the most anonymous way I can think of.

"You're amazing pequeño," I smile.

Cal hasn't taken his eyes off Crusher the whole time.

"If Crusher can't reactivate in ten seconds, he will be disqualified!" the announcer shouts.

"Although...the Anointed should direct their Droid to finish him off right about now! He's a sitting duck out there," his colleague instigates.

A countdown begins to rumble through the room. "9...8...7..." I hold my breath. "6...5...4..." My hand presses harder to K-2's as though I can feel it through the glass. "3...2...1!" The room erupts, the bell ringing almost inaudible, and it's over. He's done it. I turn to the service Droids to release K-2 and feel a commotion behind me. Cal is inches from Ren's face, hands gripping the sides of the throne. Spit flies from his mouth as he spews vile profanity, his face getting redder and redder. A member of his team rushes up and twists his hands behind his back.

"GEDDOFFF ME! What'd ya do to him ya ROYAL FUCK?!"

"I showed him Mercy," Ren responds, unflinching in his throne.

Cal is dragged away, and the security drones swarm in. Hundreds of cameras flash as K-2 joins us, and interviewers push their way through to stand beneath the platform, which is lowered to the ground. Microphones are shoved in our faces, and Ren begins to speak.

"Tonight, I have demonstrated to you all what true mercy is. This Droid was pulled together from scraps that were left for trash, and yet, he was able to smite your coveted prospect. Crusher's repairs will be simple, and Cal has lost nothing but social credit and pride. Next time, however, it will be up to you to decide whether my opponent deserves mercy. Remember this: you are all drunk on your affluence, oblivious to the truth, and it is time for you to wake up. It is time for a new King."

A few hours later, our taxi drops us off on a street a block away from Ren's place. It's late, and we're exhausted. Interviews, press releases, photoshoots. K-2 trails behind us in silence. I look up to see the glint of the city lights on the roof of the dome. Even the stars are fake here. We dip into an alley in the older part of the city, stripping off our costumes, and I begin to feel like myself again. We slide them into the packs along with K-2's exo-armor, and I use my jacket to disguise the pack.

As we come up on it, Ren's house looks eerily untouched; the lights are off and there's a small pile of leaves near his front door that the 'scapers didn't reach. It's too risky for Ren to use his credentials, so he steps forward and knocks firmly on the door. A second later, it's swung open by a figure illuminated by the street light.

"Welcome home Ren," an overly enthusiastic voice sounds from the darkness. The figure is still shrouded in shadows and ambient lights until Ren waves and the lights flip on. A house Droid. Those things really creep me out. The inside of the house is as unmoved as the outside. A coffee cup sits next to some screws he must have emptied out of his pocket, dust surrounding them. "Your 18-month reservation period has almost expired. Would you like to set up automatic renewal?

"That's fine."

"Excellent. What is my primary protocol today?" The house Droid continues.

"Um. Cleaning phase would be helpful," Ren answers, looking over the room. The Droid sets to work dusting and vacuuming the year's worth of accumulation. I want to talk, plan, and praise K-2. I'm also curious about Ren's place, but I'm just so tired. I slouch down onto the sofa and curl my legs up into myself, head lolling back onto the cushions. Ren drops down beside me. I feel my eyes drifting, despite the reorganization going on around me.

Music begins to play through my com-link, and my head snaps forward. The house Droid has settled in front of us. It stands straight, arms rigid at its sides. All the lights are off, and a projection plays from its chest.

"This is an emergency broadcast. The following people are still wanted for questioning. Anybody with any information surrounding their whereabouts is urged to come forward." Faces flash across the screen. I recognized a few UG members. Suddenly, a familiar face appears. I turn to him, and his olive skin has gone slightly gray. Though his jaw is hardened and his eyes are giving nothing away. He stands up and grabs a glass of water in silence before sitting back down on the couch beside me and staring at the ceiling.

"It's just because I was at the race," he says.

"It could be..." I trail off my sentence. I never trusted house Droids, and I'm not about to start.

CHAPTER THIRTY-SEVEN_

The feel of an icy metal hand gripping my neck wakes me from a dead sleep. I choke on my breath as two round LEDs stare into my soul. It's on top of me, bolts and cold metal digging into my forearms. I twist and turn to drag myself away, desperately trying to kick my legs as its face looms closer. It opens its mouth, and a siren begins to play, louder and louder. My eardrums are thudding, and I'm sweating as I thrash to escape the dead grasp.

"Tax? Taxia! Wake up!"

"Wha?" The sound of my voice is drowned out by sirens. It was just a nightmare. At least it was different than the ones I've been having. Wait...why haven't the sirens stopped? My stomach drops out of my ass. I jump up and raise my fists.

"We need to run," Ren says, his eyes wide. "K-2, carry mode, now!" K-2 quickly obeys and Ren hoists him up onto his back. I can tell from the strain on his face he's heavy.

Ren bursts through the door into the backyard, and I follow, reaching to grab two hoodies and our packs from the hook on the way out. My hand brushes steel, and I flinch at the sight of the house Droid in the dim of the corner. No LEDs, besides a small blinking light at its feet. I think about disconnecting its charger, but there's no time. We shrug on the hoodies as our feet fly through the shrubbery surrounding the apartments. The sky is a hazy purple, and the sun is just beginning to shed some light on the dome. Shadows dance around us, taunting as we sprint beneath the green canopies edging the buildings. My mother's voice fills my head. Songs she sang to the Allspirits. They were always for my Father. It wasn't long after that she succumbed to the same addiction, and the songs turned to shouting. I sprint faster, running from the memories, knowing the Allspirits have done no more for me than my own two feet have.

"How did they know we were here?!" I yell through panicked breaths.

"I didn't even use my credentials to get in, so I'm not sure!" he shouts back at me.

"Bet it was that weird ass house Droid," I murmur under my breath. Either Ren didn't hear me, or he's decided not to reply.

We slow down to a jog as we get further from his place, and the dense city mutes the sound of the sirens completely. We're lucky MetiCitians usually sleep in on weekdays. There aren't many jobs left to wake up for, so they'll have taken the liberty of staying up til the early hours pumping their modded bodies full of booze. Domeheads. We duck into an alcove and Ren pulls the strings of his hoodie tight, tucking his hands into the sleeves.

"You still not used to the cold?" I ask.

"There's just nothing like the feel of the sun actually hitting your skin," he replies.

"I get it; it took me forever to get used to the dampened rays."

We take some time to figure out where we are using the

map on Ren's credentials. The projection shows we're near the outer edge of the dome now. Ren deactivates the map and looks sheepishly at the floor.

"Another nightmare?" he asks, concern etched on his face. Another? I knew he heard me scream the other night.

"Just a silly dream. It's fine." I try to brush it off, embarrassed.

"You get them less now than you used to..." he states matter-of-factly. He's been paying attention.

"Yeah, once a week rather than once a day now," I laugh awkwardly.

"I get them too..." He trails off, looking up determinedly. "We should head to the Outskirtz and find somewhere to rest until the fight," he suggests. Ren could be recognized, but the tech out there is outdated, so if we're careful we're less likely to be caught. We slow to a walk and try to look inconspicuous as we head towards the docks. We're camouflaged here as colorful containers float around us, tethered to airships. A group of pilots pass inches from us as we hide behind a container labeled 'MetiCity-3.'

"Look at that scrapheap," I point to a truck that looks like it would combust into a pile of rust if you breathed on it too hard.

"Looks like home," Ren replies. He's right. It's for sure been through the Outskirtz once or twice. The back is filled with crate-shaped boxes, draped in fabric and pinned to the chassis. The driver is leaning against the door with his back to us, checking his credentials.

"I bet he's dropping Nopins off at one of those underground saloons Frank drinks at. I wonder if we can hitch a ride?"

He grabs K-2, and he's taken off before I have a chance to reply, looking back at me and smirking before sliding into the back of the cruiser and under the tarp. I sprint after him, helping him to hoist K-2 on top of one of the crates and tucking my legs up under the fabric. It's stuffy, and the smell of alcohol permeates everything. At least we were right about the import. The cruiser shifts as the driver gets in, the engine purring to life as he connects to it.

"Why does this thing have a city engine?" Ren whispers frantically.

It blows my mind that he can tell the difference from the sound. The shifting of the crates as the driver pulls a U-TURN answers his question. We're headed back into the city. I think about jumping and hoping Ren follows, but this thing can move, and I have no idea where we are. Plus, I don't fancy the idea of falling into the arms of a controller, and we couldn't just leave K-2. Twists and turns lull us into scared silence as the engine finally shuts off. I hold my breath, waiting for the door to open and our chance to run. Nothing.

"I know you're in there! Are you going to move first, or will I?"

"Go!" Ren shouts. He grabs K-2 as we dive from the back. A bolt snags on the fabric covering one of the crates and it smashes to the ground, beer lapping at our feet. It's a dead end. A garage door in front of us, the driver behind us.

"Nobody ever got in trouble for hitchin' a ride. It's the reason you had to hide that worries me. Plus, you owe me for that crate now," the driver ponders.

We turn slowly to face a tall, broad man with an equally broad smile. It's a mirror of the one Ren has, recognition washing over the men's faces.

"People that care about you been looking for you, boy." He smiles. Ren walks towards him and shakes his hand, and the driver grips it, pulling him into a hug.

"I'm not usually in the business of hugging near strangers, but you deserve that for everything you've done for my friend."

"Elli?" Ren questions.

"Frank." It's Ren's turn to look confused now. "Come on upstairs and I'll explain."

We climb the stairs into a beautifully furnished apartment. It's an eclectic mix of the old world and MetiCity, with medals lining the wall above the dining table and a replica rifle mounted over the electric fire. A well-loved and laid-in dog bed sits beneath the fire itself, filled with a few ratty old stuffed toys and a tennis ball. I swing my head around excitedly. MetiCorp has so many restrictions on pets you rarely ever see them in the city. And the ones in the Outskirtz are usually feral, with barely any fur and thickened skin adapted for the harsh sun. Tony notices the look on my face and whistles through his fingers. After almost a minute, the oldest dog I've ever seen creeps its way past the bedroom door frame. It's a tiny little mutt with scraggly brown fur and no teeth. I can tell this since its tongue is dangling loosely from the gap where teeth should be. It can barely walk, and from the glazed-over eyes, I'd assume it's blind. Yet when it passes Tony, its tiny little tail wags like crazy. He reaches down and scratches the dog on the head softly, rewarded by a few dangling tongue licks.

"This is my Bella. Best companion a man could have. She's saved my life more times than I can count. Those ones are hers," Tony nods to a smaller set of medals lined up beside the others. My heart melts, and I crouch down to stroke her. In response, she flops ungraciously onto her back and wiggles her tummy in the air, so I oblige willingly. After a minute or two, she struggles back to her feet and toddles over to the bed, curling herself into a ball of perfect fluff and snoring almost instantly. Tony has set about brewing us coffee and Ren is analyzing the medals, so I decide to reactivate K-2. He hums back to life and tests out his joints. Then, he spots Bella. His head tilts almost ninety degrees and I can hear the cameras inside focusing.

"Dog," he says, but the word sounds foreign to him.

"Pequeño, that's Bella; she's Tony's dog," I gesture to Tony across the room, who smiles at K-2. K-2 ignores him.

"Dog!" His voice is higher this time. He sounds...excited? He lowers himself down to sit on the floor, and for a moment, I think he's going to meditate; then he lies down and pulls his arms up into himself. Curling into a ball, he stares at Bella, who is undisturbed by her new observer. Stretching out a cautious finger, he brushes it softly on the fur between her eyes, making happy mechanical humming noises. It might be the cutest, weirdest thing I've ever seen. Tony and Ren look as bemused as me. I walk over to them and sit at the kitchen island.

"Thanks for the coffee, but can somebody please explain what in the Allspirits is going on?" I ask. Ren laughs. What a weird day so far, and it's not even lunchtime.

"Taxia, this is Tony. Zander took me for a drink after my first day at this guy's bar," Ren nods towards the man.

"Nice to meet you, Tony." I smile politely. His eyes crinkle.

"You said something about Frank? You know him?" Ren asks.

"Aye. Curmudgeonly old bastard he is; he was in my squadron back in 2082. Damn near blew us all to pieces with a rocket launcher once, but we were like brothers regardless. Mind, he only comes to visit me in emergencies these days. So I knew when he rocked up a few months ago looking worse than usual, something was stressing him out. At least he doesn't have any hair left to lose," Tony laughs at his own joke. "He was ramblin' away, waving the tiniest sunbleached polaroid of a dark haired little kid, 'Tony you go through punters more than I go through underwear. You must'a seen him.' I told him I had more chances of finding his hairline than finding anybody from that. 'Til I looked closer and saw the scar." He nods towards Ren's face.

"I thought Frank had retired? I didn't even think he'd notice...I didn't even know he had a photo of me." Ren stares into the distance, puzzled by this information as if the man hadn't mentored him through half his life. From what Ren had told me, Frank had basically rescued him in his teenage years. He'd given him a purpose and something he was genuinely good at. A way to survive the barren din of the Outskirtz. I imagine Ren has repaid that over a million times.

"His leg wasn't the only thing they took from him in the war, you know? He had already lost his wife in the first droughts. When his son was killed in an ambush, I thought he had given up on living...until you showed up. From the sounds of it, the stubborn old rebel told you none of this?" Tony wonders.

"Nope...but it doesn't matter. It's true. He's like a father to me," Ren answers with watery eyes.

"Aye. A father who thinks he's lost another son and is feeling terribly guilty for pushing you into the job that he believes killed you. I assume by the fact that you were hiding in my truck, it's not as simple as sending him a com-link to let him know you're alright?" Tony asks.

"It's not. If he comes back...please give him a clue. I'm okay. Tell him the thirty gauge wire was in the third drawer down the whole time," Ren replies.

"Of course kid. Happy to help, there's been too much loss after all," Tony sighs. "Every day, I expect Zander to saunter back into the bar, all the ladies' eyes stuck to him. To see Koujin and Zari straggling behind, joined at the hip. It's too quiet without them. It's not often you get to witness pure love like that these days, but it's a comfort thinking of them together. Wherever the Allspirits have taken 'em." He pauses for a second, gulping hard. "That table in the corner is always empty now, except when the little one visits," he adds.

Ren has closed his eyes, the mention of Elli and Tony's grief too much to witness. I look to the ceiling, the sting of tears threatening to fall. I'm grieving for him and the friends he's lost, and I'm grieving for me. For the part of me that died on that day. There's no getting that back. All I can do is continue to push myself as hard and as far as I can to make the loss mean something. I ball up my fists as the tears begin to stream down my face. I let them. I deserve to feel it.

Something soft brushes my hand, and I gasp, blinking the blurriness from my eyes to see K-2 placing a tissue into my palm. His innocence triggers something inside of me. I roughly drag my sleeve over my face to dry it, stand up and walk over to Ren. His eyes are still tightly scrunched for fear of the flood when they open. I open his hand gently and close it around the tissue, turning away to give him a moment.

"Thank you. I don't know what would have happened if it wasn't you we ran into today," I say to Tony, who is in the kitchen loading the dishwasher with our mugs.

"Anytime. Taxia, is it?" He holds out his hand to shake mine, dropping a piece of paper into my palm. "That's for Ren, whenever he's ready to read it. Kid's a little too emotional for it right now," he whispers into my ear. I glance down. It's some type of letter written on pastel pink paper.

"Let's get you guys ready to go wherever you need," he says, louder now.

Tony was more than happy to drop us off at a feminine facility in the City. It made me cringe to think of him putting two and two together and getting six. The last thing I'd want to do is bring a kid into the world as it is. However, this was also guaranteed to be one of the only places in the city where people aren't tapped-in, and the security drones have to maintain a two-mile radius for privacy. We duck behind the clinic and take turns to change into our disguises since it's getting riskier and riskier to change in the open. I click K-2's exo-armor into place as he stares me down through his expressionless face. The only way we could get him to leave Bella was the promise that we would go back and visit, but he's still not overly pleased about it.

We meander through backstreets until, once more, we're facing off against the arena. The rowdy crowd outside seems to have doubled since yesterday, and the tension in my body is palpable. I spot Migo thrusting his camera into the face of one of the female competitors. She's tall and imposing. Glossy black hair cascades over her bronzed skin, stopping just short of her obviously modded, um...trunk. I can't see her Droid, until I remember we were offered a lockup inside the arena for K-2 overnight. We couldn't bear to leave him in the dark like that, but I guess she isn't connected to her Droid like we are. I sneak a glance at Ren to see she's caught his attention as well. I'm sure he's just analyzing the competition.

"Just Migo's type. More alterations than a hand-me-down jacket." He grimaces. It springs a laugh from me that instantly releases the tension in my shoulders. He doesn't laugh in response.

Crossing security, Ren reaches out and scans his credentials. They flash green and we enter the building unscathed. No sirens. No controllers. Compared to yesterday, our entrance is a breeze. We're ushered back into the private waiting room by the same guard as before. I feel surprisingly good after speaking to Tony. It's nice to be reminded of the sincerity that can exist in people. Plus, crying may be cathartic, and I rarely do it. I'm hoping my renewed sense of direction will project positivity onto Ren. I don't want him to forget about his friends; I want him to remember they're why we're doing this. That we CAN do this. I close my eyes and settle into a comfortable silence with him.

"I hope she's okay," he says suddenly, pulling me from my meditative state. We can't use names here, but I know who he means.

"I may not have met her, but I feel as if I know her through your eyes. Everything you've told me proves she's tough. She's too smart to be sitting around doing nothing. I bet she's fighting her fights, just like us," I reply. He lifts his chin slightly in response. I know words alone can't fix things, but I need him to feel the force of the relationships around him. It seems to work as he gets up to go tinker with a few loose sections on K-2's exo-armor. Ren turns as the door unlocks, and our guard walks in.

"Your opponents are Saira and Stinger. Raise your arm so I can transfer their statistics," he drones.

"As I've stated previously, I do not require such things," Ren responds. This time, the guard steps forward, glaring down at Ren. His boots make him at least a foot taller. The guard speaks directly into his com-link.

"Transfer is recommended to ensure an even fight. Please note at the time of this recording, the participant is requesting to decline all future opponent statistics." He turns sharply and slaps the button for the door. "You're up next, your highness," he quips before exiting swiftly.

We enter the ArenaSphere area once more, but this time, the atmosphere is way louder. We exchange curious glances. Cheers mingle amongst angry cries, and the verdict seems to be out on whether we're power-drunk wannabees or revolutionary geniuses. Once we're on the platform, we flip our packs off our backs and our thrones assemble themselves. The audience claps, though I imagine the spectacle will get old fast. Time to up the ante. We spin the thrones to face outwards, and I carefully position the opening of my pack at our feet, pointing behind us. We hold hands with the trigger between them, and Ren speaks.

"Before we begin, ask yourselves this: have you pledged your loyalty to the one true King? Do you understand what it means to weigh the scales of life and death in your hands? It is a burden I, as King, will allow you to feel. It is simply a small taste of the power I wield. When the time comes, I shall share that power with you. Use it wisely," he roars as we push the button in tandem. I daren't turn around, but I can see the dust drifting through the projector in front of us. I know that everybody except us can see our crowns projected onto the sphere. Their eyes are wide and fixated. Suddenly, the arena falls into darkness and when the lights flip back on, our thrones are once again facing the sphere. K-2 stands inside, staring at the place where the projection had been. The room erupts into confusion and noise, only to be silenced by the sound of drums as our opponent makes their entrance.

I don't recognize the song, but it's dark and seductive. An entrancing flute whistles a repetitive melody, ominously surrounded by the beat of thundering drums. Dim lighting focuses on them. It's the girl from outside. Her hair is tied into elaborate braids, tumbling like water over her body. Her hips are accentuated by a sheer green skirt as she dips and sways to the music. It's pulled down to expose her stomach, which she rolls hypnotically. Tiny bells adorn her wrists and belt, chiming along to the beat of the drums. As she reaches us, a metallic, skittering sound begins to echo around us. It doesn't quite match the song and an excited hush rushes over the crowd. They know something we don't know. Red and orange spotlights drift in the direction of the sound, sweeping the floor and illuminating a shadow every other beat. It's too fast to make out. The music ends in a cacophony of strings and bells, and the lights flip back on. That explains the skittering. It's a giant fucking scorpion.

I hate scorpions. They're one of the only animals that can survive the world as it is outside the cities now. Insects in the twenty-second century are bigger than they used to be. The ones in the Outskirtz are nowhere near as this giant man-made nightmare, though. It stands a foot or two above Saira, its claws the size of her head. She reaches up to give it a stroke before the officials guide it into the sphere.

"I'm having holoroom flashbacks. That thing is creepy," Ren whispers.

"Glad it's not just me. What do you think their TOD is?"

"Something to do with that tail, I'd imagine," Ren says, his eyes tracing it. Saira strolls over to us and smiles. To my surprise, it's full of warmth and reaches her eyes.

"I'm sorry you had to watch that. So embarrassing. My manager thinks it will draw in the big gamblers," she chimes. Her accent is strong.

"I thought it was cool," Ren replies, his voice raising an octave. She smiles again. One of the controllers rushes over with a stool for her and holds her hand as she takes her place beside us in the viewing booth. I feel Ren's head turning as her skirt shifts up to expose more smooth, caramel skin. Several members of the crowd whistle at this. Whatever. At least I didn't need an assistant to help me sit down. I turn my attention back to the fight. We know from the entrance that Stinger is a little faster than K-2, but other than that, the stats look pretty evenly matched.

The fight begins just as the last did: announcements and the ring of the bell. I expect Stinger to make his move early, but instead, he begins to pace around the perimeter of the sphere. His claws are raised and his eyes are locked onto K-2 as he steps in pace with the scorpion. I grip the arm of my chair as they stalk each other, bracing for the inevitable first blow. Saira is whispering incoherently to herself, a smirk playing on her lips. I grow more agitated as the seconds pass, daring K-2 to make the first move, but knowing he's too clever to expose himself like that. I search desperately for any kind of pattern or reason for the standoff. K-2 is in the center, facing out towards the crowd, and on the fourth lap, I notice something glinting. Fuck. I can't be sure until the next lap and I don't want to break Ren's concentration. As they circle back around to the same section, one of the spotlights flares directly onto K-2's face plate, temporarily blinding him.

"K-2! Watch out for the light!" Ren has spotted it, but so has Stinger.

I watch in horror as his giant claw sweeps the floor, squealing metal ringing in my ears as he wipes K-2's feet out from beneath him. He hits the ground hard, and Stinger takes advantage, bracing himself as his tail comes sweeping over his head. There's a whooshing sound as the tip of it extends into a series of sharp barbed stingers. He strikes, and K-2 flips himself over just in time for the tail to collide with the sphere floor. The shockwaves rock the scorpion back slightly and K-2 takes full advantage, running and sliding beneath his opponent. He throws his full weight into a push, forcing Stinger up onto the base of his tail. His balance is off, combined with the mass of his weight, the giant scorpion crashes to the ground onto his back. His legs flail in the air, claws swinging wildly, trying to right himself. Was that enough to incapacitate him?

He stops struggling and is totally still. Until one of his legs begins to twist, sliding on an axis and clicking in place. My eyes pop as the other seven follow in quick succession. He pushes up on his newly orientated legs, and as he does so, the whirring sound of gears and pulleys heightens, his head and tail spinning 180 degrees to match. What was once his belly is now his back and he's staring down at K-2 with a fierce hunger. They charge in tandem and connect in the center with an enormous bang that rattles the arena. It's hard to tell what's happening with so many limbs in play. K-2 slams his fist down on the back of Stinger's neck, which seems to rock him for a second, but not for long. The scorpion is attack-heavy, raining down blows with massive claws in an attempt to drag K-2 beneath him. He's relentless in every move, desperate for the chance to strike again. Ren's eyes are meticulously scanning the fight, searching for any kind of chink in Stinger's armor.

"What if we turn a feature into a bug?" he asks.

"Was that a pun?" I grin. He rolls his eyes at me, activating his com-link. He whispers something so quietly I can't hear, but I see K-2's link light up in response. He stops fighting. Did he mishear? The scorpion prowls forward, looming over him. His tail begins to swing forward, claws ready to stop K-2 from escaping the inevitable sting. I scoot so far to the edge of my seat I'm almost standing. Stinger's tail swings down, in line with K-2's chest. K-2 jumps, avoiding the stinger by an inch, bolstering his shoulder against the tail hard. He grabs on and digs his hands in between the metal plates and begins to push. Slowly, the Scorpion begins to slip across the sphere. Its feet scurry, trying to grip onto something, but over half his body weight is in his tail, which is now working against him. K-2 pushes so hard I can hear the rivets in his knees popping. Finally, they're against the opposite side of the sphere. His feet are planted firmly, still pushing with all of his strength. His opponent is nipping at thin air, his claws too bulky to maneuver around his own tail to reach K-2. He shoves one final time, the barbs in the tail activating against his will.

"The time is now. Show the world the kind of king you desire. A merciful king..." Ren says, lifting his hand outward to the crowd and sticking his thumb up, "...or a ruthless king?" He flips his thumb down. The audience becomes chaotic. Confusion on so many faces as they question themselves, whispering to their peers. The noise becomes a droning melody as the hive mind takes place. The first thumb down comes from an older guy with two-bored looking kids at either side. He shoves his elbows into their ribs and they mirror him. The effect is instantaneous. Thumbs turning down, rippling outwards from the family like a wave. Any internal struggle they had over their decision was gone the minute that man chose for them. Saira looks horrified. Ren turns back towards the sphere, holding his thumb down. K-2 makes one final shove, directing the stinger towards the Scorpion. The barbs pierce into his torso, and he begins to shudder in K-2's arms as the virus takes hold. His claws open and close in reflex, legs spasming as his code is corrupted. Then, Stinger is still. The bell rings.

Saira walks over to us and curtsies, the sheer scarf over her mouth is wet with frustrated tears. I want to say something, but it's not like it was with Cal. I feel bad for her. The crowd is focused on Ren and K-2, gamesters are collecting their winnings, and chatter about us echoes around me. I watch Saira as she reaches her manager. He grips her arm and her skin blanches from the force. He leans down and whispers something viciously to her, his other hand sliding over her backside. She squirms uncomfortably and he grips tighter, dragging her away. She turns and we lock eyes. Her expression is pleading, and it breaks my heart that I know there's nothing I can do.

We use the commotion from the next fight to change and

slip out the back unseen. I think about Saira the whole time, the look on her face looping in my mind.

"How come you know where a UG hideout is in MetiCity-6?" Ren asks, disrupting my thoughts as we traipse through the overgrowth behind one of the city blocks. The UG base was the only other safe place I could think of in the city where we might be able to rest.

"One of the guys who used to come into the shop had a big mouth and a bigger soft spot for me. He invited me back to his City for a tumble in the UnderGround."

He trips over a non-existent knoll in the grass, righting himself and coughing awkwardly. "So you've...been here?" his voice raises an octave.

"If that's your way of asking if I fucked him, no, I haven't seen the hideout in person," I smirk.

We travel in silence for a while, until we see a sign for the old railway. There are stations across all the cities, abandoned when MagLevs were eventually installed. We enter the building and take the stairs all the way down into the darkness. It's quiet and the air is humid down here. My eyes adjust to the darkness, focusing on the dust dancing in the light and then beyond. Into the...rubble? The light source is coming from a hole in the ceiling where the beams have collapsed. Streaks of rust paint the earth at my feet. An iron smell fills my nostrils. It's not rust...my breath quickens as I grip onto K-2's arm for stability.

"They found them," Ren gulps.

I step forward, bringing K-2 with me. The iron smell is replaced by an acrid, rotten one. I pull my hoodie up over my mouth and nose.

"K-2. Light please." My voice trembles. He opens up his palm and an ambient white light shines from it, illuminating a palid, waxy skinned body lying beneath the destruction. My hands shake as I crouch down to check his pulse and notice he's covered in UG tats. A maggot crawls from his mouth and I pull back, falling onto my ass. Ren picks me up with ease, gripping me tightly as I bury my head into his shoulder.

"I know him," he says. "Saw him taggin' a Zelius mural a while back. Controllers got him..."

"He goes by Ghost. Or he did." My voice shakes.

"I'm so sorry, Taxia. By the looks of it this happened a few days ago at least...we should still be safe to stay here for the night. Maybe we can figure out what happened in the morning," Ren pulls away from me and strokes my shoulder, walking back over to Ghost. He rips a torn 'NO MORE KINGS' flag from the wall nearby, laying it over the body.

"Rest in peace, Anarki," he whispers. The gesture makes me want to sob. UG may make bad decisions, but they're not all bad people. These guys saved my ass on multiple occasions after I moved into the City. I dread to think of what's changed since I was last here. How many more have died? Would any of this have happened if I didn't agree to fix that fucking disruptor? I feel the crushing weight of every decision I've ever made and I can't breathe. Black spots surround my vision and my head is spinning. I'm going to die.

"Taxia. Listen to my voice." My ears are ringing. Is that Ren? Someone grabs my hand and I'm walking. My feet are moving. I'm so tired. "Sit down, Taxia. Here, sit right here." Tepid water pours down the back of my neck and over my wrists. It soaks life back into me. I gasp the deepest breath of my life and the room slowly comes back into view. I'm dizzy, but Ren is here. I'm alive. I can breathe.

"Wha..." I start, but my voice comes out stuttered and shaking.

"You had a panic attack. It happened to me too after my last meeting with Zelius."

I want to ask questions, but my thoughts are muddy and jumbled.

"What happened?" Is all I can croak.

"It only took fifteen minutes. I walked into the room and he was standing with his arms crossed behind his back." Ren nudges our packs behind us as a makeshift pillow and curls up beside me, encouraging me to lay my head on him. I'm hesitant, but I don't have the energy to fuss. K-2 sits beside me, cross-legged. The ambient light glows from both palms now. I reach out to hold his hand and the light bursts from my fingers. It warms me, though there's no actual heat. I look up at Ren from beneath my hood, encouraging him to continue.

"He just stared at me. Something about his glare makes you want to tell him all your secrets..." He starts.

"I know what you mean," I add. A blush creeps up his neck and he clears his throat.

"He asked me if I had found the hum of the frequency. I told him how I found it the very next day. That I had been ready for so long. He asked me about the plan, and I told him the truth. He asked me if I knew what I would do if I actually accomplished what I set out to. If I became a king. Asked what kind of world I would create. I told him that I would wear the crown just long enough to set things right. But once that was done, I would step down. That a king was only useful during dire times, and that the times I would create would not be. Then he stepped forward, which made me step back. He walked towards me until he was right up on me and lifted his hand," Ren says, mimicking Zelius. "I flinched, and then...he..." Ren trails off.

"Hmm?"

"He hugged me." He lets out a deep sigh. I don't know what I was expecting, but a hug was not it. I smile at him.

"I cried right there in his arms. I couldn't catch my breath, and thought I was about to die. When he disappeared, Hypatia found me and simulated an ice cold rain. Shocked me back. That's how I knew the cold water would work on you..."

"Thank you Ren," my voice is steady now. "For everything."

He pulls me in closer and we rest in silence. The tiredness is overwhelming, but it's colder down here, the air-conditioned MetiCity streets pumping air through old, waterlogged pipes. I take my hand from K-2's and shove it into my pocket, trying to warm up. My fingers brush the note from Tony. I pull it out and hand it to Ren.

"Oh. Tony gave this to me earlier...He said it was for you. I was waiting for a quiet time for you to read it," I explain. He unfolds the note. I can't read his expression as my eyes drift closed, but he's holding me tight.

CHAPTER THIRTY-NINE_

I wake to the crunch of rubble beneath someone's feet. Focusing on the tunnel ahead, I can see a short, stout silhouette dipping into one of the piles of debris and yanking out some copper piping. I can't make much out in the dim, dusty light, but I can tell that it's a guy and his face is covered with a bandana. It's emblazoned with the UG logo. A harsh, scratching discharge crackles through the air as he holds something up to his mouth.

"I told you. We got them all. It's rubble. Yes. Thank you Sir." He laughs.

My stomach turns. Slowly untangling Ren's arms from where they've snaked across my hips in his sleep, I cover his mouth with my hand and gently shake him. His eyes fly open, and I shush him softly. His gaze is questioning, but he trusts me. That thought lingers in my mind for a second. As I stand, my boot catches on a pebble, which skids across the ground and echoes in the narrow space. The guy whips his head around like a cornered dog, fists raised. Lowlife noso. Anger boils its way up my throat, threatening to expel itself from my mouth. It burns as I swallow it.

"Don't worry. I'm not here to hurt you." It's technically not a lie. Not yet, anyway. I'm met with silence, but I'm not surprised. Most of the UG won't speak until it's safe. You can wear the greatest disguise in the MetiCity, but it's useless against MetiCorp's voice recognition database. One of the biggest UG conspiracy theories is that MetiCorp taps into private com-links to monitor certain patterns of speech. It's one of the reasons I worked so hard on our vocal mods for the fights. In this case, though, I feel like he's figuring out how much we heard. I step forward into a patch of light.

"My name's Taxia. You can trust me, Anarki." The nickname is acid on my tongue.

"Taxia. That sounds familiar..." Recognition glints in his eyes. The cries of people being crushed fills my ears. It turns to a dull roar as I fight to keep my focus on the guy and nod. Ren lays his hand on my lower back, subtly pulling me closer. Sometimes, I think he can see through me like he does with his work.

"I'm Xian. And you?" Ren asks. His tone is friendly, but I know he's hesitant since he used the fake name.

"You can call me Boe, Anarki." He draws out the word, making it sound slimy, and his lips curl into a smile that doesn't reach his eyes.

"Hey, Boe. What happened...?" I hesitate.

He looks around as if he had forgotten about the bloodshed around us. His eyes linger on the covered body of Ghost.

"They came in the night. Threw down a bunch of Neuro-Pulses. I guess they thought they could disarm and arrest all of th- all of us, in one...but these tunnels are ancient. Full of water and mold, barely holding themselves up. Those cleaner Droids don't even come down here anymore. Frequency of the NP's brought the slompin' walls down. It was inevitable."

"I'm so sorry Boe. How did they even find this place?" I ask, fighting the sarcasm from leeching its way in.

"A rat." His eyes drop down to his feet. "But it's okay. They silenced him," He shrugs nonchalantly in the direction of Ghost. I squeeze my thumb in my fist, itching to leap at him. Ghost may have been a menace on a FlyBike, but he wouldn't hurt an actual fly. He was one of the first UG I ever met, and one of the only I truly liked. He came into the shop one day, bragging about how he had given himself a challenge to tag a mural in every MetiCity, but he kept getting caught. He always escaped though, hence the name Ghost. That and the fact he was paler than the MetiCity buildings. MetiCorp had used disruptors on his bike a bunch of times and the wiring was shot, so I fixed it.

"Why would they randomly target a UG base?" Ren asks. I wish he hadn't.

"Still looking for whoever sabotaged the O-Race last year," Boe smirks, coughs, and forces a frown. It's a gut punch. My head spins as the weight of more lives falls onto my shoulders. Ren and Boe continue to make small talk as I look right through them.

I'm on autopilot as we leave the ruins of the UG base, the silhouette of Boe in the distance creeping amongst the destruction. Destruction he had clearly been a part of. I shudder at the sight. Ren is my waypoint, leading me through the city and slipping my disguise over my head in a shaded corner as we near the arena. The cheering is louder than ever, and their genuine excitement gradually brings me back to my body. They hold signs bearing our name. I spot a tiny girl with a plastic crown atop her head. A fierce determination begins to grow in me, warming the blood in my veins as it trickles through. We can win this. We can make it all worth it. Barriers and controllers line the side of the entrance, blocking the onlookers from contact with us. However, a few reporters are moseying around the end of the walkway.

"...and behind us now are the up-and-coming underdogs, The Anointed. Brand new to the RFL environment, I wonder how they'll perform under the pressure of their first semi-final. Let's see if mercy truly is on the cards today!" A tall blonde woman in a pinstripe dress suit addresses a camera.

"They don't even have a fucking touch of death!" A voice sounding suspiciously like Cal yells from somewhere nearby. Security swoops in, the people dividing around them.

"A reminder to the public, we are live on air. Please do not swear," the woman warns. I try to push forward to the doors, but Ren holds back, walking up to the woman. She immediately leans the mic to him, a curious look on her face.

"I've taught my Droid to see through my eyes. That's why I'm so confident in his ability inside the sphere."

"Are you telling us you have some kind of psychic Droid?" The reporter laughs awkwardly.

"It's more like immaculate foresight," Ren replies, turning to walk away as the reporter struggles to regain the attention of her audience.

Once we're inside, the check-in is quicker than ever. The waiting room is the emptiest I've seen it, and we're guided only by the glowing green arrows on the floor. We sit down in the bright, white, familiar coffin of a room and brew our algae tea. We sip in silence, and I'm too exhausted to even overthink. I'm holding my breath for the inevitable welcoming reception from our security, but he doesn't come. After about an hour, there's a hiss as the door unlocks, leading to the empty hallway.

"I guess that means we're up?" Ren questions.

"Our guard didn't come. Allspirits, I hope he's okay..." I say dramatically, rolling my eyes beneath my mask.

Ren ignores my sarcasm, leading the way along the long hall. I can hear the shuffle of K-2 close behind. A wave of noise and light hits me as we enter the ArenaSphere. I squint my eyes as if it will muffle the sound, lifting my mask further up to dim the lights. Then, our anthem starts pumping through the speakers surrounding us. The floor is vibrating, and my skin is crawling with overstimulation as I fight not to turn and walk out. I grit my teeth as we're lifted to the owner's platform. It's empty. We follow our routine, assembling our thrones whilst K-2 is led into the sphere. There will be no extra show today; we're reserving that for the final. If we qualify.

Less than a minute after our song ends, the arena doors open once more. In walks a kid holding a doll, and I laugh, thinking about how he must have snuck backstage without his parents noticing. I wait for the controllers to swoop in, but nobody moves. The crowd watches him, snickering and murmuring under their breath as he skips down the aisle. I can't help but smile at the mischievous grin he's wearing.

"His parents gonna be mad as hell. Mine would have beat my ass for sneaking in and making a scene like this," I wince.

"Sneaking in? Look closer Tax," Ren says confusedly.

What does that mean? I'm looking. He's about thirteen or fourteen, his features cherubic on his face. Eyes wide and unfocused. They're the same blue as the simple tracksuit he's wearing. I tilt my head at Ren before staring even closer at the boy. He's almost at the sphere now and I can see it's not just a regular doll he's holding. It's one of those Defense Delilah's. I've seen them plastered all over the ads that light the city at night. Apparently, they've got some kind of inbuilt safety feature to repel danger from their owner. As I'm thinking, he steps onto the platform.

"He's our opponent?!"

"Yup. The crowd isn't shocked; it seems like they've seen him before," Ren shrugs. I didn't even notice.

"He's just a kid..."

"Well, he's gotta be at least sixteen to have qualified. Just baby-faced. However old he is, he's smart enough to have made some serious mods to that doll." He glares at it, analyzing it from the inside out.

"Isn't it weird they need to sell protection for kids in Utopia?" I grimace.

"I've heard some children can find trouble in an empty room," he responds, tentatively looking at the security drones hovering nearby.

"Lucky we're in a packed building then, aren't we?" I reply, forcing a laugh. Appearances are everything.

The kid looks taller here than he did in the din of the crowd, I guess he could pass for sixteen in this light. He doesn't come over, but smiles politely before grabbing the doll in a tight hug, and leading it to the ArenaSphere. The outfit and the skipping...it reeks of a gimmick. But that hug, it looked so genuine. The boy doesn't sit, instead choosing to stand with his face almost pressed against the glass. His expression is stoic, but determined. The stats scroll through the holoprompter as the doll toddles to stand opposite K-2. It's a ridiculous match. The doll is barely two feet tall, wearing a blue frilled dress with a painted-on smile and blonde pigtails.

The bell rings and Delilah barrels towards K-2 at the speed of a FlyBike. For a second, I think they're about to use their TOD already, but managers make money from the theatrics, and nobody wants to bet on a fight that lasts less than a minute. Instead, she sprints and slides through K-2's legs as he reaches for her, blonde hair trailing from his grasp as she escapes out the other side. He spins in confusion as the doll takes another run up, this time bounding off one of his legs, taunting him. She's a whirlwind of movement, dancing and flipping around the sphere. It's dizzying to watch. K-2 can't do anything besides try and close the gap, which Delilah widens in seconds each time. He stumbles clumsily, the doll evading him. She's almost dancing, jabbing and striking K-2 with every move. It looks insanely impressive...but her hits are weak. There's nowhere near enough weight to make a significant impact with such a short reach. I look over at the kid, suddenly realizing I don't even know his name. He hasn't moved. K-2 has, though, I notice, as Delilah slips under one of his kicks. He's closer to us now, closer to the kid.

"What exactly are those dolls designed to do?" I ask Ren.

"They're basically a magnetic repulsion airbag. Kid gets too close to danger and it projects in a twenty-foot radius. You'd get launched pretty hard, but it's not enough to kill a person, never mind a Droid. Unless..." he replies.

"Unless he modded the pulse. Made it stronger," I finish.

Delilah has stopped, forcing K-2 to step closer. He has to; it's one of the only opportunities he's gotten so far. Of course, she dodges him, looping back around to taunt him from closer to the edge. There's a definite pattern of movement now. It reminds me of the tornados that skip across the horizon beyond the Outskirtz.

"He compressed it even further. Twice as strong, but I bet the radius is compromised. They gotta be close for it to work," Ren states, eyes focused on the kid.

So they really are getting closer to us. I wait for a defining moment, something to signify they're close enough. If he compressed it by half, it's got to be around ten feet. Delilah continues to spring and spin around the sphere, capturing K-2 in her wake.

"Brace yourself K-2!" Ren yells into his com-link.

An almighty rush of energy fills the sphere, static sparks crackling around the exterior. The hairs on my arms stand on edge. The silence is the scariest part, there's no bang, yet K-2 is launched away from us, soaring through the air until his chest collides with the glass. His head snaps back, and then crunches forward as he slams back to the ground. The silence is filled by screaming from the audience. The kid finally takes his hands off the sphere, wiping them on his pants and smiling.

"DELILAH, WITH THAT DEVASTATING TOUCH OF DEATH! K-2 HAS BEEN LAUNCHED INTO THE SPHERE ITSELF FOLKS!" A commentator screeches through the speakers. It takes a second for the security to get everything back under control. The seating stands swaying from the movement. K-2 tips his head back to look at us, still in his grounded position. Thank the Allspirits his spinal connection wasn't severed. He stretches out his limbs before standing, shakily and unsurely. His disguise is scuffed and there are exposed loose wires in his torso, but he's up. Excited, hushed tones echo around us.

"Well, well, well. That's a first for the RFL. Hit by Delilah's touch of death and still standing."

"BARELY standing. K-2 is looking a little worse for wear! This could still be the end for The Anointed. Looks like the Allspirits can't save 'em. "

The commentators aren't wrong. K-2 is swaying and his movements are janky and slow. Delilah was busy skipping around the sphere in celebration, but seeing K-2 up has stopped her in her tracks. Hands on her hips, she begins to approach him, humming a sickly sweet tune. As she reaches him, his back is still to her. She huffs at this, reaching up to tap on the back of his knee. He doesn't react. I sigh worriedly.

"He's ignoring her," Ren reassures me. But K-2 is swaying even harder now, back and forth. I can hear the traction in his knees from how far he's leaning. Delilah spins around to face the kid, dramatically throwing her arms in the air in a tantrum. I look for Ren's response, and his eyes widen.

"Taxia!" he cries. I look back as K-2 takes off in a sprint away from Delilah. He reaches the glass and launches himself off it, twisting his body and backflipping over Delilah's head. His fists tighten around her hair, lifting her tiny body up above his head as he lands. There he stands, center sphere. Her head in one hand and her feet in the other, threatening to pull the tiny thing in half. She's screaming the most feeble, automated scream, kicking her tiny strappy blue shoes, short arms flailing. It's almost pathetic how small and unassuming she looks in his grasp. They're too far from the kid for her TOD, and she has neither the strength nor the size to do anything. It happened so fast.

"A valiant effort on behalf of this small boy, yet once again, my opponent stands on the precipice of defeat," Ren says, getting to his feet and turning to his audience. "Once again, I turn to you, the people with whom I have entrusted this great power. Will you choose to unleash the Anointed's violent ferocity upon this prodigy? Or will you seek a merciful resolution?" Ren is now standing with his hand outstretched like before. His thumb parallel to the ground, slightly moving up and down as they deliberate. A lone voice cascades out over the murmuring, "MERCY!" Soon, the crowd rallies behind them, crying out mercy, pointing their thumbs upward.

"It has been decided!" Ren yells. He looks over to K-2 and gives him the thumbs up. K-2 lets Delilah down to her feet and she lands in a huff. K-2 then grabs her by the ears and wiggles them in a weird motion.

"What are you..." Delilah tries to pry his hands off. "...Dooooiiiinnnnngggg...." she lets out in a stuttering whimper and then powers down completely.

"Today, I am truly proud of you all. A sovereign's duty is not just to rule, but to guide with sagacity and compassion. In the era of the Anointed, the road to salvation cannot be paved without empathy. I will not serve those whose thirst for blood and violence is unquenchable. The choice you made today demonstrates it is within you all to share the eyes of your enemy. But as we stand facing the grandeur of this arena, which echoes the mighty battles waged in coliseums of old, we cannot forget how the shadows of our past can so easily engulf the path we've illuminated. Comprehend that the choices you fashion at this juncture are imprinted upon the tapestry of time, resonating far beyond this present moment and into the next epoch. As I undertake the mantle of shepherding in this nascent dawn, I pledge the only thing that will match my contempt for the corrupt is the benevolence I extend to the vulnerable and downtrodden. Ask yourselves, who is deserving of which?"

The doors to the sphere slide open and the kid runs to Delilah, cradling the doll in his arms. I grab K-2 and we walk out of the ArenaSphere.

"What in the Allspirits is sagacity?" I blurt out as we're far enough away. Ren throws his head back and laughs, it's so genuine it makes me grin.

"Sagacity. It means foresight, perception. Good judgment," he shrugs. I mull it over for a second as we walk. He used that word to describe our touch of death.

"I like it. Although foresight is more your touch of death than K-2's" I reply, nodding my head at K-2, who is trailing his fingers through the tall grass.

"Master Ren has an extremely keen perception. I very much enjoy fighting at his command," K-2 pipes up.

Once we're out of our disguises, we head further down through the green canopies of MetiCity. I lead us around the gardens of several vacant, newly built townhouses, periodically checking my map to make sure we're headed in the right direction.

"I thought Boe said the new base was on the opposite side of the city?" Ren questions.

"I don't believe anything that snake says," I fill Ren in on what I had overheard from Boe as we hoist K-2 in carry mode up a winding staircase. Couldn't risk the security drones in an elevator.

"I wish you'd told me. I could have said anything to him..." Ren sighs.

"You're not that stupid. Plus, I couldn't let him know we were onto him, and you're a terrible actor." I stick my tongue out at him.

CHAPTER FORTY_

Darkness is looming on the horizon as we climb. The lights of the city twinkle to life as the amber and orange tones of the filtered sun in the sky begin to take on a purple haze. The rising heat of the day diffuses from the ground in waves as we close the distance between us and the dome ceiling. Reaching the top of the stairs, a large, illuminated plaque hovers in front of us. It's the memorial board for this part of the city. When idle, it cycles through the faces and names of those recently passed, but it also allows users to search for those who used to live in the area. Yet another difference between the Outskirtz and here. MetiCities don't dispose of their dead; they reuse them.

Part of the contract states you sign your body over once you're gone, so besides recycled waste, organic composting is the biggest fuel and food resource we have now. Makes me green if I think about it too hard. Not that there would be space for the burials here anyway... In the Outskirtz there are vast graveyards between the settlements, with grave markers cobbled together from remnants of stone and brick that were once houses. I only had one chance to visit my parents' graves before a massive sandstorm buried it altogether. Fortunately, I hadn't planned a second visit anyway.

"Taxia. Are we at a church?" Ren squints suspiciously.

"We certainly are. Would you like to atone for your sins?" I flutter my eyelashes at him. He shakes his head at me as I knock at the large wooden door. It creaks open an inch and a giant fills the gap.

"Password," he grumbles.

"I guess you're not the priest?" I ask, tilting my head innocently.

"*Password*," he repeats gruffly. Tough crowd.

"He is with us," I reply, holding my breath. He shuts the door on us, the sound of bolts and locks clicking on the other side. It swings open again and he steps aside to let us in. I exhale harshly.

"I guess that's the one thing Boe didn't lie about," Ren whispers in my ear as we walk inside, the giant shutting the door behind us.

Inside, it looks like a regular church, not that I've actually seen one in person before. A few 'worshippers' sit in the pews with their heads bowed. Though I notice one of them has what looks like a scabbard sitting on his lap. He leans over to conceal it as we pass.

We reach the front of the church and the giant signals us to wait here.

"I do," I whisper to Ren. He looks confused until he sees we're standing at the altar. He glares at me from beneath his eyebrows. "I wasn't even talking to you!" I tease as I lean down to kiss K-2, who is all tucked up in carry mode. He shoves me playfully as the giant returns and signals for Ren to take a seat, then directs me towards a room that looks like a wooden shower cubicle. I step inside hesitantly as he shuts the door behind me. It's dark and smells like damp. There's a tiny bench I squeeze onto before a cough makes me jump straight back up. It's coming from a set of pinholes on the right-hand wall...

"May our songs be heard, Anarki," a calm voice says. I rack my brains for the correct response.

"May harmony guide us to peace," I reply a moment later.

"Let us hear your songs and we shall recite them to the Allspirits," the smooth voice trickles through the latticework. A confessional! The memory from ranking comes flooding back.

"I'm not here to sing, Anarki. I'm here for shelter and in return, I can help you with your pest problem," I start.

"Pest problem?" he questions.

"A rat problem, specifically," I whisper.

It's silent for a moment as I hear the creak of wood beside me. My door opens and in front of me stands a dark-skinned twenty-something, who is actually wearing religious robes. He grins a toothy grin that extends across his whole face.

"It's a good thing you came today. Our regular Shaman probably wouldn't have known about our problem, but I do. Call me Avi," he says, shrugging off the robe and shaking my hand.

His tone is warm and friendly. He signals to Ren and leads us into a small back room with an antique desk, gesturing to two armchairs for us. As I sit down, the leather molds to my body, dust motes sprinkling the air from the fabric. This feels so...real. It sends a pang of longing through my chest, for home. For the Outskirtz, where furniture is recycled and reused by hand, with the memories of its past still imprinted in the padding. As I snuggle down even further, Avi hands us a pouch of water each across the desk. Maybe it's the nostalgia of the environment, or the kind look in his eyes, but I feel like we can trust him.

"We welcome our brothers and sisters with open arms. But you must first tell me what you know about pests," Avi says.

"There is nothing that I must do, except warn you that you are about to become privileged to life altering information. Dangerous information, that if shared with the wrong people, would hurt you and the UG, just as it would hurt us. So before we begin, Avi, can we trust you?"

"You need not question my loyalty to the UG. I was born, and will die loyal to its mission. This is why I'm so eager to stamp out the rodents who eat away at the pillars that support us. I treat all my Anarki as if they are my own blood."

"Well Taxia here is your Anarki, so listen carefully, because she does not like repeating herself."

The story flows easily from my lips, besides a few lies of omission. As far as Avi is concerned, we discovered a secret the Company wants to kill us for and we're on the run. He listens intently, nodding at the right time and showing sincere concern. As I describe how we found the train station and our meeting with Boe, I can see questions forming on his furrowed brow.

"Don't mistake my confusion for unwelcomeness, but if Boe guided you to our central base, how come you've ended up here? And what does this have to do with rats?" He questions.

"Well...Boe entering the base isn't the thing that woke me up. I heard him on a com-link with somebody. He was talking about how wrecked it is, how everybody was dead..." I search for disapproval at my words on his face. There is none.

"Sadly true, but I'm not hearing a cause for concern yet?" he replies.

"He was laughing," I look down.

"Laughing? Why would he be laughing?" Hurt creeps up in his voice.

"He called whoever it was, Sir. He said 'we got them all'. I'm almost sure it was MetiCorp," I finish, looking determinedly into Avi's eyes. He takes a huge breath and exhales before nodding.

"Boe has always been rebellious, for lack of a better word. However, I'm going to need some proof. I'm sure you understand."

"Zelius has no reason to lie to his people," I almost break my neck, turning to Ren as the words come from his mouth. He reaches across and places his hand on top of mine to make sure I don't freak. Avi glances around the room, a slight smile on his face.

"Alas, the great Engineer is not in this room," he throws his hands up.

"He's right in front of you drinking your water," Ren says, taking a sip from the pouch he was given.

Avi squints at Ren, eyes flickering back and forth between us. His brow is furrowed again, and I'm scared he's about to throw us out.

"I can prove it," Ren proclaims. Without waiting for an answer, he stands and clicks K-2 out of carry mode.

"I uh-" Avi begins.

"Please, Anarki. Just give us a minute to prove it and if we can't we'll leave. This isn't a trick," I plead. He sits back in his chair as K-2 comes to life, amusement playing on his face.

"Good Evening, Master Ren and Miss Taxia," K-2 surveys his surroundings before leaning over to whisper into my ear.

"Excuse me, Miss Taxia...unfortunately, Droids and humans cannot marry. But I'm quite flattered by the proposal," he says before standing up straight and setting his gaze on Avi. I bite my lip to hold back my laugh.

"I know, pequeño. It's okay. Can you do me a favor instead and enter admin mode?" I ask him. He jolts upright silently. Avi has stood now, wandering over for a closer look at him.

"Forgive me, but are you expecting me to trust the word of

a Droid and a prototype one at that? You could have modified it to say anything," Avi questions as he analyzes K-2.

"Have you ever heard of anyone being able to interfere with a Droid's admin mode?" Ren asks.

"Well, no. No one, except..." he trails off.

"Exactly. K-2. Can you confirm the true identity of the people present in the room?" Ren asks.

"Yes, I can," K-2 responds, then stands silently again. I giggle nervously as Ren rubs the back of his neck.

"Let's try that again. K-2, please confirm the true identity of the people present in the room," Ren repeats.

"K-2405812, Taxia Ishri, Avilon Achrekar," K-2 begins. A momentary blush passes across Avi's face at his full name, "and my owner, alias; Ren Unkno, true identity, Zelius Metihand," K-2 finishes. The blush on Avi's face turns to sheer disbelief. His mouth drops open and his eyes widen. A stutter tumbles its way from his mouth as he approaches Ren. He tilts his head and stares at him intently, his eyes jumping around Ren's face, examining it carefully. After a moment, his eyes suddenly widen again as the realization hits him.

"Divine Allspirits, you are Zelius...This means the prophecy..." The implications of this new information flash across his face.

"I promise we'll explain everything in detail one day soon. For now...we just need a place to sleep and some friendly faces," I beg. He smiles so big his eyes crinkle.

"He really IS with us," he can barely look away from Ren. "Come. Of course you can stay with us, we have converted rooms in the basement. I'm sorry they're not very grand!"

"We slept on rocks last night, so as long as the bed is comfier than rubble, we're happy." I smile.

"Thanks Avi. One more favor? Please don't tell anybody everything just yet. Since Boe...we're just not sure who we can trust," Ren adds as we walk out the door. Avi waves a dismissive hand in front of us.

"That is your story to tell, Zelius," he whispers back excitedly.

We're led down a steep stone stairwell lit only by candles. It opens into a circular room clad in dark woods, furnished with deep red throws and tapestries. It has the same familiar, old smell of the armchair upstairs. UG members look up at us questioningly from the various sofas and chairs they're slouched in. A few of them are reading thick hardback books from a ceiling-height bookcase that covers the back wall. I miss the turn of a page beneath my fingers. I ran through Hypatia's collection within the first month and I've been dying for something new since. K-2 lumbers down the stairs behind us, knocking out the sconces bearing candles, picking them up, and apologizing as he attempts to step more carefully.

"I must go and assist upstairs," Avi points to a bald-headed girl grinning beside us, "Lyra will show you to your room."

"Welcome! I'm Lyra. As I'm sure you can understand, we value our privacy. We ask that you please refrain from using any non-UG confirmed electronics. You may have already noticed since we block the signals, that includes credentials." She talks fast and eyes K-2 up as she talks.

"I'd very much like to be UG confirmed," K-2 jumps in. A few of the observing UG smirk at this, and Lyra beams at him.

"He's not linked to the City anyway. He runs on a closed circuit channel which transmits to my credentials only," Ren explains.

"Then he's fine," she says, turning to K-2, "I'm confirming you, Drude!" She smiles even wider, practically bouncing on her feet.

"Drude?" I ask. My stomach rumbles loudly in the open space.

"Droid Dude! Come on, I'll show you where you can satisfy that monster." She points to my stomach before flipping on her heels and taking off in the direction of a hallway.

"My name is K-2. Or pequeño. But if Master Ren appro-" he starts. I grab his hand and smile at him before leading him after Lyra. She takes us to a small kitchen full of wooden cabinets, with a large table surrounded by chairs at the center. I'm surprised to see a food printer tucked away in the corner. I guess a sandscavenger brought it. It barely looks used, the large wood fire stove beside it much more worn in. UG are very skeptical of Company property, but I'm starving.

"Your room is just through that door to the left; it's number twelve. There's a bathroom down the hall!" Lyra yells before leaving us. She seems nice, but I'm too tired to match her enthusiasm, so I'm grateful for the comfortable silence that now fills the room. I print us some protein patties and veg, heaping Ren's plate with more as he finishes his first plateful. I eat as I go, and the food fills my stomach with warmth. It's delicious. After recycling the plates, we go through to our room. It has a double bed, two wooden side tables and a rug. A dusty upright piano stands abandoned in the far corner. As I shrug the heavy pack from my back, my shoulders groan at the loss of weight. I leave to use the bathroom and wash up, and when I return, Ren is face down on the bed, his legs dangling off the end. I lean down to take his shoes off for him. When I do, he jolts up and grabs my wrists.

"Are you tapped-in? It's me!" I yell, twisting my arms under themselves to break his grip. He lets go, eyes bleary, his cheek all crumpled and red from being face down. He looks adorable. "Go and wash yourself up before you fall asleep," I command. He surprisingly obeys, leaving the room without saying a word. K-2 sits in the empty corner of the room, meditating. I lay down on the bed, basking in the feeling of a full stomach and a clean body. I'd kill for a hit of greesha right now. It's not long before the door opens and the weight of Ren pushes down on the bed. I hear the rustling of a piece of paper beside me, so I half open one eye to see him unfolding the letter from Tony.

"Lyra reminds me of Elli so much. So enthusiastic about the smallest things," he says.

"I can't wait to meet her. It's a contagious personality," I reply, smiling up at the ceiling.

"I was thinking about changing the plan a little," he says. I sit up and look directly at him now. "Listen," He walks over to the piano and pulls off the dusty blanket covering it. He springs his fingers on a few keys. It's out of tune, but it doesn't sound bad.

"Sounds like it's out of tune, but it's not un*bear*able," I smirk.

"Taxia..."

"What? I'm just here to *bear* witness to your progression as a pianist," I can barely hold in my laugh.

"TAXIA!" He picks the dusty blanket up from the floor and throws it at me.

He sits down and begins to play, for real this time. It's a slow and mournful tune, and then he starts to sing.

"I know who is forty-two, why blood alone moves the wheels of history. If not for you, hope would slip through these hands of mine. All we've been through, the loss we cannot leave behind. With this message, I know you'll view, find me with a signal or a sign."

"It was a song?"

"It's from Elli. The letter was coded using the old music cyphers they used during the rebellion. It took me some time to realize what she was doing, but once I did, it was just a matter of matching music notes to syllables. I think we should play the tune for our show at the RFL final," He responds. I should have known it was from her.

"She's gonna know it's us. Are you sure you want to put her in danger?" I already know the answer, but I feel obliged to ask anyway.

"After tonight, everyone is going to know the truth anyway. I just think she deserves to know first. She wants me to find her. Once I do, it'll be her decision to continue this fight with us or abandon the dream altogether," he replies.

Ren blows out the candle on the wall and climbs into bed beside me. He reaches over and grabs my waist, pulling my back flush against his stomach. We talk for a while and decide to tell UG the whole truth. Avi already knows the biggest secret, and the UG has the numbers we may need for protection. I can't help but think Hypatia would disapprove of these additions to the plan we had already taken a year to come up with. But she's not here. Ren's whispers make the hairs on my neck stand up.

"We're so close, Taxia. Trust in me, as I trust in you, and we can do this."

My breathing slows and I feel the soft press of lips against my shoulder as I drift to sleep.

CHAPTER FORTY-ONE_

I wake to a soft knocking on the door. After a moment, it opens a crack and Lyra pops her head in. She notices Ren flat on his back, snoring and whispers, "I thought you'd appreciate an early shower before the others get to it." Her head disappears before a huge fluffy towel is waved in its place. I jump out of bed as softly, but quickly as I can, grabbing the towel and closing the door on sleeping Ren behind me.

"I'm sorry the water isn't warm. The basement doesn't have solar amplifiers and we can't figure out how to connect it to the church's pipework without MetiCity permits," Lyra apologizes.

"I noticed last night when I washed up. It's better than nothing though, thank you," I smile as I take off down the hall before anybody gets there first. I turn on the shower and the icy water prickles my skin as it bounces off the tiled backsplash. I twist the nozzle to its hottest setting and wiggle my toes under the stream, waiting to confirm what I already knew. It's freezing. As I turn off the faucet, I spot a small panel at the base of the shower. Popping it off to take a look, I spot the issue fairly quickly. I wrap my sleeve over my fingers and grip the unruly valve tightly; it hisses as I turn it to the left. I pop the panel back on and step out, turning the shower on once more. It runs cold and I resign myself to a thirty-second rinse, but then, there's a splutter and steam rises from the stream. I'm a fucking genius.

This is the best shower I've ever taken in my life. I can't even remember the last time I washed my hair. I wring the excess water from my locs before I step out, wrapping the huge towel around me almost twice. I take a second to look at myself in the mirror. The bags under my eyes are almost gone. I sleep a lot better when I'm not alone. Closing my eyes, I relish the serenity of the moment while I can.

"Taxia? I made you some breakfast," Ren says through the closed door. Those are the kind of words I don't mind interrupting my peace.

"Thank you! Be out soon!" I yell back. I don't hear him move away from the door, though, so I sneak up to it and grab the handle, yanking the door open. Ren stumbles forward into the room unceremoniously. He catches himself on his hands before he hits the floor and looks up at me with a face as red as the roses in Hypatia's garden.

"I was trying to check if you were done showering. Because I need it. The shower, that is," he stutters. Ren has matured a lot over the past year, so I relish these moments where I can make him squirm.

"I'm done, and the water runs hot now. You're welcome! " I reply, stepping over him so the towel covers his eyes for a moment before shuffling down the corridor back to the room.

Lyra has laid some simple clothes out for me on the bed. Once I'm dressed, I wait in the kitchen, filling myself with blueberry pancakes. K-2 is already there, guarding my plate from non-existent pancake thieves. Ren appears after a while, wearing a simple white t-shirt, his hair clean and fluffy.

"It's no meditank, but at least I don't smell like a feral cat anymore." He laughs.

"You still look like one though," I giggle. He picks up a blueberry that fell from my plate and chucks it at me. I duck and K-2 catches it. Ren picks up another and readies his aim to throw it at my face when Avi walks in.

"Ahem," He tilts his head in amusement. Ren drops his hand to his side in embarrassment. "I just wanted to check if you needed anything, but it looks like you've made yourselves at home," he laughs.

"Sorry Avi," Ren says. Why do I feel like we just got caught misbehaving by a ranking coach?

"Don't be. Laughter is a blessing, unless it is at the expense of another of course," he replies, smirking.

"Oh, it was definitely at my expense. He almost took my eye out!" I pout. Avi is observing us with the strangest look. Admiration? Suddenly, I remember that he knows Ren's truth and has basically just watched Zelius assault someone with a blueberry.

"Well, I don't want to intrude too much. I just wanted to remind you of the sanctity of our residence and the importance of its anonymity," Avi begins, struggling to stop himself from staring at Ren again. I wonder if everybody will be so starstruck when the truth is out?

"We've given you more than enough leverage to use against us if we were ever to tell," I reply, almost offended that he would even suggest it.

"I appreciate that. Just looking after my own as I'm sure you look after yours," he smiles. My guard softens.

"Actually, Avi, there is something you can give us. An audience with the UG," Ren remarks all of a sudden.

"It is done. Follow me," Avi replies.

Half an hour later, we're standing in front of the bookcase

with about forty UG piled into the room in front of us. I recognize some of them as friends of Ghost, or vague passing faces that are part of the City to City backdoor trading channels I've used. Most of them, though, are complete strangers. I never realized how vast their numbers are, and this is only the members from this part of the district in this one City.

"May our songs be heard, Anarki," Avi says to the crowded room.

"May harmony guide us to peace," they all say in unison.

"We have a visitor today, one of great significance. He wishes for you all to hear him speak. I have granted him that right. Any objections?" Avi asks. He's met with silence. "Good. Then the floor is yours," he says, moving off to the side as we step forward.

"I um...." Ren begins, then turns to me. I nod reassuringly. As confident as Ren has become, the intimidating stares give the room a sense of uneasy ambiance that he can't ignore. He turns back to face them and begins again.

"Well...the truth is, as you all suspected, MetiCorp is hiding secrets from you." The room is silent. "As we speak, they're broadcasting a frequency through every credential in the city. One that subtly influences the choices and actions of docile and ignorant masses. Due to the traditions you follow, you are not fully synced with the frequency being transmitted. This makes you all especially suited to receive my message and why I've come to you for help," Ren continues as the UG exchange glances, satisfied with the possibility that their 'conspiracies' might be correct.

"Tonight is the final for the RFL title. Myself, Taxia, and K-2 will be competing as The Anointed. If we are to win, I will gain access to a secret document detailing the atrocities committed on behalf of MetiCorp. I am confident that if this happens, the Company will try and stop me from releasing this information. I need your help to ensure that doesn't happen." The UG suddenly erupt into questions, yelling overtop of one another.

"How come you know all this?"

"Why would the Company give you access to their secrets for winning some RFL fight?"

"Why should we believe you?"

Avi steps forward and holds his palms out, lowering them to the floor, and the room quietens.

"I know you're going to have many questions. The most important one I can answer for you now. Why should you believe me? Why would your leader give a sandscavenger from the Outskirtz such a platform, without evidence? Because Avi knows the truth. The reason I know that I will obtain this information upon winning, is because I'm the one who implemented the ICON system that leads to it," Ren pauses once more as confusion spreads through the room.

"Because I am Zelius Metihand."

It takes us almost an hour longer than planned to reach the ArenaSphere. It's incredible how fast we were embraced, Ren being passed around the room to be ogled and interviewed, while K-2 is being examined from every angle. I answered as many questions as I could about my part in this. It felt cathartic to talk about the race job with a wider audience. The giant drops us off as close as he can. It turns out his real name is Qonan, and he's a friendly giant. We wave our goodbyes under the agreement that UG will wait in a nearby safehouse until the fight is over.

The entrance is different today, as the fans have been separated out to either side of the building by a golden rope. In the center of the entrance is a white runway carpet with photographers on either side and a row of reporters near the end. We're really being thrust into the spotlight today. I pull my cape tightly round my shoulders and we stroll down the carpet, K-2 slowly following behind us. The flashing of cameras and the buzzing of security drones surround us. We're stopped at a backdrop featuring 'RFL - Robot Fight League' in crisp white lettering. It's odd to be concerned about them catching my best angle, considering what we're doing here, but I can't help but wonder how I look under the limelight. At least I'm wearing a mask. Once done, we're ushered past reporters who yell out questions that we have no time to answer, security continuously herding us forward. We reach the end of the carpet, and a looming figure fills the space in front of us.

"He looks different," Ren comments.

"He looks like a corpse," I scoff.

Even more so than the last time we saw him on the RFL at Hypatia's. His eyes are cold and lifeless, his skin pasty and dull. We almost bump into him as security continues to usher us on, however, once we're inside the building, we're immediately separated from him. There's no waiting with algae tea for us today, as we are the only competitors. Instead, we're brought straight out into the arena and instructed to wait near the entrance doors out of view of the crowd.

"Good afternoon, and welcome to the final of the RFL on this BEAUTIFUL day in MetiCity-6!" The announcer yells. Beautiful day? The weather here is climate-controlled; it never changes.

"We have a VERYYY special one for you today folks, the undefeated RFL champ Raven, versus our up-and-coming underdogs, The Anointed, who I believe will be performing their own entrance today!" he continues.

Since it's the final, there will be a grand performance from both sides. While it's tradition for the challenger to come out first, apparently, Raven said he wanted to go first to 'get it over with.' His entrance song begins. The notes are low and dissonant, weaving together in an unsettling harmony that echoes throughout the arena. Every chord resonates with chilling intensity, the melody twisting and contorting as it lingers in the air.

Raven is nowhere to be seen until I finally spot him, high above the crowd, perched on a ledge. The tempo shifts unpredictably, lurching forward with a jarring urgency before slowing once more to a crawl. A spotlight focuses on Raven as he dives down into the sphere from above, giant wings painting shadows on the crowd. He lands with a thud, his claws digging an inch or two into the sphere floor. The rhythm of the song pulses erratically like a heartbeat, and it sends a shiver down my spine. It ends in an unintelligible whisper, the crowd is stunned into heavy silence.

We're instructed to walk down the aisle as our performance will take place on the platform just in front of us. The lights are dimmed as we're lifted up, and rumors spread through the crowd as they try and guess what we could be doing. The hardest part about our last-minute adaptation to the plan was reprogramming the nanodroids to assemble into a piano rather than our usual thrones. But we figured it out, and they do so seamlessly now. Rumors turn to excitement as the last keys shift into place. A pristine white piano accompanied by a white wooden stool with a golden cushion sits before us. Ren holds my hand as I take my place on the right of the stool before sitting down beside me.

A spotlight is focused on the piano as Ren places his fingers on the keys and begins to play the first few notes. I desperately search for Elli in the crowd, hoping she's here. Finally, I spot a flash of green hair in the second row. Ren continues to play and her expression turns to pride and bemusement. She knew he would figure out her cypher. Although I doubt she thought he would do it in quite this way. I mirror the look of pride on her face as he continues to play. In the front row just below her, I spot Migo filming us whilst simultaneously vlogging himself and the crowd with a separate camera.

The chimes of the piano dance delicately through the air, each note resonating with a graceful harmony of melancholy and mourning. The song weaves a tapestry of bittersweet emotion, with a progression that ebbs and flows. It's beautiful, succinct and poignant. As he strikes the last few keys, the crowd erupts into applause. I'm not sure they're used to their competitors being quite so talented. We stand, and Ren takes my hand as we bow. I deserve no credit, yet I do so happily. I see him searching for her, and I nudge his foot in the right direction. The moment he spots her, his whole demeanor relaxes. They stare at each other with eyes full of shared moments and trauma. It feels...intimate. I look away. How can I possibly be jealous when he's here holding my hand? The reason is that I know he has no choice. I'm part of his plan. I wonder if it would be Elli's hand he'd hold if the circumstances were different...

Ren pulls the piano bench forward toward the sphere and encourages me to sit back down beside him. We've come so far; this is no time to get emotional. I need to focus.

CHAPTER FORTY-TWO_

The bell rings and we're immediately plunged into a hazy purple darkness as Raven takes to the air once more, his wing-span half the length of the sphere. As he reaches the top, he lets out an inhuman screech before diving feet-first towards K-2.

"Predictable," Ren murmurs.

"You knew he'd do that?" I ask, regaining some composure.

K-2 dodges at the last second to grab hold of Raven's ankle, yanking him towards the ground.

"He did the same thing to Koujin," Ren leans forward to focus just in time for K-2 to forcefully drive Raven's foot into the ground. Raven has no choice but to clench, and his claws dig into the ArenaSphere floor.

K-2 takes advantage of the momentary stillness, throwing a quick, blinding jab towards Raven's face. His fingers penetrate the helmet slightly, causing it to crack and his neck to whip backwards. On the rebound, K-2 slams a right cross into the crack, splitting the helmet wide open. Raven's expression is dark and haunted; thick, black, veined streaks creeping up his neck towards his thin-lipped smile. I shudder. The crowd is excited at K-2's efficiency; they've never seen his true speed until now. It must piss Raven off because he wrenches his leg free and swipes at K-2 with his claws. They go shooting past K-2's head as he leans on his hindleg. More screaming from the audience. They underestimated him, just as we had planned.

Raven takes a moment, stomping back and flapping his wings hard to create space, but K-2 stands firm as the breeze rushes over him. Our opponent takes another dive, hurtling forward with his claw-covered hands outstretched. K-2 dodges just in time for Raven to land behind him. I gasp as he swipes his wings backwards, gunning directly for K-2. K-2 leans forward, just barely managing to duck under the sharp, talon-like tips of the wings, but he leans too far, and it's too late to warn him. Raven quickly re-orientates himself, grabbing K-2's head. He stares down at him, the corners of his mouth curling to a demented smile. Digging his claws into the sides of his head, he headbutts K-2 in the face. Hard.

"His face almost looks human, but he must have some serious mods to headbutt a Droid. That or he's a masochist."

"I'm pretty sure it's a little of both; he just did that without a helmet," Ren replies.

To my surprise, K-2 barely flinches and instead grabs Raven's wrists. He pumps his knees towards Raven's head, backflipping them into his face. The force would have been enough to kill a human, but Raven simply stumbles backwards and releases his grip from his head. K-2 rolls forward, away from Raven, and rises to his feet. The shadow behind him swipes once more, which he simply steps back into, and elbows Raven smack in the jaw. K-2 leans forward, throwing a swift kick behind himself, hitting Raven in the stomach, pushing him back even further. Raven dusts himself off and charges once more.

"He's relentless. He barely reacted to that kick," I gasp.

"He's even further dissociated than before. There's no man

left in there," Ren worries. My confidence from earlier is rapidly dwindling. He turns to face me. "Whatever happens tonight...you must continue this fight."

To an outside listener, he's talking about Droid fighting, but the underlying meaning fills me with dread.

Raven is slowly gaining ground, cutting diagonal strikes and jabbing his claws into K-2's exo-armor. Our Droid is doing his best to keep up, but the attacks are getting progressively more ruthless and aggressive. All of a sudden, Raven's wings spread out and push into the floor, lifting him into the air and enabling him to kick both his feet into K-2's chest, but K-2 doesn't move. He's grabbed the Raven's leg armor. Raven tries to push off his wings, leaning forward so his chest almost touches his knees, but K-2 chops down at his ankles. In return, Raven's claws come screeching across K-2's chest, a screw flying out across the floor. That was a major hit.

I stand up to rush into the sphere, but Ren places his hand on my arm and ushers me back to my seat. K-2 snaps back and I sigh in relief. Not for long, as Raven's other claw comes rushing past his head. He's ruthless. K-2 kicks Raven's wings out, forcing him to fly into the air. He grabs Raven's foot and I can't quite see what's happening until a boot falls to the ground. He disconnected the mechanism, smart. Only...it's not just a boot. It's a foot. Or I assume so, considering Raven is left with a stump where his foot should be. My mouth drops open and I turn to Ren.

"That's not supposed to happen...right?" I can feel bile rising in my throat.

"Nope. That mechanism is supposed to assist him in getting out of the Biosuit. It seems like there isn't much 'him' left in there," he replies, not sounding shocked at all.

Raven growls fiercely, kicking his other foot desperately so K-2 can't remove it. He kicks once more, sending K-2 flying into the side of the sphere. As K-2 pushes himself to his feet, a small panel from the left side of his chest where the screw was tumbles to the ground. There's a flash of red from the Biosuit beneath. Raven's wings stop flapping, covering us in the purple haze once more. He stares down at K-2 like an eagle about to pounce on his prey.

"Koujin?!" He shrieks in an inhuman pitch. The sphere comes alive with a flurry of movement; Raven goes batshit, swooping circles in the air and dipping down to take repeated swings at K-2. Occasionally, he bounces off the glass like a caged animal, but the impacts don't slow him down. K-2 desperately tries to match the strikes on each descent. Raven is completely mindless in his attack, screeching and yelling.

"YOU TOOK EVERYTHING FROM ME!"

He's too livid to notice that K-2 is aiming his attacks at his wings. Eventually, his flaps are less and less powerful, barely enough to keep him up. He crashes to the ground, standing unevenly upon his stump, angrily inspecting his wings. He grabs hold of the tip of his left wing, ripping it from his own back. The audience is loud, a mixture of excitement and terror. He snaps off a piece of the wing and jams it directly into the place where his foot should have been with a gurgling scream, discarding the rest of the wing, which hits the side of the sphere with a bang. He breathes deeply, closing his eyes, and stepping down onto his newly-fashioned leg. When his eyes open, they're almost fully black.

"KOUJIN!!" He roars, running at K-2 and swinging as soon as he's in range. His movements are way more predictable on the ground, and K-2 is back to impressively dodging every one. He's faster and calmer than Raven, and slowly, the tide shifts. Ren turns, and his eyes smile at me before he stands up and outstretches his hand. His thumb is level to the ground as he addresses the crowd.

"What's this? The Anointed are so confident in the win that the King is asking for mercy before it's even over!?" an announcer yells.

"I wouldn't be so cocky if I was him. Raven is a fierce one. Even the Queen looks worried beneath that mask."

I fix my face even though I know they're bluffing.

"There once was a sovereign king who made decisions without considering the will of the people until democracy arrived. A fair, but slow and corruptible system in which the voices of the many were merely a farce to those who would hear them. Both had their ups..." Ren says, slightly raising his thumb. "...and their downs." He tips his thumb to the ground.

"But it is in times like these, when the enemy is too dangerous, and the democratic process is slow to bumble its way to the truth, I shall step forward and make the choice for us all. I shall bear the burden upon my shoulders, for I am the only one able to take that weight," he finishes, turning back to the fight. K-2 takes a quick glance at Ren, who drops his thumb all the way to the ground. He nods in response, backflipping away from Raven. Raven, of course, charges, to which K-2 slides to meet him, foot connecting with Raven's leg, which falls apart at the knee. Biosuit armor tumbles to the ground, and just like his foot, there is no leg left in its place.

"Do you see how even the mightiest of villains fall before me? On his knees," Ren yells.

Raven shrieks and stretches out a desperate hand to K-2, his arm falling to the floor from the shoulder joint. The crowd gasps as the terrifying beast begins to fall apart, limb by limb. He falls feebly to his side, using his other arm to half drag himself towards K-2.

"YOU DID THIS!" I can't believe he's still talking. I can't look away.

K-2 makes his way over and stands above him. He steps on

Raven's head, shoving it down into the ground and muffling the words still spilling from his mouth. I want to celebrate, but my mind is filled with the horrors of the fight and the anxiety of what comes next. The announcers begin the countdown, I assume out of courtesy to the former Champion, considering how badly he's been dismantled. Raven was always going to be our biggest battle, but having access to his exact Biosuit model was our advantage. I let out the biggest breath of my life as the bell rings.

I glance over to Ren, who is standing now, staring in shock at the credentials on his wrist. He taps on it with a trembling finger and slowly lifts his face to me. His eyes gloss over with tears that threaten to spill over.

"We...we did it..." he whispers in disbelief.

I leap off the bench and throw my arms around his neck in a tight hug. My body is shaky with emotion as I hold onto him. I can feel his heart thumping. The roaring crowd is music to my ears as he pulls away to address them, his arm still wrapped around my hip. He waves his hand and a hush blankets the room.

"I claim this victory in honor of Kurogane Koujin, of Zander Thorne, and of Zari Jardinera. I do so as Ren Unkno, a sandscavenger from the Outskirtz of MetiCity-6," he grips the bottom of his mask and pulls it up to reveal his face. Murmurs pass through the crowd as a few people recognize him from Zander's pit crew.

"I have come to tell you the truth. Our victory today will enable me to fulfill the prophecy of the great Mobi Kantu. I have obtained the MetiCorp Compendium, and I will use it to expose their corruption and lies," I can hear a commotion backstage as controllers burst through the far doors.

"Your reality is one of complete submission. You are under control. The very devices you've integrated into every facet of your lives have been altered to further entrap you in Meti-Corp's siren song, willingly relinquishing your free will." He holds up his wrist, bearing his credentials. The controllers are sprinting through the crowd, shoving innocents out of the way and diving over barriers as they yell commands into their com-link.

"Ren Unkno, you're wanted for questioning in connection with the sabotage of the 2120 O-Race Cup," a voice states through the speaker. We share a worried glance as he hurries to finish his speech.

"You may doubt my claims, attributing them to mere RFL theatrics, or UG conspiracy theories. But, know this, I speak the truth to you, not just as Ren Unkno... but as Z-" his microphone cuts off. A security Droid falls from the sky, narrowly missing me. I notice the reporters nearby looking around in confusion as their broadcasts disconnect. Migo looks too stunned to notice. He's staring at Ren, his cameras dangling by his sides. He lifts his arm and points to us with fear in his eyes. No...not at us. Behind us. Ren's com-link crackles to life.

"Master Ren!" K-2 shrieks robotically.

We turn to see that somehow, Raven is standing. Well, half standing, half dragging. He's making his way over towards his discarded wing. We watch in horror as he props it up and throws his body weight against it, jamming it back into place with a sickening crack.

"KOUUUUUUJINNNNNNN!" He roars, his vocal cords straining as blood sprays from his mouth. He flaps his wings, attempting to straighten them, as grinding metal sounds pierce my ears. K-2 is facing off against him as if considering the fight before turning towards the door and sprinting to join us on the platform. Ren's eyes flit between the inevitable onslaught of the oncoming controllers and the raging inhuman beast thrashing around the sphere. Lucky for us, Raven's brain seems to be shutting down completely as he struggles to even find the door. I glance down to see the crowd begin to move, clambering down the rows to escape. Elli, however, hops one row down and plonks herself beside Migo. He looks bewildered as she snatches one of his cameras, fiddling with it and yelling at him. Whatever she tells him, it works. He shakes himself out of the stupor and lifts the camera to film the horror unfolding around him. She must have fixed the interference. Clever girl.

Behind us, Raven connects with the sphere door over and over again, sending shockwaves through us. The initial impact creates a spider web of cracks, branching out like lightning. Lights bounce and glint across the fractured surface, distorting the interior into a nightmare mosaic. Hit after hit, pieces of Biosuit scatter around the floor, and feathers float absurdly through the hellscape. A cacophony of shattered glass reverberates around us, shards spinning and catching the light before surrounding us in a glittering storm. Raven plummets through the gap, wings catching on the sides of it. He's inches away from us now and we have no time to decide. Fight or flight?

"Let's go Taxia, we gotta jump." Ren looks at me with a strange expression. He grabs my hand, and K-2 grabs mine. "3... 2...1..." he counts.

I jump, but my right hand is empty. I hit the floor with a thud, rolling an ankle. Panicking, I turn back up to the platform to see Ren standing with a resigned look on his face. He pulls his credentials off his wrist and throws them down to me. He strips off his cape and steps out of his costume, now wielding his wrench.

"I'm sorry Tax. Remember what I told you. You must keep going," his voice cracks as he turns back to face his fate.

"NO! Ren!" The salt from my tears coats my lips as I scream to the sky, begging for the Allspirits to hear me. An almighty crack fills the air as Raven bursts free, screeching and heading straight for Ren. He overshoots and flies off the platform, straight towards the crowd. That section is almost empty, but the commotion amps up the fear in the room, with people scattering in every direction. They're blurred and irrelevant in my vision, as the only one I can focus on clings to the underside of Raven, having been dragged off the platform with him. Raven is erratic, smashing everything in his path as they land, his broken mind now only capable of destruction. He swings a near-obliterated wing at Ren, who dodges successfully, taking calculated swings with his wrench.

Something obscures my vision and I lose focus on them. It's Elli. She's standing in front of me now, holding my shoulders and looking me in the eye, but her words are gibberish. She leans in and presses her forehead to mine, forcing eye contact. It breaks my concentration long enough for me to notice the UG pouring in through the doors that the panicked crowd escapes through. They're regimented and focused, pointing the way to the exits, helping people to their feet and carrying children.

The controllers don't seem to have noticed me and have begun to try and climb the stands to reach the skirmish over the seats of the crowd who have not yet escaped. The UG notice this and run in to shield the innocents from being trampled in their climb. Frustrated by the perceived obstruction, the controllers pull out their batons, whipping some of the UG round the back of the knees and in the ribs as they stampede through. Cries of outrage bellow from the remaining crowd as they yell at them to leave the UG alone.

Ren and Raven are almost at the nosebleeds now, high above the top of the sphere. Ren is inevitably faster and more agile, but Raven's disregard for his own life and those around him makes him almost untouchable. Alarms begin to sound, mingling with the screaming from the crowd and Raven's gurgling cries.

"Notice to all staff and audience members: please evacuate immediately. Those who remain risk their own well-being and possible prosecution for obstruction of an ongoing investigation. This penalty is accompanied by a derogatory mark on your social credit. I repeat, all staff and audience members must evacuate immediately" an announcement cascades through the arena.

I have to help. I start to sprint, but I run into a brick wall. Qonan. He shakes his head, and won't let me move. A shout from nearby prompts me to look to the right, where I notice Migo is caught beneath a fallen strut from the platform. Elli is amongst the UG now, coordinating and helping to guide people to safety while I'm stuck by this giant oaf.

"K-2, save Migo!" I yell. Qonan tries to get a grip on the Droid's arm but is unable to without letting go of me. Ren must have assigned Qonan as a bodyguard. That noso bastard. K-2 easily frees Migo, but he's unable to walk. He hoists Migo up over his shoulder, who looks emasculated and drained, although I notice he's still filming from upside down. I'm herded towards the exit as K-2 follows, ushering us into the massive line of escaping audience members. K-2 dumps Migo into the arms of an awaiting UG. Digging my heels into the ground, I glare at Qonan. Whatever he sees on my face scares him as he stops pushing and holds me in place. Another crash, and I look past him to see a tangle of broken and disjointed limbs, wrestling across the floor beneath the platform. Raven is almost completely dismantled, his face swollen and bruised, eyes fully black with blood streaming from his mouth and nose. Ren stands over him, wrench in hand. He hesitates for a second as Raven mouths something before bringing the wrench crashing down onto the monster's head. A few controllers lie around them, armor covered in deep gouging claw marks, their limbs distorted at odd angles. Ren stands up to catch his breath as he's surrounded.

"Am I not afforded the liberty of self-surrender under section 16.3 of the contract?" Ren yells at them.

They strike him across the knuckles with a baton, forcing him to drop the wrench.

"Let him go!"

"He saved us all."

"Let him finish his speech! We demand the truth!"

Voices from the UG, but also from the crowd, bounce around the room. Cries of outrage as the controllers yank Ren's arms behind his back, kicking his wrench across the floor.

"Can you not see how the harmonious MetiCity structures crumble when just an ounce of their control is lost? Open your eyes as they rip my contract to shreds in order to maintain their control!" Ren yells as loud as he can before a glove is clamped over his mouth, muffling him. Just before I'm shoved out of the exit door, I catch the controllers strapping Ren onto the back of a controller FlyBike. My world cracks to the core as my fingers slowly lose their grip on the doorframe, and Ren is ripped out of my line of sight.

Outside the arena, a sea of frightened and confused Meti-Citians are gathered. UG have set up a temporary triage, doing as much as they can for the injuries sustained inside. Some of which they can do nothing for. People continue to trickle out of the exit; some run and don't stop, and others can't seem to find the will to move. Everything fades to a hollow silence until I'm brought back by nearby screaming.

"Elli. Let's go! Now. We're getting out of here!" A raspy voice shouts. Elli stands between us and who I assume is her manager. He stomps closer to her and yells again, demanding she leave with him. She glances at K-2 and me, a torn look on her face.

"Taxia? It's time to go. Nothing more can be done here," Qonan pleads, beckoning me into a transport that pulls up behind us. I glare at him, daring him to say another word, before looking back at Elli.

"It's time to decide Elli," I say to the Jardinera girl. She takes one last look at her manager before sprinting towards us, stopping just before diving into the back of the transport. She nods and tilts her head at K-2 reassuringly. There's fire in her eyes. We turn to the transport, and Elli darts her hand out to grab the jacket of a passerby hobbling away. It's Migo. He wears a reluctant expression as we drag him into the back of the transport with us.

I turn to Elli as the cruiser speeds off.

"What now?" she asks.

I hold up Ren's credentials. "We keep fighting."

Meet the minds behind the pen—Lando and Kori, the collaborative force known as L. K. Wintur. As a couple who met online, our cross-continental writing journey resulted in a humbling, yet rewarding experience, and we're grateful for the chance to share the fruits of our labor with you. We hope you enjoyed the blend of philosophical, scientific, and economical quandaries.

Special thanks to our editors: Jason, Makaila, Jen, and Erik. To our artist Nenshyo, and to our publishing team: Leila, Adrian, and Erin for their invaluable contributions.

Also, thanks to the insightful RoyalRoads community. Your constructive feedback was crucial in refining our manuscript, ensuring our story would resonate with readers.

Book two is already in progress! We'll take a brief hiatus to celebrate the launch of book one before delving back into the MetiCity world for an eagerly anticipated follow-up.

To all who have gotten invested in Ren and Taxia's journey, and all who follow their dreams as we have, thank you.

L. K. Wintur

VIEW MY LINKTREE

Free Gift For My Readers!

"The Art of Meticity" a look from concept art, to fan submissions of art work. This is a fun visual journey of "The Engineer's Mechanic."

This magical ride is on the house, thanks to the author,
L. K. Wintur

Scan the QR code above with your smartphone or tablet
For kindle just click the QR code